Rachael English

the LETTER HOME

HACHETTE
BOOKS
IRELAND

Cataloguing in Publication Data is available from the British Library.

ISBN 978 1 52938 071 2

Typeset in Garamond by Bookends Publishing Services, Dublin
Printed and bound in Great Britain by Clays Ltd, Elcograf, S.p.A.

Hachette Books Ireland policy is to use papers that are natural, renewable and recyclable products and made from wood grown in sustainable forests. The logging and manufacturing processes are expected to conform to the environmental regulations of the country of origin.

Hachette Books Ireland
8 Castlecourt Centre
Castleknock
Dublin 15, Ireland

A division of Hachette UK Ltd
Carmelite House, 50 Victoria Embankment, EC4Y 0DZ

www.hachettebooksireland.ie

the
LETTER HOME

Rachael English is a bestselling novelist and presenter on Ireland's most popular radio show, *Morning Ireland*. During more than twenty years as a journalist, she has worked on most of RTÉ Radio's leading current-affairs programmes, covering a huge range of national and international stories. *The Letter Home* is her sixth novel.

Twitter: @EnglishRachael
Facebook: rachaelenglishwriter

ALSO BY RACHAEL ENGLISH

Going Back
Each & Every One
The Night of the Party
The American Girl
The Paper Bracelet

For my parents, with thanks.

Prologue

She opened her eyes and tried to adjust to the dark. *Give it a minute*, she thought. *If you don't panic, the light will come.* There was always a sliver of light, a crack, however thin, that made it possible to see different shades of black and grey. While waiting for it to appear, she breathed in slowly. She paused before breathing out, but the world around her remained a seamless black.

For a strange, confusing moment, she wondered if she was dead. Was this dark place, wherever it was, the other side? Then she felt a slight, almost imperceptible, movement. It was followed by a shout. A man's voice. The noise was coming from outside. She remembered where she was and why she was there.

She listened for a sign that the others were alive, for a breath or a moan. She was certain she could smell other bodies and feel their warmth. Perhaps she should say something. But, no, this might be the wrong time. Besides, her mouth was dry as chalk, and she wasn't sure her voice would work. She was amazed that no one could hear her heart. It was in her throat, her ears, everywhere.

The boat swayed again, the movement more dramatic.

She attempted to move, only there wasn't enough room. It was cold, and she'd lost the feeling in her legs. Pins and needles ran up and down her arms.

Her breathing was shallow now, and she worried that there wasn't sufficient air to fill her lungs. Fear wrapped itself around her. They had been warned that the crossing might be rough, but this was the first time she'd realised they might not survive.

Don't fall asleep, she told herself. *If you do, you might not wake again.*

What she had to do was keep her mind active. She tried to visualise where she was going, what she would do there, whom she would meet, how her life would improve. She thought of streets, buildings, people.

It was no good. All she could picture was home.

Part One

Chapter I

April 2019, Clooneven, County Clare
Jessie

Jessie Daly had promised herself that she'd spend the journey from Dublin to Clooneven preparing her answers. By the time she reached home, every sentence would be honed, every possibility covered.

She should have remembered that bus trips made her sleepy. Barely had they passed the turn-off for Naas than her eyelids became heavy, and her head lolled to one side. She woke two hours later to the sound of rain rattling against the window and the suspicion that the lattice texture of the seat's cloth had been imprinted on her face. She ran a finger down her right cheek. Suspicion confirmed.

Waking up was always the same. For a moment, everything was bright. Then it would all come back to her, and the clouds would roll in again. She'd tried telling herself not to dwell on what she couldn't change, but it hadn't worked. Apart from sleep, nothing worked.

After two bus changes, and a further two hours, she arrived in Clooneven. The number of passengers had dwindled to six. Alongside her, there were two women with hessian shopping bags, a man who'd spent the journey from Ennis telling the driver about his cataracts, and a German couple who slouched under the weight of their rucksacks. One of the women looked Jessie up and down before tapping her companion on the arm. In the sort of whisper that could be heard two streets away, she said, 'You know who that is, Martina, don't you?'

Jessie ignored them. She also suppressed the urge to tell the tourists that they were getting off in the wrong place. With its curve of pale beach, rippling ocean and horseshoe of brightly painted houses, Clooneven was heart-stoppingly lovely. At this time of year, however, it was marked by the off-season dullness common to seaside towns everywhere. The gift shops were closed, the bars quiet, the beach deserted. The town was waiting for the summer season to unfurl.

In early April, the couple would be lucky to find a half-decent meal or a drinkable cup of coffee. If they did, chances were the coffee would be provided by the woman waiting at the town's sole bus stop. Jessie's sister, Lorna, had a navy blazer draped over her shoulders, a large pair of sunglasses on top of her ash-blonde head and a pursed-lip expression that suggested this was not how she'd wanted to spend her afternoon.

As Jessie descended the steps of the bus and retrieved her luggage, Lorna gave a quick smile of acknowledgement. 'That's a lot of stuff you have with you,' she said, followed swiftly by 'God, you're very pale.'

'Yeah, well, it's been …' Not knowing how to finish the sentence, Jessie allowed it to trail away. She'd barely spoken for five or six days, and her voice was rusty from lack of use. She heaved her black suitcase into the boot of the SUV, placed her other bag onto one of the back seats and climbed in beside her sister.

Familiar sounds and smells – the squabbling of seagulls, the tang of seaweed – filled her head. The rain had been replaced by high watery cloud. Fearing what Lorna would say next, she wished she'd chosen to walk the five kilometres to the family home. She was also annoyed with herself for not spending more time preparing her story.

At thirty-six, Lorna was seven years older than Jessie. Along with her husband, Simon Keating, she was the owner of several businesses including a café, a grocery shop and an amusement arcade. As she was fond of reminding people, she hadn't allowed her mediocre education to hold her back. 'Hard work,' she would say, to anyone willing to listen. 'Hard work and perseverance.' By contrast, Jessie with her honours-laden Leaving Cert and lah-dee-dah degree from Trinity College didn't even own a car. What Lorna chose not to say was that the most lucrative businesses in the portfolio – the shop and the arcade – had originally been owned by Simon's parents. He'd also inherited a house the size of a nursing home. In recent years, the couple had remodelled it into a palace of glass and pale brick.

When she was drunk, Jessie liked to describe herself as a Marxist. She was against the accumulation of wealth for wealth's sake. She supported public housing, rent controls, a basic income for all. In her lower moments, and there had been too many of these lately, she envied her sister. She pictured life with a husband, two children and under-floor heating. She thought about certainty, stability and the sort of comforts that came with a conventional grown-up life. Not that she'd say any of this out loud. She didn't want hypocrisy added to her list of failings.

As Lorna drove past the hotel, the seaweed baths and the golf clubhouse, she stayed quiet. Her angular face shone, like she'd taken a bath in motor oil. Maybe she'd been on a spa weekend. Or maybe it was a glow of self-righteousness.

When finally she spoke again, her words were crisp. 'They're incredibly upset, you know. I mean, they won't say as much to you, but it's difficult for them.'

'I get that. I've told them I'm sorry.'

'Everybody saw it. And, if they didn't watch it live, they've come across it on Facebook. How could you do that to Mam and Dad? What were you thinking?'

Jessie pulled at the sleeves of her leather jacket. 'Ah, Lorna. You're making it sound like I killed someone.'

'You've killed your reputation anyway. You'll be lucky to get more work.'

'If I come up with stories, I'll get work.'

Even as the words left Jessie's mouth, she knew they weren't true. The media had changed. There were too many journalists and too few paying jobs. Dublin was overflowing with young reporters who were willing to write whatever their bosses wanted while shooting a video, recording a podcast and engaging in spirited arguments on Twitter. Newsrooms were staffed either by interns or by creaking veterans with nowhere else to go. The veterans spoke about atrocities they'd covered and expenses they'd claimed, while lamenting young people's lack of initiative.

Once, she'd had notions of becoming a serious journalist, someone who wasn't ashamed to list the publications she'd worked for on her Twitter biography. She'd pictured herself filing dispatches from a Syrian refugee camp or chasing an exploitative landlord down the street. Alternatively, she'd imagined moving to London and becoming one of the blondes who wrote about sex in the *Sunday Times*. Critics would describe her as 'fearless' and 'unflinching', and publishers would outbid each other in pursuit of her take on modern life.

Instead, she'd settled for a world where 'Kate Middleton Re-wears Outfit' and 'Daughter of Famous Man Goes on Holiday' were considered stories. Her work had become safe. Shallow. She'd written soft features about soft lives, and even that was gone from her now.

Lorna glanced in her direction. 'Don't take this the wrong way, but perhaps you should consider something else.'

'Like what?'

'Oh, I don't know. What are you qualified for? Teaching? PR? Something steadier, at any rate. What does Phelim think?'

Jessie didn't answer. She focused on the road ahead, and on the patchwork of fields that lined the way to the family home. At least Lorna was direct. Being pecked at by her was easier than dealing with their parents' understated disappointment.

The Dalys lived in a pebble-dashed bungalow, one of many built in the area in the 1970s and 1980s. Compared to the two-storey houses of more recent years, with their glossy crimson doors and ornate gates, it looked insubstantial. If the building was modest, the front and back gardens were works of art, tended with care and no little skill by their mother, Maeve. As Jessie climbed out of the vehicle, it was the smell that struck her first, the blend of wallflowers and magnolia that meant springtime at home.

Having spent her school days with her nose pressed against an imaginary window, hankering after a world outside Clooneven, she'd left at eighteen. She'd been certain that everything she wanted was elsewhere. Her visits home had been infrequent.

Her father, Denis, worked in a light engineering plant in Ennis. It was skilled if unglamorous work. Although he could be great fun, he was also a follower-of-rules, a man who believed in turning up on time with a clear head and polished shoes. Maeve was a petite woman who distrusted artifice and show. She darned socks, went around the house switching off lights and took pride in her ability to make endless bowls of soup from a chicken carcass and a few wizened vegetables. If Lorna's ostentation annoyed her, she was careful not to let it show.

Jessie's father was at the front door. While usually he would have given her a hug, today he was reserved. He looked more worn than she remembered. His light grey hair needed a trim and his brown jacket shone as if given one pressing too many. He'd been wearing the same jacket, or a clone of it, for the past twenty years.

'Were there many on the bus?' he said, as he picked up her case. She decided against pointing out that it had wheels.

'It was quiet enough.'

'Not a bad old day, all the same.'

'We've had worse,' said Lorna. 'The forecast for next week is good.'

They could carry on like this for hours, batting around words while saying nothing. Eventually, though, they would have to talk, and Jessie still wasn't sure how much to say.

Maeve was in the kitchen, making tea. She also appeared tired. For someone who usually looked as if she'd stepped out of a clothing catalogue, she was surprisingly unkempt. Her shapeless camel cardigan was at odds with her blue trousers, which were at odds with her green slippers.

Jessie pulled out a chair and sat down beside the table. For once, the kitchen's comfortable clutter felt claustrophobic rather than welcoming. There were too many plates on the dresser, too many mugs on the draining board, too many magnets on the fridge.

Her mother gave a weak smile, then turned to Lorna. 'You'll stay for a cup?'

Please don't, thought Jessie.

'I will indeed,' said her sister, as she found a chair. 'Jessie, get up there and give Mam a hand. You've been sitting down all day.'

So this was how it was going to be.

For five minutes, they drank tea, picked at a currant loaf and swapped small-talk. Finally, it was Lorna who mentioned the unmentionable.

'Jessie tells me she's apologised to you.'

'She has,' said their mother, 'only that doesn't stop us worrying.'

Their father nodded. 'We should have noticed that things weren't right.'

Jessie, who'd been examining her fingernails, looked up. 'I am here, you know. You can ask me.'

'Yes,' said her mother, 'only every time we tried to talk to you on the phone, you clammed up on us. That's if you bothered answering.'

'You were very drunk,' said Lorna.

'I honestly wasn't. Well, I was, but the cameras made everything look worse.'

'What I can't understand is why they let you on in that state. Or why you didn't realise you'd stopped making sense.'

Their parents exchanged a look but remained quiet.

'Like I told you, it's kind of hard to explain. It's like …'

'Why don't you give it a go?' replied Lorna. 'We all deserve a proper explanation.'

Chapter 2

Ten days earlier

The day of Jessie's unravelling started early. Her alarm went off at seven. Without changing out of her pyjamas, she stepped into the kitchen, made a milky coffee and flicked on her laptop.

She was writing up an interview for *Inspire*, the magazine for which she did most of her work. The interviewee, an influencer-cum-online-TV-presenter-cum-eyelashes-entrepreneur called Hollie Garland, looked as though she was straight out of a box. Untouched. Untroubled. She was successful, glossy, willowy – and dull as a weekend pilgrimage to Lough Derg. On Instagram, Hollie exuded well-being and cheer. In real life, she was the same. That was the problem. She spoke in hashtags. She was truly #blessed and #livingherbestlife. She was an advocate for #metime and #selfcare. And she used these phrases without any apparent irony. She was also keen on the word 'curate' without seeming to know what it meant.

Jessie had attempted to ask about the morality of influencers shilling products they didn't use. She might as well have been asking the parish priest about death metal. Hollie had greeted the questions with a blank look before returning to her well-practised monologue on the transformational powers of clean eating and lip-liner. The only time she was even slightly negative was when bemoaning the trolls who targeted people like her. Jessie began to suspect that if she had nothing to sell, she had nothing to say.

Because of this, she suggested to her editor, Eimear Bird, they do a broader piece about what Hollie represented. Eimear wasn't interested.

'You know what Hollie represents?' she said. 'She represents a boost to circulation and a rise in advertising.'

The editor went on to point out that *Inspire*'s readers saw her as a role model, the star at the centre of their gluten-free universe. They didn't want an exploration of her psyche. They wanted to know about her new eye-shadow palette and how it would transform their lives.

Call her naïve, but Jessie would have liked to credit the readers with a little more intelligence. Still, she needed the fee, so she wrote and stared and tinkered and wrote again. If the finished piece wouldn't win any prizes, it wasn't completely embarrassing either.

Two thousand words of Hollie would sap anyone's spirit, so by the time she met her friend Shona, Jessie craved entertainment. She'd had three vodkas and was beginning a fourth when her phone rang. It was a researcher from one of the late-night TV current-affairs shows. The researcher took a deep breath before announcing that a guest had pulled out at the last minute, which meant they were without a woman on the panel, and they were in trouble for lack of gender balance so she had to find a woman, and would Jessie do it, please? The high note of desperation in her voice spoke to Jessie. Plus, Shona was being a bore about a man she might or might not have sex with. Sometimes her friend had a toddler's ability to ramble around a story without ever getting to the point, and this was one of those times.

'Okay,' she said to the researcher, barely pausing to ask about the theme of that night's show. They would, she was told, be discussing the big news of the day. Confident that she was on familiar ground, Jessie explained the situation to Shona, who insisted she finish her drink.

'You'll be fine,' she said. 'Anyone watching will probably have been in the pub themselves. And you look perfectly sober to me. Your hair's gorgeous, by the way.'

That much was true. Jessie had been to the salon the previous day to have her blonde balayage refreshed. She'd also had it cut into a long bob. That this had cost far more than she could afford was beside the point. She looked good, and with television, that was what mattered. Trite as it might sound, entire TV careers had been built on good hair and the careful use of filler. The younger and more attractive you were, the less you needed to say.

TV and radio punditry had become a useful side-line for Jessie. Although she didn't kid herself that she was in demand for her profound political insights, she could string together a few sentences. She also ticked both the 'token young person' and 'token woman' boxes. While, in the real world, few would describe twenty-nine as particularly young, on the current-affairs circuit anyone under forty was viewed as slightly edgy.

The first indication that she'd made a mistake came in the green room when one of her fellow guests, an earnest guy whose glasses needed a polish, asked what she'd made of the evening's developments in the House. She felt a twitch of panic. She was primed to talk about the story that had dominated the news all week: a row about corporate landlords buying up entire housing developments. Surely if anything important had happened in the past few hours her phone would have lit up with notifications? Then she remembered that to minimise distractions she'd turned off her alerts. She could, of course, have looked up the news sites while she was in the taxi, but time had been limited, and she'd focused on sobering up and composing some caustic lines about vulture funds.

'I reckon it's pretty serious,' she said, hoping he'd reveal more information. 'What do you think yourself?'

Before he could reply, a third panellist, a politician with boundless self-regard, slapped Mr Dirty Glasses on the back and said something about his boys being on the back foot.

With that, they were whisked into the studio.

When the producer thanked her for being available at short notice, she asked again about the topics they'd be discussing. 'Mainly the obvious,' he replied, 'and we might get to something lighter before the end.'

Jessie was in trouble. She didn't know what the obvious was and couldn't ask. She'd had to leave her phone in the green room, and the other guests – Dirty Glasses, Back Slapper and a cantankerous political correspondent called Killian McGill – were chatting among themselves. At this point, the presenter arrived. Barry Fogarty was a current-affairs veteran, who smelt of mothballs and privilege. Under the studio lights, he was as orange and wrinkled as an aged apricot. Those same lights were making Jessie feel woozy.

Focus, she told herself. *Focus*.

She asked Barry what he wanted from the discussion. With an airy wave, he said that, no doubt, she'd be able to bring her own perspective to events. For some reason, nerves she supposed, this made her laugh. The others, gathered in an insider huddle, continued to ignore her. The opening credits began, and she still wasn't sure what they'd be talking about.

The show had been on air for several minutes when she came to grips with the story. While she'd been writing about Hollie Garland and drinking vodka with Shona, vulture funds had slipped out of the news. The new political scandal centred on the premature release from prison of a drug dealer who'd gone on to commit further crimes. It had emerged that, some years earlier, the minister for justice had written a letter to the prison authorities in which she'd said that Vincent McPartlin was from a fine upstanding family and should be considered for early release. The opposition parties were demanding her resignation, as were the families of McPartlin's victims.

Jessie was feeling increasingly lightheaded. The absurdity of the situation made her face tingle, and she found her mouth curving into a smile. She shouldn't be there. She had nothing to contribute, she was exhausted – and she was drunk. She wondered if she could slip out during the break. Maybe she could say she was ill. The others were only interested in their own opinions: they didn't need to hear from her.

It was while her thoughts were drifting that Barry Fogarty asked her a question. She'd missed the start so, urging herself to stay calm, she opted for a generic answer.

'Um, yeah,' she heard herself say. 'This is what happens, isn't it, when people aren't listened to? When officialdom loses its way and ignores the consequences of its decisions.'

Killian the cantankerous correspondent squinted in her direction. 'Surely, in this instance, the problem was that no one listened to the officials. The minister paid too much attention to the convicted man's family, whose votes she wanted to secure, and ignored the misgivings of civil servants.'

'I guess you could look at it like that, but in the round, and bearing in mind what's occurred in the past ...' She searched for a coherent way to end the sentence but, when nothing came, said something about the minister's record in a previous department. The others, she realised, were staring at her.

Cantankerous shook his head. 'Were you paying any attention to what was going on today or are you spoofing?'

Barry Fogarty intervened. 'Ah, now, Killian—'

'Barry, she doesn't have the foggiest notion what she's talking about.' Once more, he turned to Jessie. 'Do you?'

She felt the heat rising from her neck. The studio tilted. They were waiting for an answer, so, with what she later saw as the worst kind of drunken logic, she decided to brazen her way through by telling the truth.

'I wasn't able to follow all of it because I had other things to do. That's what you guys tend to forget. Most people can't spend all day thinking about politicians.'

'What else did you have to do?' asked Barry. Almost immediately, he looked as though he regretted the question.

The studio tilted in the other direction. It occurred to Jessie that she might be swaying. Her tongue seemed to have swollen. 'I was writing a feature, well … it was sort of an interview, except I had to gild it a bit because the woman I was writing about … Hollie Garland, y'know? Well, she—'

Concern flashing across his face, Barry attempted to take charge. 'I'm not sure what this has got to do with our discussion. Perhaps, we should—'

'Hollie who?' said Cantankerous Killian.

'She's a famous influencer,' replied Jessie. 'She mightn't mean much to you, but I guarantee you, she means more to anyone under thirty than the minister. She probably earns more too.' For a moment, she paused. She didn't want to go too far. 'Don't get me wrong, I'm not saying that's right. I doubt Hollie could name the president let alone the minister for justice.' Again, she hesitated. 'Actually, you know what? I'm being unfair. I'd say she could buy and sell everyone here. She's got the right kind of commercial cunning. Like, she was a vegan until a burger chain offered to pay for some #sponcon. But, hey, it is what it is.'

'I think we should get back to this evening's agenda,' said Barry, the colour seeping from his cheeks.

The others, clearly enjoying the diversion, disagreed. 'What's #sponcon?' asked Back Slapper.

Dirty Glasses replied, 'It is what it is,' prompting a dry laugh from Killian, who leaned back in his chair and said, 'Hollie Garland? I'd say she's busy at Christmas.'

'Ha!' said Jessie. 'You're a very witty man, though I doubt Hollie would like you pulling the piss out of her name. She's really serious about her brand.' She attempted to make air quotes around the final word but in doing so knocked over a glass of water. It skittered across the desk and crashed onto the floor.

'Jesus,' said Dirty Glasses.

Barry, who had given up trying to restore order, leaned in and asked if, by any chance, she'd had a drink before joining them on air. Jessie, sensing there was no way back, conceded that she might have had one or two.

The rest was a blur. Well, obviously, that wasn't true. For people watching at home, and for countless others who saw the clip, it all played out in sharp focus. It was high-definition entertainment, the subject of a hundred Facebook memes, countless Twitter jokes and at least four pompous newspaper columns. She was what happened when a culture was swamped by triviality: she was the standard bearer for people who didn't know or care about their limitations; she was the self-confident face of a self-indulgent generation.

And the drink? Oh, the drink. The way the columnists carried on you'd swear she'd been off her head on red biddy. She'd been a bit jarred, that was all.

The column that hurt most was the one in which a man argued that, by turning the show into a pantomime, she'd insulted Vincent McPartlin's victims. In her mind, he claimed, they were of less significance than an online huckster.

If the men in the papers had contempt for her, the women on Instagram and the gossip forums were rougher still. Hollie's fellow influencers claimed Jessie was ignorant, jealous and a disgrace to the sisterhood. They wallowed in performative solidarity. *Can we all agree that Jessie Daly is cancelled?* one wrote.

They could.

A tearful Hollie called the editor of *Inspire* to claim that her business had been sabotaged by the cow they'd sent to interview her. (In fact, she'd gained thirty thousand followers.) Eimear Bird pledged to redo the interview herself. She also rang Jessie to tell her the magazine wouldn't be using her again. 'It's a shame,' she said, 'because you've a great eye for detail, and your writing isn't too bad either. But you need to sort yourself out. Oh, and for the avoidance of doubt, our arrangement was a casual one, so I'm not breaking any laws here.'

Jessie had identified a group of women whom she called five-star feminists. They wore jewel-coloured shift dresses in Sunday supplement features and attended empowerment conferences in expensive hotels. They had a particular skill for corporate buzzwords and phrases, like 'synergy' and 'holistic' and 'across the piece'. Their tweets were filled with admiration for Jacinda and Angela and AOC. When it came to supporting female colleagues, however, they vanished. It wasn't that they had a point to prove. They simply didn't care. Eimear was her theory made flesh.

Every time Jessie came across a mention of the incident, her name jumped out as though printed in forty-eight-point capitals, and self-loathing swelled within her. Yet some perverse part of her sought out references to the night she'd turned herself into a national joke. She doom-scrolled obsessively. Not that this required much effort: her phone was aglow with notifications.

She decided to watch the show. Could it really be that bad? She saw her flushed face, her unfocused green eyes, the way she'd appeared to smile to herself while everyone else was discussing serious crime. She heard her incoherent thoughts and mangled sentences and the way the others had laughed at her. Afterwards, she lay flat on the floor, too upset to cry. The carpet felt rough against her back; the apartment needed hoovering. The place was cold and smelt of dust and cigarettes. She wished as fervently as she had ever wished for anything that she could go to sleep and never wake again.

Friends called and messaged. Although supportive, she could tell they didn't know what to say. They asked her out, but she was reluctant to be seen. They didn't hide their relief at her refusals. She risked the local Tesco, a woolly hat pulled low, a scarf stopping at the tip of her nose like a teenage rioter.

In the main, though, she sat in the apartment and chain-smoked. She felt bad about every damn thing, but mostly she felt bad about her parents. They'd made sacrifices so she could pursue her degree in English followed by a post-grad in journalism. Even after she'd started work, they'd continued to fund her. How often had she returned to Dublin to find an envelope containing a fifty-euro note tucked into the pocket of her backpack?

If she was honest, there was more to it than that. She had diminished their achievements to magnify her own. In Dublin, her acquaintances were overwhelmingly middle class, her classmates and colleagues the sons and daughters of surgeons and barristers. They had rich-girl hair, rich-boy self-belief, and skin that revealed generations of good nutrition. Early on, Jessie had learnt how to exploit her comparative lack of privilege. For years, she'd emphasised that her background was different. She'd told stories about her family's eccentricities: the aunt who cried when anyone went to America, even for a two-week holiday; the cousin who played the concertina to his calves; the uncle who'd fallen into a grave at a neighbour's funeral. This inverted snobbery had served her well but hadn't been fair to her parents. And now she had humiliated them.

After ten days, she decided she couldn't take any more silence. Being on her own meant she spent too long indulging in self-examination, and even in good times, introspection wasn't her friend. She gathered up the remains of her dignity, did what she had to do and set out for home.

In the family kitchen, Jessie was trying to explain herself. She'd given Lorna and her parents a tightly edited version of events. Her sister had tut-tutted, her dad had rubbed his nose, her mother had dabbed at a tear. Thankfully, they'd said little.

The quiet was broken by her father. 'How's Phelim?'

'Fine,' said Jessie.

'Seriously? I mean …'

She sought refuge in inarticulacy. 'Ah, you know how it is. Like, he's kind of embarrassed … but …'

'He didn't think of coming down with you?' asked her mother, as she touched Jessie's hand. 'He'd have been welcome.'

'He's busy.'

Lorna raised a well-shaped eyebrow. 'How long are you planning on staying in Clooneven?'

'Just a week or so,' replied Jessie, hoping this was true.

Chapter 3

June 1842, Clooneven

Bridget

Bridget Markham stretched out her legs, wriggled her feet and allowed the sand to slip between her toes. In front of her, white-tipped waves eased to shore. The sky was purest blue. Within minutes, however, the sea might be agitated, the morning sun shrouded by mist. She had reason to know that, for all its beauty, you couldn't trust the Atlantic.

To wade through the water, she had tucked the hem of her long grey skirt into her underwear. Now that she had returned to the beach, the sand was warm against the backs of her legs. She tilted her head so that the sun danced across her nose.

'Are you helping me or are you going to lie about for the rest of the day?' Her mother's voice cut through Bridget's daydreams.

'I'm having a short rest. Why don't you come and sit down for a while?'

'Because I've work to be doing, and so have you. Other folk will be here before we know it.'

A high tide had thrown up strand after strand of seaweed, and her mother was determined to collect it before anyone else had a chance. Sometimes, when they were very hungry, the family ate the seaweed. Mostly, they used it to fertilise their plot.

'I promise I'll be back at work in a minute,' said Bridget.

'Well, you make sure that you are.'

This tension, this sharpness, wasn't their usual way. The events of the day before had come between them. Not that Bridget regretted what she'd said. She wished she'd said more.

While her tone could be harsh, kindness spilled out of Johanna Markham. How often had she allowed travelling strangers to sleep in their cottage? How frequently had she taken care of neighbours' children? Only a week before, she'd given a beggar the family's last sup of milk. 'God will provide,' she'd told Bridget's sister, Mary Ellen, who'd grumbled and scowled and said they wouldn't need to depend on Him if they were more careful with their rations. At nineteen, Mary Ellen was the elder sister by three years, and she was terrible for finding fault.

Bridget observed her mother pulling slimy clumps of carrageen from the water and tossing them ashore. Her face was pinched from hard work and worry, but she had the clear blue eyes of a child. She was a spare-framed woman, as tiny as her daughters were tall. Her elder son had been tall too. Still was, Bridget hoped.

'I won't ask again,' shouted Johanna. 'I know you're sulking, but you'll have to accept that you were wrong. Your sister's a grown woman, and what she does with her life is no concern of yours.'

'It is when she's making a mistake,' said Bridget, as she got to her feet and wiped the sand from the back of her skirt. Before resuming work, she turned and gazed back towards Clooneven.

Cluain Aoibhinn had got its name from neither the strand nor the sea but from the fields outside the town. In the townland of Boherbreen where the Markhams lived, the pasture had been replaced by a clutch of cottages, each accompanied by a smallholding. Some of the tenants had enough land to grow turnips or oats, and a fortunate few kept hens or fattened a pig. Mostly, though, they relied on potatoes. The greatest food on earth, Johanna would say, as she admired the plants in full bloom, their delicate white flowers more prized than any rose. Mary Ellen claimed the potatoes would be tastier if they had a morsel of meat to accompany them.

Similar one-roomed cabins dotted the surrounding land. Without exception, they were dark and sparsely furnished. Rain seeped through the thatched roofs and dripped down the walls. Bridget wished the homes were brighter and more comfortable, but her mother claimed that any hint of improved circumstances would lead to another rise in rent. Higher rent meant the family would have to work even harder for a landlord they'd never met.

She was a clever woman, was Johanna Markham.

Under the sun's glare the town itself appeared to quiver. It was a prosperous place, with two boarding houses, a dispensary and several merchants. Whitewashed houses curved around the beach, like a perfect set of bottom teeth. In the summer, the streets bustled with life. People, wealthy people, came from Limerick and Dublin to take the waters. Others travelled from England. Bridget recognised the English because of the way they looked at her. Peasants: that was what they called people like her. She suspected that England was teeming with families whose lives were no easier than her own. They were unlikely to make it as far as Clooneven, though. The overseas visitors were usually surprised to learn that not only could she speak their language, she could also read and write.

'Bridget! Do you want me to come out of the water and drag you over here? Because I will, you know.'

Bridget pushed aside her thoughts and returned to the ocean. With the frigid Atlantic around her knees, she gathered seaweed until her mother decided they'd collected as much as they could carry in their creels. They worked in silence, both conscious that if they spoke, they might fall out again.

They sat down for a short break before making the journey back to their cottage. In recent times, the ocean had brought little joy to the Markhams. Two years earlier, Bridget's father had perished when the small boat in which he'd been travelling had been dashed against rocks during a storm. The bodies of the two other men onboard had been washed ashore, but William Markham was lost at sea. For weeks, his wife had waited for news, her hands trembling, her nerves scraped raw. Bridget remembered those fraught days and nights, how they'd searched every crevice and cave, and how neighbours had joined them in prayer. When, finally, Johanna had accepted that her husband's body wouldn't be recovered, there'd been no keening or wailing. If there were tears in her eyes, she blamed them on the smoke billowing from the cottage fire.

For months afterwards, Bridget had imagined her father's voice booming through the cabin. She would dream they were all back together, a complete family, and then she'd wake, limbs stiff from the cold, sadness swirling around her.

Johanna's loss was all the crueller because of her elder son's absence. Francie had sailed for Boston in the spring of 1837. For a time, he'd written short letters. Bridget had considered it miraculous that flimsy pieces of paper could travel all the way from America. Boston was cold in the winter, he said, even colder than Clare. The snow might fall for days on end. Work was plentiful, though, and he was doing well. Soon, he'd be able to send more money home. The letters became less frequent. And then they stopped. Now, Francie's name was rarely mentioned. Outwardly, it was as if he'd never existed. This didn't stop Bridget thinking about his life in America. Was he rich? Had he married? Was she an aunt? Did he know his father had disappeared? She thought, too, of how much a letter, no matter how brief, would mean to their mother.

Her father's death meant there were just four of them at home. The man of the house, fourteen-year-old Michael, was prone to fevers and chills and not as well suited to hard labour as his mother and sisters. In similar circumstances, many families would have surrendered to their ill fortune and sought refuge in the workhouse. Bridget's mother didn't want to live among the poor and infirm.

Soon, their number would be reduced to three. The previous day, Mary Ellen had announced that she was to marry a man from Hackett's Cross. In Bridget's view, there wasn't much to recommend Thomas McGuane. He was boorish and unfriendly, with hair like freshly cut straw, but his family were better off than the Markhams, and speaking ill of them was considered a sin.

That hadn't prevented her from voicing an opinion. 'Are you a fool?' she'd said to her sister. 'You can do a lot better. The McGuanes are awful people.'

Mary Ellen had responded by getting haughty. In the end, she'd given Bridget a slap across the cheek and told her she wasn't welcome at the wedding.

Her face stinging, Bridget had squealed. She hadn't, however, backed down. 'As if I'd want to go. Honestly, he's not the husband for you, and soon enough you'll realise it.'

They'd continued sparring until their mother had intervened. She'd been annoyed that their row had taken place in full view of their neighbours. 'We'll be the talk of the place,' she'd complained. Later, she'd given Bridget a warning. 'You might not like Thomas, but you'd do well to remember that we're in no position to be choosy. We might need the McGuanes one day.'

Bridget hated the thought of relying on Thomas and his family. She also hated the idea of spending the rest of her days in poverty. She pictured places where girls slept on beds with sheets and pillows, not on the cold floor. Places where there were books to read, and no one worried about the rent. Did her brother live like that now? she wondered.

These thoughts in her head, she passed a shell from one hand to the other. It was a needle whelk, not especially rare, but pretty. She'd found it as they bundled the seaweed into their baskets. Beside her, Johanna was humming lightly to herself.

'In a few weeks, Mary Ellen will be a married woman,' said Bridget, 'and then it'll be my turn.'

Her mother rubbed Bridget's arm, her hand cold and wrinkled from the seawater. 'There's no need for you to be in a hurry. Big and all as you are, you'll always be my little one.'

Even though Johanna often gave out to her – 'Bridget Markham, you'll be the death of me,' she'd say, or 'If your father was here, he'd put a stop to your silliness' – Bridget knew she was her favourite. They laughed at the same stories and enjoyed the same songs. They had the same smooth red hair. Mary Ellen's was springy and wiry.

'Hopefully, I'll find someone better than Thomas, anyway,' she said, placing the shell in her skirt pocket. 'Someone handsome with great ideas who'll be able to make life better for all of us.'

'Oh, Bridget,' said her mother. She said this a lot. 'You'll have to accept your station. No good comes from wanting what you can't have. You'll be a lucky girl if you're able to do as well as your sister.'

Bridget disagreed. Although she longed for an easier life, she would never marry a man she didn't like, someone who bored her or was unkind. Unfortunately, only one local boy appealed to her, and John Joe Moloney's family had even less than the Markhams. Sometimes the two went for a walk and spoke about what they'd like to do with their lives. Mostly, it was foolish talk. Chances were neither would leave Clooneven.

There were things she was tempted to say, but she knew they would upset her mother. Instead, she gave Johanna's arm a squeeze and kept her thoughts to herself. The two stared out at the ocean, which shone for as far as Bridget could see. Thousands of miles of ocean and, beyond that, America.

Chapter 4

May 2019, Clooneven

Jessie

It was Tuesday. Or maybe it was Wednesday. After three weeks at home, Jessie had lost track of the days. As she walked along the prom, the evening sky was streaked with neon. Waves curled and fizzed to the shore. Two boys, who looked to be in their early teens, sat on a bench smoking a joint, the smell a reminder of her other life, the life she hoped would be hers again soon. She was about to take out her cigarettes when she spotted a familiar figure pacing in her direction. He was wearing a GAA tracksuit top and loose-fitting jeans. His dark hair was longer than the last time they'd met and his face slightly thinner. Otherwise, he appeared unchanged.

Between the ages of four and eighteen, she'd seen Ger Dillane almost every day. They'd been in the same class at St Finian's national school, studied the same Leaving Cert subjects and jumped around at the same teenage discos. If memory served, they'd once shared a fumble at the back of the arcade. It had been during the free-for-all of her Leaving Cert summer when her class had been determined to explore all available options. They'd told themselves that if quality was out of reach, they would have to settle for quantity. Jessie remembered that summer with fondness. The one low note had been provided by Lorna and Simon's wedding and her sister's insistence that the bridesmaids wear pale blue satin. Pale blue was not Jessie's colour.

In recent weeks, she'd come to realise how little contact she'd maintained with the crowd from school. A few had married, but not as many as she had expected. Like her, a considerable number had left. They were in London or Sydney or Dubai. Mostly, this separation didn't bother her. Ger was an exception. Knowing he was back in Clooneven and teaching in St Finian's, she'd considered calling him but had shied away.

She knew how her Dublin circle would view him. He'd be caricatured as the textbook 'decent guy from home': moderately good-looking, a handy footballer, clever but not showily so. The sort of man who drank a half-litre of milk with his dinner, went on stag weekends to Westport and excelled at practical things, like DIY and paying bills. That there was an element of truth to this description didn't stop it being misleading. He was also one of the shrewdest people she knew.

She'd been queasy about calling because she'd felt too low, her mood not helped by the fact that she'd entered a phase of compulsive comparing. One of the family would make a harmless comment about someone from her year – 'Did you hear Chloë Downes had twins?' or 'I gather Conor Haugh's after getting a big job in Abu Dhabi' – and a wave of inadequacy would wash over her. Did she want twins or a big job in Abu Dhabi? No, but at least her contemporaries were out there achieving something.

Her friend Shona claimed that being from a small town was a competitive sport. 'And you know the thing about sport?' she'd say.

'Strong drugs help a lot.' Behind the flippancy was a hard truth. Small-town judgement tended to be harsh. So, while she wanted to see Ger, she didn't want it to be right now, like this, when she was flat and depleted. When she was a public failure.

'Hey, Jessie,' he said, his voice as laidback as ever. 'I'd heard you were home. How are you going on?'

'I'm grand … Well, you know.' There was a world of information in her 'Well, you know.'

He gave a slight smile. 'Yeah … I was thinking of giving you a shout but …'

The past three weeks had taught her to be blunt. 'If you're going to give me a hard time, fire ahead. Only the jokes would need to be good because, believe me, I've heard them all.'

He held up his hands. 'No jokes, I promise. Are you back for long?'

That question again. Out of the corner of her eye, she saw the boys with the joint sidle away. She wondered if Ger had taught them at school.

'No, but Mam's reluctant to let me go back to Dublin. I'd be here for ever if she had her way.' She quickly realised that her tone was wrong. There was no point in causing unnecessary offence. 'Not that it'd be the end of the world or anything. I mean—'

'Relax,' he said. 'I know Clooneven's not for everyone.'

If, in Dublin, Jessie had done little apart from think about her humiliation, in Clooneven, she was trying not to think at all. She was also doing everything possible to avoid her parents' questions. When asked about her plans, she dodged and deflected until they gave up. The same was true when they asked about Phelim. She couldn't handle the conversation. Not yet, at any rate.

Her days had taken on a rhythm. She reread old books, helped her mother around the house and listened to a stream of true crime podcasts. When it came to books, she tended to choose either icy American novels with affluent characters who felt guilty all the time or coming-of-age tales where young women with no obvious source of income went to dinner parties and had unsatisfactory sex. Her taste in podcasts was lower grade. She had a particular weakness for serial killers and 'cheerleader falls on hard times' stories featuring trailer parks and rampant drug use. She told herself that this was voyeuristic brain rot. But still she listened.

On a couple of occasions, she'd taken care of Lorna's children. Seven-year-old Ethan and four-year-old Zoë were smart and entertaining, and Jessie looked forward to their teenage rebellions. Already they were wonderfully honest.

Mostly, though, she cycled around the countryside on her old purple bicycle. Clooneven was surrounded by a network of lanes. Few of them led anywhere, and Jessie assumed the houses and farms that had prompted their construction had been abandoned long ago. She thought of them as ghost lanes and doubted they saw much traffic. The late spring was as fine as she could remember, chilly mornings giving way to mild afternoons, the hedgerows brimming with life. She would look at the cloud stamped like tyre tracks across the crisp blue sky or cycle through a tunnel of trees or stop to admire a bank of cowslips and primroses, and for a moment, she'd feel something close to happiness.

She dragged herself back to the present. Ger was still talking.

'Actually, you were in my thoughts the other day,' he said.

'Oh?'

'I'm teaching sixth class this year, and we're doing a project on the Famine, so I've encouraged them to root out local stories. It makes everything more real. Anyway, one of the first recorded deaths from starvation was around here, and they'd like to find out more.'

'And that made you think of me?'

Jessie remembered learning about the Famine. She could see the black-and-white illustrations in the school history book: the blight-infested potatoes and emaciated, hollow-eyed children; the workhouses and coffin ships; Robert Peel and Charles Trevelyan. Among the litany of battles lost and punishments endured, it had always stood out.

'The woman's address was given as Boherbreen, Clooneven,' he said.

'Ah, I get you. That's Dad's home patch. Etty lives in Boherbreen.'

'That's what I thought.'

The townland of Boherbreen was about three kilometres to the north of Clooneven. Etty was Denis's eighty-five-year-old mother. Usually, Jessie avoided people who were commonly described as a 'character'. She considered it a euphemism for 'pain in the arse'. For her grandmother, she made an exception.

'What was the woman's name?' she said.

'Johanna Markham, though I'd say our chances of finding out more about her are slim. Keen and all as my investigators are, they're only twelve. Here,' he said, taking his phone from the pocket of his jeans and flicking through the images. 'I have a couple of screenshots. One's from the book where I first came across a reference to her.'

The book, a history of the Famine, said the death of Mrs Markham, a widow, had been recorded by a local newspaper in the autumn of 1846. A coroner found that she had died from hunger while walking from Clooneven to Kilrush. According to the report, she'd been trying to buy Indian meal for her family, including her daughter, Bridget, and Bridget's infant girl.

'God, that's grim,' said Jessie, handing back the phone. 'Poor Johanna. And poor Bridget, not to mention her baby.'

She knew she should offer to put Ger and his class in touch with her grandmother, but the thought of a gang of lively twelve-year-olds filled her with lethargy. Besides, she'd always managed to avoid local-history projects at school and didn't feel the need to become involved in one now. In her experience, local-history enthusiasts wore brown sweaters and ugly sandals and became unreasonably excited about old stones.

'So I was wondering,' said Ger, 'if Etty might know anything about the history of the area. Any little fact that might help bring the story to life?'

'I don't —'

'We wouldn't want to be bothering her or anything. Like, the class could write her a letter if needs be.'

Despite her reservations, something about Ger's face told Jessie that saying no would be a mistake. She'd been relieved to see that, unlike many people, he remained warm towards her. She could do with an ally. She also knew that staying completely detached from life in Clooneven wasn't a good idea. It only gave further ammunition to the gossips.

'You know Etty's spent her whole life on those few acres?' she said. 'She grew up on the next farm, and she first met my granddad when she was four or five.'

'You definitely didn't get the wanderlust from her, so.'

Jessie smiled. 'Why don't I mention the project to her, in case there's something she can tell you?'

'That'd be fantastic,' said Ger. 'The class are very keen, and they'd be thrilled to discover a bit more. They're a great bunch.'

'Okay, then. I have your number, and I can message you if Etty has anything to say. Speaking of which …' She pulled her buzzing phone from her jacket pocket. 'Bear with me a sec.'

The call was from Lorna. Jessie allowed it to go to voicemail. She noticed that she'd missed four calls: one from her mother and three from her sister. There was also a message: *A man called Dan O'Doherty is looking for you. He said you'll know who he is and why he wants to talk to you. He was VERY angry. What's going on?*

For a few seconds, she was quiet. Apart from one knee, which gave a sudden wobble, her entire body stiffened.

'Sorry,' she said eventually. 'That was a message from Lorna. She's a terrible woman. Honestly, I can't get a minute's peace. Anyway …'

Ger dipped his head, as if dealing with a troubled child. 'Is something wrong?' he asked.

Once again, Jessie should have been prepared. She should have known that Dan would find her. What she was going to do now, she wasn't sure. She could try lying to Lorna and her parents, but there was a danger that she would need their help.

'Don't worry,' she said to Ger. 'Like I say, Lorna's a demon for getting worked up about nothing.' She slipped her phone back into her pocket.

'If you're certain …'

'I am,' she said, doing her best to sound calm. 'And I promise that if Etty knows anything about Johanna and Bridget, or anyone belonging to them, I'll get in touch.'

Chapter 5

1846, Clooneven

Bridget

That she would never know the precise circumstances of her mother's death haunted Bridget. All she knew was that Johanna had died alone, at the side of the road, like a badger or a fox. The coroner said her body had been as cold as a flagstone. Bridget wondered if she had stopped for a rest and found it impossible to get up again. Or had she fallen? There were scratches on her knees, suggesting she'd attempted to crawl. If she'd called out for help, would anyone have heard? Or, by then, had she been too weak to say anything?

You mustn't blame yourself, their neighbours in Boherbreen said.

But how could she not?

Bridget pictured her mother as she'd left their cottage for the eight-mile walk to Kilrush, her lips pressed together, her black shawl draped over her head, her grey dress loose as a sack. Johanna had hoped to buy yellow meal. 'Peel's brimstone', they called it, on account of how hard it was, and how you had to keep boiling it for fear of getting sick. Before leaving, she'd kissed baby Norah's head and been rewarded with a smile. She'd doted on her granddaughter.

While she'd travelled east, Bridget's husband, John Joe, had walked north towards Doonbeg. Between them, they'd said, they would find something for the family to eat.

Bridget, her brother Michael and Norah had stayed at home. Poor Norah. At eight months old, she hadn't known a day without want. She never cried from ill-temper. When she sobbed and whined it was because she was starving. Bridget tried to feed her, but she feared the milk from her breasts was too watery. Sometimes she fretted that hunger would shape her baby's life. She worried that even if their world returned to normal, Norah would be marked by events she'd been too young to understand. Mostly, though, Bridget didn't have time for such fanciful thoughts. She didn't have time to think about the world and her place in it. Mostly, she had time only for foraging and gathering.

Everyone had been convinced that, this year, the potatoes would be better. They hadn't thought it possible for the crop to fail again. Not when the herring fishery had also failed. Not when many of the local fishermen had been forced to sell or pawn their boats, and the pigs and hens had already been eaten.

If anything, the decay was more extensive, the stench more foul. The stalks were slimy and withered, the potatoes covered with black mould. It was God's work, some said, the pestilence a punishment for their inability to appreciate what they'd been given in the past.

Using her bare bony hands, Johanna had reached into the damp earth and pulled out every potato, no matter how small. Her back was bent double, her hands black, her movements frenzied. But the potatoes were rancid with disease, every last one of them inedible. Similar scenes occurred in every plot in every townland. When Bridget tried to describe the response, she struggled for an adequate word. It was bigger than panic or fear. Terror came closest, she believed.

Every day her mother went back to the land, in the hope of salvaging part of the crop. In the end, she accepted defeat. She sat down, crying quietly, and mopping her tears with the corner of her shawl. Five days later, she set out on her mission to Kilrush.

For a time, John Joe had laboured on the relief works, building a new road from Clooneven to Hackett's Cross. Michael, never strong, had also worked. He'd broken stones until his hands were red-raw with blisters. The days had been long: seven in the morning until seven at night. The wage had been poor, and when the work had finished, they'd had little in reserve. For a month before her death, Johanna had eaten a bare meal a day. Some days, she'd had nothing at all.

Bridget had asked Mary Ellen for help. Her sister lived five miles away in a cottage with three rooms. It was difficult to fathom two people having all that space. Mrs Thomas McGuane, as she now was, said she'd nothing to give. While their situation might once have been more comfortable, they too were facing a winter without food. Their potatoes were rotten, and one of their pigs had been stolen. Bridget wasn't surprised by this miserly response. Although cordial for their mother's sake, relations between the two had never recovered from the row over Mary Ellen's choice of husband. The problem was, Bridget's sister was in thrall to Thomas and wouldn't do anything that might meet with his disapproval.

Mary Ellen advised her to go down to the shore in Clooneven. She might find crabs or other shellfish there. That would be better than going hungry, wouldn't it? Unfortunately, the rocks had been picked bare, and Bridget returned to the cabin with just a half-creel of seaweed and a few limpets.

On the day of her death, Johanna Markham had been fifty-one years old. She'd been the mother of two sons and two daughters. Her husband had been lost at sea. She'd possessed a sweet singing voice and a quiet laugh. She'd known a reasonable amount of English but had spoken mostly Irish. She'd never been to school and had been proud that her four children, including her daughters, could read and write. Although she'd rarely mentioned his name, she'd prayed every day for word of her son in America.

These were the simple facts given by Bridget to the inquest. As she spoke, shame rippled through her. Johanna had died of starvation. Or, as the coroner put it, 'in consequence of an insufficiency of food'. The facts were inadequate. The truth was that Bridget had failed her. They all had.

Michael died two months later. When Bridget went to wake him one morning, he was cold, his face waxy, his lips tinged with blue. Her brother had been suffering badly for weeks, his breath rattling, his chest wheezing, his legs buckling beneath him. She'd tried to get him to eat the stirabout she made from meal and water, but he couldn't force it down. Even warm milk wouldn't clear his throat. Somehow he'd lost his ability to swallow. He was nineteen.

'A merciful release,' John Joe said, and while she was upset, Bridget couldn't argue. She did her best to react with stoicism, the way her mother would have wanted.

Michael was buried beside Johanna. A mean wind whipped around the small crowd who'd arrived to pay their respects. They remembered how the youngest member of the Markham family had possessed the kindest nature, how he'd liked watching the birds gather on the rocks around Clooneven and how he'd been able to soothe Norah when she was crying.

After the funeral, when they were on their own in the cabin, the only light coming from the turf fire, John Joe put his arm around Bridget's shoulders.

'I promise you, it will get better,' he said.

She wept then in a way she hadn't thought possible, her chest shaking as she gasped for air.

'You can't promise that,' she said. 'None of us can.'

There was no inquest for Michael. In the space of a few weeks, death had become commonplace. Every day news reached them of another tragedy. Three children had died in Hackett's Cross, their bodies no wider than the bones beneath. Their mother was said to have lost her mind with grief. A woman sleeping beside the seashore in Cahercullen had perished where she lay. Two men had died while labouring on the relief works near Annaghcarney.

There were other stories too. Bridget heard of a widow who kept her six children indoors to preserve their strength. Another family had resorted to chewing hay in the hope it might provide nourishment. A third had killed a dog and made soup from its flesh and bones. Everywhere, people were selling or pawning their belongings so that all they had left were the four walls, a pot to cook in and a scattering of straw to sleep on.

As winter moved in, Bridget felt her mother's absence every day. Sometimes, her grief was physical. It was a rock at the base of her throat or a metal band tightening around her skull. Frequently, she thought of Francie in Boston. She presumed he knew nothing about the deaths of Johanna and Michael.

And yet her life also contained moments of joy. This confused her. What right did she have to smile?

She had no regrets about her marriage. Her mother had considered eighteen too young, but Bridget had protested that she'd find no better than John Joe Moloney. He was, she'd insisted, more intelligent than the other men in Clooneven. Oh, and he was handsome, with wavy brown hair, dark eyes and a broad back. What she didn't say was that he made her feel warm, like her insides were humming.

Finally, Johanna had relented. 'If I don't agree,' she'd said, 'there's a danger you'll end up in trouble.'

The second youngest of a family of twelve, John Joe had moved in with Bridget, her mother and brother after the wedding. His family's poverty meant he'd received no schooling, and Bridget had taught him to read. He pledged that if he ever found a way of earning money, he'd buy her an entire library of books.

When it came to politics, John Joe had educated himself. He spoke to people, and he listened. He lamented the way wheat and oats, butter and fish were leaving from the port in Kilrush. How could that be right, he'd ask, when local people were dying for want of food? He talked about the protests in Ennis where men had demanded more help for the starving. He railed against the attitude of politicians in London, who claimed that aid would encourage idleness among the poor. He discussed all of this with Bridget, asking her opinion and responding to her questions. From what she'd heard, many men didn't consider their wives capable of such conversations.

One Sunday, they were in the cabin, sheltering from a squall of rain, when John Joe asked if she would consider going elsewhere.

'America, do you mean?' she said, recalling what they'd talked about when they were courting.

'No, I was thinking of somewhere closer. We could move east. People are saying that Clare is one of the worst places to live. There are better landlords elsewhere, men who accept that times are hard and are willing to lower the rent.'

Bridget and John Joe's landlord, Sir Henry Frobisher, rarely visited Ireland. His rents were collected by agents.

She fingered the edge of her shawl. 'I don't know. I … I feel closer to Mam here. I can visit her grave.'

'I understand, but won't you think about it?'

'Maybe next year. Maybe we could move then. I'd be ready then.'

Her husband said nothing, and she worried he was about to argue. Then, as if sensing the need to intervene, Norah broke the silence. 'La la la la la,' she sang, from the floor where she was playing with some shells.

Her parents laughed. The little girl was singing with such exuberance it was impossible not to. She had two bottom teeth now, and her round blue eyes fixed upon everything that moved. While not as plump as a baby should be, she was a bonny thing. All the locals said it. Bridget was proud, not just of her daughter's loveliness, but also of her temperament. She marvelled at how Norah continued to grow despite the turmoil and poverty surrounding her. Oh, and bless her, she found delight in everything, from the shell in her hands to her mother's long hair to her father's tickles.

Even though Bridget would have liked another baby, she knew it wasn't possible. They would be bringing a fourth mouth into a house where two people had died from hunger. John Joe agreed, but staying apart was hard. It wasn't natural, he said.

'La la la,' sang Norah, as if singing was her personal discovery.

'La la la,' echoed John Joe, bending down and lifting his daughter, who gurgled her approval.

Bridget's body filled with love. She assured herself that next year would be better. The potatoes couldn't rot again. They could grow other crops too. Carrots, perhaps, or parsnips. She'd learn to be even more frugal. John Joe could continue on the relief works. And a year or two from now, when her mother's memory had receded, they'd find somewhere better to live.

All they had to do was stay alive.

Chapter 6

In the early months of 1847, fever crept through Clooneven. It was quiet at first, taking only those who'd been weakened by hunger and old age. As time passed, it became greedier, claiming young men and women. The atmosphere, already dark, became dense with fear.

Bridget watched what was happening around her. She saw the glassy eyes and jaundiced faces, heard about the sweating and vomiting, the smell that filled the cabins of the sick. It was all people could talk about.

Did you hear about Mary O'Flaherty?

About Joseph Morrissey?

About the young Griffin boy?

What was causing it? they asked. Could it be as simple as a lack of food? Or were there other reasons? Were the women who searched through dung heaps for vegetable peel to blame? Or the men who killed and ate wild animals? Some argued that if a person became infected, they ought to be banished to an empty cabin or shed. Otherwise, the entire family would fall victim to the fever. They turned on each other, neighbour accusing neighbour of spreading disease.

By now Bridget had learnt to supplement the Indian meal with seaweed, nettles and dock leaves. In the autumn, there would be nuts and berries. She dreamt of fat blackberries, the juice oozing down her chin. Her mother would have laughed at how industrious she'd become. Lazy Bridget, who'd frittered away the hours on the strand, had disappeared.

She was setting off one March afternoon, Norah on her back, feet slip-sliding in the wet clay, when she met two local women, Eliza Haugh and Cathleen Downes. Bridget was lightheaded from hunger and would have preferred to walk on, but the neighbours had been good to her when her mother died. They'd been a similar age, and Johanna's passing had been difficult for them. Nevertheless, they'd been adamant that she'd gone to a better place where she could be reunited with her husband. Bridget had her doubts about this better place, but it was a kind thought.

When she was a child, Mrs Haugh, Mrs Downes and many others had been regular visitors to the cottage. The adults had swapped songs and stories. They'd told tales about ghosts and fairies, about daring ancestors and times of good fortune. Nobody did that any more.

Bridget greeted the women and stopped to talk.

'What way is Patrick Talty?' asked Cathleen.

'Suffering no longer,' replied Eliza. 'The Lord have mercy on his soul.'

'That's terrible,' said Bridget. 'He was a young man.'

'Twenty-two,' replied Cathleen, blessing herself, 'only a gosoon.'

Eliza folded her arms. She'd once had a substantial chest and retained the mannerisms of a larger woman. 'He spent his final week in the workhouse. Would you believe that some are going there because it's the only way they'll get a coffin?'

Bridget had heard about people being buried without coffins, either because there was no money to pay for the wood or because they'd no surviving family to arrange a proper funeral. According to John Joe, the bodies were discarded at night to avoid bringing shame upon the family. While most were covered with earth, others were abandoned in fields and ditches, their remains claimed by animals or the weather.

'John Joe found two bodies last month,' she said, 'while he was building a wall beyond in Tullaroe. A woman and a child. The woman's arm was wrapped around the girl. He didn't say very much, but I knew he was distressed.'

Norah had been getting a new tooth at the time. Between her tears and John Joe's bad humour, it had been the bleakest period since Michael's death. Tullaroe was a barren spot, little of it farmed, and Bridget couldn't see any great purpose to her husband's labours. They were dividing land that didn't need to be divided. John Joe said the men joked about getting fourpence a day to protect land that wasn't worth fourpence an acre. Bridget thought they should be given a useful task, such as building fever sheds at the workhouse or repairing the homes of the destitute or sowing crops. At least her husband was able to come home at night. Some of the workers came from miles away and were forced to bed down in the wet fields. No wonder so many were ill.

'That's a desperate story,' said Cathleen. 'As God is my witness, I'll never cross the door of that workhouse. Minnie Slattery told me that an aunt of hers sought refuge there, and Hell would have been kinder. The woman was frail already, but she lasted only three weeks in Kilrush. The fever's ripping through the place.'

'Isn't that the truth of it?' said Eliza. 'I say it all the time, "The places that are meant to keep us safe are killing us." It's the same with the relief works. There are men dropping off the roads, like birds falling into a ditch.' She turned to Bridget. 'What does John Joe say?'

'He prefers not to talk about it.'

Where once John Joe had discussed the men he worked with – Packie Meleady with the torn breeches, Corney Crehan with the seven daughters – he now stayed silent or moved the conversation in another direction. He was determined not to be ground down by what he witnessed, but Bridget would have liked a return to the honest discussions they'd had in the past. Want and suffering were turning them all into other people.

It started with a headache. She might not have noticed only she saw John Joe wincing.

'It's nothing,' he said. 'There was a shocking wind out there today and it cut through all of us. Thankfully, I've no work tomorrow.'

'Well, mind yourself,' she said, as she stirred a pot of turnips. They had mussels and oat cakes too. Compared to what they'd become accustomed to, this was a feast, and she was proud of her efforts. 'The dinner will be ready soon.'

'Do you know, for once I'm not hungry. Be certain to have plenty yourself, though.'

'I will,' she said, 'only ...' She was too worried to say anything further.

By the following morning, he was burning up. His face had a grey sheen, and his eyes were rimmed with pink. Bridget instructed herself not to panic. John Joe had a temperature. It didn't follow that he was seriously ill. He might have caught a chill from being out in the elements all day. She'd make stirabout and insist that he eat.

Norah, who had begun walking, chose that moment to wobble and tumble over. Her tiny face crumpled, and she launched into a wail that would have curdled milk.

Bridget crouched down and kissed her forehead. 'Hush, pet,' she urged her daughter. 'Your daddy's not well this morning, and we have to be quiet.'

Norah sniffled and hiccuped for a minute or two before deciding to examine her father. She plodded over to where he lay, leant in and stroked his nose.

'Dada?' she said.

'Take her away,' said John Joe, his voice so gruff, Bridget barely recognised it. 'I can't risk her getting the fever too.'

Norah stumbled back, her features crinkling as if she might cry again.

'It might not be that bad,' said Bridget. 'It might be ...' She stopped. She was fooling herself.

The temperature was quickly followed by aches and pains, searing pains that caused him to cry out. Oh, and he was confused, asking after the dead and calling Bridget by the names of his sisters and rambling about people and places that meant nothing to her.

Outside, the weather had changed. A thick fog had descended over Clooneven, stripping the landscape of colour. Even nearby cottages were obscured, and everyday tasks, like walking to the well, became difficult. Bridget didn't dare leave Norah alone with John Joe, so she carried the little girl on her back. The days were so dank, the ground so sticky, that by the time she was back home, her pail was half empty. And they needed water. Lots of it. Water for John Joe to drink, water to soothe his fever and water to keep the cottage as clean as possible.

On the fourth day, two men arrived, Cathleen Downes's husband, Edward, and a fellow called Maurice Curry, who was well-known for taking an interest in other people's business. They told her they'd heard John Joe was unwell. They were here to help, they said.

'I don't follow you,' said Bridget, 'but come in out of the cold, and we'll talk.' She felt Norah beside her, pulling at her skirt.

They edged forward but stayed on the threshold.

'You have to look after yourself and your daughter,' said Maurice Curry, a man with sloping shoulders and great tufts of black hair. 'John Joe shouldn't be here in your home. It's not safe. There's a shed out past the Honan family's cabin. Patrick Talty spent a while in it. We can take him there.'

Bridget knew the shed was damp and furred with mould and spider's webs. She was thankful John Joe was asleep. 'I think my husband's safer where I can take care of him.'

'Please be reasonable, Mrs Moloney, and think of the child's welfare.' He peered down at Norah, who nestled in behind Bridget. 'You can't risk a mite like that catching the fever.'

'I'm content to keep John Joe here where I can nurse him and bring him everything he needs.' She gestured towards the bed she'd made from an old greatcoat and two blankets. 'As you can see, he's as comfortable as possible. And don't worry, I can take care of Norah too. Sure she's no bother at all.'

'You're only a young girl yourself. You don't know what's best. Your parents, God be good to them, would have wanted us to help.'

Edward Downes, who hadn't spoken, gave her a pleading look. When she was a child, he'd been the biggest man in the townland, with the heartiest voice. Now, his face was sunken, and his back had an old man's stoop.

'I'm twenty-one,' she said, 'and I know what's best for my family.'

'You'll regret this,' said Maurice Curry, poking a finger towards her. 'You'll learn that foolish behaviour has consequences.'

Tears were forming at the back of Bridget's eyes. 'I'm sure you'll remember that my mother died on a lonely road with nobody to comfort her. I'm convinced John Joe will live, but I can't let him suffer on his own. It's not human. Now please leave us be.'

Edward Downes placed a hand on his friend's back and, without a further word, the two turned and left.

A while later, Cathleen Downes arrived at the door. 'I won't come in,' she said.

Bridget didn't want to fall out with her mother's friend, but neither did she want to back down. 'I appreciate your concern, Mrs Downes. I'm not going to change my mind, though.'

'Now, Bridget, it's about time you called me Cathleen. You're a grown woman with your own family. All I'm going to say is you won't save John Joe by killing yourself and baby Norah.'

'I'm not infected.'

'Not yet.'

'Please, Cathleen. I need to do everything I can for him.' Bridget's voice was too high. She wished she sounded more like an adult. 'I let Mam down, and I can't make the same mistake again.'

Cathleen wrapped her hand around Bridget's. The skin was rough as tree bark. 'You mustn't think like that, love. Your mammy wouldn't want it.' She paused. 'How is John Joe?'

'Not well. There's a rash all over his body. I have to keep Norah on the other side of the cabin. She gets upset if she looks at him too closely.'

'And you're certain about keeping him here?'

'I am.'

'Very well. But you've got to look after yourself too.'

That evening, when Bridget stepped outside again, she found a black pot containing oats and a cabbage. Beside it was a smaller pot, half filled with buttermilk. She knew where the food had come from. Briefly, she wondered if she should accept. The Downes family had barely enough to feed themselves. But returning the gift would be considered rude. The kindness, which she might never be able to repay, caused a tear to fall down her cheek.

She remembered what her mother had said about how they might need the McGuanes one day. She could do with help from Thomas and Mary Ellen now. Even a visit would be welcome. Then she chastised herself: there was every chance her sister hadn't heard of their predicament.

That night, she lay awake, staring up at the thatch. Norah snuffled beside her. On the other side of the room, John Joe's breathing was ragged, as though every single inhalation hurt. He couldn't eat, he could barely drink and, like she'd told Cathleen, angry red spots had erupted on his skin. She fretted that she'd made the wrong decision. Might it be better if he was isolated elsewhere? Might there be some wisdom in taking him to the workhouse? As dreadful as the place was, at least there was a doctor. The McGuanes had a donkey and cart. Perhaps, they'd be willing to take him to Kilrush.

She agonised for hours, rising only to attend to John Joe when he started wandering in his sleep.

'Shush now,' she said, dipping a cloth into a pot of cold water and mopping his face. 'I'm here and Norah's here. We won't allow anything to happen to you.'

Bridget lost count of the days. She rarely left the cabin except to fetch water or search for food. As if she understood the gravity of the situation, there was barely a sound out of Norah. She sat on the ground near the door, arranging and rearranging her collection of sticks and shells.

John Joe was unconscious for much of the time. When awake, he thrashed and moaned. Bridget thought he recognised her but couldn't be certain.

A week or more after she'd spoken to Cathleen Downes, three of her husband's brothers – Andy, Dan and James – arrived, each as tall and thin as a sapling. They bent their heads to enter the room. They were even more dishevelled than the last time she'd seen them. Their clothes had been patched so often that the original cloth was barely visible.

'What way is he?' asked the eldest brother, Dan.

'Poor, to be honest,' she said.

'Mam was talking about coming to see him, only her own health isn't the best.'

'I understand.' John Joe's mother was elderly, and his father had died ten years earlier.

'We brought you these,' said James, removing a handkerchief from his pocket. It contained two hen's eggs. She couldn't imagine where he'd got them because chickens were a rarity. Most people didn't have the spare meal for their feed.

'I can't take them,' she said. 'John Joe isn't well enough to eat. They'll only go to waste.'

'They're for you and Norah,' said Andy. 'And don't worry, we didn't steal them.'

For what felt like the first time in weeks, she smiled. 'Thank you. I'm very grateful. Norah has never had an egg. Would you like to go over and talk to John Joe? He's asleep, but he might wake for you.' She took her daughter by the hand. 'Come on, pet, we'll go outside and leave the men in peace.'

It was only when she heard them praying that she realised they were there to say goodbye.

She slept for a short while that night, her lost family members flitting through her dreams. Her mother and father were there, as was Michael. Her other brother, Francie, appeared too. In her dream, he was collecting seaweed in Clooneven. He was cheerful and healthy, and had never left for Boston.

When she woke, John Joe's breathing was quieter. She wanted this to be a good sign, but she'd deluded herself for too long. He was slipping away. She lay on the ground beside him and stroked his brown curls. They had become matted with sweat. Then she drew a finger along his cheek and around his jaw. She felt impossibly tender towards him and doubted she would ever feel this way again. She considered trying to get a priest, then decided she'd prefer if they were on their own.

'Please don't go,' she whispered. 'I need you and Norah needs you. Please.'

Their daughter was asleep, and Bridget believed this was for the best.

For a while she spoke about the fun they'd had as teenagers. 'Do you remember when we went walking on the cliffs in Clooneven? That was the first time you kissed me. Mam asked why I'd been gone for so long, and I had to pretend I'd met Nellie Dillane from school.'

She squeezed John Joe's hand.

'I'm sorry,' she continued, 'I did everything I could. I hope you understand that. I'm sorry it wasn't enough, my love.'

She caressed his face again and cursed herself for not agreeing when he'd asked her to move elsewhere. If she'd been less stubborn, might he still be healthy? Might he still be talking about politics and hoisting a giggling Norah into the air?

When she kissed his cheek, she knew his breathing had stopped.

Bridget didn't want to hear that John Joe was in a better place. He belonged here with his wife and daughter. The better place could have waited.

Presently, Norah woke and toddled over to her side.

Bridget sat up and buried her face in the soft curls the little girl had inherited from her father. She remained in the dark for a long time, her sobs magnified by the silence.

Chapter 7

Mary Ellen sat beside the fire, the flames throwing amber light across her face. She hadn't attended John Joe's burial, leaving it until afterwards to offer her sympathies. Bridget was surprised to realise that she didn't hold it against her. There had been too many funerals, too many desolate scenes.

Thomas McGuane had chosen to stay outside. Although he didn't say as much, she assumed he was scared that some remnant of disease remained within the cabin.

Norah sat on her mother's knee. Mary Ellen was unfamiliar to her, and she'd wriggled away when her aunt had tried to pick her up. John Joe's death had puzzled her. Without saying anything, she kept looking for her father, tiptoeing around the room and peering into corners.

'What will you do now?' said Mary Ellen.

'I'll have to find a way of paying the rent. I'm not sure how, but I'll think of something.'

Her neighbours had been generous, donating vegetables and meal. Mrs Haugh had arrived one evening with an offering of herring. 'Your need is greater than ours,' she'd said. Welcome as these gifts were, Bridget knew she couldn't rely indefinitely on the decency of others.

'I planted potatoes,' she continued. 'Not many, but I'm hoping there'll be enough. The crop can't fail again.'

Mary Ellen stared into the fire. Wisps of smoke rose around her. 'We ... Thomas and I ... wondered if you'd considered the workhouse.'

'No.'

'You'd be able to eat there.'

'From what I hear, the only reason people go to that place is to die.'

Norah whimpered, and Bridget brushed her lips over the child's head. 'It's all right, my love.'

'It can't be that bad,' said Mary Ellen.

'Mam wouldn't have wanted any of us ending up there.'

'She was a practical woman. If she felt it was necessary, that's what she would have done.'

'I said no.'

Mary Ellen was rubbing one thumb against the other, to and fro, back and forth. For some reason, she was nervous.

'I'm sorry,' said Bridget. 'I didn't mean to sound sharp, but the workhouse is overcrowded, and I don't want to bring Norah there.' She took a long breath. 'Maybe you could help us. We're not looking for money. If you had any spare food, though, we'd be incredibly grateful.'

'I'm afraid that's not possible. We're feeding several members of Thomas's family. And, let me tell you, it's precious little we have left after the thieves get to work. They'd steal the food from our mouths if they could. When there were turnips in the field, Thomas had to mind them night and day in case some blackguard came and took them. He says people who steal food should be hanged.'

'They only steal because they're starving,' said Bridget.

A brittle silence filled the room.

Eventually, Mary Ellen spoke again. 'Do you ever think of Francie?'

'I do. Please God, his life has turned out well, but ... I have a feeling that if he was successful we'd have heard from him.'

'Have you ever considered going to America yourself?'

'When I was younger, yes. It wouldn't have been fair on Mam, though. And now ... now my memories are here.' Bridget felt her eyes burning and she willed herself not to cry. There had been enough crying. 'And I hear the conditions are rough. A ship would be no place for this girl here.' She kissed her daughter's head.

'You wouldn't have to ...' Mary Ellen's voice tapered off.

'I wouldn't have to what?'

'You wouldn't have to take Norah,' she whispered.

'I don't understand.' She did, but she needed to hear her sister spell it out.

There was another pause before Mary Ellen spoke again. Her thumbs were rotating more quickly, and there was a slight shake in her voice. 'You've asked yourself, no doubt, why I don't have children.'

'No, it's not my concern,' said Bridget. This was a lie, and Mary Ellen must have known it because she continued to speak.

'I've never been able to carry a baby for long enough. I've tried again and again. Seven times I've been pregnant, and every time I've lost the baby. Like I've explained, we're not wealthy, Thomas and I, but we could give a child ... we could give Norah ... a home.'

Despite the fire, despite the mildness of the spring afternoon, Bridget felt cold. 'She has a home.'

Mary Ellen shook her head. 'You can't take care of her. Look at this place. It's draughty and damp. There's a hole in the thatch, and loose stones in the back wall. And a man died here.'

'The cottage isn't much worse than when we were children. And the man had a name. His name was John Joe, and he was Norah's father.'

'There was food when we were children, and a father to provide for us. And we weren't surrounded by skeletons. There's every danger you won't be able to stay here either. Word has it that tenants who fall into arrears will be evicted. You must have heard that.'

Bridget tightened her hold on Norah, then looked at the woman sitting across from her, at her untidy hair, gaunt face and beseeching expression. In other circumstances, she might have felt sorry for her. But what she was suggesting, encouraged presumably by Thomas, was wrong.

'Ma ma ma ma ma,' said Norah, a shiver passing through her body.

Bridget loosened her grip and tickled one of the child's feet. 'If you took my baby, what would I do?'

'You could go somewhere else. To America or Australia. There are lots of girls going to Australia. And you could begin again, knowing that Norah was well fed and cared for.'

The sisters had never been close, but, in that moment, a chasm opened between them.

'She's all I have,' said Bridget. 'She's everything that's good in my life. And tell me this: if I left, who would visit the graveyard? Who would go and see our mother and Michael and John Joe? Because I know it wouldn't be you.'

It took Mary Ellen a small while to respond. 'I know this sounds hard, but they're dead, Bridget. It doesn't matter whether anyone visits. They're not coming back. You've got to think of the living. More than anything, you ought to think of the child on your knee. What's going to become of her? It's only a matter of time before she gets sick.'

'You didn't come here to sympathise, did you? First you wanted me to go to the workhouse, and when I wouldn't agree, you started talking about America. What you actually want is to separate me from my daughter, isn't that it? You talk about hanging people who take a few turnips yet you're trying to steal a baby.'

'That's not true.'

'Why do I get the feeling that this was Thomas's idea? You know I've never liked him. Neither did Mam, only she was too much of a lady to say so.' Bridget's voice vibrated with anger, and Norah began to cry. 'It's all right, pet, the woman is leaving. There's no call to be scared.'

'We're being sensible, that's all. You're only young. You can marry again and have other children. And we're not talking about stealing Norah. We'd give you money to pay for your passage to America or wherever you wanted to go.'

There was desperation in Mary Ellen's voice unlike anything Bridget had heard before. She couldn't listen any longer. She stood too suddenly, causing her stool to tip over. 'What I want is for you to leave my house,' she said.

By now, Norah's wails were echoing around the room.

Mary Ellen hesitated. 'When you've had a chance to consider our offer, you might think differently. Please consider it, at least.'

'I've given you my answer. Oh, and be sure to tell your husband the answer is no. And it always will be.'

The days crawled by. Bridget was tired in a way she hadn't experienced before. Every step was a struggle, a battle with sore legs and aching arms. Worry wrapped itself around her like ivy.

At night, she yearned for John Joe. To stop the tears seeping out, she pressed her knuckles hard against her eyes. Had she been on her own, she might have given up. She might have waded into the Atlantic until she lost her footing and the current dragged her under. Like her father, she would be lost to the vastness of the ocean.

While walking to Clooneven, she was struck by the absence of sound. There were no animals, no children playing. Even the seagulls were quiet. In the town, landowners and their agents continued to go about their business. There were men in fine suits and women in bonnets. A girl with blonde ringlets gazed at Norah. Mostly, however, the well-to-do stared through them.

Do you not see us? thought Bridget. When did we become invisible?

As she crossed onto Main Street, she recalled something Mary Ellen had said: 'You're strong and healthy.' While Bridget was hollow with hunger, she had to admit that, compared to many, this was true. It was then the idea came to her.

She would have to try. If he said no, and he probably would, there was nothing lost.

She rounded the corner and tapped on the door of the parish priest's house. While she waited for her knock to be answered, her knees shook with nerves.

'Please be good for Mammy,' she said to Norah.

Father McNamara's housekeeper opened the door and gave them a swift appraisal. 'No,' she said. 'You need to go elsewhere.'

'But—'

'If Father McNamara saw every woman who came to the door begging for help, he'd have time for nothing else.'

'I'm not begging. What it is—'

Hearing their voices, the priest appeared. He was a young man with rosy cheeks and furrows of fair hair. Bridget explained herself.

'You'd better come in,' he said.

The priest's front room contained a heavy brown desk and chairs upholstered in a deep shade of green. At the far wall, there were shelves with scores of books. The room smelt of wax. Bridget had to fight the urge to touch everything.

Father McNamara told her to take a seat. Norah sat on the floor, tracing her fingers along the patterned rug.

Bridget outlined her predicament. 'As you can see, Father, we're in very distressed circumstances,' she said.

When he was saying Mass, Father McNamara's voice filled the church. Here, he was more softly spoken. He told Bridget that he remembered John Joe coming to him in search of work. He remembered her mother too. 'Have you no other family who could assist you?' he asked.

'No, Father. I've one sister except …'

'She's not in any position to help?'

'She's not.' No doubt lying to a priest was an especially grievous sin, but she had no choice.

'Very well, then. I'll write a letter for you. This practice ... while uncommon ... is not unheard of, I believe.'

'Thank you, Father. You're very good.'

Norah peeped up at them. 'Be good,' she said. 'Be good.'

Bridget couldn't help but smile. 'That's what I said to her when I was knocking on the door. She has a great head on her.'

Father McNamara looked down at Norah. 'Aren't you the grand girl?' He took out a sheet of paper, began writing then stopped. 'Have you eaten today, Mrs Moloney?'

'We were hoping to get some stirabout later.'

He frowned. 'Mrs Ryan,' he called.

When the housekeeper appeared, there was a deep crease at the top of her nose. 'Yes, Father?' she said.

'I think we have some porridge left over from this morning. Oh, and we might also have a little bread to spare. Will you set up a table in the kitchen? These two ladies are in need of nourishment.'

The next morning, Bridget rose early. She tucked the letter into her skirt pocket, lifted Norah onto her back and walked the mile to the field where a group of men was gathering. They stood in a circle, blowing warmth onto their hands, clouds of breath rising into the chill air. Several young boys were there too, one no older than seven or eight. She set Norah on the ground, then approached a squat man with a narrow mouth and unruly red hair. There was a cruelty about his eyes that suggested he'd found his calling. In his left hand, he carried a whip.

He read the letter and sighed. 'You do appreciate the nature of the work here, Mrs Moloney?'

'I do, sir.'

'You understand that digging drainage ditches is hard physical labour, and that many men find it difficult?'

'Like Father McNamara says, I'm in good health. And I promise you I'm a willing worker.'

'What are you proposing to do with the child?'

Bridget was conscious that the men were staring at her. 'Norah will be no bother. She'll sit on the dry ground over there and play with her shells and cones. I can share my dinner with her.'

'I can't say I like the idea,' he replied, 'but I'll see how you get on. If I find your work satisfactory, you'll receive twopence for the day.'

'My husband was paid four.'

'You'll get twopence and be grateful for it. What sort of world would we have if women were paid the same as men?'

He laughed then, as though he'd said something amusing.

Bridget said nothing. The sun was breaking through, casting a soft light over Henry Frobisher's fields. She didn't fool herself that this was the end of her problems. Hunger was never far away. But they'd have food today, and she'd be paid for her work. For now, that would have to do.

Chapter 8

May 2019, Boston, Massachusetts
Kaitlin

Kaitlin Wilson's mother had a gift for throwing parties, and tonight she was at full tilt. Not, she insisted, that the gathering was any trouble. It was simply a casual get-together. A casual get-together involving three straight days of baking, chopping, dusting and polishing. In the lead-up to a party, Susan Wilson morphed into a blend of Martha Stewart and Rachael Ray with a dash of Katie Lee on the side.

While other women might hire caterers or wait staff, Susan did everything herself. She considered the use of professionals to be a waste of money. More than that, she considered it vulgar. She'd often been heard to mutter about women who employed caterers just to show they could afford their pricey services. It didn't seem to occur to her that not everyone enjoyed entertaining.

'Your mother was born for this,' Kaitlin's father, Kevin, would say, as he watched his wife moving between guests, replenishing glasses and gushing about new hairstyles, jobs or babies. For all that Susan had perfected an affluent suburban appearance, she was in many ways a throwback to the old days. One of those rare people who'd always known what she'd wanted, she maintained a woman's place was at home. Careers were for the young and single. While Kaitlin didn't share this view, she had a secret regard for the unapologetic way in which her mother had embraced the stay-at-home life.

If her mom enjoyed being centre-stage, Kaitlin was more of a skulker. Parties were not her natural habitat. Even as a student she'd had no love for large gatherings. Sure, she'd attended plenty, but only because not to do so would have marked her out as odd. She hadn't wanted anyone to suspect that she didn't belong.

Tonight, she wasn't just a slightly unenthusiastic party-goer. She really truly didn't want to be there. Unfortunately, she didn't have a choice. In the Wilson family, not attending a party was like working Christmas Day or missing a neighbourhood funeral. It was not what you did. You drank wine and ate finger food and, if you had tears to cry, you cried them before you came. Well, either that or you waited until the early hours so that your emotion could be blamed on alcohol.

Kaitlin had told herself to be prepared for questions. The trouble was, she felt so fragile that one misplaced word, no matter how well-intentioned, might be enough to blow her over.

Tonight's celebration was for her uncle Drew, her father's brother, who'd just turned fifty. The youngest of five, he'd insisted he didn't want a fuss. This, Kaitlin figured, was Drew-speak for 'If there isn't a huge fuss, including the presence of the entire family, most of my neighbours, the guys from high school and assorted hangers-on, I will be extremely disappointed.'

Drew was married to Orla, and they had three children, her little cousins. Only they weren't so little any more: the youngest was fourteen.

At twenty-nine, Kaitlin had passed into another world where, save for the obvious – 'What are you planning for the summer vacation?' or 'How's school these days?' – she didn't know what to say. At the same time, she wasn't sure that when platitudes about the generosity of the spread or the relative warmth of the May weather had been exhausted, she could sustain a conversation with many of the older family members either.

Luckily, they all had plenty to say to each other.

Orla had volunteered to hold the party, but in the special voice she reserved for her sister-in-law – equal parts syrup and vinegar – Kaitlin's mother had rebuffed the offer. 'Sweetheart, it's what I *do*,' she'd said.

Kaitlin sipped her chardonnay and watched and listened as tongues loosened and voices swelled. In one corner of the living room, she saw her parents' long-time neighbour, Letty Brock, exchange gossip with another neighbour, Maria Cahalane. ('I said to her, "You can't go through husbands like that. Whatever happened to perseverance, huh?"') Nearby, three uncles debated the shortcomings of various ball players. ('I think he's done. Anyone can see he's not what he was two years ago.') There, too, was her brother, Brian, and his girlfriend, Riley, whose red dress was as tight as a surgical glove. In the same dress, Kaitlin would have looked ridiculous, but no matter the outfit, no matter the occasion, Riley had a talent for looking just right. The only jarring note came from her overly whitened teeth, their shine so bright it was probably visible from another realm.

Kaitlin caught Brian's gaze and waved in his direction. He tipped his head to one side and smiled. It was a look that said, 'I'll talk to you in a bit when I've done my duty by the old folk.' Separated by less than two years, they'd long ago developed a semaphore system. They might not agree on everything but when it came to family they usually found common ground. Unlike Kaitlin, Brian was skilled at schmoozing. Not only did he remember which cousin was which, he recalled their jobs and passions and pets. Throw in the fact that he possessed the perfect combination of self-effacement and self-confidence, and he could have been a politician. No wonder he worked for one. In return, their neighbours and relatives would happily have eaten bird seed from his outstretched hand.

'Hey, kiddo,' said a familiar voice. 'No Clay?'

Kaitlin turned and gave her dad a one-armed hug. 'No, and sorry I was late. Like I explained to Mom, Clay's busy. His team has an important meeting on Monday, and he's got lots of prep to do. He sends his apologies.'

Neither statement was true. Clay had claimed he was too tired, too flat-on-the-floor exhausted, for an evening with the Wilson family, whom he'd variously described as 'full on', 'wired' and 'unrelentingly social'. He'd also been known to ask how his girlfriend could possibly be a Wilson. She was almost sure this was a compliment. She was fully sure he'd got her family wrong. Yes, her mother was hospitable. Yes, her father's extended family enjoyed each other's company. But she reckoned Clay's portrayal of them owed more to caricature than reality. Some stereotypes endured, and the raucous Irish family was one: cousins upon cousins, alcohol and religion, tribalism and sentimentality and, on top of it all, a complex system of formalities and rituals. Not that she'd say this to Clay. In her job as an associate in a corporate law firm, Kaitlin was accustomed to marshalling arguments and preparing cases. At home, she chose her battles carefully. Besides, there was no malice to his descriptions, and she joked about his family too.

She was confident that if she'd really wanted him to come, he would have. In truth, though, she didn't think his presence would have made the party any easier to navigate.

Something about her dad's face made Kaitlin suspect he didn't believe Clay's excuse. Still, he maintained the charade. 'That's a real shame,' he said, with a slow nod. 'A real shame. It would've been great to have all the family here. It isn't every day a man's kid brother reaches his half-century.'

He then lamented how much of Clay and Kaitlin's lives were swallowed by their jobs. What he chose to forget was that, at the same age, he'd been consumed by work. Kevin had helped transform the family building business into a substantial construction and property company. In doing so, he'd made it possible for them to move to a five-bedroomed white-columned house in the leafiest part of Milton – and to throw large parties.

When Kaitlin met her father's contemporaries, she was taken aback by how old they looked, their youth lost to poor diet or too much liquor or simply to the passage of time. In his blue button-down and dark khakis, sandy hair only lightly flecked with silver, he could have passed for a decade younger than his fifty-five years.

He shifted from one foot to the other and took a mouthful of beer. 'And you're doing okay, are you? I worried that tonight might be tough for you. That's why I thought Clay would be here, y'know. But—'

'I'm fine,' she said.

Her tone must have put him off because, in a voice that was almost too breezy, he asked, 'So have you been speaking to Brian about the new job?'

'Um, no. I didn't know he had a new job.'

'Ah, I see. I thought he'd have been in touch.'

'We haven't spoken in a week or two.' She widened her eyes. 'Are you going to tell me?'

'He's on the move to Washington, but if he hasn't had the chance to fill you in …' Her father paused. 'Why don't I wait until he does have the opportunity? The pair of you can talk later.'

'Come on, Dad. Spill.'

He paused again, this time for longer than was comfortable. 'It's a big job: communication specialist with the Immigration Reform Alliance of America, the IRAA. I said to him, "I'm glad they added that second A or you could have been in real trouble."'

The joke fell flat.

'Whoa,' she said. 'Are you serious?'

'I thought that might be your reaction. That's why I wish he'd kept you in the picture. I've told him a thousand times: "You've got to discuss your plans with people. That's how you avoid misunderstandings."'

'I can see why he didn't want to discuss this particular plan.'

Her dad took a long drink of his beer. 'You won't tackle him tonight, will you? This isn't really the place.'

'I can't let it slide when I think he's wrong.'

'Please, sweetheart. Think of your mother. And Drew.'

Kaitlin scanned the room. There was her mom, a gleam of satisfaction on her face as she chatted to a cousin. There was Drew, who always looked like he'd been sculpted from the side of a mountain, talking to old school friends. And there was Brian, listening attentively to one of their more voluble aunts.

For the past three years, her brother had worked for a state senator. While Kaitlin might not have shared all Mitch O'Leary's views, his multiple terms in office were based on old-school skills. He was adept at attending fundraisers, pumping hands and telling stories about his childhood in the Old Colony project ('the finest people on God's earth'). But he also delivered for constituents, and she respected that. His party affiliation was barely relevant. He had the support of the firefighters' union, of teachers, carpenters and prison officers. A political machine required attention to detail and, to the surprise of many, Brian had turned out to be good with detail. This felt different.

'You're okay,' she said finally, trying, and failing, to sound reassuring. 'You go mingle. I'll be back in a minute.'

Upstairs, she crept into her old bedroom, closed the door and sat on the bed. She didn't want anyone to know she was hiding. A few minutes, that was all she needed to compose herself. *Your brother's career choices are none of your business*, she told herself. *This isn't about you. You've got to act like an adult. Keep it light. Keep it bright.*

The pep talk didn't prevent her from running IRAA through Google.

If the organisation's title was bland, ambiguous even, a scoot through its website confirmed her suspicions. The Alliance aimed to educate Americans about immigration, especially what it called 'high-volume illegal immigration'. It assured supporters that their concerns were well-founded and legitimate, and that, while controlled immigration could be positive, the current situation was having a negative impact on healthcare, security, the environment and the economy. It repeatedly contrasted what it said was America's generous policy towards undocumented migrants – 'Numbers are soaring' – with the challenging lives of vulnerable groups, like ageing veterans and victims of crime. Kaitlin knew the IRAA's message would resonate with millions of Americans. She just wished her brother wasn't among them.

A scan of the lobby group's key employees showed a range of ethnicities. To be honest, the faces were more diverse than they were at Frobisher Hunter, the law firm where she worked. There was also a considerable number of Irish names: a Kavanaugh, a Shanahan, an O'Reilly, a Moloney.

She cleared the screen and, for a minute or so, rocked back and forth. The room was exactly as she'd left it when she'd last lived here: calm, organised, subtle. The comforter and sheets were in shades of cream. The bookshelves were ordered alphabetically. There was no mountain of furry toys, no sentimental closet of clothes, nothing chintzy or garish. The one splash of colour was provided by a corkboard on the far wall, which was layered with teenage memories including a photo from a long-ago family holiday in the Keys. Brian's thick brown hair swooped over his eyes in a way that had been fashionable back then, while, for once, Kaitlin had managed to smile at the right moment.

As she descended the stairs, she repeated her new mantra. *Light and bright. Light and bright.* Then she met Orla.

'Come here to me,' said Drew's wife, with a beckoning wave, a tinkle of bracelets and a look of concern at Kaitlin's empty glass. 'You need more wine, and we need to talk.'

The two went into the kitchen, which, right then, was quiet. It had been remodelled a couple of years earlier and was showroom perfect, the appliances gleaming. Kaitlin hadn't yet adapted to the changes. The granite surfaces reminded her of a graveyard, the pendant lights of an operating theatre. She'd preferred the comfortable kitchen of her childhood. She took a bottle of white from the refrigerator, refilled their glasses and pulled out two chairs.

'I reckon I can guess what this is about,' she said.

'I reckon you can,' replied Orla. 'First things first, though. I should have asked: how are you doing?'

'I'm … not too bad. Some days are easier than others. That's the way it goes, I guess. So about Brian …'

'When did you find out?'

'Twenty minutes ago, when Dad told me. I had no—'

Kaitlin came to a sudden halt. Riley's head had popped around the door. 'Oh, hi, you two. You haven't seen Brian, have you?'

'Last I saw of him he was in the sunroom surrounded by elderly admirers,' said Orla, with a smile that was too sweet to be sincere.

'Sheesh,' she said, when Riley was gone, 'we were almost caught there. The last thing we needed was Miss Oklahoma 1986 listening in.'

'You're such a bitch,' said Kaitlin, but she was laughing.

'Don't tell me she isn't a ringer for a 1980s beauty queen.' Orla slapped her cheek. 'Oh, listen to me. I'm jealous, that's the trouble. The woman's too perfect and, God knows, I was never Miss Ireland material myself. I shouldn't take my feelings out on Riley. It's Brian I'm pissed with.'

The Wilson family's roots had been muddied by time. The same was true on Kaitlin's mother's side. Susan was a McGrath, possibly from County Waterford. Orla, however, was part of the last great wave of Irish immigrants. She'd arrived in the summer of 1986 with three hundred dollars and the address of a second cousin in Allston. She joked about how she hadn't intended to outstay her holiday visa but had been won over by high water pressure and fifty flavours of ice cream. Her parents and siblings remained in Limerick.

Although her accent had been diluted by more than thirty years in Boston, it remained unmistakably Irish. You could hear it in the way she pronounced 'Brian' as 'Brine', or the way she used words and phrases like 'Get away out of that', 'Grand so', and 'Lookit'. Kaitlin suspected that sometimes Orla ramped up the Irishisms for effect. She'd even corrected Susan's pronunciation of her family name. 'The T is silent,' she'd informed her bemused sister-in-law. 'It's pronounced McGrah.' She'd also taken Bostonians to task for various sins including the phrase 'The Potato Famine' ('That implies it was about a shortage of potatoes when it was more political than that. "The Famine" will do') and assuming that corned-beef hash was a staple Irish dinner ('I'd never seen the filthy stuff until I came here.').

'I know I should engage with the complexities of Brian's decision,' she was saying, injecting a shot of sarcasm into 'complexities', 'but I don't want to. It's not about politics for me. It's too personal. Like, how does he think I got here? Believe me, they weren't exactly hanging out the welcome banners at Logan.'

It was no secret that Orla had spent two undocumented years working as a nanny for a couple of doctors in Brookline. She'd met Drew at a party, and they'd married a few months later.

'You're family,' said Kaitlin, 'so you're different.'

Despite being more than twenty years her junior, Kaitlin had always seen her aunt as an ally. They'd had countless conversations of the sort she would never have with her mother. It was also useful to know someone who said the things you were too timid to say.

In many ways, she envied Orla more than she envied an Insta-cutie like Riley. Drew's wife knew who she was and what she was about. She looked like herself too, if that made sense. Tonight, she was wearing a green satin midi skirt and a black peasant top. Her dark curly hair hung past her shoulders and there were silver hoops in her ears. Not visible were the tattoo of a dolphin on her right thigh and the tiny shamrock at the base of her back, which she'd shown to Kaitlin at another party when they'd both had one shot of Jameson too many.

Kaitlin, on the other hand, could never achieve the style she was aiming for. Oh, objectively speaking, she wasn't unattractive. From her father's side of the family, she'd inherited the hair that a college boyfriend had described as more amber than red. She'd received her mother's small-boned face and slender build. And yet she was never sure how to hold herself or what to wear. Take tonight. She'd considered a grey sheath, then decided it was more suited to the office. Next up had been a blue tiered Alice + Olivia number. This too she'd discarded – somehow it felt too giddy. In the end, she'd settled on a blazer and black jeans. It was not a look that said 'party'.

'Here's another thing,' said Orla, warming to her theme. 'Has he ever thought about the rest of you? Okay, your people are here for a while, but I'll bet they didn't bring a whole heap of paperwork with them. Do you know where they – where you – came from?'

Some families could rattle off names and counties of origin for several generations. The Wilsons weren't among them. Their Irishness manifested itself more in ritual than in tangible connections.

'According to Dad, we've been in America since the nineteenth century. That's all he knows. I've always meant to find out more. I've just never gotten round to it.'

'That's a shame. I remember asking Drew, and he knew even less than your father. What do your folks make of Brian's announcement?'

Kaitlin took a deep drink. 'With Mom, I don't know, though I assume she'll get a bit teary because he's moving away. And, if he presents it as a big promotion, she'll be proud. Otherwise, she probably won't take a position one way or the other.'

'He's going to Washington DC, not the south Pacific.'

'Yeah, but he's leaving *Boston*, the centre of the known universe. She likes having us both around. As for Dad, his immediate concern was that I'd start an argument and ruin Drew's night.'

Orla smiled. 'Drew loves a good bust-up. I'd say he'd be fine.'

'I'd be excommunicated, though. And I don't think I'd be able to handle the guilt.'

The one imprint a Catholic childhood had left on Kaitlin was guilt. She had enough guilt for the entire state. She felt guilty about spending too much time at work, about not spending enough time with her mother, about her lack of engagement with school friends, and her tendency to bury her true thoughts. Frequently, she felt guilty about things that weren't her fault at all.

'I think you've got Susan wrong, by the way,' said Orla, pouring more wine. 'I think she'll be keen on Brian's move.'

Kaitlin was about to ask why when, as if she'd been waiting for her cue, her mother entered the kitchen, a wad of used napkins in one hand, empty platters in the other.

'Ladies,' she said, 'I don't know what you're up to in here, hiding away from the guests.' Even though there was only a handful of years between them, Susan tended to speak to Orla like a wayward child. 'What are you talking about that's so important?'

'Nothing,' said Kaitlin.

'Brian,' said Orla, their answers colliding mid-air.

Kaitlin couldn't quite interpret the look her mother gave them, but irritation was in there somewhere.

Her mom placed the platters beside the sink and removed an enormous cake from the refrigerator. It was smothered in chocolate frosting. The numerals – five, zero – were picked out in gold. 'I know,' she said. 'It's big news, but this is Drew's celebration, and I need to bring out the cake.'

'You're right,' said Orla. 'Let's go see if he still has the puff to blow out fifty candles.'

'Hey,' said Brian.

'Well, hey yourself.'

They'd escaped to the hall, a place both private enough for conversation and public enough to make an argument unwise. Since their encounter in the kitchen, Kaitlin had sensed she was being watched by her mother. She'd been pressed into service, first handing out slices of Drew's cake then topping up drinks.

'How are you doing?' he said.

'Honestly? I'm kind of up and down, but I don't like saying anything to Mom and Dad. I don't want either of them fussing.'

'That I can understand.'

'Anyway, ahm … congratulations,' she said, more out of politeness than sincerity. 'Why didn't you tell me your news?'

'I didn't have the chance.'

'I see.'

'All right, then. Full disclosure: I was pretty sure you wouldn't approve, and I didn't think this was the place for a debate.'

'I don't want a debate either. Not here. I just …'

'Go on.'

'I wish you weren't going to work for those people.'

'It's a great opportunity.'

'You deserve better.'

Mrs Cahalane opened the living-room door, and for a few seconds, the hall was filled with the roar of voices.

Brian rubbed the heel of his hand against his forehead. 'You see, this is why I was reluctant to talk to you tonight. We were always going to end up arguing about politics.'

She remembered what Orla had said. 'It's not about politics.'

'No?'

Kaitlin's fingers clenched a little tighter around her glass. 'It's about who we are.'

He hesitated before replying. She was disappointed that when he spoke he opted for the simplistic answer.

'We were born right here,' he said. 'We're American.'

'You know what I mean. It's not as straightforward as that. Give it ten minutes, and someone in there,' she gestured towards the living room, 'will be singing "Galway Bay".'

'And there's every chance they'll be sympathetic towards the aims of the IRAA.'

'I suppose,' she said, frustrated with herself for not putting forward a more coherent argument. While she possessed a degree of vanity about her intelligence, she also knew her brother was smarter – and more charming. Often, like now, he could get the better of her without trying. What she'd always had in her favour was diligence.

'Come on, Kaitlin,' he said. 'It's a step up for me. I don't judge your decisions.'

The living-room door swung open again. Her uncle Bobby was in full voice:

'And it's no nay never
No, nay, never no more
Will I play the wild rover
No never no more'

'Right idea, wrong song,' she said, with a light shrug.

Brian smiled but stayed quiet.

It was strange. In many ways she knew him better than anyone in the world. In other ways she didn't know him at all. Normally, if she had a problem with someone's politics, she had a problem with everything about them. But she could never dislike Brian. Could she?

'I'm trying to be honest with you,' she said. 'About how I feel and about why I don't think this is a good move for you. That's all.'

'If it doesn't work out, there's nothing lost.'

That's not true, she wanted to say. Instead, she said, 'When are you going?'

'August.'

'So, we've plenty of time to talk?'

'We do, but don't expect me to change my mind.'

The following morning, sitting in her Brighton apartment, drinking coffee and regretting her dry mouth and fuzzy head, an idea came to her. Orla was right. It was a shame that the Wilsons knew so little about where they'd come from.

If Brian was better informed about their origins, if he knew more about the circumstances in which the family had arrived in America, might it … she wouldn't go so far as to say change his mind but might it give him cause to think? Might he at least be forced to acknowledge the parallels between what was happening now and what had happened then? Because if you were proud of your immigrant heritage, like their family claimed to be, you had to show generosity towards others, didn't you?

Hangover receding, she found a notepad and scribbled down some ideas. She'd watched enough episodes of *Who Do You Think You Are?* to know the information was out there. The trouble was, she didn't know how to harvest it. She had a feeling that finding out about their father's side of the family would be easier. There were more of them. And they were talkers. There was a possibility that someone would recall something useful, some scrap of information that had been passed down the generations.

What else was there? Census documents? DNA testing? Were there records in Ireland that might help? How much was online? She jotted all of this down on her yellow pad.

Clay had gone for a run, so she had the apartment to herself. She wasn't sure how much to say to him. His family lived very separate lives, never feeling the need to meddle in each other's careers. They worked on the assumption that, with a little hard work, each of them would achieve their ambition. Besides, she mightn't get anywhere. If her search failed to bear fruit, talking to him would be pointless. She would sketch out a plan and, if possible, she'd go investigating. When she'd made progress, she could tell him.

It was only as she made another coffee that something struck her: she genuinely wanted to know more about the man or woman who'd boarded a ship in Ireland and set sail for Boston. What was their story? Who had they left behind? Had they maintained any contact with Ireland? There was rarely, Kaitlin believed, one reason for doing anything. Most actions were supported by several motivations. So, yes, she was doing this for Brian. But she was also doing it for herself.

Chapter 9

Kaitlin soon understood why some people spent years piecing together their ancestors' stories. The problem wasn't a lack of information. The problem was that you could drown in information and still not find what you were looking for. There were countless websites as well as scores of message boards, books, pamphlets and videos. Helping people to learn more about themselves was a lucrative business.

Family trees were unwieldy, and she didn't have time to explore every branch. What she would have to do was give the tree a shake and hope that something interesting fell out. The task was made more challenging by her decision not to consult her parents. She didn't want to cause friction. Not yet anyway. Orla had been right about her mother. She was enthusiastic about Brian's new job. 'Who knows where this will lead?' she'd said, as though the West Wing was beckoning.

Kaitlin started her search by trying to find out more about her paternal grandparents, both of whom had died when she was in her teens. She knew they'd grown up in South Boston and had met and married there. Fortunately, the 1940 census was available online, and she was able to track down Joseph Andrew Wilson and Shirley Bridget McDonagh.

Finding them was one thing; learning more about them was a stiffer challenge. The enumerator had the worst handwriting she'd ever seen, making the census sheets all but impenetrable. Then again, he – she was convinced the writing belonged to a man – couldn't have predicted that seventy-nine years later someone would be poring over an online version of his work, zooming in and out to try to read the squiggles and loops.

In 1940, her grandfather had been five years old. Her grandmother had been two. They'd lived just streets apart. All four of their parents had been born in the United States, as had many of their neighbours. The records also showed a sprinkling of more recent immigrants. While Kaitlin had expected to see people born in Ireland, or 'Eire' as the form called it, she hadn't anticipated the neighbourhood's diversity. Not far from the McDonaghs and the Wilsons, there were families from Italy, Russia and Armenia. Another man had been born somewhere she couldn't quite decipher. Newfoundland, perhaps.

Her mind felt sharp as she examined the rows of names and occupations. Sharper than it had in months. She tried to picture what it had been like on those streets when the Second World War was young and FDR was in the White House. Had people spoken in their native languages, or had they quickly picked up English? Had there been many cars? What had they eaten for dinner? What had they learnt at school? Had they all rubbed along together, or had they formed national cliques?

Further examination revealed that her great-grandfather Wilson had been a labourer, while her great-grandfather McDonagh had been a baker. He'd been called Cornelius, and in 1940 he'd been aged thirty-six. His wife, Margaret, had been three years younger.

Kaitlin decided to follow the McDonagh side of the family. Her choice was based on a hunch. Cornelius and Margaret McDonagh sounded a shade more Irish than Peter and Helen Wilson. With any luck, this meant they were only a generation or two removed from Ireland.

'I remember that house in Southie,' said Drew. 'Mom took us visiting all the time. Her parents must have spent forty years there. Not that I ever heard them referred to as Cornelius and Margaret. They were Con and Meg.'

He was looking at the census printouts given to him by Kaitlin. If she was reluctant to involve her parents, there was no reason to avoid Drew. She had the feeling that, of all the Wilsons, he would understand.

Beside him at their large kitchen table, Orla stroked her coffee mug. A shaft of early-evening sunlight peeped through the cloud.

'I'm sorry I never knew Con and Meg,' she said. 'They'd both passed away by the time I met Drew. But I get the impression they were quite the pair.'

'They were,' said her husband. 'Even as a kid, I loved listening to them. They were great storytellers.'

'What were the stories about?' asked Kaitlin.

'Mainly about characters who lived on the block. They had the gift of making everyone and everything sound entertaining. At that time, most of their neighbours were Irish.' He winked at Orla. 'I was indoctrinated at an early age.'

She laughed and gave his arm a playful punch.

'It was a very sociable house. There were always people dropping by to shoot the breeze, and many of them were good for a spare quarter.'

In a way, thought Kaitlin, Drew and Orla's home was similar. Although not as given to parties as her mother, they welcomed a regular stream of callers. At its best, it was a freewheeling place, a house where the kids brought friends home, confident that their parents wouldn't embarrass them. There was an ease here that wasn't always present in her own family home. Built by Drew back in the 1990s, Kaitlin remembered the house growing from a skeleton to a substantial building. While the exterior was a stately grey and white, the interior was a collage of colours. Orla had a weakness for the work of student artists, and the walls were covered with bright canvases. Then there were the photos: from baby pictures to high-school graduations to significant birthdays, every occasion was on display.

If Drew had an impressive appetite for work, the same was true of Orla. Where other women might have been overwhelmed by raising three children in a new country, she'd also attended college as a mature student. She'd trained to be a teacher and now taught fourth grade in Dorchester. She explained her industriousness by saying she'd left a country that had provided few opportunities for young women like her. In America, she'd been determined to grasp everything on offer.

'Do you remember anything else about Con and Meg?' asked Kaitlin.

Drew started, 'Not really—'

'We've got pictures,' his wife interrupted. 'Upstairs in an old box. Drew's mother kept them all.'

He sent her a questioning look. 'I hope you're not going to bore Kaitlin with those photos. Besides, it'll take you all night to find them.'

'No, it won't. I know exactly where they are. They're at the back of the closet in Pearse's room. I'm sure Kaitlin would love to see them. The old black-and-white ones are hilarious.'

Before anyone could say anything further, she was halfway up the stairs. When they heard her feet overhead, there was a subtle yet distinct change to Drew's tone.

'It's fun to talk about the old days,' he said, 'but how far do you plan on going with this?'

'Ideally, I'll keep going until I find someone who arrived on the boat from Ireland. I want to be able to say, "Look, this is who we are."'

'Or "This was who we were more than a century ago."'

'I don't think it's that easy to flick away history. It matters.' Worried she sounded too earnest, Kaitlin added, 'Well, it matters to me.'

'What if all you find is a lowlife?' asked Drew. 'A sheep stealer or some such?'

'From what I've read, the sheep stealers were deported to Australia. America got the best and brightest.'

'Well, there you go. What if the family tree is heavy with bores? What if the first person to make it here was poor but honest, had an unadventurous journey and a hardworking life?' He illustrated his point with a loud snore.

'I'll cross that bridge when I come to it. It's not as if this is just about Brian. It's about all of us. I want to know where we came from. What's wrong with that?'

'He's not warning you off, is he?' said Orla, from the kitchen door. She was carrying a dusty box that looked as though it had once held a pair of boots.

'Of course I'm not,' said Drew. 'I'm asking Kaitlin what she'd like to find. Am I right?'

Kaitlin was about to reply, but Orla spoke first.

'As far as Brian's concerned, Drew and I aren't quite on the same page,' she said, putting the box on the table and sitting down again.

In truth, Kaitlin was finding Drew unusually difficult to decode. One thing was clear: he'd been keen to finish their conversation before Orla came back.

'It's not like I support the people Brian's going to work for,' he said. 'I don't. Only I'm not sure it's our … my … place to get involved. If it's what the guy wants to do, let him go. God knows he spent enough time fooling around.'

Kaitlin felt a dull pain at the back of her eyes. She hadn't expected this. Unlike many marriages, where the couples appeared to be in a constant low-level battle, Drew and Orla were almost always in agreement.

What she couldn't dispute was Drew's assessment of Brian. Until he'd found his calling with Mitch O'Leary, Kaitlin's brother had been without any obvious ambition or purpose. He'd underperformed at college and had bounced from job to job. His amiability meant everyone had indulged his behaviour. 'He's a great kid,' they'd say. 'He just needs to find his way.' Even though she'd never admitted it, this had rankled with her.

By contrast, her life had been one of clear expectations and outcomes. Her academic record had been impeccable; she'd aced her law exams before securing a job with one of the city's most prestigious firms. In her personal life too, she'd made sound choices. Not that she'd always done exactly what she wanted. But, as her mother liked to say, people who followed their heart usually did so with someone else's money. (And, yes, Kaitlin was aware that her path had been smoothed by her family's prosperity.)

For years, her father had hoped Brian would join the family construction business. It had been plain to everyone except Kevin that this was never going to happen. Thankfully, Drew's sons, Liam and Pearse, looked like they'd carry on the tradition. The difference was that both would finish college first.

'Anyway,' said Orla, opening the box and sifting through its contents, 'Brian's decision is beside the point. We're looking at family photos. That's all. And I promise you, there are some gems in here.'

The first few photographs weren't especially old. Many were from the 1970s. Hair was very big or very long, sometimes both. People smoked and goofed around. They hugged each other and flipped the bird at the photographer. Nobody seemed concerned about their angles or catching the right light. Some of the most interesting pictures were of the children. There was Kaitlin's dad, aged three or four, in striped overalls. Here was baby Drew, sitting in a stroller, a scowl on his chubby face. Oh, and there were Shirley and Joseph with all five children, their smiles as stiff as their starched Sunday clothes. The passage of time had discoloured the Polaroid so that Kaitlin's grandmother had light green hair while everything else was in shades of mud.

'Here you go,' said Orla, plucking a small black-and-white image from the box. 'This one shows Con and Meg. It's from the 1940s, I think.'

Kaitlin examined the photo of her great-grandparents. In it, a neat man, who looked far too thin to be a baker, was staring at the camera as though slightly confused. Sitting on the stoop beside him was a woman in a flower-strewn dress. Her blonde hair was rolled at the front in a style Kaitlin had only ever seen in old movies. It would be an exaggeration to call Meg glamorous, but she was very pretty. 'These are fantastic,' she said. 'Seriously. What a great collection to have.' She passed the picture to Drew.

'That's them, all right,' he said. 'Looking at them in their prime, you'd have to say Con McDonagh was a lucky guy.'

'You don't know anything else about his background, do you? Or hers?'

'Aha,' said Orla, 'it's funny you should ask because look what I have here.'

The next image was larger. While not a formal portrait, some effort had gone into its composition. It appeared to be from the 1920s or 1930s when, Kaitlin guessed, not many people had owned a camera or even had access to one. It showed a younger Con and Meg. They were beside the beach, and with them were an older couple. The men wore large flat caps, and the women had wavy bobbed hair. All four had serious faces. When, she wondered, had it become mandatory to smile in photographs?

'Who are the other two?' she said.

Drew leant in. 'Those are your great-great-grandparents.'

'Their names are on the back,' added Orla.

And so they were. In pale blue ink, the neat inscription read, *The McDonaghs, Con and Meg, Ray and Bertha. July 1930.* Kaitlin was fascinated. She was, she realised, looking for traces of herself.

'Ray and Bertha McDonagh,' she said. 'What age do you think they were?'

'I find it hard to be certain,' replied Drew. 'In those days, everyone looked old before their time. I assume they were in their forties, though.'

'Which means they must have been born in the 1880s. Have you any idea where they came from?'

'Not a clue.'

'But I'm sure you can find out,' said Orla, as she placed a hand on Kaitlin's forearm. 'You're enjoying this, aren't you?'

In the days that followed, Kaitlin thought a lot about the photo. Con and Meg, Ray and Bertha. She needed to know more about the older couple. She also needed to jump back another generation. Orla had urged her to bring the picture home, but she'd decided against. It was too rare, too precious. She wished they'd store it more carefully. It was almost a hundred years old. An antique.

She thought, too, about what Orla had asked. The answer was, yes, she was enjoying herself. Something told her, however, that the question had been as much for Drew's benefit as hers.

Ideally, Kaitlin would have spent more time searching for her ancestors, but the relentless nature of her job left few opportunities for hobbies or side interests. Frobisher Hunter was a large traditional law firm making efforts to refresh its fusty image. The aim, employees were told, was to maintain a reputation for reliability while also appealing to big tech and pharma. After all, the tech bros controlled the world: no one made serious money without them. And Frobisher Hunter was a serious-money sort of place. The firm had fifteen offices in the United

States and was also expanding in Europe. Its lawyers were expected to hustle, but to do so with subtlety.

Occasionally Kaitlin opened her page on the company website and felt overwhelmed by how grown-up she looked. How sensible. How grey. If anyone else read the page, and she couldn't see why they would, they'd learn that she worked in the business law department in Frobisher Hunter's main office on State Street, that she'd graduated magna cum laude from Boston College Law School, and that she'd interned with the Massachusetts Attorney General's Office. What they wouldn't learn was that, despite the firm's prestige, she had lingering doubts about the job. Neither would they know that sometimes, when listening to her college friends' tales of adventure, she was breathless with envy.

Every day, she considered talking to Clay about her family search. She would form the words then change her mind. She was beginning to worry that she'd left it too late. When she did speak, he would ask why she'd kept the project to herself, and she didn't have a coherent answer.

With Brian, too, she avoided saying anything of substance. In the three weeks since the party, they'd had brief anodyne chats, but nothing that could be termed a conversation. She was wary of saying the wrong thing and she suspected the same was true of him.

She was stirring shrimp risotto and listening to a podcast about a failed tech company when Clay got home.

For the past eighteen months they'd lived in an apartment near Commonwealth Avenue. It was filled with IKEA furniture and dog-eared law books. While she would have preferred more space, she loved the neighbourhood: the mix of brownstones and triple-deckers, students and families, ethnic restaurants and neon-fronted liquor stores.

Kaitlin had met Clay three years earlier at a party. She'd been in her usual position, on the fringes, trying to look as if she was having the night of her life, when they'd got talking. Initially, she'd dismissed him as one of a type. Too slick. Too unwavering in his views. Nevertheless, she'd given him her number. To her surprise, he'd called when he'd said he would. To her even greater surprise, she'd quickly grown to like him. He was neither as self-assured nor as dogmatic as first impressions had suggested. It didn't hurt that he was old-fashioned handsome, with wavy light brown hair and blue-grey eyes. By the end of their first proper date, she'd been charming him with everything she had. At the time, he'd just graduated from law school and was doing scut work at another of the city's top-tier firms. That was where he remained, steadily, assiduously, climbing the ladder. If anything, Clay's employers were even stuffier than hers.

He peeled off his suit jacket and threw it across one of the tall chairs beside the breakfast bar. She turned down the heat on the risotto and pressed pause on the podcast. Before she could say anything, he was speaking.

'I met Orla downtown this afternoon.'

'Oh?'

'She was talking about how you'd called over the other night. "Isn't it great to see the girl in such good form?"' she said.

His Irish accent was famously lame, and Kaitlin smiled.

'Why didn't you tell me?' he continued.

'That I'd been to see Orla and Drew? I did. You were working late, remember?'

'You know what I'm talking about, Kaitlin. There was Orla, rattling on about old photos and census records and whatnot, and I had to grin like a fool and pretend I was following her.'

Shit. 'I see,' she managed to say. 'I was going to tell you about that only …' Only what? When she'd run what she would say through her head, the conversation hadn't started like this.

'Do you want to put me in the picture?' he asked.

She turned off the heat and leant back against the counter. Her first instinct was to curse Orla, but she'd asked her not to say anything to her parents or to Brian. She hadn't mentioned Clay. A reasonable person would have assumed he knew what she was doing.

'Okay, I should have told you. And I was going to, only the timing never seemed right. I thought I'd put everything in train first and then fill you in.'

'Why?'

She began smoothing the front of her hair, running it between her index and middle fingers. 'I wish I could give you a straight answer. It's like it wasn't important enough and it was too important, all at the same time.'

'Have you any idea how insulting that is?' said Clay. 'How can something be too important to tell me?'

'Sorry, that sounded wrong. It's a family thing and I know you find my family a bit much so—'

'Please don't lay this on me. I'm not the one at fault here. Oh, and by the way, I still don't understand what's going on or who it is you're looking for.'

She spent the next ten minutes explaining what she'd been doing and why. Rather than emphasise her own thirst for information, something she didn't think he would understand, she focused on Brian's new job. She wanted to make her brother squirm, she said. While she spoke, Clay stalked the room. He said little and barely looked at her. When he did, she noticed the patches of red on his cheekbones. They always emerged when he was annoyed, a slight flaw in his good looks. At last, he sat down.

'I wish you weren't so hidden away,' he said. 'You disappear inside your head, and I can't reach you. I don't think anyone can. The rest of your family are all yap, yap, yap, but for some strange reason, you feel the need to keep everything to yourself. You've always been like that, but lately you've gotten worse. Much worse.'

He was right. Kaitlin was at odds not just with her family, but also with her generation. She'd never been one for pouring out her heart. In the past, she'd been told that this self-sufficiency could come across as arrogance. What people didn't realise was that she hated judgement. She liked to solve her own problems and answer her own questions without interference from others. Because she found it hard to confide in people, she didn't have many close friends. There was, she believed, something lacking in her, some skill that other people acquired without thinking.

Once, a confrontation like this would have made her cry. Lately she hadn't cried very much. She felt as if the tears were stored inside her, and that if she started to release them, she might not be able to stop.

Silence settled around them, the only noise the purr of the refrigerator.

'I didn't know I was that bad,' she said eventually. 'I'm sorry.'

He sighed. 'Is Brian's new job that big a deal? I don't agree with the people he's going to work for, but why should his background matter? I mean, is being Irish any different from being English or German or Swedish? Is it really that distinctive? When it comes down to it, you're just another shade of white.'

'I know, except to me it's more complex than that. It's ...' Her words ran dry.

Clay's last name was Abbott. He assumed his ancestors were English but had never shown any interest in finding out.

'By all means,' he said, 'try to find out more about your family's history, but please don't shut out the rest of us.' He paused, as though something had just occurred to him. 'What do your parents think?'

'I haven't told them.'

'Don't you think you should?'

'I suppose.'

Clay shook his head. 'I know you've had a difficult few months. We both have. But that's no reason to behave like this. This isn't how relationships work.'

Despite knowing that she was at fault, his comment irritated Kaitlin. It sounded so lawyerly. So smug. 'Please don't talk down to me,' she said, as she resumed smoothing her hair. 'It's really not a good time for that.'

'Okay, but what I can't understand is why you don't get help. Proper professional help. Whatever you were led to believe growing up, there's no shame in it.'

'I know there's not.'

Did she really, though? Therapy wasn't something the Wilsons did. They supported each other. They valued resilience. Shrinks were for other – lesser – families. What was more, she didn't think that therapy would suit her. If she couldn't open up to her partner, why would she talk to a stranger? Oh, and then there was the challenge of finding the *right* doctor. How many articles had she read about people who'd tried out three or four therapists before they'd found one who suited them? Kaitlin didn't have time for doctor-shopping.

'Will you do it, then?' asked Clay. 'For my sake as well as your own?'

'I'll see,' she replied.

It wasn't an honest answer, but right now it was the easiest one.

Chapter 10

May 2019, Clooneven
Jessie

An hour had passed since Jessie had been wrenched from Ger Dillane's easy company, and every minute yielded another tough question.

'And you thought you'd get away with it?' said Lorna, patent navy stilettos clickety-clacking on their parents' kitchen floor. 'Like, did you think the man was stupid or something? Because take it from me, Jessie, stupid people rarely get to own property portfolios.'

'To be honest, I didn't do a whole lot of thinking. After the TV thing, I kind of panicked.'

'Could you not have spoken to him?' said her father, from the other end of the table. 'Could you not have explained the situation you'd found yourself in? I'm sure you could have come to an arrangement.'

Jessie wished her parents weren't there. Handling Lorna was one thing. Lorna saw life as a profit-and-loss sheet. She didn't take Jessie's failings personally. Also, she tended to act like she was playing a scene in a secondary-school pantomime. She did what the audience expected, subtlety wasn't part of her repertoire, and she didn't necessarily mean everything she said.

Their parents were different. They were emotionally involved.

'I was nervous,' she said, shifting in her chair, 'and I made a mistake.'

Click-clack. Lorna did another lap of the kitchen. She appeared to crackle, as if her movements were generating electricity. 'You owe him six thousand euro. He was always going to track you down.'

'Five thousand six hundred. And that's pushing it. I haven't been there for the past three weeks.'

'Oh, for fuck's sake,' said her sister, drawing a wince from their mother. 'This isn't the time for pedantry. You did a runner owing the man four months' rent. You also owe the ESB money, the gas and the broadband, so six grand's a conservative estimate. You're lucky he didn't set the guards on you.'

Jessie had a hunch that Dan O'Doherty wouldn't want the police involved in his affairs. Her former landlord wasn't overly keen on forms or paper trails. She kept this thought to herself. She was in enough trouble without throwing out theories she couldn't prove.

'When did you split up with Phelim?' asked her mother.

'January.'

The twenty-fourth of January, to be precise. The day was marked on her brain. Despite their topsy-turvy history, she'd known the relationship was over.

Click clack. 'And did he move out straight away?' said Lorna.

'We'd January's rent paid, so there was nothing stopping him. He gathered up his gear and went to a friend's place.'

Not to his best friend's place, obviously. Or, to be more accurate, his former best friend.

'Please sit down, Lorna,' said their mother. 'Those shoes will ruin the floor.' She turned to Jessie. 'When did you last see him?'

89

'I haven't seen him since.'

'But you've broken up before,' said her father.

'It's different this time.'

Oisín McNeill made it different. While Phelim had been away with colleagues from the advertising agency where he worked, Jessie had slept with his friend, Oisín. It hadn't been planned. They'd bumped into each other, gone for a drink, and ended up in bed.

Afterwards, they'd sworn each other to secrecy. It had been fun, they said, but it wouldn't happen again. It did. They'd spent the next two months looking for – and finding – opportunities to meet. By the time they agreed that it honestly, truly, couldn't happen again, it was too late. There was something about them, a residue of sex that marked them out as different. Phelim tackled her. She confessed, and he left.

Before leaving, he told her the truth about herself. They'd been together since they were twenty-four, so there was plenty to tell. She was entertaining but not as entertaining as she thought. She was talented, but the world was full of talented people. She was self-centred, self-indulgent. She'd squandered opportunities that should have gone to other, more deserving, people. He'd loved her for years, but he'd grown up and needed a grown-up relationship. Oh, and Oisín's girlfriend was pregnant. Did she know that? Did she even care?

(No, she hadn't known. And of course she cared. The information brought bile to her mouth. Four months later, she was still thinking about it.)

Obviously, she said none of this to her sister and parents. In the family-friendly version of the split, she and Phelim had simply grown apart.

'What I don't get,' said Lorna, who'd joined them at the table, 'is why you didn't move out and find somewhere more affordable.'

That was hard to explain, especially to Lorna, who viewed procrastination as the eighth deadly sin. No matter that Jessie's relationship with Phelim had already been in its death throes, she had been flattened by his departure. That his words were spoken in anger didn't make them untrue. He'd waved her shortcomings in front of her, and she hadn't been able to argue.

In the self-help-manual version of life, this would have forced her into a radical rethink. Instead, it had knocked her into a stupor where even a straightforward task, like interviewing Hollie Garland, had felt arduous. Dealing with Dan O'Doherty and finding somewhere new to live had been beyond her. She'd frittered away the modest amount of money she did have on new clothes and nights out. She'd kidded herself that she was presenting a positive face to the world and that this was the best way to start over.

'I should've found a smaller flat,' she said, 'only I kept putting it off. I did look at a couple of places, but they were unbelievably dingy. And I suppose I was a bit … a bit down.'

She was slow to use the word 'depressed'. It was thrown around too easily. Yet there had been days when her head had been packed with sawdust and she'd felt physically and mentally incapable of doing anything productive. She'd sat in the apartment counting her regrets and asking why she was so given to self-sabotage.

'Yes,' said Lorna, 'so down you were able to go out on the lash and then appear on television.'

Their mother cleared her throat. 'How did you get away without paying rent for four months? Did you lie to your landlord?'

'Phelim had always handled the payment, and I gave my share to him. So when the money stopped arriving in Dan O'Doherty's account, he got my number from Phelim. I managed to string him along for a few weeks. Then I stopped answering his calls and messages. And finally … I disappeared.'

'Why didn't he call around to the flat?'

'He lives in Spain.'

'You must have known he'd catch up with you at some stage,' said her father.

'I guess I shoved it to the back of my mind.'

That was the truth. Dan O'Doherty had been towards the bottom of a catalogue of worries. She'd obsessed about what she and Phelim had shared: attraction, intimacy, conversation and, middle-aged as it might sound, companionship. Like all couples, they'd had in-jokes, phrases and customs. She'd also realised that, even though the relationship had grown stale, it had insulated her from loneliness.

'Where's your stuff?' asked Lorna.

'Down the corridor in my room.'

'No, I mean the rest of your belongings. You've got to have more than two bags.'

'I left a few bits and bobs with my friend Shona, and gave everything else to a couple of charity shops.'

Lorna's eyes roamed the ceiling.

With hindsight, Jessie feared she'd been too impulsive with her donations to Oxfam and the St Vincent de Paul. She'd abandoned her favourite little black dress on the grounds that it had also been Phelim's favourite, and she'd discarded an expensive suede skirt because it reminded her of Oisín.

'Could you not have stayed with Shona or one of your other friends?' said her father.

'I didn't want people to know I wasn't coping.'

Her mother spoke next, the weariness of her tone more wounding than Lorna's pyrotechnics. 'I'm disappointed,' she said. 'The television show was pure silliness, but this was dishonest. Poor Mr O'Doherty, what must he think of us? And I know it's what parents always say, but I thought we'd raised you to be better than that. Isn't that right, Denis?'

Her father nodded.

'How are you going to pay him back?' asked Lorna. 'I take it you've got savings?'

Jessie swallowed. 'Not really.'

'You're nearly thirty years old. Were you not saving for a deposit?'

'God, Lorna, do you not listen to the news? I live in Dublin. Even if we'd both saved every cent we earned and eaten nothing apart from porridge, we couldn't have afforded a house. Well, maybe we could. But it would have been out in the sticks somewhere.'

'Other people manage. Mind you, they're not going through a never-ending adolescence.'

'It must be great to have all the answers. If you'd ever moved further than five minutes from home, you'd learn that everything's not as simple as you think.'

'Where I live is irrelevant. We're talking about you.'

Their father slapped the table. 'Come on now, girls. Falling out isn't going to solve anything.'

'Sorry, Dad,' said Lorna, 'but Jessie needs to hear this.' She paused and leant back in her chair. 'Anyway, I have a suggestion.'

'Go on,' said Jessie, who found she couldn't look Lorna in the eye. She focused on her multicoloured necklace. The square beads reminded her of a child's toy bricks. She was annoyed with herself for rising to Lorna's goading. She'd said too much. She was always saying too much.

'Between us, Mam, Dad and I can pay Mr O'Doherty what you owe him. And you can pay us back by working in the Seashell Café for the rest of the season. I'm down a worker, and I'm sure you could do the job. You've worked in a café before.'

'You're not serious?'

'Why wouldn't I be?'

'Because I'm not staying here all summer. I'm going back to Dublin.'

Lorna gave her parents a look that said, *You talk to her.*

It occurred to Jessie that her sister had been toying with this idea all along. Now she had an opportunity to act. After all, Jessie was the perfect employee. She had neither children nor a social life.

'I'm afraid I agree with Lorna,' said her mother. 'I'm not saying you shouldn't go back to Dublin at some stage, but you've got to sort yourself out first.'

'We'll pay the landlord what you owe him,' added her father, 'and we'll pay the other bills too. Your sister's right, though. It's not our debt.'

Her mother nodded. 'We'll expect you to pay us back. And I really do think you should ring Mr O'Doherty and apologise.'

Jessie looked from face to face to face. 'I don't exactly have a choice here, do I?'

Her father rose, walked over and patted her shoulder. 'This could be the making of you,' he said.

Jessie propped her bicycle against Etty's gable wall, knocked on the brown front door and let herself in. At this time of year, the neat white bungalow was draped in wisteria, and the garden dazzled with flowers.

'Come in, come in,' called Etty, from the front room. 'Isn't that one powerful day? Oh, and put the kettle on before you sit down, will you? I'm parched.'

Jessie was convinced that this was how her grandmother had reached such a good age in such fine health: she was skilled at getting others to do her bidding.

The house was of its era. A brown three-piece suite dominated the front room, while the floor was covered with pink and blue carpet. In a china cabinet, Aynsley and Belleek jostled for space with souvenir knick-knacks from Bundoran and Lanzarote. There were numerous photos from family occasions, including one of Jessie on the day of her university graduation.

Her memories of that day were strong. Her wild happiness had been joined by concern that her parents might say something to embarrass her. This, in turn, had been joined by shame that she was capable of such thoughts.

Boherbreen was a place of small farms, marshy land and crooked trees. The fields adjacent to Etty's house were farmed by Jessie's uncle,

Pat, better known as Rusty. He frequently complained about how hard it was to stay afloat. 'The government will only be happy when all the farmers are in a museum,' he claimed. Still, he'd been scratching a living for more than forty years and showed no sign of retiring.

It was only when the blue and white teacup was safely in her hand that Etty raised her granddaughter's latest disgrace. 'I gather things weren't going too well for you above in Dublin.'

Jessie placed her cup on the coffee-table. 'The Clooneven bush telegraph has been busy.'

Etty laughed. She had a gorgeous laugh, a healthy chuckle that didn't match her narrow frame and delicate features. She was an active, and competitive, grandparent. She liked to know what everybody was doing, and she enjoyed collating and passing on the news. She also had a habit of speaking her mind. This, it seemed to Jessie, was the joy of being either very old or very young: you could say what you wanted without fear of the consequences. Lorna claimed their grandmother talked so much because she knew her time was running out.

'I'm glad you'll be in Clooneven for the summer. Your mother loves having you around. You were always the favourite in that house … which probably accounts for why you are the way you are.'

'What way am I?'

'Spoilt.'

Et tu, Etty. 'You're terrible for handing out insults. I won't come and visit unless you start being kinder to me.'

'I'd a husband and three children when I was your age.'

'You lived in Clooneven. There wasn't anything else to do.'

Etty laughed again, displaying her old-style dentures, which were a shade too long. 'You want to be young for ever, that's your trouble. I mean, look at the cut of you.'

'What's wrong with shorts?' Jessie looked down at her denim cut-offs, which she was wearing with a lilac vest. Her long legs were her best feature, and if she could wear shorts every day of the year, she would.

'Not a thing if they were shorts for a grown woman, but those are like the ones the teenage girls in the community school wear.'

'I'll bear your views in mind the next time I go shopping.'

Etty shifted her gaze towards her granddaughter's graduation picture. 'Don't pay any heed to me, I'm only jealous. I wouldn't mind being twenty-nine again. There's no decade to compare to your twenties … not that they're always easy, mind. Back in my day, we were told to keep our heads down and ask for nothing. Your generation was told to ask for everything. And I'm not sure which was more dishonest. Or unkind.'

Jessie would have liked to argue, but much of what her grandmother said was true. At college, they'd been encouraged to see themselves as special. It was a designation they'd willingly accepted – and they'd expected it to continue. Why shouldn't older people respect their talents and imagination, their new way of looking at the world?

Now, she saw how naïve they'd been. In the main, her college friends had been met by a great rush of indifference, their perceived privilege mocked and used against them. Six years after graduation, she was still adjusting to the fact that no one wanted to see her and her contemporaries as unusual or revolutionary.

If the stereotyping of her generation irritated her, Jessie was honest enough to admit that she was guilty of doing the same to older people. Having Etty in her life was a reminder that, while seductive, judging people by the number of candles on their birthday cake was often a mistake.

'So,' she said to her grandmother, 'what I'm here for, the pleasure of your company aside, is to see if you know anything about what happened around these parts during the Famine.'

She ran through what Ger had told her about Johanna and Bridget.

When she'd finished, Etty took a while to respond. 'Isn't that very sad?' she said. 'Those were brutal times. Johanna can't have lived far from here. A man named Henry Frobisher was the landlord. People still spoke about him when I was a child in the 1940s.'

'Do I take it he wasn't much good?'

'By all accounts, he was one of the worst. Not that he spent much time in Ireland. He had his henchmen do the work for him.'

She stopped to drink some of her tea. Jessie looked at her thin hands with their dark blue veins, and, fleetingly, thought about all her grandmother had lived through. Her husband, Flan, had died twenty years earlier. One of her children had also died young.

'I don't know if this will be of very much help to the young people,' said Etty, 'but I do remember how my grandfather would get agitated when the Famine was mentioned. He wasn't old enough to remember it, but his mother was. Some people … well, it was as if they were ashamed to have survived when so many others had perished.'

'Like survivor's guilt?'

'Exactly. I always think that if these fields could talk, they'd have quite a story to tell. And it wasn't that long ago, you know. Not in the grand scheme of things.'

'What was your grandfather's name?' asked Jessie.

'Seánie Nugent. I was a Nugent before I married. He hated seeing food wasted – that's the other thing I recall. One of my brothers, Colm, the Lord have mercy on him, was a fierce picky eater, and Granddad would give out if he didn't clear his plate. He used to say it was sinful to leave good food behind.'

'Really?'

'Oh, yes. I can still remember how he used to react.'

'When was he born?'

'Now you're asking.' Etty stopped to think. 'Back in the 1870s, I'd say.'

'So it's possible he knew Bridget or her daughter?'

Again, her grandmother's answer came slowly, and Jessie wondered if she was all right. Perhaps age was finally getting the better of her.

'It is,' she said at last.

'I'd say Ger's class would love to hear all this.'

'I'd be happy to call down to them, if he'd like.'

'That'd be great. I'll let him know.'

Etty smiled and folded one hand neatly over the other. 'Wouldn't it be wonderful to discover what happened to Bridget and her daughter?'

'It would,' said Jessie, surprised to realise that she meant it.

Chapter 11

'Are there no names?' asked Jessie, as she walked the perimeter of a small grass plot at the rear of the graveyard.

Ger leaned against the ivy-smothered dry-stone wall, which ran around three sides of the ground. 'No, all the graves are unmarked, and I can't find any records, but it's a safe bet that this was where Johanna Markham was buried.'

A breeze rustled through the nearby trees. A lone magpie made an *ack ack ack* sound, like a machine-gun. The only indication that scores of bodies had been interred here came from a decades-old stone, its surface splotched with lichen. *In Memory of Those Who Lost Their Lives in the Great Famine*, it said. Jessie must have walked past these walls a thousand times, but now that she was inside, and now that she knew what had happened here, she found the experience unexpectedly moving.

Ger had finished work for the day, and she was having a late lunch.

This was her fourth day at the Seashell Café, and while she wouldn't admit it to Lorna, the job wasn't as bad as she'd feared. Her colleagues, Ashling from Clooneven and Ivana from Croatia, were a laugh, and she'd yet to come across any completely obnoxious customers. Given that they sold only sandwiches, pastries and ice cream, there was nothing overly onerous or foul-smelling about the work. And who didn't like the scent of fresh coffee?

She'd forgotten some of Clooneven's qualities: the long, long evenings, the people who insisted on swimming regardless of the weather, and the fact that sea and sand retained the power to excite children. She'd also forgotten how people changed when they went on holiday, how even the weariest mothers and most semi-detached fathers tried on different lives. Oh, and corny as it sounded, she'd forgotten what it was like when the night sky was filled with stars. In Dublin, they were usually masked by an orange haze.

Several of the girls from her year at school had called in on the pretext of buying coffee. Their real mission, she sensed, had been to check if the rumours were true. They'd wanted a side order of smugness with their flat white.

'Yeah, I'm giving Lorna a hand,' she'd said to Venetia Lillis, as though she was making a charitable donation to her sister.

'You're constantly surprising us,' replied Venetia, who was engaged to the local GP and wore her status like a crown.

Jessie suspected the girls' WhatsApp group was hopping with confirmation of her return. Lads, it's true! Hilarious to see her with the hair tied back and the apron on. 😂 No, I didn't mention the TV show. 🫢 The state of her! 🙈

She told herself not to worry about their judgement. She couldn't allow herself to think of this as going home. As retreating or bailing out. She was performing a four-month act of contrition, and when her duty was done, she could go back to her old life.

'Why didn't they teach us things like this – interesting things, I mean – when we were at school?' she asked, as she joined Ger beside the wall.

'They did, only your head was elsewhere.'

She smiled. 'I can't argue with you there.'

She'd told him why she was working for her sister but only in the most general terms. 'I'm at a loose end,' she'd said, 'and Lorna needs a dig-out.' Although he hadn't questioned her story, she had the feeling he was suspicious.

'I suppose there's every danger Bridget was buried here too,' she said. 'It'd be good to learn more.'

'I've done a bit of work,' said Ger.

'Have you found her?'

'If only it was that easy. For a start, I assumed she was married, which means her last name was no longer Markham. And, if you look at the records, there were thousands upon thousands of Bridgets. Not to mention all the Biddys, Bríds and Bridgies. I tried to see if I could find a Bridget whose maiden name was Markham, but didn't have any luck.' He took a sheet of paper from his pocket and unfolded it. 'Many of the online search sites have quite high charges, which you might pay if you were an American looking for long-lost family, but ...'

'... Bridget isn't our family, and we're not looking to go the full toora-loora-loora on this.'

'Exactly. So I had a look through a lot of what's available for free. This is my list.' He held up the paper, allowing it to flap in the breeze. 'The parish register only began after the Famine. By that point, there were no Markhams in Clooneven.'

'Are there any census records?'

'No. Some were burnt in a fire during the civil war, and others were deliberately destroyed ... which I suppose goes to show how much interest the authorities had in recording ordinary people's lives.'

'Typical.'

'Anyway,' he said, easing another piece of paper from his pocket, 'just as I was about to give up, I found this. It's in the County Library's archive. If it does refer to the correct Bridget, and the details are accurate …' He handed over the paper. 'Here, have a look for yourself.'

The sheet, which had been printed from the library's website, was headed, *Reports and Returns Relating to Evictions in the Kilrush Union. 1847–1849. List of Families Ejected and Houses Levelled in the Townland of Boherbreen, Clooneven. Property of H. Frobisher.* Jessie's eyes scanned the page until she found what Ger was talking about: *Head of Family: Bridget Moloney, Widow. Number in Family: 2 Females. Cause: Non-Payment. Quantity of Ground in Holding: 2 acres. Ejected in the superior courts in Dublin by Sir Henry Frobisher or his executors.*

'It's her,' she said. 'Isn't it?'

'More than likely, yeah.'

She looked again at the details. There were twenty-six families on the sheet, some of them with eight or nine children.

'All that hassle over a cottage and two boggy acres,' she said. 'Who else was he going to rent them to? I mean, can you imagine evicting people who were already starving?'

'I've been reading about Sir Henry. He had his defenders, you know. Apparently, he gave a small bit of money to the Church. Oh, and he claimed he couldn't afford to pay the rates for tenants who weren't producing anything.'

'There's always an excuse for the likes of him.'

That was the trouble with Ger: he was too reasonable. He was forever on the hunt for the other side of the story.

'So,' he said, 'Bridget's husband must have died from starvation too. Or else he caught some form of Famine fever.'

'It's unbelievable, isn't it? She was probably younger than us and she'd already lost both parents and her husband. I've never been a fan of all that it-puts-everything-in-perspective guff. It just seems like another way of making you feel guilty. In this case, though, I'll make an exception.'

'That makes two of us. Actually, you can include the class, so that makes twenty-eight of us.'

She folded the evictions list and handed it back to him. 'Did you find anything else?'

'Once I reckoned I had her full name, I tried to see if I could find a notice of her death. A lot of the records are online, so I looked up women called Bridget Moloney whose deaths had been registered in Clooneven. There were a few, but none sounded right. Either their age or place of birth was wrong.'

'So either our Bridget didn't die around here, or she married again.'

'Or she died before 1864 when the records began.'

Jessie checked her watch. She should have been back in the café ten minutes ago. 'I wish I could stay and talk this through. I can't risk falling out with my new boss, though.'

'Maybe we could have a chat later in the week? Go for a drink or something?'

After her conversation with Etty, it had occurred to Jessie that tracing her own family's story might make more sense. Even if they hadn't made the history books, it would be interesting to know how they'd fared during the Famine. She was already invested in Bridget's story, though: a life so different from her own yet lived on the same fields and streets.

'You're on,' she said to Ger. 'In the meantime, I'll see if I can find out anything else.'

The Seashell Café was quiet, so Ivana went home early, leaving Jessie to clean up and count the takings. Say what you like about Lorna, and Jessie said plenty, she had built an attractive business. The front of the café was painted pistachio green while the interior was decorated in cobalt blue and white. Small stoneware vases stood on the bleached-wood tables, and seaside-themed paintings dotted the walls.

She was about to put the 'Closed' sign on the door when a man arrived. Before she could stop him, he'd swerved past and was standing in front of the stainless-steel counter.

'I'm sorry,' she said, 'you're too late. I've already switched everything off.'

'Nah, you're all right, love,' he replied in a south Dublin drawl. 'I'm not here to buy anything. I'm looking for Lorna.'

Jessie bristled at his use of 'love'. She didn't mind local old lads calling her 'pet' or 'sweetheart'. She'd grown up with it. This guy, however, with his dark goatee, expensive runners and cheap leather jacket, was too smooth for her liking.

'As you can see, she's not here. I haven't come across her since this morning. Why don't you try the arcade?'

He tipped his head to one side. 'If I'm not mistaken, you're the famous sister, aren't you?'

Here we go again. 'Yep, that's me.' She tried to keep the impatience from her voice. 'What's your name? I can tell Lorna you were looking for her.'

'There's no need to tell her anything.'

'Why's that?'

'Because here she is.'

Lorna pushed open the door and entered the café. She placed her large cream handbag on the counter.

'I called you,' said the man, jangling the change in his pocket. 'You didn't answer, so I thought I'd come and find you. Instead, I met … it's Jessie, isn't it?'

'It is,' said Lorna. There was an unmistakable smell of salon shampoo from her hair. 'I didn't hear my phone.' She checked the clock on the far wall. 'You're early.'

'Only a minute or two. You know how much I hate poor timekeeping.'

Silence stretched between them. Jessie, still wondering who the man was and why he was there, sent a questioning look to her sister. 'Is everything okay?'

'Never better,' replied the man.

Lorna pulled at one earlobe. Her gaze slid towards him, but she addressed Jessie. 'Weren't you about to finish up?' She was speaking slightly differently, as if trying to make her accent less rural.

'I've got to wipe down the fridge and count the takings.'

The silence returned. Lorna and the man continued to look at each other, like they were sharing secret signals.

Jessie picked up a cloth. 'Don't worry, I can be speedy when I have to be.'

'You can leave that to me,' said her sister.

After dinner, Jessie went to her bedroom, took out her laptop and opened the website where Ger had found the list of evictions. She scrolled down, seeing townland after townland, family after family. She assumed that many of those forced out of their homes had ended up in the workhouse in Kilrush.

Another file contained a record of workhouse deaths. It covered only 1850 and 1851, but again the list was lengthy. The family names, all of them familiar, filled the screen: Harvey, Haugh, Hayes, Hehir. It read like a roll call of her class at school. Her own family name was there, as was Ger's. The records showed that people had died of dysentery, consumption, smallpox and typhus. They had suffered from measles, bronchitis, fever and jaundice.

Biddy Bourke had been four months old when she died, Connor Corbett, six weeks. Pat Crowe had died on the day he was born. Michael Cunningham had been eighty-three. Few others had been older than sixty. There were notes beside some of the deaths. One man had been admitted in 'a hopeless state'. Another was described as 'a mere skeleton'. A third had been admitted 'when all but dead'. Mary Cavanagh, aged fifty, was described as 'a feeble old woman'.

Part mesmerised, part fearful, Jessie moved slowly down the page.

Finally, she arrived at the Moloneys. There were three Bridgets. She breathed in quickly, then looked again. One had been fifty-nine, one forty-seven, the third just five.

It was entirely possible that her Bridget had died before 1850. She knew that. All the same, she was relieved.

The next file was different. It contained a series of reports from a London news magazine. A journalist and an artist had travelled to west Clare to document the catastrophe. The style was of its time, but the writing was compelling. The third dispatch was particularly moving. Halfway through, Jessie paused and returned to the start of the paragraph. She reread it. Then she read it once more. Even though the name wasn't quite right, she was hit by a jolt of recognition. She looked at the accompanying sketch. Without going any further, she rang Ger.

'I've found her,' she said.

Chapter 12

February 1848, Clooneven

Bridget

Bridget tried to think of reasons to be grateful. It was something her mother had taught her, and even in good times, she hadn't found it easy. Now, it was almost impossible. Under pressure, she would probably say that at least they no longer had to sleep on the floor. There were beds in the workhouse. There was food too, albeit not enough.

If gratitude was hard, fear was easy. Fear was always at her shoulder. She was scared that Norah would fall ill. Scared they'd never leave the workhouse. Scared she'd become disfigured by hate.

She didn't hate the men who'd forced them from their home. They were idiots, following instructions without heed for the consequences. Her hatred belonged to the man who'd ordered their eviction. The man who thought it right to tip families onto the side of the road when they had nowhere to go. Although it was unlikely she would ever meet Henry Frobisher, if she did she would spit in his face. Her mother would have said that such thoughts were sinful, but their world had changed, and the old ideas of right and wrong didn't make sense any more.

For months, she'd lived with a fool's optimism. After the relief work had ended, she'd been forced to rely on the soup kitchen. Often, all they received was salted water. On other days, they were given meal to which she added nettles or seaweed.

For the first time in three years, some of the potato crop was edible. The shame was that most of them hadn't been able to sow many seeds, so their yield was low. If she couldn't say that Norah was thriving, neither was she reduced to bone and sinew, like many of the local children.

Still, they had no money for rent, and rumours flew like dandelion seeds. All over the county, people were being cleared from their homes. In Boherbreen, they knew their turn would come and they braced themselves for the inevitable.

In early December, the eviction notices arrived. Shortly afterwards, an army of men appeared, some of them on horseback. The animals were better fed than any of Henry Frobisher's tenants.

Bridget tried to stand her ground. 'Do you not understand?' she said, as Norah nuzzled into her. 'We can't pay. We haven't any means. Forcing us onto the side of the road isn't going to make Sir Henry any richer.'

The bailiff's face was empty, his voice stripped of emotion. 'That's not our concern,' he said. 'We have a court order.'

'But it doesn't make any sense.'

'I promise you, Mrs Moloney, if you stay, you'll be a sorry woman.'

Nearby, an elderly man showered curses upon the eviction party. They would spend eternity in Hell, he warned. The men laughed at him, harsh cackling laughs that made anger rise within her. The only other opposition came from Cathleen Downes's eldest grandson who sat on their roof and threw stones. One of the agents warned that if he didn't stop, he'd be shot. Everybody else appeared resigned to losing their home.

To make sure there was no backsliding, the landlord's men tumbled every cottage. The thatch was sheared off or set on fire, the flames crackling, then roaring to life. Some people stood and wept. Others scattered. More, like Bridget and Norah, gathered up their few belongings and set off for the workhouse.

Icy needles of rain fell as they walked to Kilrush. Night was closing in around them. There were a thousand reasons to worry, yet one thought lodged in her brain: even if Francie wrote a letter home, she wouldn't receive it. The family home, the place where she'd been born and had given birth to Norah, was gone.

The other women wondered why she wouldn't go to Hackett's Cross. Couldn't Mary Ellen help? they asked. Hadn't she a decent house and means to pay the rent? Bridget said nothing. She couldn't explain that her sister's help would come at too high a price.

The workhouse was an enormous gloomy building surrounded by high stone walls. Some days brought a torrent of new people, others a trickle. In every case, they were there because they had no choice. Where once men and women had been reluctant to spend time in the workhouse, now they fought for admission. There were people in every inch of every room and on every step of the staircase. Many were listless. Others, delirious with fever, rambled and shouted. It was the noisiest place she'd ever been. Oh, and the smell was vile: urine and vomit, sweat and putrefying flesh. Bridget thought of it as the smell of hopelessness. While a doctor did his best to treat the sick, there was no remedy for most ailments.

Often, the children were in the worst condition. Clumps of hair were missing from their heads, and a light down coated their faces. Their stomachs were bloated, their limbs wizened. They tottered rather than walked, their eyes full of milky uncertainty. There were schools for both boys and girls, but many were too weak to learn. When they were old enough, they were put to work mending clothes or tending the garden.

Norah, her second birthday approaching, didn't seem to notice her friends' strange appearance. Or, maybe, she considered it normal. She was talking all the time now, even if not everything she said made sense or was easy to understand. Among her closest companions was three-year-old Honor Guilfoyle whose family had been evicted from their home in Cahercullen. Honor was a spindly girl with wisps of white hair and grey half-moons beneath her eyes. Several of her teeth were misshapen, others had fallen out. But she was a sweet-natured child who appeared to view herself as Norah's protector.

In early February, something unusual happened. The sky turned a stark white, and it snowed. The flakes came slowly at first, then blurred into a steady fall. Bridget recalled her father saying they hardly ever got snow in west Clare because they were too close to the sea.

Norah's eyes were out on stalks. 'Look, Mammy,' she kept saying, voice laced with wonder. 'What that?'

In the yard, flakes as big as Norah's fist swirled by. Thrilled by this strange substance, the children ran wild. They began throwing snowballs. The adults joined in, so that crystals flew in every direction, reflecting the light like showers of jewels. All the while, the snow tumbled down, and everything was fresh and clean.

Norah, Honor and the other children stuck out their tongues and allowed the flakes to settle there. Bridget picked her daughter up and twirled her around. Norah squealed with delight. Then, cheeks pink from the cold, she kissed her mother's nose and said, 'Thank you, Mammy.' There was a pure happiness in that moment and, however briefly, Bridget felt like the wealthiest woman in Ireland.

Honor had never been strong, and in the weeks that followed, her health deteriorated. She died in the middle of March. Typhus, the doctor said.

Immediately, Norah noticed her absence. She was ill at ease, looking for her in the same way she'd looked for her father the year before. Bridget didn't know if their daughter had any memories of John Joe. She hoped not. Forgetting was easier.

Twenty people died that week, and only a few mourners attended Honor's burial. Once, funerals had been sacred. Showing respect for the dead and for the journey they were about to take was considered important. Those days were gone.

There were no individual graves at the workhouse. Men dug pits ten feet deep and put seven or eight bodies, sometimes more, into each one. The shoulders of young men were sore from carrying corpses. Honor, bless her, was too light to hurt anyone. At three years of age, she'd weighed scarcely more than a baby.

Bridget prayed with Honor's parents and older brother at the graveside. The weather remained cold, and the ground was crusted with frost. She hadn't brought Norah with her. This didn't stop her daughter asking questions. She wanted to know why her friend had disappeared and if she could go to see her.

Bridget said that Honor had gone to Heaven. 'Like Daniel,' she added, referring to a boy who had died the previous week.

Norah gave her an earnest look. 'Me go too,' she said.

That night, Bridget lay awake. She always made sure that Norah didn't see her crying, but in the dark, she could allow the tears to run down her cheeks.

She'd heard that some families had gone back to Boherbreen. They were camped out by a stream with little by way of shelter. Food remained scarce, and Frobisher's men might try to move them on again. That wasn't all: for such a young child, Norah had travelled too many miles. If they stayed here, however, she would suffer the same fate as her friends. They were surrounded by people whose lives were disintegrating. Whatever chance there was of crafting a new life, it wouldn't happen in the workhouse.

The next morning, she gripped her daughter's hand. 'We're going on a small journey today, pet.'

'Where?' asked Norah.

'Home,' she said.

Five families had returned to Boherbreen. They were living on common land close to the old cottages. The only shelter was provided by the scalpeens they'd built from turf sods and branches. There wasn't enough ground to grow vegetables, nor did anyone have seeds to sow. They were reliant on charity.

When Bridget saw their cabins, damaged beyond repair, she was hit by a renewed surge of anger. While far from perfect, the buildings had provided good homes. Families had been happy here. Men and women had led productive lives. Her dark humour was tempered by the sight of Cathleen Downes striding across the bog to greet them.

'Welcome home,' she said. 'Welcome home.'

Like the others, the Downes family were living in a makeshift structure, cooking on a communal fire and washing in the stream.

'I won't lie to you,' said Cathleen, as they crouched beside the fire, 'it hasn't been easy. There have been days when I've been tempted by the workhouse. It'll be the summer before we know it, mind. And everything's better in the summer.'

The Moloneys had been gone only three months, but in that time, several of their neighbours had perished. Eliza Haugh had died in January, and Cathleen's eyes filled with tears as she spoke about her friend's last days.

'She was a decent woman. No matter how little she had, she was willing to share. There are plenty who could learn from her.'

'There are,' said Bridget, thinking of Mary Ellen and Thomas. 'What about the others?'

'Maggie and John Tubridy are gone to America. More are headed the same way, but you need money for the passage, and few enough have it. I've heard that in some places, the landlord is paying for people to go, just so he can be rid of them.'

'If you had the money would you go?' asked Bridget.

'I'm too old, my love. America's not for the likes of me. If I was young, though, that's what I'd do. There's nothing left for anyone around here. I usen't think they'd deliberately set out to kill us, but now … now I don't know. What I can't fathom is why those men beyond in London hate us so much. Are we that different from their own people?'

Cathleen's words echoed Bridget's thoughts. What had once looked like an unfortunate series of events had begun to feel like a plan.

'What are you doing for food?' she asked.

'The soup kitchen opens most days in Clooneven. When it doesn't …' Cathleen paused. 'When it doesn't, people eat whatever they can find, even if it's only seaweed or a few tufts of grass. I've seen children with green juice trickling down their chins. It's not right, but, sure, what is right any more?'

Bridget soon discovered that every day in Boherbreen was about survival. They had to be careful where they foraged in case anyone accused them of trespassing on Frobisher's land. While Bridget was relieved to be home, she'd underestimated how difficult Norah would find it. Staying warm was a constant challenge. She rebuked herself for leaving Kilrush without so much as a blanket.

The little girl, who'd endured endless privations without complaint, started to grizzle and moan. 'I cold,' she'd say, her teeth chattering as she spoke. Sometimes her clothes were stiff with frost.

Bridget thought constantly about death. At her lowest, she decided it wasn't a case of if they died, but how and when. She couldn't say that leaving the workhouse had been a mistake because staying would have been a mistake too. At night, she dreamt of her childhood and of the days when they'd had enough to eat. It had never occurred to her that an existence like this was possible. At other times, she fantasised about food. She imagined what it would be like to eat an entire pot of potatoes. She thought of salty fish and sweet apples and warm oat cakes.

One night, as she attempted to get Norah to sleep, she realised that her daughter looked like the children in Kilrush. Her wrists were so thin it appeared as if they could snap at any moment. The same was true of her ankles.

I'm killing you, thought Bridget.

As much as I love you, I'm killing you.

If she could have done so, she would have given Norah whatever warmth was left in her own body. She would donate her blood and breath. But it wasn't enough. She hadn't been able to save her mother. She hadn't saved Michael or John Joe. She might not be able to save herself. But she could save her daughter.

It didn't end there. Even if Norah lived, she deserved better than this. She deserved a house, a bed, clean clothes. She deserved oatmeal with milk, eggs, bread. She deserved laughter.

The offer remained open. Continuing to spurn it was selfish. She would give Norah to Mary Ellen, and then she'd return to the workhouse.

Bridget pulled Norah close and whispered into her hair: 'You've got to go to sleep, pet, because we'll be busy tomorrow.'

In the morning, as they prepared for the walk to Hackett's Cross, Bridget saw two men striding across the bog. From their heavy coats, hats and sturdy boots, she guessed they were English. She might be leaving, but the others weren't, and they didn't deserve any more upheaval.

She walked towards the men. 'No one here is doing anything wrong,' she shouted. 'Go away and leave us be.'

Several others joined her. One of Cathleen's grandsons, the boy who'd thrown stones at the eviction party, urged the men to turn back. 'Can you not allow us to live in peace?' he said.

'That's right,' added Cathleen. 'We've no more to give. Ye've already taken it all.'

The men continued towards them. The taller of the two raised a hand. 'Please,' he said, 'we mean you no harm.'

'What are you doing here then?' said Bridget. 'What do you want?'

'We want to ask about your lives,' he replied.

Chapter 13

If Mary Ellen was taken aback by Bridget's change of heart, she didn't let it show. She acted as though what was happening had been inevitable. Maybe it had. Bridget was trying not to think. Thinking would lead to resentment.

When she'd spoken to the newspaper men, she'd still had some fight. She'd said everything she'd wanted to say, and the others in Boherbreen had supported her. She wondered if her words would appear in the newspaper. She assumed not. Papers were for politicians and landlords and important men. Not for women like her. The journalist and the artist had been kind, but when they went back to London, their superiors would probably dismiss her story.

Now, numbness had taken hold of her. Words came slowly and voicing them was difficult.

'I'd like one last day,' she said. 'One good day.'

Mary Ellen, clearly nervous that Bridget would change her mind, took a deep breath. 'I don't think that would be wise.'

'It's not a lot to ask.'

'How can we be certain that one day won't turn into two, and two days won't turn into a week?'

'Because you have my word.'

'You say that tonight, but what if you feel differently afterwards? No, it's best that you leave tomorrow.'

Bridget despaired of her sister's pettiness. Was there a danger she would treat Norah in such a cold way? Briefly, she considered taking the little girl from her bed and leaving again. But that would be heartless. Norah was having her first proper sleep in weeks.

It would also be pointless. They had nowhere to go.

To her surprise, Thomas spoke up. 'One day won't hurt. Bridget can spend tomorrow with Norah and leave on Thursday.'

Mary Ellen's jaw slackened, but she didn't argue. As far as Bridget could tell, she never said anything to contradict her husband. 'Very well,' she said. 'One day it is.' She turned to Bridget. 'Only you're not to go upsetting the child. You're to leave quietly, like we agreed.'

'I've no intention of unsettling my daughter.' She found herself emphasising the last two words. She might be entrusting Norah to the care of Mary Ellen and Thomas, but this didn't mean she was truly theirs.

The three were sitting around the kitchen table. Norah was in the room next door. Weary from another walk, mostly on her mother's back but occasionally on her own small feet, she'd fallen asleep as soon as Bridget had blown out the candle. Before going to bed, she'd eaten some oatmeal. Not too much, though. They'd spent so long on starvation rations that a large meal would have made her ill. It was also clear that Mary Ellen had not been lying when she'd said their circumstances were straitened. They had more to eat than Bridget and Norah, but so had birds and mice.

Mary Ellen had given Bridget a grey dress to replace her ragged workhouse uniform. It hung about her like a man's greatcoat, but it was clean. For the first time in weeks, she'd had a proper wash with water heated on the fire. Her sister had insisted on washing Norah, who had wriggled and cried. Bridget had forced herself to turn away. Afterwards, she'd soothed her daughter, telling her that Mary Ellen loved her and would never hurt her. She prayed that this was true.

Initially, she'd intended to return to the workhouse. But Mary Ellen and Thomas had persuaded her to leave the country. For more than an hour, they'd argued and cajoled until she'd given in. They would pay her fare and give her a small amount of money. Not much, because they didn't have much, but enough for her to get started elsewhere. She was clever, they said. She'd been the brightest girl at school, the one the master had chosen to read out loud. In another country, she could make something of herself.

There was only one place for her to go: Boston, where her brother was. She didn't know if it would be possible to find him. All she could do was try.

Now they sat in silence, scared a stray word would cause their agreement to fall asunder.

It was Bridget who spoke first. 'I know you'll be able to give Norah what I can't, but I hope you can also … I hope you can love her the way she deserves to be loved. For such a young girl, she's had a hard life. Everyone has left her. She must think the world's a very cruel place.'

Bridget worried that Mary Ellen would be offended. Instead, her face softened. 'I promise you, we'll mind her and love her. We will, won't we, Thomas?'

He gave a small nod.

'And, one day, when she's older, will you tell her why I had to go? Will you explain?'

'I don't—'

'I couldn't bear her thinking I hadn't loved her enough. That I'd abandoned her because I didn't want her.'

'We'll have to see what happens,' said Thomas.

She wondered then if they intended to say anything to Norah. If they didn't, she would grow up thinking that Thomas and Mary Ellen were her parents.

Bridget had decided not to tell her daughter she was going away. She would only get upset. Of course, she'd be confused and anxious when she realised her mother had disappeared, but how long would that last? She'd already lost so many people, she would probably consider it normal. Soon, she would forget.

'Please,' said Bridget. 'Please tell her about me. And about John Joe. And about Mam and Dad and Michael. She ought to know about us.'

She closed her eyes to stop the tears sliding out. She wasn't as numb as she'd thought.

Eventually, Mary Ellen spoke again. 'I'll tell you what we'll do. You can write her a letter, and when I think it's appropriate, I'll show it to her.'

Bridget wasn't sure she believed this, but there was nothing else she could do.

It was important that their final day together was calm. The less fuss she made, the less likely Norah would worry that something strange was happening. They went to the beach in Hackett's Cross. While not as impressive as Clooneven, there was plenty of sand, and they gathered shells to replenish Norah's collection.

Out of habit, Bridget also began to collect seaweed. Then she stopped. When they were growing up, Mary Ellen had hated seaweed, and it was unlikely she would want it now.

Already, Norah looked healthier. Her curls, stripped of dirt, had regained their shine. Her cheeks were pink from running about in the breeze. Most striking was the way her face had relaxed, as if two meals and a night's sleep were enough to make her forget months of hunger. Oh, to be so resilient.

The day was gentle, the pale blue sky speckled with light cloud. A hawk sailed above them. Behind the beach, the land was flecked with the colours of spring. Yellow and purple and white. For a minute, Bridget considered picking Norah up and running away. They could travel to Galway and get the boat to America. They'd arrive in Boston together.

Then the truth returned. According to everything she'd heard, the boats were infested with desperation and disease. She remembered a man in the workhouse who'd claimed the Atlantic was rotten with Irish flesh because of all the bodies thrown overboard. Anyway, without money from Thomas and Mary Ellen, she couldn't afford the fare.

While Norah splashed about at the water's edge, Bridget sat and watched. The sea stretched out before her in different strips of blue. Its scent filled her head. Although she had scant idea what the rest of the world looked like, it was hard to picture anywhere more beautiful. But what did beauty matter? What was this place? Only soil and stone, sea and sand, grass and clover. Why should she feel attached to it? Save for a two-year-old girl, there was no one here for her. Most people didn't care whether she lived or died. Indeed, they might prefer her dead. Hers was one more mouth in need of food, one more body looking for a place to sleep, one more face in the ranks of the destitute. She was a walking, breathing inconvenience.

When it was time to go, she crouched down and kissed Norah's head.

'Have you enjoyed yourself?' she asked.

'Mammy, that was a good day,' replied Norah, her face serious, her voice content.

Back in the cottage, Mary Ellen was doing her best to pretend that everything was normal. She made a pot of vegetable broth. It had been months since Bridget had tasted anything so good. While they ate, Norah chattered. She was growing accustomed to her new family.

Bridget fought to keep the emotion from her voice. There would be time enough for emotion. She wanted to eke out every second of the evening. Every word, every smile, every glance. They were all important.

By the time Norah went to bed, her eyes were drooping with tiredness. 'Can we stay here?' she asked Bridget, who kissed her cheek.

'Yes, you can, pet,' she replied.

In the main room, Mary Ellen was parcelling up some bread. 'It's not much,' she said, 'but it'll get you on your way.'

'What are your plans?' asked Thomas, as he threw another sod of turf onto the fire.

'I'll sleep out here and leave early. If I sleep beside Norah, there's a danger I'll wake her. Oh, and if you give me some paper, I'll write that letter.'

Mary Ellen tensed. All the same, she provided two sheets of paper and some ink. 'Be careful with that,' she said. 'It's all I have.'

Later, when the others had gone to bed, Bridget sat and concentrated on her letter. She tried not to dwell on the fact that Norah might never read it. All she could do was hope.

My darling Norah,

I trust you're safe and well and that life is being kind to you. I doubt you remember me, but believe me when I say I will never forget you. You were my light in very dark times. I could not have survived without you. It's my dearest wish that, by the time you read this, conditions have improved.

In the short time we spent together, we shared many happy moments. Our last day, on the shore in Hackett's Cross, was perfect. I've decided that when life feels too difficult, those are the hours I will try to recall. Once, I thought we were all better off without happy memories. Now, I understand that they're what make life bearable. To know that we were happy once is to believe that it might be possible again.

Bridget's hand was unsteady, and she put down her pen. She told herself to remain composed. Presently, she continued.

We all want to know what we were like in our earliest years, and be assured, you were a lovely little girl. When I had to work, you came with me and played beside me. All the men said what a good child you were and how I was blessed to have you. They were right.

You were very small when your daddy was taken from us. He was a fine man, and you were the centre of his world. I remember him picking you up and twirling you around. You laughed then like you were the luckiest girl in the land.

I don't know if you can understand why I left. Please accept that I did what I thought was best. It was the most difficult decision I ever had to make, but I could offer you nothing apart from more suffering. I wish all that's good for you, not simply material comforts but love and happiness and fulfilment.

As I write this, I'm preparing to leave. In the morning, I will make a start for Galway where I plan on boarding a ship for Boston. In truth, I'm very scared but I'm sure everyone feels the same. What strange times these are.

I'd like to think we will meet again. Even if we don't, I pray that you will look upon me fondly and with mercy. You will always be in my heart.
All my love, now and for ever,
Your mother,
Bridget Moloney

Afterwards, she lay on the floor. She didn't expect to sleep. She was wrong. When she woke, light was beginning to wash through the windows. The sky was tinted with lemon and rose. Ribbons of mist clung low to the ground. She was tempted to take one last look at Norah but couldn't risk disturbing her. She wrapped her black shawl around her shoulders and picked up the bag containing her few possessions, including a blanket given to her by Mary Ellen. She was about to go when she remembered something. She went back to the table, took one of her daughter's new cockle shells and dropped it into her pocket.

When she left the cottage, she didn't look back. Neither did she follow the obvious route. Rather than walking north towards Galway, she turned south and travelled in the direction of Clooneven. Without Norah, she moved swiftly. She kept thinking of how John Joe had helped to build the road.

The graveyard was quiet. She suspected that nowadays this was a rare occurrence. She paused to consider her surroundings. She was standing among the missing. These had been her neighbours and friends. Some had been cantankerous, others mild. Some greedy, others generous. Some workshy, others industrious. But, like her mother, brother and husband, they had deserved to live. She imagined their ghosts rising up around her.

Although no cross marked the spot where Johanna, Michael and John Joe were buried, she knew exactly where to go. That she wasn't especially religious didn't matter. She dropped to her knees and spoke to them.

'I'm sorry I won't be here to talk to you,' she said, 'but I hope I have your blessing. I'll think of you every day. And, Mam, I promise I'll try to find Francie.'

It struck Bridget that if anyone saw her, they'd think she'd lost her mind. No matter. Hunger had brought madness to them all, twisting their minds as well as their bodies.

When she'd said her goodbyes, she left the graveyard and headed towards the town. She pictured John Joe walking alongside her, Norah on his back. That was how it should have been.

There might, she thought, be someone in Clooneven with a donkey and cart. Someone who could help her on her way. If not, she would begin her long journey on foot.

Chapter 14

May 2019, Clooneven

Jessie

The night after her discovery, Jessie met Ger in Sexton's lounge. In her view, Sexton's was the best of Clooneven's bars. It was basic without being dirty, busy yet calm. There was no television, and stags and hens were banned.

She'd been useless at work, forgetting who'd ordered what and handing out the wrong change. Cappuccino, latte, flat white: it was all just milky coffee, and she didn't believe anyone from Clooneven could tell the difference anyway. When Venetia Lillis complained, she'd wanted to shout, *Look, love, you grew up with a mug of instant, and you were glad to get it. Do you have any idea how much important information is in my head? Cut me some slack here, would you?*

The words had remained unspoken. Not only would Lorna have given her a talking-to, no one, apart from Ger, would have understood why a news report about a woman who'd lived almost two hundred years ago could be important.

'Are you sure it's her?' he asked, from behind his pint of Guinness.

'I am. I know the name's slightly different, and I know there were a million Bridgets, but on balance, it has to be our woman. Doesn't it?'

'I reckon you're right. I'm kicking myself I didn't come across the article. I suppose the different spelling didn't help.'

Although the *London Illustrated Gazette* had spelt her name as Brigid Malowney, everything else was a perfect match. She'd been living on boggy ground in Boherbreen, having been evicted from her cottage some months previously. Her husband had died from Famine fever, and she'd had one daughter, whom they now knew had been called Norah.

Other details were new. Her father had been lost at sea some years earlier. She'd had a sister called Mary Ellen McGuane who'd lived in Hackett's Cross. On the day the journalists had met her, she'd intended travelling there to leave two-year-old Norah in her sister's care.

These basic facts were only part of the story. What captured them both was the picture the article painted of Bridget's life, of the poverty and hunger but also of her intelligence and determination. There was a rare honesty about her comments. She'd had nothing left to lose and nothing to sell. She was described as a 'pauper', as part of the 'great mass of peasantry', yet in the article she came alive. She was fierce in her love for Norah and her home. 'We're entitled to better than this,' she'd told the reporter. 'The failure of one crop shouldn't mean we have to die like neglected animals. My girl is no less important than the children of landlords and gentry.'

The descriptions of Clooneven and its surrounding townlands were graphic. According to the journalist, in the space of a few hours, he had counted ninety-two roofless houses. The whole district, he wrote, had been swept of food. Jessie tried to imagine what those familiar fields must have looked like.

The article was accompanied by a portrait. In black ink, it showed

Bridget, her tattered clothes dripping from her thin body, holding a curly-haired Norah.

Ger kept picking out different words and lines. "'The present condition of the Irish," he read, "has been mainly brought on by foolish and vicious legislation. Surely, there can be nowhere else on earth where misery and neglect are so rife."'

Jessie sipped her wine. 'He didn't hold back, all right. I stayed up half the night trying to get more information. Apparently, the piece caused a stir because interviewing "real people", especially someone as young and poor as Bridget, was unusual.'

'So both Bridget and her mother made the headlines?'

'Mmm. Only I don't think anyone's ever made the connection between the two.'

'We'll be professors of history before we know it,' he said, with a wink. 'Another glass?'

'Go on. I'm not working till ten in the morning.'

It had been the best part of two months since she'd spent Friday evening in a pub. The last occasion had featured a large group of friends, too much over-priced prosecco and unwelcome attention from a guy who worked at Facebook and planned on retiring at forty. She knew this because he'd talked about his achievements in the sort of run-on sentences that made it impossible to interrupt. He'd also spoken at length about his dislike of authority, without appearing to recognise any contradiction. His name escaped her, but she couldn't picture him enjoying a quiet pint in Sexton's. Back then, she'd still been mourning her relationship with Phelim.

Little by little, she was filling in the gaps with Ger. She'd known that he'd spent several years in Cork. What she hadn't realised was that his return to Clooneven had been involuntary. Three years ago, his father had been diagnosed with a rare form of cancer. A permanent job had become available in St Finian's, and before you could say, 'Only son does the decent thing', he was back in Clare. He shared a rented house in

Kilrush with two other teachers and didn't know whether he was home for the long haul.

That he enjoyed his work and devoted so much energy to it made Jessie feel all the more inadequate. Oh, she knew she was being self-indulgent. Compared to Bridget and Irish women of almost every other generation, her life was a bounty of gifts. But coming across the article had deepened her angst. The correspondent for the *London Illustrated Gazette* had done genuinely important work. It was hard to picture him wasting ink on the nineteenth-century equivalent of Hollie Garland.

At the next table, three women were moaning about a neighbour. 'No harm to her,' said one, 'but talk about losing the run of yourself. I remember her at school, and the family were so poor she wore sandals in November.' On the other side, two men were discussing a recent funeral. 'Ninety-nine's a grand age,' said the elder fellow, 'though it's a mighty shame he didn't make the hundred. Not that he'd have spent the cheque from the president. May God forgive me, but he was tight.' Maybe it was the alcohol, but Jessie found herself enjoying the conversations. There was little to match the sound of small scores being settled.

When Ger returned, they discussed what they should do next.

'I've been thinking about it all day,' she said, 'and, bleak as this sounds, I don't reckon Bridget could have survived much longer. When she spoke to the reporter and illustrator, she was in a very bad way and, apart from Norah and Mary Ellen, everyone belonging to her was dead.'

'What about her sister?' said Ger. 'From what she said, Mary Ellen was better off. Plus, she wasn't that far away. Mary Ellen could hardly have taken Norah and allowed Bridget to fend for herself.'

'I know it wouldn't have been the kind thing to do, but perhaps they'd never been close.'

Ger paused to drink some of his pint. 'There's one way we might find out. Back around 1860, a curate called Father Kelly carried out an informal local census. Presumably, the Church wanted to see who was left. He surveyed most of the area including Hackett's Cross. I think that's where he was based. If Mary Ellen McGuane and her husband were still alive, they should be on the list. And who knows? Bridget and Norah might be there too.'

'You're a genius.' Jessie picked up her phone again. The drink was definitely kicking in, and she felt her shoulders loosening. 'Is the priest's census online? I'll look it up.'

'I'm afraid it's not. Copies of the records are available from the current parish priest in Hackett's Cross, though. We can go and have a look if you like.'

'Absolutely. I'm at work all day tomorrow, but I'm free on Sunday evening. How are you fixed then?'

Ger picked up his glass. 'Ah, I won't be here. I'm going down to Cork to spend the weekend with Rosemary.'

Jessie must have given him a confused look because he quickly added, 'My girlfriend, you know? I'm sure I mentioned her. She's a nurse in the University Hospital.'

'I'm sure you did,' she said. 'Don't mind me, I've an awful memory.'

Of course he had a girlfriend, and of course she had a wholesome name and a wholesome job. No doubt they did wholesome activities together, like hill-walking and watching GAA matches. Oh, and going to christenings. In her experience, wholesome people attended a lot of functions involving either children or religion. At their family gatherings, they played card games for small change and shared photos of their pets. Their WhatsApp groups were filled with jokes and affection and entirely free of snark.

Using Ger's Facebook page as a starting point, Jessie found Rosemary O'Donovan's social media. Her Instagram page was private (Why? What could she possibly put on there that required privacy?) and her Twitter barely used. Her Facebook account was more useful. Post after post showed Rosemary walking in the countryside or on a night out with the girls. You could practically smell the fake tan and floral perfume. Ger made an occasional appearance, usually as part of a large gang of friends. Everyone was as stick-thin and rosy-cheeked as Jessie had feared. Rosemary was also a regular 10K runner, and a range of children's and mental health charities had benefited from her efforts. Truly, she was the patron saint of wholesomeness.

Twenty-four hours later, and she remained annoyed with herself for becoming interested in Ger. It was beyond cliché: small-town girl goes home and falls for small-town boy. If any of her friends behaved in such a pathetic needy way, she wouldn't be long in putting them straight. Not, she assured herself, that she had fallen for him. It was more a case of wanting a distraction and thinking he might provide it. And wasn't that one of her weaknesses? She'd spent her life being driven by boredom or the fear of it. She'd hooked up with men, not because she found them particularly appealing but because she'd fancied the adventure or, worse, because she'd been flattered by their attention.

Okay, she'd been with Phelim for five years, but they'd had several breaks. She'd been unfaithful before Oisín and, deep down, she suspected Phelim had too. If it was ridiculous to claim that such a lengthy relationship hadn't been particularly serious, it was also the truth. A long time had passed since she'd expected them to have children, get married or save for a house. Like the worn-out couples she saw shuffling down the prom, they'd stayed together because it had been easier than splitting up. Their relationship had been like a starter marriage, only without the certificate and the chocolate fountain.

In frustration, she considered going to Hackett's Cross without Ger, but that wouldn't be fair. Besides, her free time was limited. She'd spent most of Saturday in the café and now she was on her way to Lorna's house for a few hours' babysitting.

After Lorna and Simon had renovated his family home, they'd renamed it Clevedon. To Jessie's ears, the name was out of place. It sounded more suited to a prosperous part of England than to the marshy end of west Clare. There were six bedrooms, four bathrooms, a kitchen the size of a football field, and a dining room with French windows and a chandelier. 'I wouldn't like to be paying the heating bill,' had been their father's assessment. Jessie thought the house was fine, in an antiseptic, generic sort of way. Then again, she'd never been particularly interested in furnishings.

A sweep of trees masked the view of the old farm buildings at the back of the property. The sheds hadn't been used for years, and the time must have come to level them. The garden was largely untouched, which was a shame. It was as if Simon and Lorna had spent every last cent on the house and had run out of cash for the grounds. Come to think of it, that might be the case. Making money in a seaside town wasn't easy. If they could afford it, many Irish people chose continental heat rather than a soggy week in a west-coast caravan.

As she cycled up the tarmac, past the clusters of ragwort and dandelions, she wondered why Lorna hadn't asked their mother to look at the garden. She was sure Maeve would be able to work her magic at minimal expense.

Money worries would also help to explain why Simon looked so worn out. One of the worst things you could say about anyone was that they weren't ageing well, and it was definitely true of her brother-in-law. Although still in his late thirties, he looked a decade older. There were pouches of flesh beneath his eyes and his hairline edged backwards by the week. Even his voice sounded too old. Oh, and he was crabby. No matter what Jessie said, he found fault with it. He reminded her of the guys who hung out on Twitter with a contrarian take for every occasion, the guys who liked to say, 'Fixed it for you' or 'Do better.'

She'd never liked Simon, a view bolstered by the fact that he didn't have much time for her. In his eyes, she was a messy, unpredictable presence, who liked poking at things and asking questions. Once upon a time, she'd made an effort to meet him halfway. She'd told herself that even Lorna wouldn't marry for money alone. There must, she'd reasoned, be a softer, more inviting side to him. She'd conceded then that he was warm towards his children, was on friendly terms with her parents and didn't appear to be mean with money.

None of this was enough. If you asked Jessie, Lorna was too compliant. Too willing to follow her husband's line. It was as if her high-handed behaviour with other people was compensation for her far meeker attitude at home. No doubt the Clooneven gossip-mongers would maintain that Lorna had 'done well for herself'. In Jessie's opinion, she could have done far better.

That her sister wouldn't stray far from home had always been clear. To this day, she had an old woman's perception of Dublin, seeing it as a noisy, smelly place filled with fumes and chancers and criminals. 'I wouldn't have the patience for it,' she liked to say. 'I mean, it's not the 1980s. We have everything in Clare now.' Once, after several glasses of sauvignon blanc, she'd become philosophical about her sister's determination to travel. 'I think it's in your blood,' she'd said. 'Because previous generations left, you were convinced you had to leave too.'

Jessie had pointed out that wanderlust couldn't be in her blood because she was descended from people who'd stayed. Her pedantry had received a cool response.

Lorna met her at the door. She was wearing a white towelling bathrobe and pink flip-flops. 'There you are now,' she said, with a smirk. 'I gather you were in Sexton's with Ger Dillane last night.'

'That's right,' said Jessie, following her up the stairs and into the master bedroom. 'I've invited him over so we can have wild sex in front of the kids.'

'You're joking me.'

'*Duh*. Of course I am.'

'What's the story, then?'

'There's no story. Well, actually, there is … only not what you're thinking.'

She perched on the powder-blue chaise longue and told Lorna about Bridget.

Her sister, who was at the dressing-table, frowned. 'That's a terrible tale, but, if you don't mind me asking, what's it to you?'

'It's interesting. I might write about Bridget and her mother.'

'They're a long way from your usual fodder.'

'That's for sure but, like you keep reminding me, it's time for a change.'

Lorna, who'd been applying bronzer with the precision of a portrait artist, paused. 'The best of luck with it, anyway. Oh, and sorry if I've come the heavy lately. I've been under a bit of pressure. Believe it or not, Ash and Ivana are full of your praises.'

This, thought Jessie, was classic Lorna. Nothing was clear cut. Every time she felt as if her sister's judgemental tendencies had gone too far, Lorna would say or do something thoughtful. It would be easier if Jessie could dismiss her as an uncaring social climber, a self-obsessed money-grabber, but she was more complex than that. Despite their disagreements, they'd often looked out for each other. For every petty argument, there had been a moment of solidarity, for every frosty exchange, an evening of laughter.

Lorna had spent seven years as an only child, and according to family history, the Dalys had expected her to be jealous of baby Jessie. Instead she'd been delighted with the new arrival, forever offering to push her buggy or play games. Later, she'd been generous and protective, her sharp tongue and even sharper elbows a shield against the likes of Venetia Lillis.

This was the first time Jessie had been alone with her sister since the unknown man had walked into the café. Now, with Simon and the children in the kitchen, she had an opportunity.

'You know what I've been meaning to ask you, who was the chap who came into the Seashell looking for you?'

'People look for me all the time.'

'You know who I mean. The fellow with the goatee and the south Dublin accent.'

'Him?' said Lorna, picking up her mascara. 'He's an ice-cream rep.'

'Oh, right,' said Jessie, confident that whoever the man was, he hadn't been there to sell ice cream. Unfortunately, before she had the opportunity to probe any further, Simon's head appeared around the door.

'I thought we'd agreed that tonight we'd be on time,' he said.

'And we will,' replied Lorna. 'Give me five minutes, and I'll be with you.'

'Not if you stay up here gossiping, you won't.'

Jessie took her cue and got to her feet. 'I'll go down and say hello to Ethan and Zoë.'

'That's a good idea,' said Simon.

It was as she was going down the stairs that something struck her. She thought of how nervous her sister had been when the – still unnamed – man had come into the café. In her desire to get rid of Jessie, she'd practically pulled the cloth from her hand and shooed her out the door.

If there was one skill Jessie possessed, it was the ability to spot a couple having an affair, and that was what she believed was happening.

Chapter 15

May 2019, Boston
Kaitlin

'Brian and Riley are in Washington for the weekend,' said Susan, voice varnished with pride. 'They're looking at apartments. Otherwise, they'd be here.' She picked up a serving bowl. 'You're too pale. You ought to eat more vegetables.'

'Thanks,' replied Kaitlin, accepting the dish. 'That's nice. About Brian and Riley, I mean.'

'Well, I think it's very exciting,' said her mother, her tone implying that Kaitlin hadn't shown sufficient enthusiasm. She insisted on providing regular updates on Brian's new job, whether they were wanted or not.

Kaitlin's tame response was at odds with the turmoil in her stomach. She felt like she was at the top of a rollercoaster, seconds away from the swooping descent. She reminded herself that being nervous was stupid.

Attempting to trace your ancestors was normal. Hundreds of thousands of people were out there right now, wading through names and putting saliva samples in the post.

Telling her parents would be different if she'd made more progress. If she could surprise them with a *ta-dah* moment. A revelation. That was what she'd hoped for. Instead, all she had to offer was a lengthening list of humdrum relatives who'd lived and died within a ten-mile radius of their birthplace.

It was Clay who'd insisted that she talk to them. 'Your father might be able to help,' he'd argued. Anxious to prove that she wasn't as secretive as he'd claimed, she'd given in. At least he'd reconciled himself to her search. He could see why she might find it therapeutic, he said.

In the two weeks since her conversation with Orla and Drew, she'd located the older couple from the Revere Beach photo. Like Drew had said, they were her paternal great-great-grandparents, Ray and Bertha McDonagh. Unfortunately, the 1940 census had told her little she hadn't already known. To find out more, she'd signed up to several genealogy websites. When she'd run 'Raymond McDonagh, South Boston' through the first, it had promised – or should that be threatened? – hundreds of matches. Thankfully, the real figure was closer to thirty. She'd whittled them down until she'd isolated the right Ray. Then, slowly, methodically, she'd spooled back through the decades. 1930, 1920, 1910: every census had captured Ray, Bertha and family. They'd had seven children, and it occurred to Kaitlin that Boston must be dotted with cousins she'd never met.

The previous evening, courtesy of the 1900 census, she'd had a breakthrough of sorts. Ray had been twenty years old then and living at home. Bertha had been seventeen and living less than a mile away. Kaitlin now had the names of their parents, her third-great-grandparents: Patrick and Finola McDonagh, Edmund and Edith Lankford.

To dig deeper, she'd have needed to pull an all-nighter, but with Sunday lunch looming at her parents' place, she'd decided against. At the best of times, a meal with her mother required all her energy. The records would have to wait.

Although simple, the meal was wonderful. Herbed roast chicken, mashed potato, roast root vegetables, crisp green beans: her mother always went the extra mile for Clay. The house was pristine, the smell of lemon Pledge lingering in the air, the vacuum cleaner's lines visible on the carpet. She'd also taken care with her appearance. Her blonde hair was blown out, her make-up buffed and blended. (Orla had once described her mother's look as 'senior news anchor with dermatologist on speed dial', prompting laughter and feelings of disloyalty from Kaitlin.)

Lunch with her parents didn't unnerve Clay in the same way as larger family gatherings. All the same, she couldn't avoid the sense that he viewed spending time with them as an obligation rather than a pleasure. To be fair, she had a similar attitude towards his parents. While she couldn't claim that Landon and Hilary Abbott had ever been anything but polite, she suspected she wasn't quite what they'd expected. Something about Landon in particular made her feel more like a recipient of his benevolence than a member of the family. No matter her expensive education and successful career, she was, and always would be, the daughter of an Irish builder. Her people had carried hods rather than bank files. The Irish might have gained political power, but they weren't on the boards of galleries or tasteful charities. They were sentimental and brash and overly obsessed with the slights of the past.

For twenty minutes, Kaitlin swung between telling her parents and remaining quiet. Why was it that small issues were harder to raise than significant ones? In the end, as she'd feared he would, Clay forced her hand.

'Has Kaitlin told you about her search for long-lost Wilsons and McDonaghs?' he said.

'Sorry?' replied her mother.

Her father put down his knife. 'Tell us more.'

And so she did. She managed to outline the steps she'd taken while gliding over the reasons why. She talked about the satisfaction the task gave her. And she mentioned the importance of heritage – because who could argue with heritage? As she spoke, her confidence returned. Clay squeezed her knee. He had been right. This was the ideal place to discuss her project.

Her mom made the occasional noncommittal noise. Her dad asked a question or two. Otherwise, they said little. It was only when Kaitlin mentioned the help she'd received from Drew and Orla that her mother's expression changed.

'Orla certainly knows plenty about landing in America without papers or permission,' she said.

No one replied.

Eventually her dad lifted his glass. 'Well, I think it sounds interesting. I'd love to know where we all came from. Have you ever tried to trace your ancestors, Clay?'

Kaitlin waited for one of them to raise Brian's new job. No one did. Neither, she noticed, did her father offer any information about the family.

The phone calls came the next morning. Kaitlin ignored the first two, then muted her phone. The screen continued to light up. By call five, she gave in.

'Hi, Mom. Is anything wrong?'

'No, not really. I want a quick word. That's all.'

'I'm afraid I'm kind of busy. Can I call you back later? I'll look forward to a chat then.'

This was a lie twice over. Rather than working on a document for an energy analytics company, something that bored her into a stupor, she was browsing a genealogy forum. (The message boards had become her secret addiction, her version of dating apps or real-estate sites or TMZ.)

And the last thing she wanted was a chat, especially when she knew what it was likely to be about.

'Now, Kaitlin, I'm sure you can afford to down tools for five minutes.'

Okay, she said to herself. *Just get it over with.* 'All right, but you'll have to bear with me for a minute or two.'

She rooted around for the shoes she'd kicked off an hour before. Then she looped her purse over her shoulder and walked out to the corridor. She didn't need eavesdroppers.

'I'm all yours, Mom. Shoot.'

'I wanted to ask about this family search idea you sprang on us yesterday. I was reluctant to say anything in front of Clay, but are you sure it's wise?'

Stay calm. You've got this. 'Um, is there a reason why it wouldn't be?'

'Wee-ll, a lot of those stories can be very dark. I'm not sure you're in a good place for them right now.'

Kaitlin hesitated before replying. The corridor smelt of cleaning fluid. She rubbed her free hand over her forehead and down the side of her face.

'I promise I'm fine. Both Clay and Orla think it's a good project for me. It's a challenge and it stops me thinking about myself, you know?'

'Whatever about Clay, I wouldn't pay a lot of attention to Orla. Her own story is hardly one to be proud of.'

Kaitlin gripped the phone more tightly. She hated arguing with her mother. That Susan wasn't always logical didn't make her any less formidable. In fact, it was her ability to weave off topic that made her such an awkward opponent. She had a knack of lobbing in the sort of statements that were guaranteed to rile her daughter: 'You can't say anything these days without someone finding offence,' or 'Women would be happier if they accepted that sometimes men deserve to earn more.'

Over the years, Kaitlin had taught herself to think before giving a snippy response. Her mom had grown up clipping coupons and sharing a bed with her sister. Susan's own mother had worked a succession of low-paid jobs. Her father had been drunk as often as sober. By comparison, Kaitlin's early years had been a stroll down Easy Street. Still, this was the second time in as many days that her mom had thrown a grenade at Orla, and her claims had to be challenged.

'She's been in America for more than thirty years. I don't think you're being fair.'

'*Tuh*. To listen to her, you'd swear she was forced into exile at gunpoint. I hope you don't buy any of her nonsense. She left a country that was perfectly capable of supporting her. She preferred life here, that's all.'

Kaitlin had the impression that there was a subtext to her mother's words. Maybe she'd fallen out with Orla. Again. 'You're talking about the 1980s. At the time—'

'You don't have to tell me about the eighties. I was there. Besides, I didn't call you to talk about Orla. It's Brian we need to talk about. Have you considered him at all?'

'In what way?'

'You know the importance of this job with the IRAA, but you seem determined to set off on a crusade about immigrants.'

'That's not what I'm doing,' said Kaitlin. 'I'm curious, that's all.'

A sigh fluttered down the line. Her mother had an extensive range of sighs, an entire repertoire of them. 'You're my daughter. I know you better than I know myself. You don't approve of his choice, and you want to make things uncomfortable for him.'

'And suppose that was my aim, what would be wrong with it?'

'He doesn't interfere with your decisions.'

'He doesn't have to. I'm not a hypocrite.' She was aware that this sounded pompous, but it was how she felt.

'We're all hypocrites to one extent or another. When you're older, you'll appreciate that.' Her mother paused. 'I'm only saying this because I love you, and because I realise that, right now, you're probably asking yourself a lot of big questions. If you want my advice, you ought to focus on Clay … and allow your brother to do what he thinks is best. Your life would be a whole lot easier if you could just be happy for him.'

Big questions. That was new. Over the past three months, she'd grown accustomed to euphemisms. To slippery-slidy language. To diffident enquiries and well-rehearsed platitudes. She knew people meant well and that their sympathy was genuine. Yet somehow she found expressions of pity more corrosive than offhand or tactless remarks.

Of course she'd heard those too. The previous week, a colleague with childcare issues had put down her phone and said, 'Kaitlin, never have children.' Immediately her hand had gone to her face. 'Oh, hell,' she'd said. 'I'm sorry. I didn't think.'

'It's cool,' Kaitlin had replied, for what else could she say?

She told herself that by now she should be getting over the miscarriage. Some women lost five, six, seven babies. And, while it wouldn't be accurate to say that they carried on and never looked back, they coped.

Losing one baby wasn't unusual. Having a miscarriage at nineteen weeks was. By nineteen weeks, Kaitlin had been noticeably pregnant. She'd been making assumptions and plans. Miscarriages were something that happened early on when the foetus was little more than a cluster of cells. At nineteen weeks, her daughter had been as long as her hand. She'd had a button nose and tiny arms and legs. All her fingers and toes had been in place. She'd been a perfect person.

But if the baby had been flawless, the fault must lie with Kaitlin. That was why every day she asked herself, *What did I do wrong?*

Logically, she knew the answer was 'Nothing.' Logic didn't matter. She would think she had recovered, that everything was fine, and then the questions would find their way in. She would look at women pushing strollers and wonder how they'd brought another life into the world when she had failed. Teenagers carried babies to full term, as did women in their forties. Women with cancer. Women with drug habits. They all succeeded. She was the right age and in good health. She had every advantage and privilege. Yet her body had rejected her baby.

Her unhappiness was compounded by the sense that she'd also let her family down. She didn't voice these thoughts, not even to Clay. He would tell her she was being absurd and urge her to get help.

Although her pregnancy hadn't been planned, she'd quickly come around to the idea. So had Clay. Within a couple of days, his initial shock had been replaced by enthusiasm. They told each other that their lives would change and that a baby would swallow every minute of every day. They decided they were ready for change. For the time being, they would stay in the apartment, but they'd start looking for somewhere new. They'd buy a family home in a neighbourhood with good schools.

Until that point, Kaitlin had retained doubts about their relationship. In many ways, it was what she wanted. (Or what she believed she wanted. Was anyone ever fully sure?) Certainly, it was the sort of relationship that someone in their late twenties *should* have. They were an adult couple with adult responsibilities. What concerned her was the way she could fall in and out of love. Sometimes she would think Clay was everything she needed. At others she would find herself asking, *Is this it? Is this enough?* His reaction to her pregnancy had helped to push those doubts aside.

Her parents, too, were happy. Okay, they would have preferred a wedding first, but they were thrilled about becoming grandparents. Her mother saw the announcement as an opportunity to put her homemaking skills to full use. The baby would have set a world record for ownership of delicate knitted goods.

Kaitlin worried about work. She was supposed to be on the conveyor-belt to better things. It wasn't the right time for a baby. Her boss, a fifty-something partner called Barrett Weston, was too experienced to let his annoyance show. In the rarefied atmosphere of Frobisher Hunter, people used language carefully. The woman in the HR department was even smoother. She told Kaitlin about the resources at her disposal but was careful not to display any actual humanity.

When the first pink dots appeared on her underwear, Kaitlin didn't panic. She didn't want to be one of *those* women, the ones who treated even the slightest twinge as an excuse to stay in bed and self-obsess. Throughout the day, the pain became more insistent, gnawing at her until it dawned on her that panicking was appropriate.

She remembered walking into the hospital, the February air so cold that she struggled to breathe, her pain at Emergency Room levels. After that, her memories were less distinct. Clay arrived. They hugged and pretended that everything would be all right when they knew it wouldn't. The following hours were so physically gruelling that thinking was impossible. She was vaguely aware of doctors' instructions and whispered conferrals. For the first time in her life, everything was out of her control.

Later, they learnt that the baby had been a girl. They were asked if they'd like to see her. Kaitlin had expected this to be the hardest part. She'd been wrong. The hardest part was watching Clay struggle. She had failed him too. She wept then for her empty womb and their dead daughter. They decided to give her a name. She was Stella, their star.

Three months on, Kaitlin was trudging through life. She liked to think she was skilled at hiding her grief. There was no point in upsetting people or making them uncomfortable. This was especially true at work. Even when focusing was difficult, especially when it was difficult, she put in the hours and tried to deliver what was expected. Everything took twice the effort. For all their stated commitments to equality and employee welfare, there was no scope for slackers at Frobisher Hunter.

She also did her best to avoid magazines and their obsession with motherhood. The headlines – 'My Mom Guilt', 'My Miracle Child', 'The Greatest Love of All' – brought a tightness to her chest. On the rare occasions when she did feel like talking about her lost baby, she couldn't find the right words. She couldn't stand anyone telling her she was young and that there would be other children.

Until the day Stella died, Kaitlin hadn't appreciated real sadness. How heavy it was. How suffocating. It was a bag of rocks on her back and a coating of lead on her feet. Mourning, she discovered, wasn't simply what you did at a wake or a graveside. It stayed with you. It was what you did every day.

Two days after her mother's call, Kaitlin received a message from Orla: Hope all's well. Your mother says we shouldn't encourage you. Was she very pissed off when you told her? Thinking of you ♡

She tapped out a reply: Not quite sure why she's so agitated. Has she been bothering you? All you did was show an interest in what I'm doing ♡

In a nanosecond, her phone pinged again: Should have warned you this would make your folks uncomfortable. Thought you knew that. It's a sensitive subject. ☹

Increasingly confused, Kaitlin replied: Oh??

She waited, but there was no response.

Later that evening, the unfinished conversation ran around her head. While she wanted to think of the messages as straightforward statements of solidarity, she sensed that Orla had been looking for information. She'd been trying to find out what Susan had said about her.

Kaitlin decided to rekindle the exchange: Is everything ok? Thought I'd hear from you.

It was the next morning before the answer came: OK-ish. Drew and I had a talk. There's something we want to talk to you about. Would it be possible to meet up this evening? Please say yes. 🙏🙏

Chapter 16

'We grew up assuming we'd have to leave,' said Orla. 'And, in some ways, that was what we wanted. I can hear people saying, "She could have stayed in Ireland," and, yeah, we weren't being persecuted or anything but, God, it was dreary. Besides, there were no jobs. Even though I'd done well enough at school, college was never really an option.' She took a swig of her beer. 'I remember people here being surprised that so many of us had left, and I used to say, "Listen, the surprise is that anyone stays."'

They were sitting on rattan chairs in Drew and Orla's backyard. The evening was mild, the air scented with lilac and sweet peas. In the near distance, someone was cutting grass. Despite the tranquil setting, there was an unfamiliar tension about husband and wife, a tightness to their shoulders, a wariness around their eyes. Kaitlin was puzzled by this because so far neither had said anything she hadn't heard before.

This time, she'd made sure to tell Clay about her visit. He'd chosen not to join her.

Orla put down her bottle and continued. 'We arrived in June '86. I can see the day. The weather in Ireland had been miserable, but Boston was scorching. Within a couple of minutes, sweat was collecting along my spine, and I thought, This is it. This is the place for me. And I hadn't even left Logan.' She smiled and shook her head at the memory. 'Up until then, I couldn't have told you much about Boston. I'd wanted to go to New York. But Shay – my boyfriend back then, Shay Drennan – had a cousin in Allston, which meant we had a floor to sleep on. So Boston it was.'

This was new. Kaitlin couldn't recall hearing Shay's name before. She'd always had the impression that Orla had arrived with a gaggle of girls. Also, in earlier versions of events, the Allston cousin had belonged to Orla. She glanced at Drew, but his face gave nothing away.

'All we knew about America was what we'd seen on TV,' said Orla, 'which meant I was expecting a cross between *Hill Street Blues* and *The Waltons*.'

'You must have been disappointed,' said Kaitlin.

'Not a bit of it. The city was everything I'd hoped for. It was so ... so *American*. Does that sound mad?'

'Yeah, I think I know what you mean, though.'

'Let me try to explain. If I was arriving now, the experience wouldn't be so mind-blowing. The differences between Ireland and Boston have become less obvious. But back then? Back then everything was different ... the high-rise buildings, the stores, the cops with guns, even the traffic lights ... Oh, and the cars! In the 1980s, everyone here still drove those long, long cars. It was all Chevys and Oldsmobiles. I'd watch the traffic and laugh.' She brushed back a strand of hair. 'You wouldn't believe the things I found exciting. Like CVS. Imagine being thrilled by a drugstore. The biggest difference, though, was the people. When I was growing up, Ireland must have been the whitest place on the planet. In my whole life, I'd only met two or three black people.'

Orla stopped for another drink. 'I revelled in the differences. Most of us did. I remember going up the John Hancock tower one evening, watching the lights blinking across the city, and loving every inch of the place. Compared to Limerick, it was so … liberating. There was nobody to watch you or tell you how to live. You've no idea how refreshing that was.'

Kaitlin tried to imagine her exhilaration. She reminded herself that Drew's wife had been eighteen when she left home. At eighteen, life should be filled with excitement.

'Like I've told you before,' continued Orla, 'I was undocumented. I don't recall that word being used, mind. "Illegal" was what people called me, but that didn't colour their view too much. Once you were willing to work, folks were happy to let you. And, let's be honest, I was helped by the fact that it was such an Irish city. There were networks in place, you know? At home, jobs were few and far between. In Boston, it was boom time, and there were "Help Wanted" signs everywhere.'

'That's how I remember it as a teenager,' said Drew. 'There was a real expectation that the good times would keep on rolling.'

Keen to steer the conversation back to Orla's boyfriend, Kaitlin asked if he'd had a visa.

'God, no. For most of us that wasn't the way. In the main, people arrived on holiday visas and stayed. We assumed we'd get sorted, that somehow a green card would turn up. We had this notion that being Irish gave us a superior status. And the truth was, even if we'd gotten into trouble, we were less likely to be deported than someone from, say, Haiti or Mexico.' She fingered the cuff of her chambray shirt. 'Looking back, I suppose we understood white privilege before we'd ever heard the term. We knew that life was more straightforward for us.'

'Did you stay with Shay's cousin?'

'No, we moved on pretty quickly. After a month or so, we found another place in Allston, near Packard's Corner.' Orla tipped her head towards Kaitlin. 'Not a million miles away from where you live now, though nothing like your apartment, obviously. It was fairly seedy, and when I say there were a lot of us, I mean *a lot*. There were always at least seven or eight people in a two-bedroom place, with others coming and going. New people arrived every week. And some of them ... well, talk about lost souls. It's a miracle they managed to book a plane, let alone take care of themselves in America.'

As she spoke, the years fell away. The spray of fine lines around her eyes appeared to fade, and she became the young woman Kaitlin had seen in photographs: black curls frizzing in every direction, a splash of freckles across her nose, her mouth in a full-wattage smile. In those photos, she looked sharp and three-dimensional, even when everyone else was out of focus.

Drew was harder to gauge. While it would be an exaggeration to describe him as ill at ease, he was more tense than usual.

Still unsure where the story was heading, Kaitlin asked if Orla had ever been homesick.

'At the risk of sounding like a total bitch, not often. I didn't come from the happiest of homes. But, yes, there were days when I longed for a good natter with my mother. Back then, staying in touch wasn't easy. A lot of the time, I had to call home from a phone booth on Comm Ave. You should have seen me with my pile of quarters.'

'She was doing that when I met her,' said Drew.

'I probably asked if you had any spare coins.' They both smiled.

After a short while, Orla had got a job minding children for a Brookline couple called the Whitmers. Meanwhile, Shay was working in construction – and doing well. He was clearing more in a week than either of his parents was earning at home.

Orla, who for the most part had been looking at Kaitlin, allowed another glance to slide in Drew's direction. He gave a slight nod.

'I haven't spoken enough about Shay,' she said. 'In one way, everything between us was fine. But as the months went by, I worried that we were living in an Irish cocoon. And as much as I liked my fellow immigrants – some were the soundest folks you could ever meet – I was keen to hang out with different people.

'Heidi Whitmer was a major influence on me. She was forever encouraging me to go places or to see particular movies or whatnot. Like, she knew I was keen on art and design, so she brought me to the Isabella Stewart Gardner and the MFA. That doesn't sound like a big deal, but I was flattered. She also encouraged me to go to university. Shay took against her, though. He claimed she was filling my head with nonsense and that I was forgetting who I was.'

'How did you react?' asked Kaitlin, who could picture a young Orla striving to broaden her horizons while a jealous boyfriend attempted to hold her back. It was a potent image.

'Not well. I said, "Listen, I didn't come all this way to spend every waking hour with characters we could have met at home." We argued for ages, and it was only then I realised he wasn't enjoying America like I was. That he was one of the people who wanted to go back.' She stopped for a drink and drained the bottle. 'At that point – we're talking the early summer of '87 – I should have reassured Shay, met him halfway. Instead, I resented his attitude. I resented his dissatisfaction.'

'You were incredibly young, though. What were you? Nineteen?'

'Except I was old enough to … to be a better person.'

Drew rose from his chair. 'Anyone for another beer?'

'I thought you'd never ask,' said Orla. 'My throat's dry from all this talking.'

Kaitlin was surprised to see that her own bottle was nearly empty. By rights, she should say no. The sun was slipping away, however, and she sensed that Orla's story had a way to go. Presumably, it ended with poor Shay going home to Limerick, though why that should be such a secret, she didn't know.

'I'd love a beer,' she said, 'but it means I'll have to stay the night. Is that okay?'

'Of course,' said Orla, patting the back of her hand. 'There's plenty of room.'

'Three beers coming up,' said Drew.

While Kaitlin messaged Clay to tell him about her change of plan, Orla was quiet.

'I've wrestled over what to tell you,' she said eventually. 'We both have. And it's important we give you the full picture.'

'No, that's fine. It's fascinating, only …' Only what? Kaitlin wasn't sure how to finish the sentence and she was relieved when Drew returned with three bottles of Sam Adams.

'So,' said Orla, 'it was around then that Shay began working for Wilson Brothers Construction. In those days, the brothers in the company title referred to the previous generation. Drew's dad, Joseph, was the boss.' She looked at Kaitlin. 'Your father was in his early twenties and already heavily involved in the business.'

'I'd just left high school,' said Drew, 'and I was finding my feet. We were all working on the same job. At the time, it was probably the biggest contract the old man had ever won. We were subcontractors on a housing development in Dorchester. And the thing about a contract like that is, if you prove your worth, you can be certain that bigger paydays will follow.'

'That's how we met,' said Orla. 'At a birthday party for one of the guys on the site. I was there with Shay. It was one of those crazy Saturday nights you only get when you're very young. There were scores of people, all jammed into a tiny apartment, high on beer and weed. Everyone flirting like demons. You should have seen the state of us: all the girls wanting to look like The Bangles. Our hair was *biiig*.' She placed her splayed hands about six inches from her head. 'And all the guys were thinking they were Mickey Rourke. Somehow, I got talking to Drew.'

'We hit it off immediately. I remember we went out to the stoop ...'

'... to "get some air",' added Orla. 'Everyone was so blitzed, I doubt Shay even noticed I was gone.'

Kaitlin turned the beer bottle in her hands. She could picture the party – smell it, almost. The sweat and hormones and sickly eighties perfume. 'Did you know Shay was working for Drew's dad?'

'Not to begin with. They were co-workers as far as I was concerned. We sat there, chatting about this and that. Someone played "Livin' On A Prayer" over and over again, and everybody was singing along. Jesus, the noise. It was banging through the walls.'

'Gradually,' said Drew, 'the chatting became flirting. We went for a walk and ...'

'... the flirting became kissing.'

'We knew straight away. Well, I did.'

'We both did. I thought he was the finest thing ever.'

Drew gave Orla his number, and a few days later they met again.

'Going back to the apartment was tough,' she said. 'I kept wanting to drop Drew's name into the conversation. That's what it's like, isn't it? When you know, you know.'

Once upon a time, Kaitlin had wondered what Orla saw in Drew. A green card, her mother would probably have said. But that was too simplistic. As she got older, she saw how evenly matched they were. It reminded her of how, as a kid, she'd automatically thought the tanned blonde girls were the pretty ones. It was years before she recognised the subtleties that made the quirkier girls more attractive. So, yes, Orla was the more immediately glamorous of the pair, but Drew with the short neck, square body and slow laugh was in every way her equal. His quiet intelligence and pure, practical kindness set him apart.

'When did you break up with Shay?' she asked.

'That ...' started Orla.

'... wasn't what happened,' said Drew.

Silence fell between them. The trees at the bottom of the garden were in silhouette now, the sky a heavy shade of blue.

The silence lengthened.

At last, Orla spoke. 'I was getting together the strength to tell Shay. I wasn't going to mention Drew. I reckoned I'd fall back on the old clichés: we'd grown apart, we wanted different things … because in many ways they were true.'

'Surely he was going to find out?'

'We were going to say we only hooked up afterwards. I know, I know. It wasn't the most inspired of stories. At the same time, I was trying to sort out the practicalities. Splitting up with Shay meant moving out of the apartment and finding somewhere new to live. I'd arranged to get a bit of floor space with a girl I knew over on Kelton Street. I was all ready to go. That was when—'

'To give you a clearer picture of what was happening,' said Drew, 'we were working long hours on the site. Crazy hours. Dad kept stressing that if we did well and finished on schedule, there'd be better days ahead. I can't say that corners were cut, but we put in longer days than I'd expect anyone to work now. Don't get me wrong, Dad was a great guy, but when it came to growing the business, he tended to lose perspective.'

A picture of her grandfather, Joseph, entered Kaitlin's head. She could see him in this very garden, a broad-shouldered man with huge hands and the sort of booming laugh that had seemed obligatory among men of his generation. He'd called her sweetheart and teased her about her red hair. 'The most Irish of us all,' he'd said, meaning it as a compliment. He hadn't understood that looking Irish meant having blue-white skin and a face like a dumpling, thin pale lips and thick freckled arms. She'd been seventeen when he died. That had been the first time she'd seen her own father cry. The second time had been when they'd talked about Stella's death.

'What happened?' she asked.

Orla pressed her palms together. 'There was an accident. Shay was working on the roof of an apartment building ... and he fell.'

'I wasn't there at the time,' said Drew.

'Because he'd bunked off to meet me.'

'I don't know exactly how Shay came to fall. I do know an ambulance was called straight away, the fire service too. They did everything they could. But the poor guy died almost instantly.'

Kaitlin inhaled with surprise. A moment ago, she'd been visualising a lost era when girls wore a pound of hair gel and guys wore top-to-toe stonewashed denim. In an instant, those carefree images had been swept aside.

'Shit,' she said. 'That's awful. I had no idea.'

'They took him to the hospital,' said Drew. 'But it was too late.'

Recounting what had happened was costing him some effort. All the same, when Orla went to speak, he gently waved her away.

'When I got back to the house, Dad was at the hospital. Mom was sitting at the kitchen table, chain-smoking. Kevin and Susan were there. Everyone was twitchy.'

'Wasn't that the summer my parents got married?' asked Kaitlin.

'They'd got back from their honeymoon in Aruba the day before. What a welcome home, huh? We were all shocked. I asked if anyone had been in touch with Shay's family. Kevin wasn't sure. Then I asked about Orla. "He has a girlfriend," I said. "Has anyone told her?" I already knew the answer. We'd been together until a half-hour before. Without thinking it through, I said, "I can find her."'

'And that's what he did,' said Orla. 'We went to the hospital. It was so bizarre. Jesus, I'll never forget it. There were people swarming around: doctors, nurses, cops, a priest. I could barely talk. They must have thought I was a complete eejit.'

Drew paused for a drink. 'If anyone was taken aback to see the two of us together, they didn't say.'

'I was upset, obviously ... but, to be honest with you, my head was in about fifty different places. I'd been going out with Shay since I was fifteen. I'd also been a day or two away from breaking up with him. And when he'd fallen to his death, I'd been fooling around with someone else. I felt guilty, as if I'd pushed him. Everyone was asking questions – "Does he have any family in the United States?", "Do you have a number for his parents?", "Will they want his body returned to Ireland?" The only person I could think of was Clem, the cousin we'd stayed with when we first arrived. Thankfully, he took charge because I'd have been hopeless.'

Kaitlin noticed tears in Orla's eyes.

'In the middle of all of this,' said Drew, 'there I was, mooching around, not knowing what to do. By that point, Dad was panicking. Even though the regulations weren't nearly as tight as they are these days, the cops were involved. I figured he was worried about safety violations. I was wrong. What worried him was that Shay was undocumented.'

'Would that have been a big problem?' asked Kaitlin.

'It wasn't as much of an issue as it is now. There'd been a crackdown a year or so earlier, though, and the law had been tightened up. The thing was, the company was in line for more government contracts so …'

'You didn't want to be the guys who played fast and loose with the regulations?'

'You got it.'

'What did your father do?'

'Lied, basically. He insisted that, as far as he knew, Shay had been legit. He pointed out that he'd given the company a social-security number and all the rest of it. Now, everyone knew there were lots of ways of getting a social-security number. It was no harder than getting a fake ID. There wasn't any comeback, though, so the excuses must have worked.'

'And Shay? Was he buried here?'

'No,' said Orla. 'One of his brothers came over from Limerick and took his body home. There was a row because everyone, including my parents, presumed I'd go back. My mam didn't speak to me for ages afterwards. She said all the neighbours took a dim view of my behaviour.' For a moment, she faltered. 'And Mrs Drennan, Shay's mother, was very sour towards her. There I was, she said, living it up in America when my boyfriend was in Mount Saint Oliver's. You can guess her reaction a few months later when I called to say I was getting married. Mrs Drennan is dead now, but she never spoke to me again. As she saw it, I married into the family that killed her son.'

'If you'd gone home for the funeral, would you have been able to come back to Boston?' asked Kaitlin.

'Considering I'd arrived a year earlier on a three-month visa, there wasn't a prayer I'd get in again.'

'That was what worried me,' said Drew.

Kaitlin's forehead throbbed. She was trying to summon an appropriate response. A proper family response. Something empathetic. Unfortunately, all she had were lawyer-like questions. 'Were there other undocumented workers on the site?'

'Several,' said Drew. 'They were told to lie low for a while. A couple got work elsewhere. A couple more came back. If you're wondering whether the company kept hiring undocumented guys, the answer is yes. Everyone did.'

Kaitlin thought of the Immigration Reform Alliance of America's website. She'd been a frequent visitor in recent weeks. In particular, she recalled the section that criticised employers for ignoring American workers in favour of cheaper foreign labour. She was afraid to ask about Wilson Brothers' practices now.

For a short while they sat in the dark, each captured by their own thoughts. The only sound came from the distant swoosh of traffic and the occasional whine of a neighbour's dog.

Orla was first to speak. 'Those first few weeks were difficult. I felt so bad about Shay, about everything. And we were scared of anyone seeing us together. After that, though ... if anything, we became closer. We met up as often as we could. Then, shortly before Christmas, Drew asked me to marry him.'

To begin with, Drew said, his parents weren't keen on the idea. Gradually, however, they changed their minds. Others were more hostile.

'When your mother heard the news, she cornered me,' said Orla to Kaitlin, a tear dropping down one cheek. Drew reached over and squeezed her hand. 'Not unreasonably, she didn't believe I'd only started seeing Drew after Shay's death. The rest of her comments ...' She hesitated, and Kaitlin saw that she was trying to be tactful. 'Let's just say they were less reasonable. She accused me of setting out to snare him. I was the scheming older woman taking advantage of Drew and his family. No matter how much I protested, she wouldn't listen. That set the tone for our relationship, I suppose.'

Kaitlin had a sense of pieces slotting into place. Seen in this context, her mother's microaggressions towards Orla made sense. Susan valued her hard-won respectability. Social ambiguity scared her. Orla was a reminder that even if the family money wasn't exactly dirty it was tarnished.

'We got married the following April,' said Drew, 'right before my nineteenth birthday. It wasn't a big occasion. We were very young, and Orla's family were three thousand miles away. All my friends joked that I was the only eighteen-year-old Irish guy in history to marry a woman who wasn't pregnant.'

'Even my mother asked when the baby was due,' added Orla.

'For years, Shay was barely mentioned. If anyone referred to Orla's arrival in America, they tended to do it in a light-hearted way.'

'But with my mother there was always an edge,' said Kaitlin.

'You could call it that,' said Orla. 'Or you could call it distaste.' She shook her head. 'Sorry, that's going too far. Most of the time she's cordial, but Brian's job has dragged everything up again.'

'That and my questions about the family's background.'

'I hope,' said Drew, 'you can see why I was wary of getting involved.

You were looking for a story from a hundred years ago, when the story was right in front of you.'

'I understand.'

'After you left that evening, we argued.'

'I reckoned we should get everything out in the open,' said Orla.

'I didn't agree.'

'And then, the other night, your mother called. She lost her cool. I knew she'd be super supportive of Brian. He's her son, after all. There was more to it than that, though. It's like she's frightened I'll stick my nose in. That I'll confront him and say, "Lookit, pet, your family thought nothing of employing undocumented people and lying about it. I should know. My boyfriend was one of them."'

She spoke in an exaggerated Irish accent, and Kaitlin couldn't help but smile. She swallowed the last of her beer. 'So why did you decide to talk to me?'

'I still wasn't one hundred per cent sure,' said Drew. 'But, on balance, it's best that you know. It might help you grasp some of your mother's …'

'… issues,' finished Orla. 'You're an adult. You've been through a lot lately. You deserve better than the rest of us whispering in corners and throwing jibes you can't understand.'

Kaitlin's head was whirring. She was struck by how little she knew about her family – and about the issues simmering just beneath the surface. Briefly, she wondered if she should reassess what she was doing. No, she decided. If anything, this made her more determined to press on. There must be other family stories, and she would like to hear those too.

'I take it I'm to pretend this conversation didn't take place?' she said.

'Oh, God, yeah,' replied Drew. 'We don't want to make everything worse.'

Chapter 17

June 2019, Clooneven
Jessie

As Ger drove north along the coast road, the green-grey water hit the rocks and exploded into spray. Clouds bounced in from the Atlantic. The weather in Clooneven tended to follow a pattern: every shimmering wonder of a day was offset by a handful of stormy ones. Given a choice, Jessie would have picked the sun, but she had to admit there was something impressive about the ocean's violence.

Since becoming interested in Bridget, she'd found herself looking at the landscape in a different way. The dry-stone walls she'd taken for granted might first have been built by Famine relief workers. The holy wells she'd dismissed as slightly ridiculous might have provided solace to the destitute. A scattering of square stones might once have been a family home. To paraphrase her grandmother, the land had a story to tell.

It had taken them three weeks to make the short journey to Hackett's Cross. If she wasn't working, Ger was. Or else he was playing football or at training. His girlfriend was rarely mentioned, and Jessie got the impression that she, too, would have to wait until Clooneven's progress was halted. Ashling, her colleague in the Seashell Café, was going out with the centre forward and spent her days chattering about who was flying in training and who had a tricky hamstring. Jessie had forgotten how much these things mattered.

Now that the tourist season had begun and the Americans had returned, Ashling was up to high doh. 'Jesus, I love them and the happy heads on them,' she'd say. Jessie suspected that what she loved most was their generosity. Like much of the west coast, Clooneven had grown accustomed to visitors from the other side of the Atlantic. While some were lured by images of a dramatic unspoilt landscape, a significant number came in search of their roots. They carried notebooks filled with names and places. Many of the stories dated back to the Famine.

Etty had once told her that when she was young there'd been a popular phrase: 'You can't eat scenery.'

'Isn't it funny how wrong that turned out to be?' her grandmother had said. 'People will pay an awful lot of money for a fine view, fresh air and a bit of peace.'

Ger's voice pulled Jessie back to the present. 'I'd say we'll get rain this evening,' he said, as they passed the lighthouse at Cloonmara.

'There's a novelty.'

'It doesn't rain in Dublin, I suppose.'

'It's a scientific fact that it rains more in the west.'

'I didn't know you'd had time to pick up a meteorology degree. Fair play to you.'

If necessary, they could carry on like this for hours. The rapid-fire banter reminded Jessie of their school days when the entire class would trade jokes and insults. She found it strangely comforting.

She'd hoped that by this point, the Hollie Garland episode would have been forgotten. Unfortunately, Hollie continued to see Jessie's humiliation as a commercial opportunity. Over five pages – five pages! – of the sort of Sunday supplement that usually viewed influencers as a tawdry blight on humanity, she spoke about her trauma. The article was accompanied by misty-hued photos in which an under-styled Hollie stared mournfully at the camera. *I find it harder to trust people, especially journalists*, she told the journalist. *You have no idea how many young women contacted me to say my success mattered to them. Then, all of a sudden, people who knew nothing about my world were laughing at my name and my business. I felt like I'd been stripped naked in front of the entire country.*

Even Lorna had reckoned that this was going too far. 'That girl would want to cop on to herself,' she'd said.

Nevertheless, the hate had flooded in again. There was a limit to how much half-baked malice Jessie could take, so she'd deleted Twitter and Instagram from her phone.

There had been no further sighting of Lorna's lover, as she now thought of him. This disappointed her. As engrossed as she was in Bridget's story, she would have liked some present-day intrigue. She'd outlined her theory to Ger, who'd said she was seeing things that weren't there.

'Who do you think he is then?' she'd asked.

'An ice-cream salesman,' he'd replied. 'You've an unbelievable imagination. There's no reason to believe your sister's having an affair.'

That was the trouble with straightforward people. They assumed everyone was like them.

Jessie consoled herself with the knowledge that, every week, her debt dropped a little. By the autumn, she'd be free. Her friend Shona, with whom she'd been drinking on the night of the TV disaster, was urging her to return to Dublin as soon as possible. She'd also broken the news that Phelim was going out with a theatre director called Roseanne Lane.

A scan of Roseanne's social media suggested her creativity was focused more on seeking Arts Council grants than staging plays.

To Jessie's surprise, what she missed most was writing. She missed the craft and challenge of it as well as the feeling of achievement when the finished article appeared.

Hackett's Cross was a throwback to bleaker days. While most west-coast villages had benefited from the tourism dollar, the Cross, as it was known, remained a standard bearer for austerity and decay. Wind and salt water had combined to give the buildings a battered appearance. The fascia board on the Cross Tavern was peeling, while the door looked ready to splinter apart. The few trees were buckled and bent.

'Surely even you couldn't see any merit to this place?' said Jessie, as Ger parked his car, an unobtrusive blue Corolla.

Ger laughed. 'It's not the best the county has to offer, all right.'

St Aidan's Church, where they'd arranged to meet the parish priest, was mottled with lichen and moss. The door was newly varnished, though, and the grounds well kept. Jessie had read that some of its graves dated back to the 1830s, so if Bridget and Norah had stayed in the area, they might be buried there.

She'd once been to a small-town museum in Croatia where the attendant had explained a lengthy gap in the local records by saying that no accounts existed because, during those years, the area had been peaceful and prosperous. Part of her desired something similar for the Moloneys, for the story to be that there was no story. Having been through so much, Bridget and Norah had been entitled to decades of uneventful plenty.

Father Enda McElligott was younger than she'd anticipated. Not that he'd sounded old on the phone, but she was preconditioned to think of clergy as white-haired and slow-moving. The man who met them was tall with a head of brown curls and the rolling stride of a farmer inspecting his land. He was also blessed with a melodic voice. She had the feeling he would give good Mass.

He ushered them into the room at the back of the altar and pulled out three hard chairs. It was the first time Jessie had been in a sacristy, and she was disappointed by how unremarkable it was. She guessed the chalice, altar cloths and suchlike were stored in the rosewood cupboards that lined the walls.

'As I think I told you on the phone,' said the priest, 'we no longer have the original 1860 census. It's too precious … too valuable, I dare say … to keep here. We do, though, hold a copy.' He picked up a large red-covered ledger. 'Ideally, the contents should be online. One day soon, please God. Now, you're interested in a family called the McGuanes, is that right?'

'Yes,' replied Ger. 'We're trying to find out what happened to Mary Ellen McGuane's sister, Bridget, and her daughter, Norah.'

'Ah, the famous Bridget.'

'You know about her?' said Jessie.

'When you gave me her name on the phone, the details rang a vague bell. So, I looked her up, and it all came back to me. I'd read about her years ago. She was the woman who spoke to the newspaper men from London.'

'That's right,' said Ger.

'It was the drawing I remembered as much as anything. The one of her and her daughter? Of course, when I first read about her I was only a student, so the Hackett's Cross reference didn't mean anything to me.'

He opened the ledger at a bookmarked spot. 'I hope you don't mind. I've done a small bit of work.'

Jessie, apprehensive about what the records contained, didn't reply.

'Not at all,' said Ger. 'Did you get anywhere?'

Father McElligott handed the book to Jessie. 'I'm nearly sure these are the people you're looking for.'

And there they were: Thomas McGuane, aged forty-two, Mary Ellen McGuane, aged thirty-seven, and their daughter, Norah McGuane, aged fourteen.

Still without speaking, she passed the book to Ger, who gazed at the names before asking about Bridget.

'I'm afraid there's no mention of her,' said the priest. 'I've looked through all the records. There was no Bridget Moloney of the right age in Hackett's Cross or Clooneven or any of the surrounding townlands.

Jessie felt so deflated she could cry. 'So Mary Ellen really did take Norah and allow Bridget to fend for herself? What sort of sister would do that?'

'Bridget might have gone elsewhere,' said Ger. 'She might even have left the country.'

'We'll never find her, so.' She took back the ledger and stared again at the rows of names.

'I'm sorry you're disappointed,' said the priest. 'I can tell you some more about Norah if you like. She was considerably easier to find.'

'I suppose,' said Jessie. It was brave, outspoken Bridget who'd captured her imagination. She returned the red book to Father McElligott, who got up and removed several sheets of paper from a desk drawer.

'It seems,' he said, 'that Norah McGuane didn't stray too far. According to the parish records, she got married in 1864 to a local man called Barney Nugent, and they had two sons, James, born in 1866, and Seán, born four years later.'

'James and Seán Nugent,' said Jessie. It took her a few moments to recall where she'd heard one of those names before. Was it possible that …? She shook off the thought. It was a fairly common name. She was getting ahead of herself.

'There were no marriage or death records for the boys, so I assumed they must have left the area.' He paused, as if for dramatic effect. 'In my experience, people either move to the other side of the world or they go down the road. I thought I'd give a neighbouring parish a try. I approached Larry Punch, my counterpart in Clooneven. You know Father Larry?'

Ger nodded.

'I reckoned I'd start with him because he's good at this class of thing. I asked if the parish records contained any reference to either a James or Seán Nugent. Obviously, I gave him their dates of birth and all the rest of it.' Another pause.

Jessie felt a tingling sensation at the back of her brain. 'Go on,' she said, with more force than she'd intended.

'He told me there were several mentions of Seán.' Father McElligott looked down at one of the pieces of paper. 'In 1900, he married a woman from Boherbreen named Gertrude O'Meara. They had five children. One of them, Peter, stayed in the area and married a Mary Meaney.' Yet another pause. 'They also had five children, the youngest of whom was born in 1934. Her name was, or should I say is … Eithne.'

'Better known as Etty,' whispered Jessie. The tingling had become a buzz. It was joined by a skittering sensation down her spine, and, finally, by a burst of exhilaration.

'No!' said Ger, clapping his hands. 'You're having us on.'

'Eithne,' added the priest, with a grin of satisfaction, 'married Flannan Daly. They had two sons and two daughters. Her younger son is named Denis.' He stopped and smiled. 'I don't need to go any further, do I?'

'Denis married Maeve McMahon. They have two daughters,' said Jessie, following his template. 'The younger one's called Jessica. I can't …'

'You must have had an inkling?'

'I promise you, I hadn't a notion. Not a clue.' For once, she couldn't think what else to say.

Ger made a woo-hooing noise. 'This is unbelievable,' he said. 'Un-buh-liev-able.'

Father McElligott handed the sheet of paper to Jessie, who spluttered out a thank-you.

'To be fair,' he said, 'most of the credit belongs to Larry Punch. I said to him, "It's not a priest you should be at all, Lar. You should be above in Dublin running the national archives." He said he'd spent so many years helping Americans and Australians that it was no bother to him.'

Bit by bit, the room was becoming darker, and Father McElligott rose to turn on the light. As he did, Jessie studied the paper on which he'd drawn a rudimentary family tree. It began with the woman whose mother, brother and husband had been killed by hunger – and ended with her.

Bridget Moloney born 1825

|

Norah McGuane (originally Moloney) born 1846 – Barney Nugent
Married 1864

|

Seán Nugent born 1870 – Gertrude O'Meara
Married 1900

|

Peter Nugent born 1901 – Mary Meaney
Married 1924

|

Eithne (Etty) Nugent born 1934 – Flannan Daly
Married 1954

|

Denis Daly born 1958 – Maeve McMahon
Married 1981

|

Jessica Daly born 1989

She traced her finger over the names. 'There's no chance Father Punch made a mistake, is there?' she asked, eyes pooling with tears.

'It's highly unlikely,' said Father McElligott. 'Highly unlikely. There was always a chance that Bridget had family still living in the area. The miracle is that you turned out to be one of them.'

'Okay, so this means she was my …'

'… great-great-great-great-grandmother,' said Ger, counting off the generations on the fingers of his left hand.

'Thanks. When I spoke to Etty she told me her grandfather used to give out if they didn't eat up their dinner. Imagine: he was Norah's son. And Bridget was his grandmother. Small wonder the poor man got rattled if he saw food being wasted.' She shook her head. 'Etty also said that, in the grand scheme of things, the Famine wasn't too long ago. At the time, I was all "Yeah, right." Now I see what she meant.'

Ger turned to the priest. 'You're some showman,' he said. 'You managed to feed us that information drop by drop.'

Father McElligott's smile returned. 'There was no point in giving everything away at the start, especially when I knew the pair of you would be disappointed not to find Bridget. I had to hold something in reserve.'

'You did it well.'

'I'll be honest with you: I only got the final details from Larry last night, and I was fairly shocked myself. I rang him again this afternoon to make sure he'd got everything right.'

Jessie rubbed a hand over her damp eyes. It wasn't that what they'd learnt had made her sad, more that she was overwhelmed. An hour ago, Bridget had been a figure from history, a black-and-white sketch from the archives. Now she was part of the family. She was also tickled by how much the priest had enjoyed his big reveal. In a village like this, he probably performed far more funerals than weddings and christenings. It must be a relief to talk to people who were neither sick nor in mourning.

Father McElligott broke the silence with a slap of his knees. 'While that's sinking in, I have some more news for you. Mary Ellen, Thomas and Norah are all buried here.'

'I'd hoped that was the case,' she said. 'Have you any idea whereabouts? Is there a headstone?'

'A headstone, no. I do have the locations of the graves, though.'

He turned to the final sheet of notepaper. 'Over the past while, we've had a fantastic group of volunteers helping us to map out the graveyard. Mighty young people altogether. They've been here on and off, trying to make sense of the records. When they're finished, we should be able to say definitively who was buried where.'

'I've heard about them,' said Ger. 'Aren't they working on several of the older graveyards in the area?'

'That's right. We've been inundated with visitors looking for the graves of their ancestors. Please God, this will help. Like I say, the work isn't finished, but the volunteers have been able to identify Norah's grave.'

Once again, he gave the paper to Jessie. This time, it contained a rough map. Some of the old graves were numbered, and for every number there was a corresponding name and year of death. It showed that Thomas McGuane had died in November 1879 at the age of sixty-two. His wife, Mary Ellen, had died two years later. Norah Nugent, their daughter, Bridget's daughter, had lived until 1928. She was buried beside her husband, Barney.

The paper quivering in her hand, Jessie asked if they could go outside and see for themselves.

The old part of the cemetery appeared to contain about a hundred and fifty graves. Some were headed by crumbling stone slabs, the names and dates barely legible. Others were marked by modern marble headstones. Presumably, these had been erected by people who'd wanted long-dead family members to be remembered. Mostly, however, the graves were unmarked. These were the people who had stayed behind while their relatives had fanned out all over the world. Perhaps Ger was right, and Bridget had found a better life elsewhere. Jessie hoped so.

Having examined the map, she pinpointed where Norah was buried and walked in that direction. The others followed. The sky was fully grey now, the rain only minutes away. A swirling wind buffeted the grass and blew her hair into her face. Like Father McElligott had said, there was no headstone. Instead, there was a small, rust-scabbed iron cross. She stood in front of it. Ger joined her. The priest stood apart, his eyes closed, his hands clasped together.

'Bless her,' she said, 'what an awful start she had. I keep seeing her as the toddler in the newspaper drawing, a small scrap of a girl with big eyes and curly hair.'

'At least she had a relatively long life,' said Ger. 'She was, what, eighty-two when she died?'

Jessie nodded. 'When you think about it, not only did she live through the Famine, she also lived through the war of independence and the civil war. It's hard to fathom how much she must have seen.'

'Have you recovered from the surprise yet?'

'I've a feeling it'll take a while. It's as if some part of me knew I was connected to Norah, Bridget and Johanna.' She raised a hand. 'And, yes, I know that sounds mad. Don't worry, I haven't gone soft in the head.'

'You're grand. I'd be thinking the same if I was you. Do you reckon Norah remembered Bridget?'

'I'd love to think so,' she replied, 'but I doubt it. The sad thing is, we'll probably never find out.'

By the time they got back to the car, rain was dotting the windows. Jessie's mind was in overdrive. As Ger started the engine, she voiced something that had been bothering her since she'd first heard about her connection to Bridget.

'Etty must have known.'

'I don't think so,' he said. 'You asked her about Johanna Markham, and she said the name didn't mean anything to her. Even if she does know about Bridget – which I doubt – there was no reason for her to connect the two.'

'Except I told her that Johanna's daughter was named Bridget.'

'It's a bit of a stretch. At that point, we didn't even have Bridget's married name. And, like we've said before ...'

'... the place was coming down with Bridgets. Listen, I can see why you mightn't think Etty's capable of skulduggery, only I'm not convinced. That woman could outwit most of us.'

'I wouldn't doubt it,' he said. 'Why would she lie, though? Why not just say, "It's funny you should mention that, Jessie, because we happen to be related to Johanna"?'

'You don't know her as well as I do.'

'True, but I don't see why she wouldn't tell you. She was really helpful with the class. They thought she was brilliant. If she'd had an even better tale to tell, surely she'd have told it.'

Jessie groped for the right words. The rain was becoming heavier by the minute, a curtain of water obscuring their view of the sea, the windscreen wipers swishing to and fro. Although logic was on Ger's side, she was confident the truth was on hers. She recalled how hesitant her grandmother had been when they'd discussed Johanna and Bridget. At the time, she'd worried that Etty's brain was slowing. Now, she believed she'd been putting on a show.

'Don't take this the wrong way,' she said, 'but I think you're making the mistake of assuming that a woman who's pushing towards ninety can't be a schemer.'

'If you're suggesting she's been manipulating you, I can't see why.' He hesitated. 'It's like the way you met that ice-cream guy and immediately thought the worst of Lorna. You're very tough on your family.'

'Whatever,' said Jessie, and then more quietly, 'You're still wrong.'

'I'd forgotten how stubborn you can be.'

'You say that as though it's a bad thing.'

'If it means you insist you're right when there's every chance you're wrong, it's hardly a good thing, is it?'

'(A), I guarantee you I'm not wrong. And, (B), in my experience, stubborn is one of those words tossed out by men when women won't roll over and agree with them.'

'Yeah, yeah, yeah,' said Ger, like he was fourteen.

For a couple of minutes, they drove in silence. Jessie was surprised by how quickly her joy had been replaced by irritation. Having half of the internet judging her was bad enough. She didn't need Ger joining in. It wasn't the substance of his accusation that annoyed her so much as the casual way he'd thrown it out. She was exhausted from other people's opinions.

'I'm going to ask Etty,' she said.

'This evening?'

'Why not? Either way, I want to talk to her about what we've discovered.'

'I suppose there's no harm in giving her a ring.'

'No,' she said, bringing her palms together. 'I'm going to call over to her.'

'I'm not sure if you've noticed,' said Ger, as the car sloshed through a puddle, 'but it's a filthy evening. How are you planning on getting to Boherbreen?'

'I thought you'd come with me.'

'Ah, Jessie.'

'You can "Ah, Jessie" me all you like. I'm sure I'm right about Etty. Would you not like to find out?'

'Nope.'

'Right so. You can drop me at the turn-off. I've an umbrella in my bag.' The part about the umbrella was a lie, but she didn't want a lecture about getting wet. He was starting to treat her like one of his class. Second by second, her irritation was turning to indignation.

'Okay,' he said, with a sigh. 'But this isn't one of your better ideas. It's too windy for an umbrella. It'll just get blown inside out.'

Her indignation deepened. 'Actually,' she said, 'you can pull over here. I'll walk the rest of the way.'

'You're not serious.'

'Yes, I am.'

'Now you're being stupid. We're more than a kilometre away from the turn-off.'

'I asked you to pull over and let me out.'

'All right,' said Ger. 'Have it your way.'

And so she did. Even as she climbed out of the car, and even as the first blast of rain hit her face, Jessie knew she was making a mistake. Still, she was worn out from everyone automatically assuming she was wrong about everything. Tonight, she would prove she was right about Etty, and after that she'd prove she was right about her sister.

Chapter 18

'As soon as I heard the knock on the door, I knew it was you,' said Etty, as Jessie squelched into her hall. 'No one else would be mad enough to go out in this rain. Get yourself a towel there so you can dry off.'

Chastened by half an hour of trudging through the downpour, Jessie did as she was told. She wasn't just wet, she was completely saturated. Her T-shirt and jeans had become glued to her body, and her light summer jacket was heavy with water. Her runners were soaked through and chafing against her heels. Her hair hung in damp ropes.

'On second thoughts,' said her grandmother, 'you need to take off those clothes. I'll get you a dressing-gown.'

Jessie went into the bathroom and wriggled out of her clothes. She was at least five inches taller than Etty, and the lavender candlewick dressing-gown barely reached her knees. Still, it was an improvement on what she'd been wearing.

She hung the sodden clothes on the back of three kitchen chairs and placed them beside the range.

'Put on the kettle as you're there,' called Etty. 'I could use a cup of tea – and an explanation.'

'No bother,' replied Jessie. 'I'd prefer something stronger myself.'

'Oh?'

'I've had a bit of a shock. That's why I'm here.' She'd decided not to mention falling out with Ger. There was a limit to how much questioning and emotional wrangling she could take. Besides, she wasn't here to talk about herself.

'You'll find a bottle of Jameson in the press beside the fridge,' said Etty. 'I'll have a drop of water in mine.'

Jessie poured whiskey into the sort of tumblers that had once been free with a large fill of petrol. Her hands were blue and orange from the cold. Fat drops of rain continued to slide down the window.

The first slug of whiskey had the desired effect, stinging and burning all the way down. The second and third were even better. The tension in her shoulders eased. From her brown armchair, she watched Etty take careful sips.

'So,' said her grandmother, 'are you going to tell me about this shock?'

Jessie put down her glass. Beside it on the coffee-table were the previous week's *Clare Champion*, a glossy magazine and a Michael Connolly novel. Etty was a woman of diverse tastes.

'It's connected to what I asked you about a few weeks ago,' she said.

'You'll have to refresh my memory.'

'You know what I'm talking about: the story of Johanna Markham and her daughter, Bridget.'

Etty put down her whiskey. 'And?'

For the next ten minutes, Jessie outlined what she had uncovered about Bridget. Throughout, Etty's face was opaque. Save for a couple of questions about how her granddaughter had unearthed various facts, she was quiet.

Jessie concluded with the evening's discoveries. 'That means Norah Nugent or McGuane or Moloney or whatever you want to call her was your great-grandmother,' she said.

Etty made a slight sound, softer than a sigh. 'She passed away before I was born.'

Jessie continued. 'So I'm joining the dots and …' The implications of what she'd heard hit home. 'Sorry?'

'You heard what I said. Norah died a few years before I was born. I've seen a picture of her, though. She was a lovely gentle-faced woman. A lady, by all accounts.'

Despite her suspicions, Jessie was taken aback by her grandmother's admission. 'Right,' she said. 'Just so as I have this clear: you've known all along that we're related to Johanna Markham and Bridget Moloney?'

'Bridget, the Lord rest her soul, was my great-great-grandmother on my father's side. Johanna was her mother.'

'Why didn't you tell me? And why didn't you tell Ger? He was the one who started this. Why give him and the kids only part of the story?'

Etty's face tightened. 'Answer me this. What would you have done if I'd told you everything on the first day you called up here?'

'I can't say.' Jessie sipped her whiskey. 'Actually, I can. I'd have told Ger, and he'd have told the kids in his class.'

'And there's every danger you'd have walked away and forgotten about it all.'

'You don't know that.'

'Well, I can't be certain, but you're an awful young one for flitting from this to that. When you came to me with Johanna's name, I got a right land. I hadn't heard anyone refer to her in years. I was about to tell you. Then I had second thoughts. *No*, I said to myself. *The girl's at a loose end. A bit of work won't do her any harm.*'

Jessie was in awe of her grandmother's ability to deflect. It truly was her special skill. She was making her deviousness sound like an act of charity. 'I do have a job, you know.'

'I'm well aware that you're giving Lorna a hand, but I thought you'd like a problem to solve. Otherwise, you'd keep fretting about the carry-on above in Dublin.'

'What if I hadn't got anywhere with my search?' asked Jessie, before swallowing the last of her drink. 'What then?' She was deliberately minimising Ger's part in the process. The knowledge that she'd been played was tempered by the fact that she'd been right about Etty's duplicity. She felt almost drunk with vindication.

'I'd every faith in you,' said Etty. 'In fact, I thought I'd hear back from you before now. I was beginning to think I'd have to throw a few hints in your direction.'

'You're something else. There I was, traipsing around the county and examining every website I could find, while you were sitting here with the full story.' Hardly had the words cleared her lips than it struck her that Etty might also know what had become of Bridget. Before she had the opportunity to ask, the elder woman raised her glass.

'I'll have another tot if you wouldn't mind.'

Jessie returned to the kitchen and poured them both a strong measure.

Back in the sitting room, she asked how long Etty had known about the family's history.

'For as long as I can remember.'

'Why didn't you make more of a fuss about it? Hollywood movies have been made out of less. What Bridget said to the journalist was amazing. Aren't you proud to be related to her?'

'I am, only … you're forgetting that almost everyone around here has a family story. All you have to do is lift a few stones, and the truth comes crawling out. Most of us are descended from someone who lived through the Famine. The only thing that sets this family apart is that we're related to a woman who left.' She paused. 'Actually, that's not quite true. There are a couple of other differences, including the fact that Bridget's experience was written down.'

Jessie pushed her fingertips against her forehead. 'Does Dad know about Bridget and Norah?'

'I'd say he was told at some stage, and he put it to the back of his mind. I wouldn't go giving out to him, mind. Until fairly recently most folks weren't too interested in that sort of thing.'

'I see,' said Jessie, far from certain that she did.

As if sensing her scepticism, Etty continued, 'Not that long ago, family trees were only for Americans or film stars on TV shows. You know the sort I mean: the ones who get all dewy-eyed about their ancestors' suffering. It's easy for them because they're so far removed from it. Few people around these parts wanted a reminder that their ancestors were so poor they searched dung heaps for vegetable peel and died at the side of the road.'

On this count, Jessie was forced to agree. 'You said there were a couple of things that made our story different. One was Bridget and Norah being in a newspaper. Is there something else?'

'I've something to show you. Normally, I keep it upstairs, but I got it down a couple of weeks ago.' Etty stopped for a drink. 'Like I said, I've been expecting you.'

She rose and went to the wooden sideboard that ran along the far wall. From it, she produced a maroon-covered photo album embossed with crumbling gold leaf. It appeared to be several decades old.

'Here we go. Be careful now because, as you'll see, some of the contents are very old.'

The first page contained a photocopy of the familiar drawing of Bridget and Norah. The accompanying article took up the next few pages. After that, there was a photograph of an elderly woman sitting in front of a whitewashed cottage. White curls poked out from beneath a pale headscarf. She was wearing a black dress and scuffed boots. Her face was heavily lined but, like Etty had said, there was gentleness to it.

For the second time that evening, Jessie's eyes watered. 'Norah?' she asked.

'That's her. The photo would have been taken a few years before she died. It's unusual enough to have a picture of an ordinary country woman from those days. God only knows what she would have made of the modern mania for picture-taking.'

Jessie took a minute to look at the woman whose grave she'd seen only an hour before. 'What's been bothering me is whether she knew about Bridget. She was only a baby when her mother left.'

'Turn over the page, and you'll find out. If you can't read it, don't worry. My father had it copied out in darker ink, and that version is a couple of pages on.'

Stuck to the next two pages was a letter so old the paper was nearly brown. It was creased in several places, and one corner had been torn. The ink had faded until it was barely legible. That the letter was covered with a sheet of cellophane didn't help. All the same, Jessie could make out the opening words. *My darling Norah*, and the final ones, *All my love, now and for ever, your mother, Bridget Moloney.*

Jessie gathered her thoughts before moving to the next page. As promised, the letter's contents had been transcribed in black ink. Bridget had written it before leaving Norah in Mary Ellen's care. Before she'd begun her journey to America. She'd told her daughter about their time together and about why she'd had to go. She'd also asked for mercy.

This latter request hit Jessie hard. Bridget's love for Norah was spelt out in every loop, slant and line. The magnitude of her pain was beyond comprehension. The passage of more than a hundred and seventy years had done nothing to diminish her words. On the contrary, it had amplified their power.

'It's a remarkable letter,' she said, conscious of the crack in her voice. 'She wrote well.'

'When you add that to what she said to the newspaper man, she must have been very clever,' said Etty. 'And it's unlikely she got to spend many years at school.'

A stream of questions were on Jessie's tongue but, to her

embarrassment, she couldn't voice them. Her chest constricted and the tears that had been building all evening emerged. She had a proper old-fashioned cry with spasms, hiccuping and, presumably, a shiny red face. At least she remembered to hand back the album to Etty. The last thing she wanted was to stain it with tears.

'I'm sorry,' she said, when her hiccups finally came to a halt. 'I feel like a fool, crying over something that happened the best part of two hundred years ago.'

'You're grand, pet,' said her grandmother, handing her a packet of tissues. 'In a way, I'd be disappointed if you weren't upset. It's a desperate story, and you've learnt an awful lot today.'

'Do you have any idea what age Norah was when she found out about Bridget? Like, did she see the letter when she was a child, or did she only find out later?'

'I'm afraid I don't know. She gave the letter to her son, Seánie, who was my grandfather. He handed it on to his son, Peter.'

'Your father,' said Jessie, still trying to get the family chain clear in her head.

'That's right.' Etty paused to sip her drink. 'He put the book together.' She tipped her neat white head towards the photo album. 'I don't know how he came across the *London Illustrated Gazette* article about Bridget and Norah. But, considering he didn't have much schooling, he was quite a learned man, so I assume that, like you, he did his research.'

'He probably found it in the library. They've lots of Famine records.'

'That'd make sense, right enough,' said Etty. 'He was a great man for the library.'

'There's no mention of Johanna there. How did you hear about her?'

'Again, my father told me. Mary Ellen must have told Norah.'

Jessie reached for her glass. 'Mary Ellen sounds like a right piece of work.'

'To be fair, you don't know the woman's circumstances. People can do desperate things when they're under pressure. She'd no children of her own. Who knows how her husband was treating her? Or how his family behaved?' She took another drink. 'In those days, ordinary women didn't have many choices. Not compared to the way things are these days, at any rate.'

Fearing this could veer into a homily about Jessie's generation not appreciating how easy their lives were, she raised a hand. 'All right, we'll give Great Aunt Mary Ellen the benefit of the doubt. Anyway, the big question is, what became of Bridget?'

'That I can't tell you.'

'For real?'

'I wouldn't blame you for doubting me but, as God's my witness, I never heard anything more about her, so I doubt the family did either.'

This came as a blow. Given how much Jessie had unearthed about the people who'd remained, she'd expected a snippet of information about the woman who'd been forced to leave.

'We know she went to Boston,' said Etty. 'Or, to be more accurate, we know she intended to go to Boston. Whether she ever got there is another question.'

Jessie swirled the last of her whiskey around the tumbler. 'Shouldn't Bridget's letter and Norah's photo ... shouldn't they be in the National Museum or somewhere? I mean, from what I've read, letters from that period aren't overly common, especially ones as eloquent as this. And that's before you consider the interest in the pair because of the article in the *London Illustrated Gazette*. In historical terms, Bridget's a star.'

For a minute or more, her grandmother was quiet. 'I hear what you're saying to me,' she said eventually. 'The way it is ... well, I've always thought of that letter as belonging to the family. I can't tell you how happy I was to see you taking an interest. Maybe you're right, though. Maybe other people deserve to see it. Not yet, mind. I was hoping you'd do some more digging first.'

'You hope I'll be able to find out what became of Bridget, you mean?'

'I've every faith in you. And Ger Dillane will be getting his summer holidays soon. Won't he be able to give you a hand?'

'You're overlooking the fact that, unlike me, he has a life.'

Etty laughed. 'Still and all, I've a feeling he'll help.'

'I'm not so sure about that,' said Jessie. 'We've had a bit of a falling-out.'

'Does that explain why you were tramping around in the lashing rain?'

Jessie reversed her earlier decision and outlined what had happened.

'Well,' said Etty, shaking her head, 'at least you'll be able to tell him that you were right.'

'That's if I decide to talk to him.'

'Of course, you'll talk to him. Nobody misses an opportunity to say, "I told you so."'

'We'll see,' said Jessie. 'Going back to Bridget, the whole thing is devastating, isn't it? It's like in one way I find myself wondering if any of it matters now. They're all a long time dead. And in another it's all I want to talk about. Bridget, Norah, Johanna and the rest of them are constantly in my head … if that makes any sense.'

'It does,' said Etty. 'It does. I've had many years to consider it all.' She paused. 'I think what matters most is that we remember.'

Outside, the wind was dying down, and the rain had been replaced by a fine mist. Despite the late hour, light remained in the sky. At this time of year, night fell slowly in Clooneven.

Thankfully, Jessie's clothes were dry again, as was her hair. She thought about Ger. Perhaps he'd like her to speak to his class. She was, after all, a living, breathing relative of Johanna Markham. She wouldn't call him yet, though. Actually, now that she thought about it, she'd wait for him to ring her. He was the one who'd been in the wrong.

Before going home, she decided to go for a short walk up the lane. Apart from Bridget's weeks in the workhouse, this had been where she'd spent her first twenty-two years. This had been her home.

The hedgerows were threaded with honeysuckle, its scent strengthened by the damp air. Jessie wondered if the families who'd lived here in the nineteenth century had been allowed time to enjoy their surroundings. She wanted to believe the answer was yes.

After a couple of hundred metres, she stopped beside a farm gate and lit a cigarette. She leant back and took a deep pull. Despite the poignancy of what she'd learnt, and despite her row with Ger, she felt light. It would be great to say that the feeling was pure, that it was based solely on her discovery of a personal connection to the Moloneys. But that wouldn't be true.

When she'd told Lorna she was thinking of writing about Bridget, she hadn't meant it. She'd been scrambling for a way of making the project sound less fanciful. But it *was* a good story, and if she could discover where Bridget had gone next, it would be a great one. Not in a hold-the-front-page way. A 170-year-old yarn hardly qualified as a scoop. The letter was gold dust, however, as was the photograph of Norah. She pictured them as part of a feature in an upmarket newspaper or magazine.

Cigarette finished, she walked on. She wasn't far from Lorna and Simon's place. She ought to turn around and head towards home. Even though the rain had eased, it wasn't a night for rambling around the countryside.

She heard the car before she saw it. Keen to avoid being splashed with puddle water, she jumped in by the ditch.

'Watch where you're going,' she shouted after the vehicle, a silver-coloured Honda with a Dublin registration.

To her surprise, it slowed and stopped. The driver lowered the window. 'Hop in there, and I'll give you a lift. Are you on your way up to Lorna?'

It was only then that she recognised him. 'Eh, no,' she replied, blindsided by his sudden appearance. 'I was in with our grandmother.

I'm about to go home.'

'I'll bring you to your folks' place so. It's a miserable night.'

Her first impulse was to decline, but she was curious. She assumed he'd been to Lorna's house. Perhaps Simon was working. Or perhaps he was out with friends. Then again, would her sister bring home a lover when the children were there? Young as they were, little escaped their attention.

She might have to rethink this one.

'Thanks,' she said, as she slid into the passenger seat and fastened her seatbelt. 'The last day? In the Seashell? I didn't get your name.'

'It's Dave,' he said.

She waited for him to elaborate, but when he spoke again it was to ask whether she was okay.

'I'm fine. Why do you ask?' Then she remembered that she'd been crying. There was every danger her face was a tear-smeared mess. She pulled down the mirror and her fears were confirmed. Her mascara and eyeliner had resettled under her eyes, so that she looked like a refugee from a glam-rock group. *Thanks for telling me, Etty.* 'Don't worry about the makeup,' she said. 'I heard something sad about a relation.'

'Oh?'

'No one you'd know.' If he was going to be cagey, she could match him all the way.

They'd arrived at the turn-off for her house. 'It's down that way,' she said, 'past the ruined church and the "No Hunting" sign.'

'Cheers. I always get confused around here.'

'What brings you to this part of the world on a wet Tuesday night?'

'Oh, you know. A bit of this, a bit of that.' They rounded the corner towards Jessie's house, and he laughed. If she was honest, it was a pleasant, throaty laugh. She had the feeling he was aware of this. 'Don't mind me trying to wreck your head,' he said. 'I was over with Simon and Lorna. We were tying up some business, that's all.'

'I get you,' she said, even though she didn't. 'It's the third house on the left. The one with the flowers.'

'That's an impressive garden.'

'It is.' She unhooked herself and opened the door. 'Thanks for the lift. No doubt I'll see you around.'

'No doubt,' he replied.

Chapter 19

May 1848, Galway

Bridget

Only when she reached Galway did Bridget fully appreciate the scale of the leave-taking. They were everywhere: townsfolk and country people, families and couples. Almost without exception, they looked as if they were struggling to survive. Some were clearly unwell. All were reed-thin and dressed in flimsy clothes. At times, there was a hysteria about them. They panicked for fear they might not have enough money for the fare or because they'd been separated from their family. When the crowd moved, they didn't walk so much as swarm. Nevertheless, after the lonely journey through Clare and south County Galway, she welcomed the noise and bustle.

She hadn't spent every day on her own. Along the way, she'd met and walked with countless people, many of them America-bound. 'I've a brother in New York,' they'd say, or 'Half our parish is in Philadelphia.'

Others were going to Canada, yet more to England. There were ships galore in Galway, she learnt, but the fare was expensive, and you needed to bring as much food as possible because the rations onboard were meagre.

Frequently, people asked why she'd chosen Boston. She told a version of the truth. 'I've a brother there,' she'd say. 'Francie Markham's his name.' What she didn't say was that she had no idea how to find him. When he'd left, she'd been a child. It was doubtful she would even recognise him now.

Some of the places she passed through had been stripped of people, the houses levelled, the fields abandoned. In others, life remained. In a village in the Burren, she watched three small girls at play. The youngest had the same enquiring look as Norah, the same wide smile. Bridget imagined picking her up and kissing her and was forced to turn away. She came close to changing her mind and returning to Hackett's Cross.

It wasn't the only time she considered going back. Early one morning, she was climbing a wind-battered hill when, amid the sparse grass, she noticed a lone daisy. Bridget believed she'd been hardened by everything she'd witnessed. Yet, for some reason, that one miserable flower, clinging on despite the elements, brought tears to her eyes. She wondered if she was losing her mind. What sort of woman could walk past dead bodies and ruined villages but cry over a wild flower?

It occurred to her then that she felt empty because she had no one left to love. Most of those she'd loved were dead while Norah was no longer hers. Her love had turned to grief. Shortly afterwards, she fell into step with a family from Doonbeg, and their company helped to sweep aside her melancholy.

During the weeks it took to reach the city, she became accustomed to sleeping outdoors. On some nights, she found a lovely soft bed of new grass. On others, it was almost impossible to stay dry and warm. In Galway, she slept on the streets. The local people were frightened of newcomers and reluctant to give them shelter. The workhouse on the Newcastle Road provided refuge for some but, remembering the hardship in Kilrush, Bridget balked at sleeping there.

On her second day in Galway, she found the shipping office and took her place in the queue. A ship was due to sail for New York the next day. Another was bound for Québec. Then she saw the notice she'd been looking for. The following week, a boat would leave for Boston.

For the Flourishing city of BOSTON
The splendid ship, the *Mary and Elizabeth*,
will sail for the above port (wind and weather permitting)
in or around Monday, the 22nd of May
Commanded by men of experience in the Trade

When she reached the office, she asked for one ticket.

The man behind the counter gave her a concerned look. 'Have you no husband or children?'

'I'm on my own,' she replied.

From a distance, the *Mary and Elizabeth* was impressive. While not as large as other ships, her two masts stood clean against the blue sky. Closer examination revealed that the timber was in poor condition and, in places, was rotting away. As they waited to board, Bridget pointed this out to the heavily whiskered man in front of her.

He laughed, displaying a mouth with more gaps than teeth. 'If you're waiting for better, you'll be a long time here. Every ship in the port's the same. No one would waste a valuable boat on the likes of us.'

Bridget pushed aside her misgivings. She'd spent most of her money on the fare and the rest on food and a thin mattress. She couldn't afford to be fussy. She'd passed the week in Galway trying to find someone, a woman preferably, who would be making the crossing on the same ship, but with so many people travelling in so many directions, it had been impossible.

As they boarded, the passengers' names were checked against a roll and a doctor gave them a brief examination. Even though most were pale and weak, and many were coughing, none was considered unfit to travel. She suspected a person would have to be wrapped in a shroud for the doctor to reject them.

Moments before they set sail, she shut her eyes, pressed her hand around the shell she'd taken from Norah's collection and asked for strength. When she opened her eyes again, the crew were scurrying about. A series of shouts and a clang of the brig's bell announced their departure. On the quayside, those left behind waved with an enthusiasm they couldn't have felt. Seagulls circled overhead.

Standing beside her on deck, a young boy began to cry. He made small snuffling sounds, as if embarrassed by his tears. She placed a hand on his shoulder. His name was Anthony McDonagh, he told her. He was twelve and would miss his friends in Claddaghduff.

'I promise you, it will get better,' she said, echoing John Joe's words on the day they'd buried her brother, Michael. She needed to believe them.

Within a short while, they were sailing past Mutton Island lighthouse and along the Connemara coast. Like Anthony, many on board were from that part of Galway and they wept as the land faded into the silvery distance. Others gripped rosary beads and prayed for a safe journey. When next they saw land, it would be their new home, America.

As the *Mary and Elizabeth* gathered pace, it started to sway, and the sea spray hit Bridget's face. Taking in the keening and praying around her, she wished her own feelings were more straightforward. She was fleeing from a place where her family had been persecuted and allowed to die, so of course she felt sorrow. But she also felt anger. A hot, unrelenting anger. Shame was there too. Shame that she hadn't saved them or been capable of looking after her daughter. And, finally, there was another sensation. As small as a ladybird and as delicate as a butterfly wing, it was so unfamiliar that she barely recognised it. The sensation was hope.

The ship's hold was gloomy and cramped, with rows of narrow bunks, one stacked on top of another. Voices rose around her as men and women argued over who should sleep where.

Advancing as swiftly as the tight space allowed, she claimed a lower bunk. She sat with her belongings spread around her, determined not to be moved.

Almost immediately, a young woman arrived. She had light brown hair, large brown eyes and was carrying a baby. Starvation had made it increasingly difficult to gauge a child's age, but Bridget guessed the baby was no more than eight or nine months old.

'We have to share,' said the woman.

Bridget stared as her, as if to say, *No I don't.*

The woman raised her chin and tried again. 'Are you on your own?'

'I am.'

'So am I.'

'Can't you find another berth?' asked Bridget. 'There isn't room for three of us.'

'If you don't share with me and Delia,' the woman dipped her head towards the baby, 'you'll find yourself sleeping beside a man. Or someone who's sick. Or mad. Then where will you be?'

Bridget looked around. People were still entering the hold. Others were shuffling and squabbling. She did a quick calculation. There were more than a hundred of them on board. The woman was right. There wasn't a berth for everyone.

She gave a nod of understanding. 'All right,' she said. 'We can share.'

'I'm Alice,' said the woman, as she eased herself onto the bunk. 'Alice King from Tulla in County Clare.'

Bridget introduced herself.

Alice smiled. 'We're pleased to meet you, aren't we, Delia?'

The baby sent a shy smile in Bridget's direction.

'That's her way of agreeing,' said Alice. 'Not everyone gets a smile.'

'She's a beautiful girl,' said Bridget.

'She is,' said Alice. 'She's an absolute blessing.' She squinted at Bridget. 'What's your story then?'

Little by little, they got to know each other. Alice was twenty years old, and her husband had died shortly before Delia was born. Both of her parents and three of her five siblings had also passed away. Her fare to America had been paid by their landlord, a man called Crofton Blake, who was desperate to be rid of them. She had an uncle living outside Boston but hadn't been able to contact him. Despite this, and despite the tragedies that had befallen her, she was strangely confident about life in the new world.

What was most impressive about Alice and Delia was their ability to sleep. No matter that they were crushed into the hold like sheep, no matter the coughing and hacking of others, no matter the putrid smell, the blistering heat and the scuttling rats, both mother and daughter slept as soundly as princesses on a feather bed. Bridget was less fortunate. Their surroundings were too rank, and she missed Norah too much, for her to settle properly.

Alice maintained that when Bridget was established in America she could send for her daughter. She said as much one evening as they prepared their shared dinner. Cooking on the *Mary and Elizabeth* was an ordeal. The fire on the deck was small and contained by bricks and two iron bars. People queued from morning till night for their turn.

If their food portions were mean, the allocation of water was even more miserly. The captain, a huge slab of a man named John Talbot, insisted it had to be rationed. 'If we run out, you'll know all about it,' he'd said, in a voice that suggested he might welcome such a calamity.

Bridget and Alice were making stirabout with their oatmeal. They were ten days into the journey, and the extra food they'd brought on board had been eaten. She thanked her new friend for her thoughts about Norah but doubted a reunion would happen.

'When I gave her to Mary Ellen,' she said, 'that was the end of it.'

'What if she's unhappy without you?' replied Alice. 'When she's older, she might come and find you.'

'But I don't want her to be unhappy.'

'Well, then, perhaps she'll decide that, as good as life is in Hackett's Cross, it would be even better with her mother in America.'

'Ba ba ba,' said Delia, in what sounded like agreement.

Bridget had to laugh. 'I don't know how you keep on seeing everything in such a positive way.'

'Our fortunes will have to change,' said Alice. 'No one can have bad luck all their life.'

Bridget wanted to say that what had happened to them was more than bad luck. They'd been allowed to starve in a country with plentiful food. She held her tongue. It was at times like this that she yearned for the conversations she'd shared with John Joe. And yet she'd also come to admire Alice's attitude. Given the tragedy she'd endured, it took more than resilience to face into every day as though it held promise. It took bravery.

Her own pleasure came from the sea around them. Unlike many passengers, who became ill when the ship rolled, Bridget found that she enjoyed the thrashing of the waves. On the calmer days, when others complained they'd be stuck on the boat for ever, she sat and looked at the ocean as it took on different colours. Depending on the angle of the sun or the type of cloud, the Atlantic could be twenty different shades of blue. Or it could be green or grey or black. She also kept watch for flying fish or for the grey-headed dolphins that leapt through the foam.

'Look at them dancing,' she'd say to Delia. 'They're putting on a show for you.'

She liked to think her love of the water had come from her father. But if, in life, William Markham had encouraged her to appreciate the Atlantic, his death had taught her how cruel and unpredictable it could be.

From the day they'd left Galway, there was sickness on board. Not just vomiting caused by turbulence and the stagnant air below deck, but more serious illness too. The further west they travelled, the more people fell ill.

Bridget was terrifyingly familiar with the symptoms: the headaches and dizziness that became a swelling pain until the patient felt their head might burst; the throbbing temperature; the disfiguring rash. At night, as the *Mary and Elizabeth* creaked and groaned, she listened to the moans of her fellow passengers. Some became delirious from pain and fever, their voices changing from an incoherent babble to a hideous roar. More struggled for breath, their chests wheezing and rattling. Others lost control of their bowels so that the stench below deck was worse than anything she could recall. No matter how hard she tried to keep the smell at bay, it filled her nostrils until she too felt ill. Accustomed as she was to hardship, she was shocked by the intensity of the suffering. And, unlike the workhouse, she had no means of escape. There was no doctor on board, so passengers with a small bit of learning or experience attempted to tend the sick. For the most part, their efforts were futile.

When John Joe was ill, Bridget had been able to ease his thirst with fresh water. It might not have saved his life, but it had helped to alleviate his distress. On the ship, water remained rationed. Not only was there not enough to drink, there wasn't a spare drop to clean their living quarters.

The families of the sick pleaded with the crew to show some generosity. Every time, the answer was no. A deputation of men went to the captain. He, too, rejected their request.

Afterwards, they were divided over what to do. Eugene Hester from Ballinasloe, who had the spindliest arms Bridget had ever seen, suggested they try to seize a barrel or two and distribute the water themselves. Others cautioned against. Billy Joyce from Clifden pointed out that even the sturdiest of them was malnourished while the sailors were strong and well fed.

'It's likely they'll batter any man who tries to take the water,' he said.

Reluctantly, the others agreed.

The first person to die was an elderly woman, Biddy Feerick from County Mayo. Within a week, six others were gone, among them a young mother who left behind a husband and four children. There was a brutality about the treatment of the dead that made Bridget's heart ache. In the absence of a priest, the family of the departed prayed over their remains. They were given only a sliver of time to mourn before their loved one's body was thrown overboard.

Bridget thought of the man in Kilrush who'd claimed the Atlantic was rancid with Irish flesh. He'd been wrong. The water was still rippling when the sharks arrived. Within minutes, there was no flesh left to rot.

Eleven people died the following week, including Anthony McDonagh, the young boy whom Bridget had attempted to comfort as the ship set sail. Although she knew the tears weren't hers to cry, she wept as if he'd been her own brother.

When his body splashed into the water, she looked up towards the hard sun and square white sails and prayed that she, Alice and Delia would keep their health.

Chapter 20

In the days that followed, Bridget spent as many hours as possible on deck. She peered out to sea and inhaled lungfuls of clean air, hoping it would safeguard against fever. Had it been allowed, she would have slept under the stars.

She was sitting on deck when Alice found her. As usual, Delia was in her arms.

'Will you feel her head?' said Alice. 'She's too hot.'

Bridget stood and did as she was asked. In truth, she didn't need to. Even in the murky evening light, she saw that the baby's fair hair was dark with sweat, her face a dappled pink.

While she thought of the softest way to say this, Alice began to tremble. 'She's after getting it, isn't she?' she said. 'She's going to die, isn't she?'

'She's not going to die,' replied Bridget, although she had difficulty believing her own words.

Delia made a rasping sound, suggesting she was finding it difficult to breathe.

'No, she will,' said Alice, her tone matter-of-fact. 'Everyone else did. Why should she be different?'

Bridget ran a hand along Alice's shoulder, the bone so close to the skin that it felt as if it might break through. 'We can't allow that to happen. We'll have to do everything we can to save her.'

'You don't ...' started Alice, before her voice came to a halt. 'I was going to say, you don't know how much I love her. Only that would be wrong. I love her the way you love Norah. She's all I have left.'

If Bridget felt fear, she also felt guilt for all the times she'd compared Delia to Norah and found her wanting. She was a dear little thing. Already, you could see how she was destined to have the same snubbed nose and pointed chin as her mother. Alice always cared for her with great tenderness, ensuring she was fed before eating as much as a mouthful herself. She also kept her as clean as conditions allowed. Unlike some of the other children, Delia carried no lice or fleas. Her head smelt as sweet as a baby's head should.

The days blurred together, with the two women taking turns to nurse the sick child. Occasionally, they disagreed. Bridget thought Delia should sleep as much as possible, while Alice worried that if she did, she might not wake again. The child suffered dreadfully. A dry cough caused her body to shake. Frequently, she struggled for air. Her lips and hands were tinged with blue, and the muscles in her tiny neck became strained. A rash bloomed over her body, and there were watery pimples on the soft skin of her arms and legs. Bridget had seen similar markings on others and knew that, if they became infected, Delia would grow sicker still.

They tried bathing her limbs in salt water, but the stinging and irritation made her fretful. What they needed was fresh water, only supplies remained limited. They set aside the modest amount they were given for drinking and cooking and used this to clean and soothe the child. They had underestimated the ferocity of the July sun, and, within hours, lack of water caused them both to become dizzy and weak.

All the while, Alice grew more despondent. She ate like a small bird, and when Bridget attempted to reason with her, she turned away. Not only was her optimism gone, her gift for sleep had disappeared. Beside her in the bunk, Bridget, too, lay awake. If she managed an hour's rest, she woke to find her body stiff with dread. For the first time in weeks, she was relieved she'd left Norah behind.

This pattern continued until one afternoon, when the heat was at its most stifling, Alice keeled over and hit her head against one of the masts. Bridget realised that action was called for. If she didn't intervene, both mother and child would perish. Yes, she knew that water had to be used sparingly. But she also suspected the captain of being meaner than was necessary. Several of the seriously ill were either very old or very young. Reasoning that these were the most likely to die, she felt it should be possible to increase their allocation.

Her resolve was strengthened by Delia's deterioration. Every day, she slipped a little further, her plight all the more poignant because she was too young to describe her pain. She whimpered and gasped but no longer had the energy to cry.

Consulting the other passengers would be pointless. A fatalism had taken hold among them. Anger had been replaced by lethargy. They would either do nothing or, worse, they would discourage her from acting. She reminded herself that she'd done a man's work in Clooneven. She shouldn't be afraid to take on a similar role here.

She decided to seek out the captain. She also did her best to summon the hope she'd felt at the start of the voyage. There were good people on the ship, and they deserved better.

John Talbot wasn't hard to find as he spent a portion of the day on the bow, sucking on his pipe. Unsure how to address him, Bridget settled on 'sir', and with only the briefest of preambles, explained her mission.

'No,' he said, his pale eyes assessing her. 'If conditions below deck are lamentable, which they are, you have only yourselves to blame. You were warned of the need to be frugal with the water.'

'A child is dying, sir. She's not yet a year old, and her father passed away before she was born. Whoever's to blame, it's not Delia, but she's the one who's suffering.'

'I said no.'

'Surely a baby born into such dreadful circumstances is entitled to a chance at life?'

Captain Talbot tilted his head to one side. 'Are you simple? I gave you my answer, and your display of stubbornness isn't going to change my mind. Now return to your bunk. Why America should want to accept any of you, I don't know. You're nothing but a mass of disease and idleness.'

Conscious that they were attracting an audience, Bridget felt her back stiffen. She suspected that he was motivated more by arrogance and expediency than any desperate desire to conserve supplies. He didn't want to accede to her request because it might be inconvenient. And because she was a woman. What man of the captain's standing would want to be seen doing a young woman's bidding?

'Twenty-seven people have lost their lives on your ship,' she said. 'If that continues, there won't be anyone still alive when we reach Boston, so you won't have to worry about who the Americans will or won't accept. Would you like that on your conscience? Would you like the death of a baby girl on your conscience?'

'I've warned you,' he said, frost in his voice. 'Go back to your berth.'

'All I'm asking for is a small concession for those whose lives are at risk. For the very weakest. Have you no mercy or compassion?'

With that, he passed the pipe to his other hand, leant forward and slapped her across the face.

Because his hand was calloused and rough, and because it was supported by considerable bulk, Bridget felt as if she'd been hit by a length of timber. She staggered back but was able to stay on her feet. The pain surged across her face and around to the back of her head. For a moment, she was too winded to speak. When she recovered her voice, she willed herself to sound firm.

'I asked you a question, sir,' she said. 'You haven't answered.'

The captain moved his weight from one foot to the other. She feared he was about to strike her again, but before he had the opportunity, a man stepped forward. She recognised him as Martin McDonagh, father of Anthony, the boy who'd been among the first to die.

'You won't hit her again,' he said, his robust voice at odds with his skeletal body.

The captain went to reply, but as he did, several others moved closer.

'She made a fair request,' said Eugene Hester, the man who'd argued they should steal some barrels of water. 'And the rest of us support her.'

'We have to try to put a stop to the sickness,' added a woman. 'From everything I've heard folks say, we're only a week or two out from Boston. We're not going to run out of water.'

Bridget touched her cheek. The woman was right. They'd been at sea for six weeks, and they'd made good progress. Still, as heartened as she was by everyone's support, it was hard to see the captain changing his mind.

From her rear, she heard a mumble of voices: three, maybe four, men were talking. She turned to see several of the ship's crew. Two of them peeled away from the group and approached Captain Talbot. They stepped to one side, their discussion taking place in animated whispers. Everyone else, Bridget included, remained quiet.

Finally, the captain walked towards them again. He cleared his throat and spat. A great green dollop landed directly in front of Bridget's bare feet.

'I have discussed this with the crew,' he said, 'and it is apparent that some of these fine men are willing to use less water, if it means there will be more for the weakest among you. While I question whether any of you is capable of the gratitude their generosity deserves, they are insistent.'

'Oh,' Bridget heard herself say.

The captain ignored her, choosing instead to address the older men and women who had gathered behind. 'However,' he added, 'any further insubordination will have consequences of the most severe kind. Troublemaking will not be rewarded. Is that understood?'

A murmur – part gratitude, part surprise – passed through the throng, and they began to disperse.

Afterwards, the situation improved slightly. Even a small increase in water was sufficient to quench the thirst of the sickest passengers. Alice was able to drench a cloth and use it as a cold compress on Delia's forehead and chest. She also bathed her sore legs and arms. Gradually, the child responded. Although frail and listless, her temperature dropped, and her breathing became less laboured.

At first, they were scared to mention the change. Bridget worried that acknowledging it would bring bad luck. In the end, it was Alice who chose to speak. A week or so after the scene with Captain Talbot, she took Bridget's hand.

'You saved Delia's life,' she said.

Bridget wasn't innocent enough to believe she was responsible for the baby's recovery, but she hoped she'd made a contribution. She also liked to think that standing together had made it possible for the passengers to achieve their aim. Perhaps if they did so more often, it would make a difference. Her mother had frequently used the Irish word *meitheal*, which described neighbours coming together to help each other. She thought of Johanna now. How would her mother feel about what had become of her?

The improvement in their circumstances wasn't enough to save everyone. Six people died that week, including a four-year-old boy named Owen McGirr. He was the second child the family had lost, and his mother's sobbing sent shivers down Bridget's back.

As America drew nearer, she thought more and more about Boston. Not just about important matters, like how she would find work or how she would locate her brother, but also about lesser considerations. What did they eat there? How large were the buildings? What did women wear?

She and Alice joked about finding prosperous husbands.

'I want a fine big American man,' said Alice, 'with a large house and an important position. We'll have a maid, which means I can be as idle as I choose. Oh, he'll love Delia like she was his own daughter. No, he'll love her more because he'll have sympathy for her poor start.'

Bridget laughed. 'You're not asking for much.'

'You can laugh all you like, Bridget Moloney, but I look at it like this. We won't be in Ireland any more, so we won't be treated as inferiors. No one will sneer at us … or claim we're dirty or feeble-minded. We'll be free to live our own lives.'

Although Bridget doubted it would be that straightforward, she didn't have the heart to say so.

That night, the sea caught fire.

Sparks of white light surrounded the ship, as if reflecting the multitude of stars overhead. Underneath, the water glowed blue and green. For as far as they could see, the Atlantic glistened.

Alice squealed with pleasure. 'Look,' she said to Delia, 'someone has put thousands of lanterns in the water.'

The baby smiled her anxious little smile.

'I've never seen anything so lovely,' said Bridget. 'It's like magic.'

'It's real enough,' said Martin McDonagh, who was standing nearby. 'I heard about such a happening once, but I never thought I'd see it.'

'Better still,' added a passing sailor, 'it means our journey is nearly over. They say this occurs when land is near.'

Bridget sighed. The voyage had been arduous, and only two thirds of their original number would make it to America. Nevertheless, they were almost there.

'How far away from Boston do you think we are?' she asked.

'Only a day or so,' he said, 'which is just as well. Captain Talbot claims the weather's about to change.'

Chapter 21

In the morning, there was a jagged grey strip on the horizon. Bridget, an early riser, was one of the first to see it. For a long moment, she savoured the view. Then, she returned to the hold to tell Alice.

Her friend's eyes widened as she picked up Delia and danced towards the steps. 'Let's go and see America,' she said.

As the word spread, people poured onto the deck and competed for space. Parents lifted children into the air. Even those who'd barely been able to stir from their bunks made their way up to have a look. The only shame, they agreed, was that such an important day hadn't been blessed with better weather. The morning was grey, and the breeze carried spits of rain. The sea churned, its spray slapping their faces. But what of it? Their destination was within reach.

'We could swim to Boston from here,' said one man, as he hoisted up his son for a better view.

'That we could,' said a woman. 'Before we know it, we'll be there.'

Their excitement lifted Bridget's heart. Soon, their new lives would begin.

The crew said the weather would grow stormy and that this might delay their arrival. The warning was enough for some passengers to take shelter in the hold. More remained where they were, anxious not to miss anything.

Hour by hour, the north-easterly wind strengthened until Bridget, always one of the last to leave the deck, decided it would be better to shelter below. The gale kept lifting her skirt, and the rain stung her face. With every gust, the brig gasped and creaked, a reminder of how flimsy it was. How ill-suited to a storm. By this point, the Massachusetts coast was shrouded by the downpour. There was nothing to see.

On her way, she met the sailor who'd first warned that the weather was going to change. He appeared worried. 'The wind's blowing us too far to the south,' he said.

'What are you going to do?'

'Everything we can, but we won't reach Boston today. We'll have to hope we stay safe, and then we'll plot a new course tomorrow.'

Down below, the mood remained buoyant. If the rolling of the sea was making people ill, at least they were confident that their journey would soon be over. All they had to do was wait, and they were accustomed to waiting.

Periodically, Bridget and some of the others went up to have a look. Within minutes, they were forced back down again. With every hour, the weather became more violent. Lightning flashed across the sky, followed immediately by growls of thunder.

In the early evening, she noticed that the ship's sails had been torn and were no longer working. Again, she met the sailor, who explained that they'd dropped both anchors. Nevertheless, the force of the waves continued to push the vessel to the south-west.

For the first time, she was afraid. A sudden vicious gust forced her to cling to one of the masts.

'Where are we?' she asked.

'Heading towards Cohasset Bay.'

'Isn't that good news?'

He paused before speaking again. 'Maybe ... if we can avoid the rocks.'

Her fear became more urgent. 'What can we do?'

'Pray,' came his reply. Quickly, he thought better of it. 'Please don't say that to the others. There's a danger they'll become hysterical.'

'Should you not talk to them and explain the situation?'

'No,' he said, and hurried away.

In the hold, there was growing understanding of their predicament. Several people were saying the rosary. Others were singing a hymn. Alice gripped Delia as though the child was in immediate danger of being torn from her arms. Nearby, a man attempted to reassure his wife. All of this was being done in the dark: no sooner had someone managed to light a candle than the rolling of the ship would extinguish it.

Bridget wondered if she should tell them what she'd learnt. She decided there was nothing to be achieved by causing panic, for panic there would surely be. She was considering what to say to Alice when Eugene Hester entered the hold. Even in the grainy light, she could see that his eyes were as large as those of a cornered animal.

He began to speak, except between the wailing wind and the crying and the singing and the praying, it was hard to hear.

'Will ye listen to me?' he roared. 'If ye value yeer lives, will ye listen to me?'

It took a few seconds, but the commotion died down.

'They say there's a danger we could be washed ashore, and the problem is ... the area we're in ... well, there are rocks.'

A woman screamed.

'Hush,' snapped a man.

'How close are we?' asked someone else.

'I believe we're close enough,' said Eugene. 'And if we do hit the rocks our chances of survival are poor.'

'Why didn't you tell me?' said Alice to Bridget, in a furious whisper. 'I didn't realise,' she lied.

Already, people were scrambling towards the steps. Others looked to be gripped by fright, unable either to stir or speak. More were too sick to move and would have to remain in the hold no matter what happened. Two men started reciting an act of contrition.

Eugene flapped his long arms as if trying to scare away crows. 'We need a plan,' he shouted. 'We can't all run onto the deck. That won't help.'

No one was listening. 'It's too late for a plan,' someone yelled. 'It's every man for himself.'

'Where does that leave the women?' asked Alice, before kissing Delia's head. 'Come on,' she said to Bridget. 'We'd best go up and look.'

'I'm not sure you understand how bad it is.'

'You stay here if you like. I want to see for myself.'

'Fine. I'll – I'll come with you.'

As stark as Eugene Hester's words had been, Alice appeared shocked by what she saw. In front of them, the waves were crashing against the rocks, causing great plumes of water to rise into the air. So ferocious was the Atlantic that it looked capable of reaching in, picking someone up and tossing them about. Terrified for their lives, passengers clung to the gunwales. Others huddled in prayer, their precise words lost in the wind. The sky was the greyish brown of dried mud.

I'm going to die like my father, thought Bridget. I'm on a bigger boat, in a different place, but I'll die the same way.

'What are we going to do?' said Alice, wrapping her arms around Delia.

Before she had the chance to answer, the ship was swept forward. Then, with a thunderous crack, it slammed into a wall of stone. A splintering sound filled their ears. The *Mary and Elizabeth* was going to break apart. Those who had remained below would be dead within minutes. It wouldn't take much longer for the entire ship to sink.

Despite the spray lashing her face, Bridget noticed activity to their right. She turned and saw several people, Captain Talbot among them, attempting to launch the long boat, a rowing boat, which, in better circumstances, would be used as a tender. While their chances of reaching the shore were slim, staying on the main ship meant certain death.

'Over there,' she shouted at Alice, who immediately saw what was happening. They began to run, but a sudden lurch threw them onto the deck. Mercifully, Alice was able to keep hold of Delia. They picked themselves up and proceeded, more carefully this time, towards the long boat. All the while, they were battered and pummelled by the storm. Breathing was almost impossible.

Somehow, the small craft had been eased into the water. It was overcrowded. Bridget counted fourteen people on board: five women, the rest men.

Everything was happening quickly now. If they didn't move, they would be killed. Stubbornness took hold of her. She had travelled too far and endured too much to accept death without a fight. This was their chance for survival, and she couldn't let it pass.

Beside her, Alice was crying. 'Please save my baby,' she screamed at the people in the smaller boat. 'Whatever about me, you've got to save my baby.'

Throughout, Delia remained mute. Perhaps she was too scared to make a sound.

'We're all leaving together,' said Bridget, doing her best to sound emphatic. No sooner had she spoken than a woman tried to elbow her to one side. The push, though weak, caught her by surprise. She took some seconds to recover. As she did, the *Mary and Elizabeth* smashed into the rocks again. This collision was even more powerful.

'If you give Delia to me,' she said to Alice, 'you can climb down to the boat. There's a rope over there.' She gestured to their left. 'I'll pass her to you before climbing down myself.'

Alice hesitated.

'Go, will you?' she shouted. 'You have to trust me. There's no other way.'

Alice followed her orders. She took hold of the rope and jumped. She almost fell into the water, but, with the help of one of the men, managed to struggle on board.

When Bridget attempted to follow, the woman who'd pushed her a minute before did so again. As the woman clambered onto the long boat, a huge wave toppled the craft and sent everyone spilling into the water.

For a few seconds, Bridget could see Alice's terrified face. She was trying to reach the upturned boat. Every time it looked as though she was about to do so, it bobbed away again.

Never had Bridget felt so powerless. 'Please,' she roared into the wind. 'Please help.'

But there was no one to come to their aid. When she looked again, Alice had vanished into the froth of the ocean.

Before she could draw breath, the main ship was thrown against the rocks once more. The force sent her staggering back. An almighty groan indicated that the *Mary and Elizabeth* had been torn asunder.

The ship tipped forward, and Bridget felt water lapping at her feet. The sensation paralysed her. A shrieking sound filled her head. All she could see was black. If she was conscious of anything, it was of the baby pressed tightly to her chest, like a barnacle to a stone.

'I'm sorry,' she whispered to Delia. 'I'm sorry.'

The water was enveloping them. As cold as the grave. As dark as purgatory. Soon, it would swallow them.

Memories rained down on her, her thoughts not of what she'd lost but of what she'd had: the happy days at home; John Joe who'd promised to buy her a library of books; Norah who'd brought nothing but joy. Even on this journey she'd had the friendship of a fine woman who'd done her best to raise everyone's spirits. But Bridget couldn't dwell on these memories. Nor could she fight any further.

Her story had come to an end.

Part Two

Chapter 22

June 2019, Clooneven

Jessie

To begin with, Jessie was confident that Ger would contact her. As pointless arguments went, theirs had been on the higher end of the scale. He'd understand that, wouldn't he? She also reasoned that, even if he wasn't minded to apologise, curiosity would win out. Surely he'd want to know if her hunch about Etty had been correct?

A day passed. Then another. Then three. Then ten. Every day, she contemplated calling or sending a message. She was desperate to tell him about Bridget's letter and Norah's photograph. But her desperation was fused with anger. She'd been right about her grandmother, and he'd been completely wrong. He needed to admit that. She tended her grievance with care, taking it out and polishing it every evening.

Okay, she'd probably been wrong to suspect Lorna of having an affair, but something strange was going on there. Whatever Dave did for a living, she doubted it involved selling choc ices and tubs of raspberry ripple.

All around her, the summer was taking shape. The fine weather had returned, and the beach hummed with sunbathers and sandcastle builders. Jessie served golfers in salmon-coloured chinos and women in jewelled sandals and ill-fitting white jeans. She sold ice-cream to small children and strong coffees to hung-over parents. She watched flirting teenagers, the girls in bikini tops and denim cut-offs, the boys in board shorts and flip-flops, and envy rose within her. What she didn't envy was the girls' obsession with taking and uploading photos. It was as if their family holiday had been turned into a personal marketing campaign.

Lord, she thought, I sound old.

Without Ger, Jessie had no one to knock about with. There was no one to listen to her stories about the café's more eccentric customers or to take an interest in what she'd been reading about the Famine. She missed his company, but could only assume that he didn't miss hers. He, after all, had friends, a girlfriend, a demanding job. His life was full. She decided to invite Shona and some of her other Dublin friends to Clooneven. All found reasons to say no.

Still determined not to contact Ger, she thought she'd try to engineer a meeting. She remembered that, despite the breath-taking cold of the Atlantic, he was one of those people who enjoyed swimming. She took to walking the beach. Once or twice, she thought she saw his dark head bobbing between the waves. On other occasions, she imagined she saw his loping walk. Each time, she was wrong. She told herself that in such a small town she'd have to bump into him eventually. But she didn't.

More than two months in Clooneven had honed Jessie's knowledge of home. She saw that, just as she'd caricatured her family for a city audience, she'd done something similar with her town. She'd long been irritated by the tendency of Dubliners to view the west of Ireland as a rural Disneyland where all was tranquil and picturesque. An oasis of fiddles and fishing rods and hampers of artisan food. A place where all the fires burnt turf, all the bread was homemade, and all the locals were self-effacing charmers. But by dismissing Clooneven as bland and parochial she'd fallen into another trap. If the sense of community was real, so were the fissures that ran through the town. It was a more complex place than she'd been willing to acknowledge. A place of three-day weddings, wellness seminars and cars the size of minivans, but also a place of peeling paint, potholed roads and young guys in court for heroin possession.

She would have liked to share her observations with someone. Oh, let's be honest, she would have liked to share them with Ger. But that was no longer possible.

Since hearing about her connection to Bridget, Jessie's compulsion to find out more had strengthened. Her fourth-great-grandmother felt as real as her colleagues in the Seashell or the sunbathers on the beach. On her days off, she sought information about boats leaving Galway for Boston in the spring and summer of 1848. She scoured websites and forums until, finally, the County Library's archives provided her with a result, albeit not one that she'd hoped for.

Initially, she didn't want to believe the words in front of her. Maybe the documents related to a different Bridget Moloney from a different Clooneven. Maybe Bridget hadn't tried to go to America. Maybe she'd ended up moving to Dublin or Liverpool or London.

But Jessie was deluding herself. In her heart, she knew she'd found the right woman.

On the bus home, she considered her options. Climbing down was against her nature. All her life, she'd waited for people to come to her. The trouble was, she really wanted to talk to Ger. Without him, she wouldn't have known about Johanna, Bridget and Norah. After ten minutes of shilly-shallying, she found her phone and sent a message: Have found out what became of Bridget. If you're still interested, let me know. BTW I was right about Etty.

It wasn't the most gracious of messages, but it would have to do.

Twenty minutes passed without a reply. School was finished for the day, so she assumed he was ignoring her. This was disappointing, and not just because she was keen to share her knowledge. She was disappointed that someone whose opinion she'd valued had turned out to be so petty.

And then, just as the bus was about to turn off for Clooneven, her phone pinged. Still very much interested. Sorry for late reply. Cleaning up after school sports. If you're around, I can meet you on the prom in ten minutes.

The first few minutes were as awkward as Jessie had feared. She sat on a bench, eating an ice cream. One scoop pistachio, one scoop salted caramel. Ger paced. He looked tired.

He conceded that he'd been too hasty to dismiss her theory about Etty. He was sorry for that. She could tell that he felt slightly foolish. She did too. She admitted she'd been too quick to take offence. All the while, they avoided eye contact.

'It was a stupid row,' she said, ice cream dripping onto her hand.

'It was,' he replied, sitting down beside her. 'But isn't that the problem with stupid arguments? They're the hardest ones to back down from.'

'You should have got in touch.'

'Maybe so, only I wasn't the one who stormed off in the rain. I'd have been happy to drive you to Etty's house.'

'I think "happy" is a bit of an exaggeration. As I recall …' Jessie stopped and looked him in the eye. 'Please can we not have another dumb argument?'

'I can agree to that,' said Ger. A long pause. 'I kind of missed our conversations … about Bridget and that, y'know?'

'Me too.'

Another long beat of silence followed. There they were, with thousands upon thousands of words available to them, and still they couldn't find the right ones. She crunched the last of her cone while trying to think of a way to move the conversation on.

Thankfully, Ger broke the silence. 'So what have you found?' he asked.

Jessie started by telling him about Bridget's letter to Norah. Given what she'd learnt a couple of hours previously, it was difficult to recount the story without feeling emotional.

'What a fantastic woman she must have been,' he said.

'A total star. And you should see the photo of Norah. I still have difficulty believing we're part of the same family. Anyway, this afternoon I managed to discover what happened next.'

In front of them, the sun was creeping across the sky. The beach had its distinctive end-of-day look: crumbling sandcastles, bins erupting with bottles, cans and wrappers, hundreds of footprints leading in all directions. It was hard to reconcile the calm, glistening water with the pitiless ocean that had torn apart a ship and taken the lives of more than eighty people. Because, as she explained to Ger, that was what had happened.

'There were seven survivors,' she said. 'Two women, four men and a baby girl. They were able to cling to part of the ship's hull until a rescue boat reached them.'

'By the sound of things,' he said, 'it was a miracle anyone made it ashore.'

'Oh, God, yeah. According to reports from the time, the men who pulled them from the water in Cohasset were lucky not to lose their own lives.' She took out her phone and passed it to him. 'I've got a few screenshots. Here's the list of survivors.'

'Patrick Hassett, Gort, County Galway, aged eighteen,' he read. 'Nancy Quinn, Ennistymon, County Clare, twenty-nine; Martin McDonagh, Claddaghduff, County Galway, thirty-eight; Michael Slattery, Galway city, nineteen; Tom O'Meara, Doonbeg, County Clare, thirty-one; Alice King, Tulla, County Clare, twenty; and Delia King, daughter, ten months.'

'Awful, isn't it? Because the tragedy happened so close to Boston –

Cohasset's only a short distance to the south, apparently – there were several newspaper reports. One said the survivors wouldn't let go of the men who rescued them, even after they were all back on dry land. If you swipe to the next image, you'll see Bridget's name.'

Ger moved on to the following page. 'List of the dead and lost,' he said. 'Bridget Moloney, Clooneven, County Clare, aged twenty-two; Eugene Hester, Ballinasloe, County Galway, forty-three; Maria Hester, wife, thirty-six; James Hester, son, sixteen; Annie Hester, daughter, twelve; John Talbot (Captain), Dublin, forty-eight …' He allowed his voice to fade away.

'No one knows the exact number of dead. According to the survivors, more than thirty people had already died on the journey. Oh, and one of the articles made it clear that this wasn't considered a particularly high number. It was just your regular common or garden coffin ship.' She took back her phone and put it into her bag. 'It's enough to make you scream, isn't it?'

'Except you can't get angry with bad weather.'

'But if the ship had been in a better state, there's a strong chance it would have survived the storm. The *Mary and Elizabeth* might have had a fancy name, but it was a heap of junk. The reports said it was rotten from top to bottom.'

'Okay,' he said. 'Point taken.'

'And you know what? Bridget didn't even get a proper grave. None of them did. The bodies washed ashore were all buried together. Seriously, you'd have to be raging. As Etty might say, I'm pure vexed.'

'She's going to be disappointed too.'

'She is. I'll drop up to Boherbreen later and tell her. We'd all hoped for a happy ending, but I guess it wasn't to be. I'd even planned on writing something about Bridget, only I'm not sure it would work now. Ah, well.' She sighed. 'I'll have more time to devote to being Lorna's dogsbody.'

'I thought you liked the café?'

'Oh, yes. Because my life's ambition was to earn the minimum wage in a coffee shop owned by my sister ... and to spend the rest of my day running errands and minding her children. I said as much to the career-guidance teacher in sixth year, and she said, "Fair play, Jessie Daly. That sounds like a worthwhile career."'

Ger laughed. 'Why don't you go back to Dublin then?' He raised a hand. 'Not that I'm telling you to go or anything.'

Jessie was about to sidestep the question. Then she changed her mind. Chances were she was making another mistake. Chances were she was giving him another reason to judge her. But she felt an urge to tell the truth.

'It's not that simple,' she said, before outlining how she'd fled Dublin and how her sister and parents had settled her debt.

When she'd finished, they sat in silence. Two blonde women in garish exercise clothes sat down on the next bench. A young boy on a black scooter zoomed past.

'I can see why you feel trapped,' said Ger. 'I'd be the same, but to be honest—'

'It's my own fault? Do you not think I know that? Have you any idea how rubbish it is when you can't blame other people for your troubles? And that's not all. I've managed to tear up the narrative on landlords. Who ever heard of the landlord being the good guy, huh?'

Jessie worried that she sounded too sharp. Perhaps it would be difficult to put their argument behind them. Perhaps her ears would be on constant alert for slights or putdowns.

That was when Ger did something unexpected. He touched her hand, not in a condescending way, or a let's-have-sex way, but in a friendly way. It was a gesture that said, 'I understand.'

'Sorry,' he said. 'I didn't mean to be unsympathetic. If I can roll out the clichés, this won't last for ever, you know. You'll move on soon enough. You've got to decide what you want.'

'Ah, Ger. Whatever the self-help books claim, good stuff doesn't happen just because you visualise it. I'll have the debt paid off by the autumn but getting started again in journalism is going to be tough, and I'm not sure I've got the stomach for it.'

Mostly Jessie avoided thinking about what she'd do when her job in the Seashell ended. She was starting to accept that her old life was gone. Doors had closed behind her, and she didn't have the strength to reopen them. Salvaging any part of her career would be difficult, and without regular work, she couldn't afford somewhere to live. Meanwhile, many of her friends and acquaintances were coupling up and moving on. Soon they'd be obsessed with babies, yoga classes and garden furniture. They'd begin reminiscing about the days when they were young and wild and effortlessly thin; the days when their boasts had been about body counts and three-day sessions, not promotions and engagement rings.

This realisation hadn't come in a sudden burst of enlightenment. Rather, it had arrived in a series of dull thuds. Occasionally, one of those thuds brought a reminder of what Phelim had said about the opportunities she'd squandered. He'd been right, and it hurt.

As Etty had predicted, her mother was pleased to have her at home. Maeve had been enthusiastic about what she'd uncovered and urged her to find out more about both sides of the family. Suspecting this was her mam's way of encouraging her to stay in Clooneven, Jessie felt grateful and guilty in equal measure. Being at home brought numerous benefits: ironed sheets, nutritious dinners and a drawerful of clean underwear among them. It also brought regression to the age she'd been when she'd last lived there. She was twenty-nine, not eighteen. Being back under her parents' roof was never going to feel right.

'Does Lorna really pay the minimum wage?' asked Ger.

'Uh-huh. I'm sure she pays a bit more to Ivana and Ashling. They're on the books, though. I'm strictly cash – or no cash – in hand, so she can do what she likes.'

'She gives you nothing?'

'Well, she gives me enough to pay my phone bill and buy the odd drink or pack of smokes.' She put up her hands. 'And, yeah, I know. It's a terrible, dirty habit. Other than that, everything goes towards paying what I owe to her and my folks.'

'Right. Just so we're entirely clear about this: officially you're not employed, which means Lorna doesn't have to pay any employers' tax. She holds on to most of what you earn, and she also keeps what you'd expect to get for minding your niece and nephew.'

'That's about the size of it,' said Jessie, staring down at her chipped toenail polish. God, she'd love a pedicure. 'Like you said, though, I've only myself to blame.'

'That's not what I'm getting at.'

'No?'

He turned, angling his body so he was speaking more to her, and less to the prom-walkers. 'I've been thinking about that guy, Dave. The "ice-cream salesman".'

Catching the scepticism in his voice, Jessie smiled. 'You've changed your tune. Does this mean you accept that he's dodgy?'

'To be fair, I've never met the fellow.'

'He's not Mr Snuffleupagus. He does exist.'

'If you remember your *Sesame Street* correctly, so does Mr Snuffleupagus. Anyway, back to the enigmatic Dave. I'll admit I still have a problem with your theory about him being Lorna's lover.'

'I've moved on from that idea,' said Jessie, trying not to make it sound like a climb-down. 'On the night of the … On the night I went to see Etty, I met him up near Lorna and Simon's house. He'd been talking to both of them. Also, I decided … well, he's a bit too Dublin for Lorna's tastes, if you get my drift.'

The more she thought about their encounter, the more uncomfortable she became. It was clear that Dave got a kick from knowing more about her than she knew about him, and she couldn't figure out why.

'Fair enough,' said Ger. 'Listen, you were right about Etty playing games with you. And I reckon that, in a way, you're right about Dave. What you've said about your arrangement with Lorna has confirmed my theory.' He hesitated. 'Nah, confirmed is too strong, but it certainly gives it more weight.'

'Go on.'

'I haven't seen their house since it was done up, but I gather they spent a fortune.'

'Two fortunes,' said Jessie. 'It's like something out of *Real Housewives of Beverly Hills*. And my sister's not exactly low-maintenance either.'

'If you look at their businesses, though, it's hard to see any of them bringing in huge money. Not when, for a lot of the year, Clooneven's a ghost town. I mean, the arcade and the shop probably have a decent turnover in the summer, but the season's short. And, yeah, the Americans are great, only they don't stay for long. They're more interested in the Cliffs of Moher and the Burren. So I was thinking that, maybe, Simon and Lorna owe money to Dave.'

'*Duh*,' she said, ears filling with the sound of pennies dropping. A few weeks ago, the idea of her sister being in debt would have seemed absurd. Taking everything into account, however, it made sense.

She slapped her cheek. 'I did wonder if a lack of cash might explain why they'd done nothing with the garden in Clevedon. And why Lorna couldn't bail me out on her own. Mam and Dad put up half the money.'

'Not to mention,' said Ger, 'why Dave, if that is his name, is hanging around.'

Jessie was annoyed with herself. She'd invented all sorts of explanations for Dave's connection to Simon and Lorna, but it had taken Ger to spot the truth. Everything came down to money in the end. That had been the case in Bridget's day, and it remained so now.

'Do you think he's a moneylender, then?' she asked.

'Obviously I can't say for sure, but I think it's the most likely explanation. Don't you?'

'I do,' she said.

Chapter 23

July 2019, Boston
Kaitlin

The breakthrough came on a warm Wednesday night when Clay was at work and Kaitlin had the opportunity to spend three uninterrupted hours in front of her laptop. She'd already tracked back through her paternal grandparents, Joseph and Shirley Wilson, and through Shirley's parents, Con and Meg McDonagh. Con's parents – her great-great-grandparents – had been Ray and Bertha McDonagh. Ray's parents had been Patrick and Finola McDonagh. All had been born in Massachusetts.

Once or twice, she'd considered putting an end to the search. There were, she told herself, more appropriate uses for her energy. Her relationship with Clay topped the list, but she also needed to do better at work. In a company that demanded all her brain power and commitment, she was increasingly distracted, lacklustre, uncommunicative. Because of the miscarriage, she'd been given some leeway, but continuing to take advantage of it would be a mistake.

Every morning, as she joined the dark-suited hordes on her way to Frobisher Hunter, she reminded herself of her good fortune. There she was, amid the steel and concrete towers, where the successful people worked. Where the money was. *This is what you wanted*, a voice would say. *This is what everyone aspires to.* Unfortunately, it was usually quashed by another, more insistent, voice. *Who are you kidding?* it replied. *This means nothing to you, and it never did.*

Some days, she imagined reaching the office and walking on by. She pictured herself boarding a bus or a boat. After a few days, she would contact Clay and her parents and tell them not to worry. Where precisely she'd go she wasn't sure. California, perhaps. Or Oregon. Or another country entirely. The destination didn't matter so long as it gave her the chance to begin again.

She'd spoken to Clay about her discontent. He'd listened sympathetically before pointing out that most of their contemporaries felt the same. 'It's the level we're at,' he'd said, as he stroked her hand. 'All the pressure, none of the power. Everyone says it gets better. We've got to knuckle down for a while. If we put in the hours, we'll get the rewards. That's how it works. You know that.'

Later, he'd returned to the subject. It was a mark of adulthood, he'd said: persisting even when the going was tough, *especially* when it was tough. It was also one of the things he admired about her, her ability to persevere. He would like to think it was a quality he shared.

That was Clay, so invested in his own career that he couldn't countenance Kaitlin questioning hers. She decided not to raise the subject again.

She'd said nothing further to her parents about her search. Nor had they asked. Her mother was organising a going-away party for Brian. Between that and planning their vacation in Maine, her scope for interfering was limited. There was no indication that either parent had spoken to Brian about what she was doing. Although Kaitlin chatted to her brother from time to time, their conversations remained excessively polite. They were more like acquaintances than siblings.

Frequently, she found herself thinking about Orla and Drew. Shay's death had been a tragedy, and she felt desperately sorry for his family. She could understand why they'd been hurt by Orla's behaviour. Truth to tell, though, her feelings didn't end there. She would never say it out loud, but the envy she'd felt when Orla had spoken about her first months in America had returned. She envied her aunt's sense of adventure and the abandon with which she'd lived. Kaitlin couldn't imagine taking so many risks. She also envied Orla's relationship with Drew. She'd always been sceptical about love at first sight, considering it a hokey concept belonging to drugstore novels and daytime soaps. Yet, to listen to Orla, not only was it possible, it was what you should expect.

What sort of person behaves like this? she asked herself. *What sort of person thinks such self-serving thoughts?* An unhappy one, she supposed.

If Orla and Drew's story had highlighted how little Kaitlin knew about her family, she was also starting to realise how little she knew about herself. She hadn't thought she wanted to be a mother until the prospect had been placed in front of her. She'd been convinced that she wanted a career with a big law firm, yet now the job felt more like a burden than a prize. What else didn't she know?

Every single day, she thought about Stella. As twisted as it might sound, she'd begun to wonder if she'd lost her baby for a reason. If her body had rejected the little girl because it had known she wouldn't be born into the right circumstances. Then Kaitlin would round on herself. There was no logic to her meanderings. Bad things happened, and she had to accept that, for once, something bad had happened to her.

It was while she was contemplating all of this that the 1860 census delivered the information she'd been hoping for. It told her that while

Patrick McDonagh had been born in Boston in 1852, his parents, Martin and Alice, had been born in Ireland. On the night of the census, Martin had been fifty years old, Alice thirty-two. He was described as a dock worker. Unlike her husband, Alice could read and write. The couple also had a twelve-year-old daughter, Delia, who'd been born in Ireland.

A fizz of excitement rising in her chest, Kaitlin turned to the records for the Catholic Archdiocese of Boston. While she'd hoped to find a baptism notice for Patrick, and possibly for other children, what she read surprised her. Martin and Alice had got married in Boston in 1850. Before her marriage, the bride had been Alice King. She was a widow, Martin a widower.

This discovery made Kaitlin pause. If she was no expert in Irish history, she knew a little about what had happened in the mid to late 1840s. Delia had been born in 1847. Black '47, the Irish called it because of the scale of the destruction and suffering. For a few moments, Kaitlin didn't move. This was what she'd hoped for: definitive evidence that her own family had escaped poverty and found shelter and succour in America. Now that it was in front of her, she found the knowledge overpowering. She was glad she was on her own.

She waited until she felt calm again before opening her notepad and sketching out a basic family tree:

Alice King – Martin McDonagh
Married 1850
|
Patrick McDonagh born 1852 – Finola Ryan
Married 1875
|
Raymond (Ray) McDonagh born 1880 – Bertha Lankford
Married 1903
|

Cornelius (Con) McDonagh born 1904 – Margaret (Meg) Bannon
Married 1935

|

Shirley McDonagh born 1938 – Joseph Wilson
Married 1961

|

Kevin Wilson born 1966 – Susan McGrath
Married 1987

|

Kaitlin Wilson born 1989
Brian Wilson born 1991

Amid the fog of detail in her brain, Kaitlin remembered one website in particular. She scrolled through her folder of notes and found the address. The site had gathered hundreds of ships' manifests and, if you were lucky, could offer a few facts about when your ancestors had arrived in the United States. She decided to try Alice first. Hers was a slightly more unusual name, which meant she might be easier to locate.

The results revealed that twenty-year-old Alice King had reached America in July 1848. She had been accompanied by Delia King, aged ten months. There had also been a Martin McDonagh onboard the ship, the *Mary and Elizabeth*. He was born in the same year as the man Alice would later marry, so Kaitlin had to assume he was the same Martin. What startled her was that only four other names were listed. Even though she'd read that considerable numbers had died on the Famine boats, it seemed unlikely that just seven people had survived the voyage from Galway.

A suspicion entered her head. She opened another window and searched for 'Mary and Elizabeth ship 1848'.

Her theory was confirmed.

For the next half an hour, she read about the ship that had run aground and broken into pieces near Cohasset. Some bodies were washed ashore, many of them cut and mutilated by the jagged rocks. Others were swept away, never to be found. A priest was summoned from Boston to perform the funerals. While the rescuers were hailed for their heroism, all spoke of their regret at failing to save more lives. Yet, somehow, through a combination of determination and luck, a tiny band had lived, among them Alice, Delia and Martin. Along with the others, they were taken to a nearby boarding house to recover. A reporter who'd met two of the men struck a cautionary note. *Given the scale of this catastrophe,* he wrote, *it is unlikely that these misfortunate souls will ever be the same. Such an unseaworthy vessel should never have set sail. That it did was an act of villainous negligence.*

Kaitlin had expected that if and when she found the family's Irish connection, most of her work would be done. Now she saw that her task had a way to go. In particular, she was fascinated by Alice, her fourth-great-grandmother. At an age when Kaitlin had still expected Susan to do her laundry, Alice had been a mother and a widow. She'd survived a famine and a shipwreck, and made a new life in America.

Because she knew so little about Alice's background, she decided to seek help on a message board. There was a strong chance that nothing would come of it, but if someone else was interested in the *Mary and Elizabeth*, they might be able to provide information:

Hello, I'm writing this from Boston, Mass. I was wondering if any of you know anything about the Irish ship, the Mary and Elizabeth, which broke up during a storm off the coast of Massachusetts in 1848. It had set sail from Galway two months earlier. There were seven survivors, among them my great-(x4)-grandparents, Alice King and Martin McDonagh. Alice's baby daughter, Delia, also survived. Alice and Martin weren't married to each other when they left Ireland. I can't tell whether both were already widowed when they boarded the M&E or whether their original spouses were killed in the shipwreck. I'm overwhelmed by the discovery and would welcome any information about the ship or its passengers. Thank you.

It was only after she'd posted the message that Kaitlin realised there must be other people out there who'd had relatives onboard. But would any of them be aware of that? After all, it had taken considerable work, and a pinch of luck, for her to get this far. Even if they did know about the *Mary and Elizabeth*, it was unlikely they would come across her post. Unlikely, she thought, but not impossible.

Chapter 24

July 1848, Cohasset
Bridget

What Bridget saw first was the sunlight. It crept through the thin curtains and across the panelled white walls and wooden floor. The room had a high ceiling. There was a dark wooden chair and a small table with a porcelain jug. Two paintings hung on the far wall, one of the sea, the other of a woman with a long neck. She'd never been in such a place before, somewhere so ordered and pristine. Nor had she slept in such a bed. The sheet that covered her was as soft as a rose petal, as was the blanket that lay on top. The pillows beneath her head were firm.

The silence was shattered by a crying baby, the thin wail of a small girl. Norah wasn't far away. In the next room, perhaps. Bridget needed to go to her, but when she moved, pain cracked through her body. Up her legs it ran, and down her arms. In some places, it was no more than a dull ache. In others it was sharper, more insistent. Her shoulders were heavy, and when she looked at her hands, she saw that they were raw with blisters. Her arms were black with bruises.

Still, she had to get up and comfort her daughter.

Then the truth broke through. The cry was that of a younger child, not Norah. And Norah was in Ireland with Mary Ellen and Thomas. This place, with the white walls and the soft bed, wasn't Ireland. She attempted to take a deep breath, but a spasm of pain hit her chest. She closed her eyes.

When she woke again, the light had dimmed. Two people sat at the end of the bed, an elderly man with wings of grey hair and a younger woman. The woman, who wore a blue and white dress, had shiny dark hair and a round face. Slowly, Bridget rubbed her eyes, which were crusted with sleep. Noticing her gesture, they smiled and exchanged a glance. The man, whom she saw was a priest, rose slowly. Then he picked up his chair and moved to the head of the bed.

'*Conas atá tú?*' he said, as he sat down again.

Briefly, she wondered if she was at home, after all. Why else would he speak Irish? There was, though, something strange about his voice. He pronounced the words too deliberately, as if scared of stumbling over them.

He tried again. '*An cuimhin leat cad a tharla?*'

The honest answer to his second question was that she remembered little. Images danced through her head. She had thought she was going to die, but following the example of some of the others, she'd clung to the wreck of the ship. She recalled screaming into the wind, screaming at Delia to keep holding on, and screaming at the rescue boat which she feared wouldn't see them through the waves and the spray. Whatever had happened next had been stripped from her memory.

'*An bhfuil aon Béarla agat?*' he asked.

'Yes,' she told him, 'I can speak English.'

'That's a relief,' replied the priest, who had the brown face of a field-worker. 'We weren't certain. I rarely have the opportunity to speak Irish these days, and I've grown slightly slow. At least we'll be able to understand each other.'

'Where am I?' she asked, her mouth dry as slate.

'You're in Mrs Florence Stanhope's boarding house in Cohasset, Massachusetts.' He gestured towards the woman, who smiled again. 'My name is Father Paul Garrity. Oh, and you're welcome to America.'

'I …' she started. Her jaw ached.

'You were pulled from the ocean. You and your baby. Do you remember?'

Bridget went to speak again. Her voice cracked.

Mrs Stanhope got to her feet, picked up the porcelain jug and poured water into a cup. 'You need a drink,' she said, 'but take care or you'll be sick. It's four days since you've had anything to eat, and you swallowed a lot of seawater. And don't worry. Now that you're awake, we'll get you something to eat. Something light tonight, I think.'

Four days, she thought. She'd been here for four days. With difficulty, she propped herself up on the pillows. Once more, she felt a surge of pain. She noticed she was wearing a white nightgown. Someone, presumably Mrs Stanhope, had dressed her. She had difficulty holding the cup but managed to take a few sips. No drink on earth could have tasted sweeter.

Her mind working more quickly, she realised that when Father Garrity had spoken of a baby, he'd meant Delia. He assumed she was Delia's mother.

'Is Delia alive?' she asked.

'She's in the next room,' said Mrs Stanhope. 'One of the other survivors saw her and told us your names. "That's Delia King," he said, "and her mother's name is Alice." What a brave girl Delia was, holding on until the two of you were rescued. You should be very proud of her.'

Bridget knew she should explain. *You think I'm Delia's mother,* she should say. *But I'm not. I was about to pass her to Alice, only Alice disappeared under the waves.* Instead, she asked another question. 'How is she?'

'Oh, she's thriving! If only you had seen her crawling around the room earlier. She'll be walking before you know it. Admittedly, she was weak when she first arrived, but the doctor examined her – we have a splendid doctor here in Cohasset – and he's satisfied she'll make a full recovery. Isn't that magnificent news?'

'It is.' She hesitated before asking her next question. 'How many of us are there?'

'How many survivors, do you mean?' asked Father Garrity.

'Yes.'

'Only seven, I'm afraid.'

Bridget gasped. He went on to explain that no other child had survived and only one other woman. 'Nancy Quinn,' he said. 'She's also from County Clare. She's …' it was his turn to hesitate '… not well. From what we can understand, she's lost her husband and two daughters, may the Lord have mercy on them. She's keen to go back to Ireland.'

Nancy Quinn. While the name wasn't familiar, Bridget assumed the woman's face would be. If Nancy was the only other woman to survive, Alice – the real Alice – must be dead. She shivered, prompting a look of concern from Mrs Stanhope.

'And the men?' asked Bridget, before taking another sip of water.

'They're in better health,' said Father Garrity. 'In fact, two have already left for Deer Island.'

Bridget must have appeared confused because Mrs Stanhope intervened to explain that this was a quarantine station in Boston Harbour. Her tone made it clear that she didn't approve of the men's transfer. 'We gather there was a considerable amount of illness on the ship,' she said. 'The doctor who examined Delia believes she had typhus. That must have been a frightful worry for you.'

It's not too late, Bridget told herself. *You can tell them you're not her mother. You can claim you were confused.*

'The doctor thinks that more people might have lived if they'd been stronger,' added Father Garrity. 'The poor souls were in no condition to fight such a terrible storm. No wonder so many lost their lives.'

Tell them. They will understand. 'Is there a chance that anyone else will be found?' she asked.

'Alas, no. There's a vigil near the shore in the hope that more bodies might be recovered, but even that's not likely now.' He pinched the bridge of his nose. 'I'm here to conduct the funerals. I live in Quincy. It's not far away. Very few of the people in this town are Catholic. They're fine people, all the same,' he added, as though this was in doubt.

From the next room, they heard a shout. Delia.

'Are you strong enough to see her?' asked Mrs Stanhope. 'I should imagine she would be delighted to see you. We were reluctant to bring her in before this, for fear she became upset.'

This is your final chance. Tell them. 'I'd like that,' said Bridget. 'Thank you.'

When Florence Stanhope left the room, Father Garrity urged Bridget not to fret about anything. The locals were generous, he said, and would provide clean clothes and anything else she required.

'Unfortunately, your own dress was badly torn,' he said, 'but Mrs Stanhope did find this in the pocket.'

From his own pocket, he produced a shell. Norah's shell.

Bridget felt tears at the back of her eyes. She took the shell and passed it from one hand to the other. She closed her fist around it, making her blisters sting. 'Thank you for keeping it safe,' she said. 'It's all I have left.'

'That's not true, Alice. You have Delia, and what could be more important than your beautiful girl?' He turned towards the door. 'Here she is, bless her.'

There were bandages on Delia's arms and a thin cut on one cheek, but otherwise she appeared unscathed. She was wearing a white cotton dress and the tiniest socks Bridget had ever seen. A lady's daughter couldn't have looked prettier.

'Look at you,' she said to the little girl in Mrs Stanhope's arms. 'All dressed up in your finery.'

'The clothes belonged to my own daughter,' said Mrs Stanhope, 'and there are more where they came from, aren't there, Delia?'

The baby made a hiccuping sound, as if she might cry. Bridget felt a flutter of panic. Suppose Delia failed to recognise her? Suppose she whimpered and wriggled? They would know then that Bridget was an imposter.

'Hello, little one,' she said, holding out her arms and praying the baby didn't make strange.

Delia was wary, her brown eyes uncertain. Bridget's body tensed under the scrutiny of Father Garrity and Mrs Stanhope. *What am I doing?* she thought. *I might have fooled the adults, but I can't fool a ten-month-old.*

Then, as if her memories of the days and nights on the boat had come back to her, Delia stretched out her short arms and settled into Bridget's embrace.

Mrs Stanhope wiped away a tear. 'Isn't that wonderful to see?' she said to the priest, who agreed that it was.

Bridget inhaled the scent of Delia's freshly washed hair and kissed her face. She couldn't turn back now. Her words and actions were a bell that couldn't be un-rung. She'd lost her own daughter, but another child had been given to her. A child with whom she had a bond. A child who'd twice cheated death. Her mind returned to the *Mary and Elizabeth* and to Alice's claims that Bridget had saved Delia's life. If it wasn't true then, it was now. She'd saved her from drowning.

Alice would have wanted this, she said to herself.

Afterwards, when Delia was asleep, Mrs Stanhope assured Bridget that they could both stay until they had the strength to move on.

'And when you've recovered sufficiently,' said Father Garrity, 'you can go back to Ireland if that's what you'd prefer. Like I explained to you, it's what Nancy – Mrs Quinn – hopes to do.'

Bridget couldn't go back. Not because she was afraid to take to the sea again, or because there was nothing for her at home. She couldn't return to Ireland with a baby girl who didn't belong to her. Instead she would go to Boston. She would find work, find her brother, and take care of Delia as best she could.

She wept then for Alice, a brave woman who'd faced every day with enthusiasm and who'd been steadfast in her belief that their lives would improve.

'Thank you,' she said, the words barely audible through her tears, 'but Delia and I will try our luck in America.'

Chapter 25

Two months later, Boston

At the start, becoming Alice was a challenge. People in Cohasset would address Bridget by her new name, and she would fail to respond. Or they'd ask a question about her life in Ireland, and she'd take too long to answer. By the time she left Florence Stanhope's care, however, she'd perfected her act. She was Alice Ann King, widow of Bernard, from Tulla, County Clare. Her daughter was Delia Mary. She'd learnt to shave two years off her age and to say little about her upbringing. Slipping into Alice's identity became as easy as slipping into the new dresses provided by Mrs Stanhope.

She'd assumed that when she reached Boston she'd be able to revert to her real name. True, her paperwork was in Alice's name, but she would think of ways around that. She'd underestimated the diligence of Father Garrity, who'd arranged for her to stay with an Irish family. As far as they were concerned, she was Alice.

'It's only for a week or two,' he emphasised. 'The Russells scarcely have room for their own family. They're good Catholics, though, and they wouldn't want to see the two of you on the streets.'

Peggy Russell was a stout woman with a puff of orange hair, a reedy voice and a burning need to warn Bridget that 'her kind' weren't popular in Boston.

'You shouldn't expect much sympathy,' she said. She also maintained that Bridget would find it impossible to get work as a domestic servant. If being Irish was an impediment, being Irish with a baby was too high a barrier for any young woman to scale. 'No,' she concluded, 'the best you can do is find yourself another husband.'

Delia, just past her first birthday and starting to take small, uncertain steps, chose that moment to fall over and bump her head on the hard floor. She let out a high wail, Bridget dashed to her aid, and Peggy folded her arms across her chest in a way that suggested her point had been well made.

As she tried to pacify the child, Bridget wondered again about the wisdom of her decision. What, though, if she'd been honest? Where would Delia be now? Would she have been sent to a home? Or would she have been given to a family who knew nothing about her or where she came from?

The Russells lived in the North End, an area of tenements, lodging houses and warehouses. Its streets teemed with Irish faces, more faces than she had ever seen. They dug trenches and worked in stables and textile mills. They cleaned houses and cared for children. They came from Kerry and Tipperary, Donegal and Armagh. For the first time, Bridget heard how many different Irish accents there were. Someone from Wexford or Louth sounded as unusual to her as someone from Texas or New York.

Along with her husband, Ned, Peggy had been in America for twenty-five years and, in her own eyes at least, was of a different standing from the Irish who'd landed in more recent times. That her family of seven lived in the same ramshackle conditions as the new arrivals didn't weaken her conviction. She was also blessed with a religious fervour that Bridget had rarely seen in Clooneven. While she railed against sinfulness of all types, her strongest condemnation was reserved for an area known as the Black Sea, which was home to many of Boston's gaming houses, dance halls and brothels.

'It's the women who need to take most of the blame,' she said. 'The men can't help themselves, but the women have neither modesty nor shame. I look at them and say to myself, *Is this what we've become?*'

While never as optimistic as Alice, Bridget hadn't expected to find hostility in Boston. Her time in Cohasset had bolstered that view. Those weeks had been misleading. In a seaside town, she'd been a novelty, a blameless young widow in need of support. In the city, she reverted to being another unwanted body. Under Peggy's tutelage, she soon learnt more about her status and about how her own people were to blame.

'The trouble with the newer Irish,' said her landlady, 'is that they're determined to bring their worst habits with them. They'll have to realise that begging and pilfering aren't acceptable here. And as for all those men going to grog shops and saloons, if I had my way, they'd be sent back to Ireland on the next boat. Decent American people aren't accustomed to public intoxication.'

'But most people don't behave like that,' said Bridget. 'And considering what they went through at home, is it any surprise that their behaviour has been affected?'

'They've got to leave Ireland behind them. My American friends say it to me. "Peggy," they say, "Ireland isn't sending us its best people any more. Why is that?"'

To Bridget, a considerable number of the newcomers seemed too gentle for the streets of Boston. They were country people who, until they'd arrived in the city, had known only the company of others like themselves. Her heart hurt when she came across a lost-looking man or a frightened woman.

Despite Peggy's sermons, the first time she saw an advertisement that stated Irish people weren't welcome, she inhaled with shock.

WANTED

A reliable woman to take care of a small boy in Brookline.
Good recommendations as to character and capacity demanded.
Positively No Irish Need Apply.

After that, she saw the notices everywhere. Some outlined the employer's requirements in more diplomatic terms. Rather than saying that Irish people weren't welcome, the family emphasised their preference for a Protestant girl. Others were more specific still. The position was for a German Protestant, they said, or a Scotch Protestant.

Nevertheless, Bridget continued to look for work. Leaving Delia with Peggy, she presented herself at door after door. Sometimes, the rejections were polite. More often, they were accompanied by advice. 'Bostonians are generous,' one woman said, 'and we know life has been very cruel to the Irish. That's why we've sent money. But you're not wanted here.'

Others were scornful. 'You're taking food from American mouths,' a man told her, 'and you're lowering standards. You should go back to where you came from.'

She attempted to press her case. She was a hard worker, she said. She could read and write. She was willing to clean and cook and take care of children. After her stay in Cohasset, she was in robust health. Didn't she deserve a chance?

Every fruitless day lowered her spirits further. She'd return to the Russells' house where Peggy would narrow her eyes and mutter about young women needing to heed the advice of their elders and betters. To this end, the names of various men were mentioned. Almost without exception, they were the sons of families who'd been in Boston for decades. Decent people. The problem was, Bridget didn't want to be paired with a man she barely knew. It was only eighteen months since John Joe's death, and she still sought solace in her memories of him. The thought of being touched by another man, especially one favoured by Peggy, repulsed her.

She regularly thought of how America would have disappointed Alice. This mean-spirited, stone-hearted city wasn't what they'd hoped for.

As the days became weeks, Bridget's despair deepened. Peggy's warnings about limits to the family's generosity became more frequent. Not only that, she began musing about the differences between Bridget and Delia.

'She doesn't look like you. Not a bit,' she'd say. 'Her with the big brown eyes and the fair hair, and you with blue eyes and red hair. And that tiny nose. She didn't get that from you, that's for sure. She must take after her late father, does she?'

Bridget assured herself that the woman couldn't know what had happened on the *Mary and Elizabeth*. Even so, the questions made her anxious. Uninformed as she was about the law in Boston, she had the feeling that, no matter where you went, stealing a dead woman's baby was a serious crime.

There was another reason she needed to leave the Russells. For as long as she remained, searching for Francie was impossible. Once, shortly after she'd arrived in Boston, she'd thought she'd seen him on Hanover Street. She'd called his name, softly at first, and then with more vigour. 'Francie! Francie Markham from Boherbreen!' The man had stared at her as though she was simple-minded before giving a slow shake of the head. She had smiled and apologised. It struck her then that she didn't know if her brother remained in Boston. He might be a thousand miles away. He might be dead.

There was a nip of frost in the morning air as she made her way to the Edgecombes' house on Beacon Hill. This was, she feared, a futile journey, but her love of the area had won out. The maze of cobbled streets, the grace of the red-brick houses, the grandeur of the State House, the trim grass and towering trees of the Common: this was the America she'd dreamt of. Every inch was bright and clean. She'd also been lured by the prospect, however slim, of gaining entry to the Edgecombes' home. Just once, she'd like to see inside one of the city's most sophisticated houses.

When she arrived at the address, the building in front of her was even more impressive than she'd anticipated. Unlike many houses in the neighbourhood, it had a front garden with thin black railings. Steps ran up to the front door, which was painted the rich green of a duck's head. A white column stood at either side.

The notice had made clear that the family required a housemaid who could also serve meals. If she was honest, Bridget knew nothing about either of these tasks. How could someone who'd spent most of her days in a one-room cabin know anything about the intricacies of a grand house or the correct way to serve a lavish meal? She decided this wouldn't stop her pressing her case.

Every day in Boston taught her something about how people lived their lives – and about how they perceived others. About what was deemed respectable and what was considered backward. One of the lessons she'd absorbed was this: no matter where they lived, the rich were allowed to occupy more space. The poor were expected to take up as little room as possible. She'd also learnt to recognise Irish people. Not by their worn clothes or thin frames, for clothes could be changed and frames could fill out, but rather by their distinctive faces. They had blue-white skin, narrow mouths and a wary, watchful look, as if permanently worried about what would happen next.

The woman who answered the door shared none of these characteristics, but as soon as she spoke, it was clear that she was Irish. Bridget explained why she was there.

'You're not the sort of person we're looking for,' said the woman, who had large grey eyes, a thin nose and a general air of satisfaction. 'You don't have the experience Mrs Edgecombe requires.'

'I'm a quick learner. If you show me something once, you won't need to do it again.'

'I've told you. The answer is no.'

Even though this was what she'd expected, Bridget's eyes watered. 'That's fine,' she said. 'I'd hoped there might be something. It's a lovely house, the nicest I've ever seen.'

The woman softened. 'I'm from Tipperary, myself,' she said. 'I've been in America these past fifteen years. And they haven't always been easy years, let me tell you.'

'You're lucky to work somewhere like this, though.'

The woman nodded before introducing herself as Mrs Johanna Hogan. 'You look like you need to warm up,' she said. 'You can spend five minutes in the kitchen. It's quiet at this hour of the day, and you won't be disturbing anyone.'

Although she didn't get to view as much of the house as she would have liked, Bridget was in awe of what she did see. Like Mrs Stanhope's boarding house, it was clean and quiet, but it was also far more luxurious, with ceilings so high that even a giant could hold up his head. The walls were pale gold, while elaborate rugs covered the polished wooden floors. She felt she should say something about their surroundings but couldn't find the right words.

The kitchen was larger than her family's cottage in Boherbreen, and its shelves were stacked with bowls and pans of every size. A variety of unfamiliar implements hung on the walls. Warm light fell through the window. A girl a year or two younger than Bridget was kneading dough. And the smell? Oh, the smell. It was of spices and ham and freshly baked bread and all the good things in the world.

'I was about to have a cup of tea,' said Mrs Hogan. 'Will you join me?'

Surprised by the offer, Bridget almost declined. 'Yes, please,' she said eventually.

They sat at one end of the large table, and within a minute or two the girl, whose name was Lydia, produced tea in delicate china cups. The taste, too, was delicate, unlike anything Bridget had come across before.

'My mother was called Johanna,' she said to Mrs Hogan. 'It's a lovely name.'

The housekeeper peered over the top of her cup. 'When did she die?'

'Two years ago. Her anniversary was last month.' The kitchen's heat was spreading through Bridget's body, and she began to relax. 'My younger brother died a short while afterwards. And then my husband.'

'I can understand why you left,' said Mrs Hogan. 'My own family are all in America, thank God.' She was about to continue when a tall woman with fair hair entered the room. The woman had perfect posture, as though her head was held up by an invisible string, and she was wearing a deep blue dress with a neat white collar. Plain as the dress was, Bridget could tell it had been very expensive.

The housekeeper got to her feet, a move Bridget quickly followed.

'I'm sorry,' she said, feeling her face colouring. 'I don't want to be a nuisance. I'll go, if you'd like.'

'Stay where you are,' said the new woman. 'I'm Charlotte Edgecombe. Lydia, may I have a cup of tea, please?'

Mrs Edgecombe offered her hand. Bridget, feeling uncharacteristically timid, took it. The skin was as soft as she had expected. By contrast, her own hands were rough, the legacy of both hard physical labour and the shipwreck.

Mrs Hogan, who appeared at ease in her employer's company, outlined why Bridget was there and what she'd been telling her. 'While Alice isn't suitable for the current position,' she said, 'I felt she would benefit from five minutes in the warmth.'

'Goodness,' said Mrs Edgecombe, her face tight with concern. 'I've read about the situation in Ireland. It sounds frightful. And, of course, we're all aware of the numbers arriving here in recent months. What I find impossible to fathom is how entire families could die. There must have been some assistance, surely.'

Bridget could have spent the day explaining how the landlords, politicians and relief schemes had allowed them to starve. At the end of it all, however, she feared the elegant woman on the other side of the table wouldn't understand. She was from a different world. A world of smooth linens and silk dresses and perfumed tea. A world where the important people were on your side and didn't view you as disposable. The simplest option was to tell her own story. Well, not her actual story, but a version that brought together her old and new identities. When she reached the part about also having a young daughter, she nearly called her Norah. But her own name was Alice now, and Alice's daughter was called Delia.

Charlotte Edgecombe told Bridget that, while she'd read about the *Mary and Elizabeth*, she hadn't expected any of the survivors to remain in America. 'But here you are,' she added.

'Yes, here I am.'

She finished her tale with reluctance, not because she took any pleasure from talking about her struggles, but because she knew the time had come to leave.

'Where are you living?' asked Mrs Edgecombe, as she placed her cup on the saucer.

'In the North End with a family called Russell,' Bridget replied, before describing the situation there.

'And is that where Delia is at the moment?'

'Yes.'

'Would you excuse us for a minute, please, Alice?' she said. 'I want to have a word with Mrs Hogan. And you too, Lydia We can talk in the parlour.'

Bridget suspected that Mrs Edgecombe would give her money. While money was always welcome, she didn't want charity. She wanted to work. She wanted somewhere to belong.

After five minutes or so, the two older women came back and sat down again.

'I believe I may have a solution,' said Mrs Edgecombe. 'As Mrs Hogan has pointed out, you don't have the necessary experience for the position we advertised. However, Lydia has been with us for some time and is ready to step up and assume more responsibility. This means that we need a kitchen maid who can also take on other chores around the house. The space we have for servants isn't as large as I would like, but it's adequate.' She paused and smiled, revealing small, bone-white teeth. 'I'm being impulsive here, but would you be interested in the kitchen maid's position, Alice?'

Bridget replied immediately. 'Oh, yes, Mrs Edgecombe. Yes.' Then, she chastised herself. What about Delia? She hadn't mentioned Delia.

'Very well. I shall leave Mrs Hogan to sort out the arrangements. Cook will be here presently, and you'll have to take most of your instructions from her.'

'I'm sorry,' said Bridget. 'I should have asked about my daughter. I can't—'

'No, I'm sorry,' said Mrs Edgecombe. 'I should have made it plain that Delia must come with you. While it's unusual for one of our staff to bring a young child with them, in this case we shall have to make an exception. You say she's a very well-behaved little girl, so I'm sure she can stay in the kitchen with you. You'll have to confer with Mrs Hogan and the others.'

Two days later, Bridget said goodbye to the Russells. Toting Delia and the small bag of possessions given to them in Cohasset, she returned to the Edgecombes' house on Mount Vernon Street. Mrs Hogan showed them to their room, which was in the attic. Compared to the splendour downstairs, the furnishings were Spartan. There was a bed, a chair, a washstand but no carpet or decoration. In one corner, there was a bell, which would sound when she was required downstairs.

Bridget was a little confused about how her new arrangement would work, a little nervous about being part of such a grand house. Most of all, though, she was excited. Finally, she felt as if a door had opened on the wonders of America.

Chapter 26

Never before had Bridget been forced to learn so much so quickly. Every day was a series of requests and demands. She became accustomed to using the cast-iron range and the numerous strange utensils: the fish kettle, the cake moulds, the infinite varieties of knife and fork. She learnt about foods she'd never seen before: lobster, cranberries, lemons. Quite often, she'd find herself staring in bewilderment at a fruit or fish. 'What are you?' she'd say. 'And what am I supposed to do with you?'

The one thing she never had to fret about was running out of food. There was enough in the Edgecombes' larder to satisfy the entire town of Clooneven.

She found herself wondering if it would be possible to take items that wouldn't perish – a loaf of sugar, say, or a pot of jam or a package of cured meat – parcel them up and send them to Norah. Her more sensible side knew this was an outlandish idea, and one that would get her into trouble, but still it lingered.

Much of her day was spent in the small scullery to the side of the kitchen. Here, with Delia at her feet, she peeled and chopped. When not preparing food, she cleaned. Cook insisted that everything be scoured with camphor, lye and scalding water. One spot of grease on the floor, and she'd sigh and tut and ask if she had to do everything herself.

Bridget had also to help in the laundry, a room she found impossibly hot and steamy. Sometimes, she would feel a complaint rising in her throat. Then she would remember that earlier in the year she'd worried about freezing to death and she would swallow her grievance.

Cook's real name was Mrs Eula Miller, and she was American through and through. (Or so she liked to claim. It seemed to Bridget that if you went back far enough almost everyone was from somewhere else. As far as she could tell, the only true Americans were the Indians, and they were treated little better than Henry Frobisher's tenants.) Mrs Miller devoted a portion of every day to telling her how lucky she was. In some houses, she said, the kitchen was in the basement, and the smoke-filled air made the staff ill. In others, the domestics only ever got to eat leftovers. Thankfully, she doted on Delia, and had no quarrel with the child's presence in the scullery.

'Keep her away from the range. That's all I ask,' she said.

Cook vied with Mrs Hogan for household supremacy. The contest manifested itself in various ways, the most obvious being the battle for Mrs Edgecombe's ear. On occasion, Bridget found herself becoming involved.

'What sort of area is Tipperary?' Cook asked, about her rival's birthplace. 'Are there many educated people?'

Bridget replied, truthfully, that she couldn't say because she'd never been there.

On another occasion, Mrs Hogan asked if she'd ever heard Cook speak about her husband. 'I haven't,' she said, 'and I'd be very surprised if a Mr Miller ever existed.'

If the two had a common devotion to Mrs Edgecombe, they shared a distaste for her husband. Their criticism was rarely voiced. It didn't have to be. Their response to his name was enough. Mrs Hogan would throw her eyes heavenwards, and Cook would give an impatient wave of her hand.

Frederick Edgecombe was a substantial man with ruddy cheeks and bushy side whiskers. He looked to be at least ten years older than his wife. In the main, he avoided domestic matters. Occasionally, however, when annoyed by some oversight or other, he would summon one of them to his study and scatter orders like whitethorn petals on a breezy day. Bridget had no particular quarrel with him, and she suspected that Mrs Hogan and Mrs Miller would resent anyone who intruded on their domain.

The Edgecombes had two sons, aged twelve and eight. Delia was intrigued by the presence of humans who, while much bigger than her, were not yet fully formed. She tended to stare at them in silent awe before scuttling back to the scullery.

Bridget's hours were long and irregular. She received one half day off each week; which day depended on how busy they were. Mr and Mrs Edgecombe entertained frequently. The dinners were elaborate occasions with multiple courses and abundant wine. On the most special nights, the guests drank champagne. By the end of them, Cook's face was the colour of plum jelly and Bridget's hands were white and wrinkled.

Because this was the first time she'd been in close contact with very rich people, she enjoyed studying the family. She soon appreciated that, aside from the material comforts provided by their wealth, the main difference between the Edgecombes and anyone else she'd known was their expectation that life would always be good. In their world, there was a solution for every problem, a remedy for every ailment. If you wanted something badly enough, it would eventually be yours. They would grow ever more prosperous, as would America.

The family had been in Massachusetts for more than a hundred years. While their wealth was based on shipping, they'd also expanded into leather and textiles. Mr Edgecombe's grandparents had lived in the North End but, according to Cook, all the best people had abandoned the area because it had been overrun by the Irish. She said this in such a matter-of-fact manner that Bridget found it amusing rather than offensive. In truth, she understood why rich people would prefer to live on Beacon Hill. She doubted there were prettier streets anywhere in the world. What captivated her was how the neighbourhood was constantly changing. Be it as small as a fresh window box or as significant as land being cleared for houses, there was always something new to see.

Charlotte Edgecombe told her that once upon a time the hill had been much steeper, but that builders had cut sixty feet off the top.

Bridget thought Mrs Edgecombe was teasing her. 'No!' she said. 'You can't change a hill just because you'd like to build more houses.'

'In America, you can do whatever you want,' said Cook, from the other end of the kitchen table. 'There's even talk of filling in the Back Bay so people can live there.'

Bridget thought, as she often did, how much John Joe would have loved this strange place.

In January, it snowed. The feathery flakes gathered and folded themselves around the city until everything was white. The snow encased the trees and bushes and became so deep that a small person like Delia could disappear. The sky, too, was a brilliant white and, save for the children's shouts of delight, everything was quiet.

All Bridget could think of was Norah.

Less than a year earlier, they had played in the snow together. Norah had thanked her, as if the magical substance had been her personal creation. They'd been barefoot then. Already, that was hard to fathom. Bridget had warm, comfortable boots now and a substantial winter coat.

Of course she played with Delia. They crunched and slithered and laughed at how beautiful everything was. When they were back indoors, though, and Delia was sipping a restorative cup of warm milk, Bridget had to force back her tears.

Delia was a lovely child, straightforward in her likes and dislikes. She was polite and rarely drew attention to herself. But, and Bridget hated herself for thinking this, she wasn't as clever as Norah. At the same age, her daughter had known more words. She'd been friendlier and more inquisitive. When she'd been quiet, Bridget had sensed it was because she knew that making a fuss was pointless. When Delia was quiet, she feared it was because she had nothing to say.

She wondered if any part of Delia remembered the real Alice. If sometimes she looked at her and thought, *Who are you? And what have you done with my proper mother?* Then Bridget would be forced to accept the truth. What she really wondered was if Norah remembered her.

She considered writing to Hackett's Cross to let them know she was alive. One letter, that was all. Then her pragmatism returned. She had left that life behind, and a letter might well be thrown into the fire. She had been gifted a new life with a new child and would have to make the most of it.

After the snow had melted, she redoubled her efforts to find Francie. She walked the streets of the North End, Charlestown, South Boston and anywhere else with substantial numbers of Irish people. She spoke to sailors and dockers and domestic workers; to men in shops and women she saw on the street. For fear she encountered anyone who knew her as Alice, she'd prepared a story. She would pretend that Francie Markham was the brother of a woman she'd met on the ship.

Once or twice, she met someone who claimed to be familiar with the name. Then they hesitated and announced that, no, they were thinking of someone else. Their Francie had been from Fermanagh or Cork or Leitrim. Or maybe he hadn't been called Francie at all. It was a lonely, frustrating task, and as the months wore on, and spring became summer, Bridget despaired of finding her brother.

At work, she was entrusted with more delicate tasks, such as maintaining the family's collection of Chinese porcelain. While she dusted and polished, Charlotte Edgecombe would come and talk to her. To begin with, she asked about Ireland. Bridget found it hard to respond, not because she worried about revealing the extent of her duplicity, but because she found it difficult to discuss her homeplace without becoming emotional.

Over time, their conversation broadened. One day, while Bridget polished silver spoons with a linen cloth, Charlotte told her that she was an abolitionist.

'Do you know what that means?' she asked.

'It means you think black people should be free,' said Bridget, as she examined her work. 'But they are, aren't they? In Boston, anyway. The people on the other side of the hill go about their business the same as I do.'

Prior to her arrival in America, Bridget had only ever seen white faces. At the start, she'd had to stop herself staring at the dark-skinned people who lived on Beacon Hill's north slope. Cook had told her that some were slaves who'd fled the south. They lived in fear of their owners capturing them and taking them back.

'Massachusetts isn't America, Alice,' said Mrs Edgecombe. 'Elsewhere, black people are still slaves. That's wrong.'

'I appreciate that, only ...'

'Only what?'

'Mrs Russell, the woman we stayed with when we first arrived in Boston, used to say that if all the slaves were freed, they'd travel north and take the work the Irish are doing now.'

Charlotte Edgecombe had a small, expressive face so that when she smiled or frowned, it crinkled. Even the slightest movement, and her face could change completely. Right then, it showed extreme displeasure. 'I don't believe that's true,' she said. 'And even if it was, you mustn't think like that. Everyone is entitled to their dignity.'

Bridget felt silly for repeating what Peggy Russell had said. The same woman had been wrong about a million other matters. Why should her views on slavery be worth recalling?

It occurred to her that, just as she'd had to learn about unfamiliar fruits and strange fish, she also needed to educate herself about her new country. There was tumult all around, but she knew little and understood less. She had no idea what life was like outside Boston. Were there similar houses in the south or the west? Or did people in other parts of America have an altogether different existence?

Later, when she was back in the kitchen, she recounted the conversation to Cook.

'I don't doubt her sincerity,' said Cook, 'and I agree with her. All right-thinking people do. I wonder, though, if she ever pauses to think about how her husband's mills rely on cotton picked by slaves. I've heard him say he's in favour of abolition too, but you can be certain that if everyone was freed in the morning, he wouldn't be a happy man.'

The next day, Bridget was in the scullery peeling potatoes. (She was baffled by people's dislike of the skins. They were the best part.) Mrs Edgecombe appeared at the door.

'I have something for you,' she said, as she placed a pamphlet beside the bowl of peelings. It was called *Appeal to the Colored Citizens of the World*. 'This was written by a man called David Walker who lived not far from here. It's an important work, I think.'

Bridget dried her hands and picked up the pamphlet. 'Thank you,' she said. 'I don't have a lot of time to …'

'No. I understand that. Between your work and taking care of Delia, you don't have very much time at all. But you're obviously an intelligent young woman, and I think you might find Mr Walker's words helpful.'

'My husband was the clever one. He liked to talk about politics.'

Mrs Edgecombe stared at the floor. 'I'm sorry, Alice,' she said. 'Sometimes I forget how much you've lost.'

Chapter 27

November 1849

'This will be a significant occasion for us,' said Mrs Edgecombe, voice more strained than usual, 'and it's important that everyone has a memorable evening.'

Cook and Mrs Hogan muttered and clucked and assured her that the celebration would be flawless.

From the scullery, Bridget could decipher only a sentence here and there, her ability to eavesdrop not helped by Delia's new-found fondness for talking. From what she could gather, there would be eight guests for Thanksgiving dinner, including a couple from England who were in Boston for a mixture of business and pleasure. Like Mr Edgecombe, the man owned a textile mill.

'More work for us,' she whispered to Delia, who insisted on repeating the words in her best sing-song voice.

'More work, more work,' she said. 'More work, more work.'

'Sssh,' said Bridget, with her finger in front of her mouth.

'Sssh,' echoed Delia, forcing a laugh from Bridget.

'If you stay quiet for Mammy, you can have a story later.'

'Sssh, Mammy,' said the child.

Mrs Edgecombe had continued her practice of lending books to Bridget. Some were political. Others focused on American history or the wonders of distant parts of the world or the glories of nature. More told stories, and these were her favourites. In particular, she loved ghost tales like *The Legend of Sleepy Hollow*. She also liked making up her own stories to entertain Delia. Often, the two women discussed what they'd been reading, with Mrs Edgecombe confiding that her husband had no interest in books, especially novels.

In the days before Thanksgiving, anxiety was high. Cook reprimanded Bridget for even the most inconsequential mistake while Mrs Hogan took to wringing her hands and asking unanswerable questions. 'Will the mashed potatoes be sufficiently creamy?' she would say, or 'Can we be certain the champagne will be served at the correct temperature?'

The preparations were meticulous. The dinner would begin with beef consommé. This would be followed by turkey, ham, mashed potatoes, sweet potatoes, stuffing, cranberry sauce, turnips, cabbage and creamed corn. Afterwards, the guests could choose from a variety of pies along with custard and jelly. They would drink the finest wines available in Boston. As well as her work in the kitchen, Bridget would assist Lydia with serving the meal. She would wear her best uniform with a starched white apron.

If part of her relished the challenge of such a grand event, a larger part felt queasy. Was there not something distasteful about so much food being served to such a small collection of people? She made the mistake of voicing this thought to Cook, who told her it wasn't her place to question Thanksgiving.

'I'm not,' said Bridget. 'I'm simply asking why there's so much fuss over this particular meal.'

'As I understand it, Mr Edgecombe has introduced a new production method. He's hoping that if the gentleman from England is sufficiently impressed, the English mills will place orders for his machinery.'

'He's expecting to make a lot of money, then?'

'Heavens, Alice, the questions you ask. But, yes, I think we can assume that substantial sums are at stake.'

Thanksgiving was a piercing cold day, with banks of grey cloud hanging low over the city. From before dawn, Bridget was busy in the kitchen, so busy that by the time the most challenging part of the day arrived, she was fit for bed. The atmosphere was frenetic, the work unrelenting. Cook bustled to and fro while Mrs Hogan checked that everything was exactly as it should be. Armies had gone to war with less preparation.

Bridget was determined not to make a mistake. This was not the night for dropping a hot plate or for pouring sauce onto a lady's lap. So absorbed was she by the minutiae of the meal that she gave scant attention to the guests, save to notice that they included a young man who was as bloated as his wife was haggard, and a handsome couple whom she decided must be the visitors from England. Both had the firm rosy skin that came with being very young or incredibly rich.

She did try to have a look at the finery. How could she not? In the year she'd spent with the Edgecombes, she'd become increasingly interested in the work that went into Charlotte's dresses. Tonight, she was wearing a lilac silk gown with a boned bodice and a full skirt while the lady from England was in a cornflower blue dress with gold embroidery around its low neckline. Bridget tried to imagine what such elegant clothes would feel like against the skin.

As the evening passed, and the champagne loosened tongues, the guests' voices filled the house. Each time Bridget returned to the dining room, the noise had swelled further. The Americans, she noted, were copying the English way of speaking.

'The weather is *frightful*.'

'The soup is *exquisite*.'

'The situation in Ireland is *lamentable*.'

This last line cut through the hubbub, and she strained to hear more. It had been voiced by the large young man.

Mrs Edgecombe agreed. 'I understand the distress is considerable.' She turned to the English man. 'You must have noticed the thousands of Irish exiles here in Boston?'

He leaned back in his chair. 'I'm afraid the situation in Ireland is vastly more complex than the newspapers here would have one believe. A great many remedies have been tried.'

He pronounced it 'Ahlund', as though he didn't want the word to spend too long in his mouth. As though it was dirty. Desperate as she was to stay and listen, Bridget was also conscious of Mr Edgecombe sending an impatient look in her direction. Lingering was not allowed.

Back in the kitchen, a melancholy feeling came over her. She was curious too.

'Do you know anything more about the English couple?' she asked Cook.

'Well,' said Cook, face shining from heat and exertion, 'if Johanna Hogan is to be believed, he's one of the wealthiest men in England. Not only does he have extensive business interests, he also owns a large amount of land.'

'By any chance, is some of it in Ireland?'

'Johanna claims it is ... except she could be wrong.' Cook raised a sceptical eyebrow. 'Let's be honest, she often is.'

'What's his name?'

Cook tutted. 'What has Lydia been doing? She should have given you all the names. He's called Henry Frobisher. *Sir* Henry Frobisher, if you don't mind. And his wife is Lady Harriet.'

'No.' The word had left Bridget's mouth and was hanging between them before she was able to consider the full implications of what she'd heard.

Cook didn't seem to notice. 'Here's a list of the guests,' she said, as she removed a slip of paper from the pocket of her apron. 'You ought to have been shown this earlier.'

Bridget ran her eyes across the names, then allowed the paper to fall from her hand. She shuffled towards the back door. In the garden, she closed her eyes and took one, two, three large breaths. Her heart was so loud, she could feel it everywhere. It was in her throat, her breasts, her fingertips. The last time she'd felt like this had been on the *Mary and Elizabeth*, when she'd been convinced her life was about to end.

When she opened her eyes again, Cook was standing in the gloom beside her. 'Was he …?'

'Yes.'

'I see.' She moved a step closer. 'Now, listen to me. The meal is almost over. If you go back in and help with serving the pudding, Lydia will finish the evening on her own.'

'I can't. I can't serve that man.'

'You can,' said Cook, her tone firm. 'It will take ten minutes, that's all. Ten minutes of your life. You've endured far more.'

'I swear to you I can't.'

'You can and you will. The Frobishers aren't spending the night here, by the way. They're staying with friends on Chestnut Street. After you've brought in the next course, you'll never have to see them again. Tomorrow, if Mrs E asks any questions, I'll explain the situation. Do you hear me?'

'Yes,' said Bridget, in a tiny whimper of a voice. Short of walking out and never coming back, she couldn't see that she had a choice.

'I can understand why you're upset, but you don't want to let Mrs Edgecombe down, do you?'

'No.'

'Come on, then,' said Cook, taking her arm.

As Bridget climbed the stairs with an apple pie and a lemon cream pudding, her hands trembled. She reminded herself of Cook's words. She had been through worse than this. All she had to do was serve the food. Then she would be able to escape.

The dining room was airless, the heat overpowering. The noise, however, had subsided. The guests were full, she assumed. Sated. And yet they would eat more. They could keep on eating for as long as they liked. She placed the dishes on the table and warned herself not to look at Henry Frobisher.

It was a warning she couldn't heed.

The room appeared to tilt. She was no longer at an ocean's remove from Boherbreen. She was back among the starving and the delirious. Their cottages had been tumbled. There were grass stains around their mouths, and a smell of death in the air.

Everything was clear and sharp-edged.

A dark anger came over her. Who was this man to sit in a gilded room and claim to know what had happened in her country? How could he claim to understand her townland, a place he owned yet rarely visited? He had inherited the land and its tenants and had never seen them as real people.

The noise receded further. She found herself looking at him. No, staring at him.

'May I help you?' he said at last.

'If you'd cared to help any of my family or neighbours, they wouldn't be dead.'

Around the table, the smiles withered. One of the women unleashed a nervous whinny.

'Alice!' said Mr Edgecombe. 'You'll apologise to Sir Henry, and then you'll leave the room.' He grimaced. 'My sincere apologies, Henry. She doesn't usually behave in this manner. The pressure of the occasion must have affected her.'

'I'm sorry, Mr Edgecombe, but the only person who should apologise is that man.'

Henry Frobisher turned to face her. 'My dear, I don't think you know what you're talking about.' He glanced back at the table. 'Is this the best help a family can find in Boston?' he said, his lips twitching, as though he'd said something amusing. 'I employ more intelligent mill girls.'

A woman tittered. It was an ugly, hollow sound.

'I know exactly what I'm talking about,' said Bridget. 'I'm talking about your treatment of people in Boherbreen in County Clare. The way you killed men, women and children.' Someone, Mrs Edgecombe perhaps, gasped. 'Because, take my word for it, you killed them as surely as if you'd rampaged through their cabins with a knife.'

'Alice, apologise now,' said Frederick Edgecombe, his voice quivering with anger.

She ignored him and continued to stare at Frobisher. 'Do you ever think about the people who died there? Or about the people who worked on your land for a pittance? I helped to dig a ditch through your fields, you know. I was paid twopence a day. Some of the men beside me were so weak they could barely stand. But if they didn't work, they couldn't eat.'

Frobisher squinted at her. 'Don't be ludicrous, girl. You're awfully young to possess such bile. I've found that's one of the problems with girls of your background. You're not capable of rationality.'

'I'm not a simpleton. I know how you behaved. You were aware that people were starving to death on your land, yet you did nothing to help them. My mother died. And my brother. And my husband. And when those who'd survived couldn't afford the rent, you tipped them onto the side of the road and destroyed their houses. They were decent, hardworking people – as fine and as intelligent as anyone at this table – and you allowed them to die like rats in a trap.'

The thin woman began to cry. There were heavy footsteps on the stairs.

'You have your liberty,' said Frobisher, with calm precision. 'There are plenty who would be grateful for that. You were free to leave your backwater and travel to America. Whatever nonsense may have been put in your head, I'm not an ogre. I'm someone who was forced to make difficult decisions. I was paying rates for tenants who contributed nothing.' He looked around the room, then waved a hand, as if flapping off a wasp. 'Yes, that's right. Rather than providing an income, the land was costing me money. I think the gentlemen at this table, businessmen all, will understand the dilemma I faced. If blame must be attributed, let it go to its rightful place: the government and those other fools in Westminster.'

There was a murmur of agreement from one man and a snorting sob from the crying woman. Otherwise the room sat in icy silence.

Bridget's entire body was shaking. 'I'm sorry you lost money,' she said. 'But you're alive. My family and neighbours are dead. You'd do well to remember that.'

She heard the door opening behind her and felt a hand on her shoulder. There was nothing to be gained by saying anything further. She followed Cook out of the room.

The tip of Charlotte Edgecombe's nose was pink, her eyes bloodshot. 'You know we won't be able to supply you with a reference?' she said.

'I do,' replied Bridget, who perched at the edge of her chair. She was fragile this morning, her bones sore, her bravery extinguished. 'I wouldn't have chosen to embarrass you, but I had to speak.'

Mrs Edgecombe gazed out the parlour window. Not that there was anything to see. The city was cloaked in freezing fog. 'No,' she said. 'You didn't have to speak. I'm so deeply sorry for everything you've been through. You've endured more than I could ever imagine, but that doesn't mean we can forgive your outburst.'

Earlier, a sombre Mrs Hogan had informed Bridget that she would have to leave immediately. Frederick Edgecombe wouldn't tolerate her under his roof a minute longer than necessary. Because of the circumstances of her departure, she would forfeit her final week's pay. Mrs Hogan had also revealed that the proposed deal between Mr Edgecombe and Sir Henry Frobisher had been cancelled. Like the Thanksgiving dinner, their business association had ended abruptly.

Bridget would miss this room. She would miss the golden drapes and the walls painted the same light green as a spring leaf. She would miss the warmth of the kitchen and the rivalry between Cook and Mrs Hogan. Most of all, she would miss Charlotte Edgecombe. Her thoughts went back to the day they'd met when she'd decided that Charlotte would never grasp how people in Ireland had suffered. Nothing had changed. As decent and generous as she undoubtedly was, she couldn't understand that the agony in Clooneven ran through Bridget's veins.

In the workhouse, Bridget had pledged that if she ever met Henry Frobisher, she would spit in his face. She hadn't done so, but her words had been enough. Despite the consequences, she had no regrets. Her loyalty to her family would always come first.

'I don't expect you to agree with what I did,' she said. 'But I'd like to thank you for how kind you've been to me and to Delia. Bless her, she's very fond of you. We've had some good times here.'

There was a lengthy pause before Mrs Edgecombe spoke again.

'Very well,' she said at last, as she continued to look anywhere but at Bridget's face. 'Have you packed your belongings?'

'I have.'

She produced a small parcel. 'These are for you. If by any chance you see my husband before you leave, please don't …'

'I won't say anything.'

Mrs Edgecombe escorted her downstairs and into the hall, where Delia was waiting. Cook had given the little girl her breakfast, and there was a frill of milk around her mouth.

Bridget crouched down so they were at eye level. 'Let's put on your coat,' she said. 'We've got a journey to make today.'

Delia folded her arms. 'This my house.' For confirmation, she looked at Charlotte Edgecombe, who said nothing.

Bridget held out Delia's coat. 'We have to leave, my love.'

'I like here.'

'I know you do, but you'll have to trust Mammy. Please?'

Reluctantly, the child agreed to put on her coat.

'Where will you go?' asked Mrs Edgecombe, her voice less precise than usual.

'I don't know but I'll think of somewhere. I always do,' said Bridget, as she picked up their bags and walked into the raw winter morning.

Chapter 28

July 2019, Clooneven

Jessie

Despite her disappointment at Bridget's fate, Jessie couldn't let go. The story of the *Mary and Elizabeth* continued to tug at her. Having read everything in the library, she returned to the internet in the hope of finding out more. When it seemed that she'd tracked down every possible article and reference, she began reading about other ships. She also combed forums and advice pages. That was how she found the message board post from a woman in Boston whose fourth-great-grandparents had survived the shipwreck.

Jessie clapped with joy. She could scarcely believe that someone else out there had a connection to the boat on which Bridget had perished. She replied straight away, outlining what she knew about Alice and Delia King, and Martin McDonagh. After a further exchange of messages, she swapped emails with the woman, who was called Kaitlin Wilson. Kaitlin was also twenty-nine, and Jessie was intrigued. She'd expected that an American tracing their family roots would be older.

At this point, she made the mistake of running Kaitlin's name through Google. Instantly, she regretted it. The woman who appeared was too accomplished. Too straight-toothed and shiny-haired. It turned out that she was a lawyer with an über-prestigious Boston firm. Her Instagram showed she had an unnaturally tidy apartment and a boyfriend called Clay. Another search revealed that he, too, was a lawyer.

Jessie obsessed over Kaitlin's perfection. Chances were that she attended daily spin classes, always remembered her sunscreen and knew how to wear stilettos without ripping her feet to shreds. She'd probably passed every exam she'd ever taken and had a small but devoted circle of friends. Hopefully, Kaitlin wouldn't be tempted to search for her. The thought of Hollie Garland articles cascading down the screen made Jessie want to hide under the bed.

'You should see the place where she works,' she said to Ger. 'I'd say you'd need five degrees to be allowed in the door. Funnily enough, it's called Frobisher Hunter. Do you think that's where old Henry went next?'

He laughed. 'I doubt it. I'd say he'd enough to do without becoming a corporate lawyer, or whatever they were called in those days.'

'I wouldn't be so sure. A ruthless business like that would have suited him.'

'Are you jealous of Kaitlin?' he said, a teasing note in his voice.

'I am. Not of her job, mind. It sounds like a total head-wreck. I envy the fact that her relatives were pulled out of the ocean. Unlike our woman, they got to see America.'

While she would have loved to say her feelings ended there, the truth was that Kaitlin's conspicuous achievements had resurrected Jessie's self-doubt. There she was in Boston with her career and her tasteful apartment and her successful, conventionally good-looking boyfriend. And here was Jessie with a list of mistakes as long as the strand in

Clooneven. She was single, practically unemployable and sleeping in a room with faded posters of The Killers and Arctic Monkeys on the walls.

Again and again, she looked at Kaitlin's most recent email. Replying should be straightforward. All she had to do was send a few anodyne words, some polite lines about how, if she learnt anything further, she'd be in touch.

If only it was that easy. Every time she tried to tap out the letters, her mind drifted away. When it came to Kaitlin – lithe, poised, talented Kaitlin – Jessie had a mental block. She disliked herself for being so superficial, but that didn't change how she felt.

The following day, another email arrived. Again, it was brimming with enthusiasm and questions. *Please stop*, she thought. *Please take your perfectly ordered life elsewhere. I'm not able for you right now.*

Ordinarily, Ger might have been expected to show more interest in the American connection, but like the rest of the town, he was distracted by Clooneven's continued presence in the county football championship. 'It's our year,' Jessie's colleague Ashling kept saying, her voice suggesting that any attempt to question this would not be tolerated. Having beaten Liscannor in the previous round, Clooneven were due to play Doonbeg the following weekend. Ger's girlfriend, Rosemary, was travelling up from Cork for the occasion.

Almost alone among the town's population, Jessie wouldn't be there. Lorna and Simon were going to the game and were joining friends for dinner afterwards. She'd been drafted in to babysit.

Ever since they'd decided that Lorna and Simon owed money to Dave, she'd been trying to dig a little deeper. So far, she'd made no progress. The more she thought about Ger's theory, the more sense it made. She blamed Simon. While Lorna had never wanted for any of the basics, there had been nothing showy about the Dalys' early years. Their clothes had been from Dunnes and Penneys; their holidays had been spent in Kerry or Donegal; restaurant meals had been an occasional treat. Simon, on the other hand, had grown up in a house of plenty. He'd been accustomed to holidays in Marbella and trips to matches in Dublin. He'd ridden the newest bicycle and worn the best football boots. He'd become entrenched in a life of high spending, and had brought his wife along with him.

The thought of Lorna being in serious debt was an uncomfortable one. If their parents knew, they'd try to help. But until she had more than hunches and suppositions, Jessie couldn't say anything. Not that her motives were entirely pure. No matter what she did for a living, she would never lose her journalist's nosiness.

Chapter 29

July 2019, Boston
Kaitlin

This was the week that Kaitlin should have arrived home from hospital with a baby girl in her arms. By rights, she should have been tired, sore, apprehensive – but elated. By now, she would have been taking calls of congratulation while quietly fretting about how she'd adjust to her new responsibilities. Instead, she was in the office, advising on the stock market floatation of a mid-sized pharmaceutical company. She hoped that, aside from Clay and her immediate family, no one would remember the week's significance. The best way to get through this was quietly.

She was muddling along, doing as well as possible, until an encounter on Franklin Street with a law-school classmate. Mallory Sorenson was very tall and very blonde with a wide coral-lipsticked mouth and a rasping laugh. Her friends would describe her as ebullient. Charismatic, even. She also had no filter. Her every thought had to be articulated. If you asked Kaitlin, self-censorship was an undervalued skill. Had she been able to stride past with a wave and a too-busy-to-talk look, that was what she would have done, but Mallory seemed to expand until she filled the sidewalk.

'Kaitlin Wilson,' she said, as though announcing her arrival on stage.

Before Kaitlin could come up with an excuse, she was being herded away from the street and into a pool of shade in Post Office Square.

'I don't know about you,' said Mallory, 'but this weather's getting to me.'

Kaitlin agreed that the heat was uncomfortable. It was that time of year when her hair became a mass of damp tendrils and sweat gathered along her spine. While engaging wasn't easy, she was anxious not to come across as unfriendly. Mallory was an accomplished gossip, and any perceived rudeness would be widely shared. A minute or two of small-talk and she'd be able to escape.

'Now, forgive me if I've got this wrong,' said Mallory, 'but did I hear that you and Clay were expecting a baby?'

Do I look pregnant to you? Kaitlin was tempted to say. She'd lost weight in recent weeks, and her expensive charcoal suit hung around her like a garbage bag. Like so much else, this hadn't been deliberate. The weight loss had crept up on her until she'd realised that her clavicles were protruding like shards of metal and her face was all eyes and bone. Even her underwear was too large.

'Eh, no,' she said, her voice a hesitant squeak.

'Leave it to me to get the wrong end of the stick. I could have sworn ... Oh, well, you want to put a ring on it first, I guess.'

Kaitlin told herself not to get upset. Not here. Not now. And definitely not in front of Mallory Sorenson. Somehow, she forced out the truth. 'I had a miscarriage.'

Mallory, who wasn't completely without shame, turned Pepto

Bismol-pink. 'Oh, shit,' she said. 'I'm sorry, Kaitlin. I had no idea. I heard a whisper of something, but obviously I didn't pick it up right.'

'You weren't to know.' With relief, she realised she wasn't going to cry. She was too listless for emotion. She just wanted this to pass. She wanted to walk away and be on her own, but doing so would leave a residue of embarrassment. They needed to move to safer ground. Work: that was what they needed to talk about. Safe, predictable work. First, though, she decided to make Mallory squirm a bit more. 'Actually,' she said, 'my due date was around now.'

'Ah, hell. Please forgive me. I'm usually more tactful than this. Are you all right? Can I—'

Kaitlin cut her off. 'It's cool. Honestly. Tell me about you. You're working with ...?' She hoped this wouldn't be read as bitchiness, as if she was suggesting that her former classmate's employer was too inconsequential to recall, but the name genuinely eluded her.

'Sullivan, Garcia and Rogers.'

A moustache of sweat had formed over Mallory's top lip.

'And are you specialising in any particular area?' asked Kaitlin.

'Are you kidding me? We're not Frobisher Hunter. I handle whatever's thrown my way, but I'm enjoying the work.'

Mallory went on to give a spirited monologue about the joys of small law firms. She was working on a couple of employment cases and had also handled some immigration work. The strange thing was, the more she spoke, the more her words and enthusiasm rang true.

When Kaitlin's turn came, she kept it snappy. She was part of a large team; she found it challenging; the hours were long; yada-yada-yada. She did her best to sound upbeat, but had the feeling she fell short.

'I'd better let you go,' said Mallory, eventually. 'I'm sure they keep you on a tight leash over at Frobisher's. And apologies again for being such a great big doofus.' She raised her palms to the sky in what she probably thought was an endearing gesture.

As Kaitlin walked back through the forest of skyscrapers, she considered the encounter. It occurred to her that the standout part hadn't been Mallory's blunder and subsequent discomfort. The memorable part had been the passion with which she'd spoken about her work.

More and more, Kaitlin found herself engrossed in the story of her Irish ancestors. To her delight, the message-board post had put her in touch with an Irish woman who'd also had a relative on the *Mary and Elizabeth*.

Jessie Daly's fourth-great-grandmother had been among the dead. She'd sent screenshots from a document containing the names of those who'd died and those who'd survived. It revealed that Alice and Delia had been from County Clare while Martin had been from the neighbouring county, Galway. As far as Jessie could tell, Alice had been a widow when the boat set sail, but Martin's original family, his wife and three children, had died on board. The news brought Kaitlin up short. It was hard to comprehend the scale of the poor man's loss.

Jessie had also asked a throwaway question about Frobisher Hunter. She wondered if there could be a connection between the company and a man called Sir Henry Frobisher who'd evicted huge numbers of starving tenants, including her own ancestor, Bridget Moloney. A few hours' research confirmed that she was on to something. The firm's co-founder, Walter Frobisher, had been Sir Henry's youngest son. He had emigrated to America as a young man and had been called to the Suffolk bar in 1875. What was unclear was how much he'd known about the deaths on his family's land in Ireland. Kaitlin didn't think of it as a coincidence, more as proof of how the world was connected – and of how the powerful remained so.

She was about to email the news to Jessie when she stopped to reconsider. She'd already written twice without reply. Clearly, Jessie had a lot going on. There was no point in annoying her.

From their first email exchange, she'd sensed that her Irish counterpart was reluctant to talk about herself. An internet search revealed why. A series of articles popped up, all of them based around a clip from a TV show in which a pretty but seriously drunk blonde derailed a discussion about the victims of crime. Although the onscreen Jessie seemed far removed from the smart woman in Kaitlin's inbox, they were definitely the same person. In the articles, she was described as 'the poster girl for self-absorbed privilege' and 'a millennial nightmare brought to life'. No wonder she was seeking refuge in the past.

Kaitlin spent an hour reading about the debate ignited by the TV show. Then she read some of Jessie's published articles. A few of them, including a profile of a toxically ambitious news anchor and an interview with an actress who'd been abused by her partner, were impressive. Eventually, Kaitlin had to remind herself that she was supposed to be researching her fourth-great-grandparents, not Jessie Daly.

As well as trying to find out more about her family, she'd been reading about how challenging life had been for those who'd arrived in the 1840s and 1850s. Many Bostonians had considered them a nuisance, a sickly tattered bunch who drank too much and stole food from American mouths. Others had gone further. In their minds, the Catholic newcomers hadn't simply been a drain on resources, they'd been an out-and-out menace, a violent, unpredictable mob.

Had Alice been treated unkindly? she wondered. Or had the dramatic way she'd arrived encouraged a more charitable response? Kaitlin recalled what Orla had said about her path being smoothed by the millions who'd made the journey before her.

It had been people like Alice and Martin who'd removed the stones and pushed open the door.

Kaitlin decided not to tell Clay about her encounter with Mallory Sorenson. Of course she knew this was wrong. Stella would have been his child too. But there was a wide chasm between accepting the illogicality of your behaviour and doing something about it.

Apart from one question about how she was coping, he didn't raise the week's significance. It had been a while since they'd discussed anything of substance, even longer since they'd talked about marriage or buying a house or other children. It was her fault. Her secrecy had infected the relationship. They were treading warily, frightened that a misplaced word would turn their carefully constructed world to rubble. Even when they spoke about mundane subjects, there was tension humming underneath, and she wasn't sure they would ever be free of it.

Chapter 30

Brian's message caught Kaitlin off guard. He was in the area, he said. Was she free for lunch? Her first instinct was to say no. She had an important afternoon meeting. But she hadn't seen him in the longest time, and thirty minutes couldn't hurt. They arranged to meet in a bar and grill a few minutes from her office.

That morning, her boss had summoned her for a talk. Her work was lacking its usual finesse, he'd said. Her input wasn't matching her ability. 'I'm not annoyed,' he'd added, 'just concerned. Do you need to talk to someone?'

She'd given a mechanical answer. It was nothing, she'd insisted. She would try harder. How could she explain that she was trapped in a place where she found the job both difficult and dull? That even when information worked its way through the sludge of her brain, she lacked the motivation to do anything with it?

Brian was in the restaurant before her, sitting in a booth with a beer. He waved and smiled. Her carefree brother in shorts and a polo shirt, his face tanned from a weekend on the Cape, was another reminder of how drained she was, her eyes so heavy she could barely open them.

'I'm off the clock,' he said. 'I'm tying up a few odds and ends for Mitch O'Leary. He keeps calling, and I keep saying, "I'm on it." But I'm not really. I like being a free man.'

'Lucky you,' she said, shuffling into her seat. 'I could go for some of that freedom.'

'No offence, but you look like you could do with it. You've gotten too thin.'

Brian ordered the shrimp plate with fries while she asked for a chicken caprese sandwich. He tried to coax her into a beer, but she insisted she couldn't.

Although the restaurant was close to her office, Kaitlin had never been there before. It was a masculine sort of place, the walls decorated with black-and-white prints of ball games and ball players, the clientele dressed in business suits with loosened ties. They barked about contracts and vacation plans in a way that suggested they'd be disappointed if someone wasn't eavesdropping.

After the ritual swapping of news – Riley had found a job in a DC gym; Clay was working on an important, possibly career-changing, case – Brian asked the question she'd been fearing.

'I don't know if we've ever gone this long without seeing each other. Have you been avoiding me?'

'No,' she lied.

'Maybe we've been avoiding each other, then.'

'Maybe,' she said, tearing her napkin into thin strips.

'I'm reluctant to ask, but wasn't the baby due around now?'

'It's okay. Yes. Yes, she was.' Kaitlin put down the shredded napkin. She gripped the table, as though its solidity might provide her with more mental strength. 'It's ...' She couldn't think how to finish the sentence, so she allowed it to slide away.

Brian leant in, like he'd done when they were children and he'd had something important to say. 'You don't have to talk about it. I wanted to let you know I haven't forgotten, that's all.'

'Thanks, I appreciate that.'

'I've been talking to Mom,' he said.

'Why does that worry me?' she asked, her tone lighter than she felt.

'She told me about your project. The family tree thing, I mean.'

'No doubt she put her own slant on it.'

'Wee-ll—'

'Sorry. That came out wrong. It's just I could live without her interference right now.'

This wasn't how Kaitlin had planned their conversation. She needed time and space, and she needed to finish her research. She'd wanted to be able to say, 'Look at these brilliant people. Look at what they went through. They walked away from a shipwreck, for God's sake! And we wouldn't be here without them.' Instead, she was in a downtown restaurant, rock music with neither rhythm nor tune was slicing through her, and she was due back at work in twenty minutes. Oh, and once again, she'd been bounced into something by her mother. She could have stamped her foot in frustration only stamping would have required too much energy.

By the time their food arrived, she'd decided that alcohol might be a good idea after all. She could brush her teeth before the meeting. She ordered a glass of white wine. She also asked if the music could be lowered a little. Brian asked for another beer.

The waitress, who looked like she, too, was having a bad day, turned to Kaitlin. 'And I'll get you a fresh napkin, honey. I find the ones that come in twenty-five pieces aren't very effective.'

'So,' she said, when they were on their own again, 'what exactly did Mom say to you?'

Between mouthfuls, Brian told her about calling around to their parents the previous day. Their father had been at work, which had given their mother an opportunity to air her frustrations.

That was how Susan worked. She was serene and long-suffering until some minor issue tipped her over the edge. A leaking faucet would be the catalyst for a diatribe about how, if it wasn't for her, the house would fall down around them. Someone failing to call on her birthday would provoke a speech about how the entire country had forgotten their manners. Give it an hour or two, and she would regret her outburst. Not that she would ever say as much. Instead, she would put on a sheepish face and become overly solicitous.

'She was on edge,' said Brian, a fry in one hand, his beer in the other. 'She's convinced that you've joined forces with Orla to try to sabotage my new job.'

Kaitlin pushed her food across the plate in annoyance. 'That's one way of putting it. I wouldn't choose it myself, but there you go. And why she has to drag Orla into everything, I don't know. Well, actually I do, but she's got to stop.' She took a gulp of wine. 'You know Mom has this long-running issue with Orla over something that happened before we were born? More than thirty years have gone by, and she still can't let go.'

Immediately, she regretted her words. Drew and Orla had asked her to keep the story to herself.

Before she had the opportunity to backtrack, Brian answered. 'As it happens, she told me about it yesterday.'

'We're talking about the same story here? Shay Drennan's accident?'

'Uh-huh. Was that the poor guy's name? Mom went on about how shocked she'd been that the family employed undocumented workers.'

'I don't know what planet she was living on if she was shocked. According to Drew and Orla, the city was overflowing with young Irish people. Where did she think their green cards were coming from?'

'You know as well as I do that she's always had a talent for ignoring the inconvenient. Plus, I guess she put Dad's family on a pedestal because they seemed so much more respectable than hers. Anything that suggested Wilson Brothers was less than one hundred per cent clean was going to be tricky for her. And, if you don't mind me saying so, she doesn't like the fact that you're tighter with Orla than you are with her.'

Kaitlin almost challenged his final point, but how could she when it was true? She reminded herself that there was nothing spiteful about their mother. Susan liked everything to be orderly, and when it wasn't, she lashed out.

'I still can't understand why Mom would tell you all that,' she said to Brian. 'I'd assumed she wouldn't want you to know.'

He took a long drink of beer. 'I reckon she thinks it paints Orla in a poor light. Anyway, why don't we forget about Mom for a minute? I want to hear about my Irish roots.'

It struck Kaitlin that the more she found out about her family, the less she understood. She'd expected Brian to address the fact that their family business had employed undocumented immigrants. Surely he had an opinion? Instead, he seemed keen to move the conversation in another direction. Maybe their mother wasn't alone in her ability to ignore the inconvenient.

'Okay,' she said, 'but please don't be flippant. When you hear what our family survived, you'll be – I hope you'll be – impressed. I'd planned on having more information by now, but … well, the past few months have been tougher than I'd expected.'

'I'm not being flippant, I swear. I genuinely want to hear about them.'

She looked at her phone. Her meeting was due to start in ten minutes. If she left immediately and moved quickly, she could make it. For a moment, she wavered. Then she put the phone on mute and nodded towards their waitress. 'Could we get two more drinks, please?'

Over the next twenty minutes, she outlined what she'd discovered about the *Mary and Elizabeth*. She spoke about the conditions their ancestors had left behind and about the city that had become their sanctuary.

'That means,' she said, 'that our American story began with people fleeing the Famine. Can you imagine what they went through?' She took a drink. 'But, like I say, I'm quite a distance from having the full picture. I'd love to know how Alice and Martin became a couple. Like, did they stick together because they both survived the disaster or what happened?'

Although people were drifting back to their offices, a background hum remained. There was a burst of raucous laughter. A phone jangled.

Brian was quiet. Without making it obvious, Kaitlin searched for a reaction. She hoped for a sign, no matter how slight, that he'd been moved by what he'd heard. Moved or embarrassed or intrigued or something.

There was nothing.

She checked her phone. Four missed calls.

She'd always feared that, as far as Brian was concerned, this was a hopeless mission. Some days, she didn't know why she'd embarked on it. No, scratch that. Of course she knew. Like Orla had said, this was more personal than political. She had difficulty, would always have difficulty, with someone so close to her disagreeing about something that felt so fundamental. She'd accepted that she couldn't change his mind, but she'd wanted, at the very least, to give him pause for thought.

Brian wasn't just part of her childhood memories. He *was* her memories. They'd been as close as twins. A conspiracy of two. Now, she had to admit that, in important ways, they weren't alike at all. Perhaps they never had been. Her brain, her straightforward logical brain, couldn't accept that. No matter how often she said, *Listen to me, see it my way*, he wouldn't.

He ran a finger down the side of his glass. 'It's fascinating, and they all ... Well, "brave" doesn't begin to describe them.'

'You don't think they should have been locked up and sent back to Ireland, then?'

'Come on, Kaitlin. That's not fair.'

'You're right,' she said. 'It's not. But you know what? Nothing feels fair at the moment.'

Her voice must have been too loud because a woman in a perfect white linen blazer swivelled around and frowned. Kaitlin gave her a broad smile, and the woman turned away again.

'I don't want to lose your friendship,' she said. 'And I don't want us to feel we have to vet every word we say.' *Because I get enough of that with Clay*, she could have added.

'That's not going to happen,' said Brian, his denial unconvincing.

'But you're not really interested in Alice and Martin, are you?'

He shook his head. 'I'm not saying I don't feel any obligation to the past. I do. I get that. But I feel more of an obligation to now.'

'Please don't give me the spiel. I've read the Frequently Asked Questions page on the IRAA's website. Believe me, I could do a master's on that site.'

'Okay,' he said, 'I understand why you don't agree with my decision. And listen,' he sighed as though needing more time to compose his answer, 'it's not like I support everything the Alliance stands for. I'm not that wild about family separation or kids in cages either.'

She looked down at the sandwich she hadn't been able to eat. 'Why work for them, then?'

'Because I do share some of their aims … which, if you ask me, are more nuanced than you're willing to admit.'

'That,' started Kaitlin, 'isn't exactly—'

Brian refused to give way. 'But the main reason I'm taking the job is because I can't stay with Mitch for the rest of my days. I don't want to spend my life writing speeches for the official opening of Pat O'Donnell's new grocery store and making sure Mitch remembers to wish Connie

O'Brien a happy birthday and Joanie Fallon a contented retirement. And if I stay in Boston, that's what's going to happen.'

Despite herself, Kaitlin smiled at his job description. It was bitingly accurate.

'It's all right for you,' he continued. 'Everything's on track for you. It always has been. But I've got to move on, and this is an entry to Washington for me. Is it everything I've ever dreamt of? No. But it's a start. I'll get the chance to meet people and to hear about vacancies. And then I'll look for other opportunities. It's politics, Kaitlin. That's how things work. You've got to compromise.' He paused and sank the rest of his beer. 'One more?'

By now, the lunchtime crowd had thinned to a sprinkling of customers. She risked another look at her phone. Six missed calls. 'Why not?' she said. She couldn't recall when she'd last had three glasses of wine in the middle of the day. Already, she was feeling blurred.

While Brian took a call from Mitch O'Leary about a row on the health finance committee, she considered what he'd told her. She'd assumed he was working for the Immigration Reform Alliance because he was the truest of true believers. It turned out that he saw it as a stepping-stone. She didn't know whether this cynicism made his decision easier to accept. On balance, she thought not.

Kaitlin switched off her phone. She would have to think about all of this, but not now.

After the restaurant, they ambled towards the harbour. It was another violently hot day, and as they crossed Atlantic Avenue, the sky opened out and they entered a different city. People stood in untidy lines for lobster rolls and bus tours. They spilt out of Legal Sea Foods and the aquarium, all wearing the tourists' uniform: shorts and tanks, backpacks and baseball caps. Here was a bachelorette party in cerise T-shirts and too-short shorts. There was a group of baseball supporters, telling everyone within earshot that they'd travelled from LA. The holidaymakers chattered and laughed and squabbled, and Kaitlin envied them with a ferocity bordering on resentment.

Perhaps it was the alcohol, but she talked more than she had in weeks. Their conversation careened from childhood adventures to their mother's eccentricities to anecdotes about work. They remembered vacations and punishments, parties and mishaps, as though their shared history was enough to override their differences. Without acknowledging it, they were trying to re-establish connection.

Finally, she opened up about the miscarriage.

'I'm not the same person I was a year ago,' she said. 'I wish I could be, but I'm not. And, I don't care what Mom thinks, finding out about the generations before us helps a little. It gives me a chance to care about another world.' She lifted her sunglasses. 'That probably sounds crazy to you, but it's how I feel.'

They found a free bench and sat down. On the other side of the harbour, they could see Logan Airport, its planes scoring lines through the blue sky.

'You're not the first person to show interest in our family tree, you know,' said Brian, as he searched through his backpack.

'Really?'

'Uh-huh.' He pulled out a notebook. 'Do you remember Gina Queally?' He stretched out an arm and placed his hand about three feet from the ground. 'About this high? White spiky hair? Slightly gravelly voice?'

'Vaguely.'

'She's a second or third cousin of Dad's. Don't ask me which. There are so many of them, even I lose track. Anyway, I'm pretty sure she's keen on this stuff. In fact, I know she is because I was talking to her at one of Mom's parties.' He tore a page from the notebook. 'That's her number. She gave it to me because she wanted Mitch to fix the sidewalk in front of her house.'

'I think I know who you're talking about. Isn't she married to a great big wall of a guy?'

'That's right. Greg Queally's his name. Mom doesn't like putting them together in photos because she says the height difference makes the pictures untidy.'

'And you're sure she was doing the same work? Like, looking for the same people?'

'I'm not one hundred per cent. She didn't give me names or anything … or if she did they've slipped my mind. If I recall correctly, she was talking about letters that had been passed on to her when another relative died.'

'That sounds promising.'

'You should give her a call. Even if she can't answer all your questions, she might be able to point you in the right direction.'

Kaitlin watched two planes land, the air shimmering around them. She thought of the stories the harbour and the airport had heard. Of the nervous newcomers and the optimistic ones. Of the people who'd fled persecution and those who'd wanted an adventure. She thought too of all the people, from whatever part of the world, who still arrived in hope.

Then she took her brother's peace offering and tucked it into her purse.

When he'd left, she checked her phone again. It was late in the evening in Ireland, and she was convinced that an email from Jessie would be waiting. She was wrong. Apart from a handful of news alerts and a series of emails about 'Summer's Defining Looks' and 'Fall's Fresh Offerings', her personal inbox contained nothing new.

Had she said something to offend Jessie?

The tally of missed work calls had risen to eleven. She promised herself that she would listen to the messages, and then, when the wine had started to clear her system, she'd call to apologise. She assumed that some sort of disciplinary process would kick in. The thought made her feel ill.

For a few moments, Kaitlin sat with her head in her hands. She pressed her fingers hard against her eyes so that stars and spirals popped up against the black. Now that Brian was gone, her despondency had returned. She was adrift, unhappy but incapable of tackling the root causes of her unhappiness.

Once again, she checked her inbox. Once again, there was nothing new. She decided to send one more email to Jessie.

Chapter 31

July 2019, Clooneven
Jessie

The night before the football match, Jessie received another email from Boston. She didn't open it. She'd had a fraught day at work with too many customers making too many bizarre requests. Seriously, what sort of person asked for banana slices and ham in the same sandwich? Or three different types of cheese? As if that wasn't enough, a woman had thrown up all over the toilets and a young guy had given her a hard time about her TV appearance. Oh, and her hands smelt of mayonnaise. In Jessie's opinion, mayonnaise was the work of the devil.

She tried telling herself that she would feel better if she replied. Procrastination was never a sound policy. She did nothing.

'Go away,' she said to Kaitlin's latest message. 'I can't handle your

American perfection right now. Go and screw up your life and then come back to me.'

With the injustices of the day zipping around her head, she couldn't sleep. She listened to a podcast about poison-pen letters in South Dakota, did some social-media stalking (Phelim and his new girlfriend were having a wildly photogenic time in Santorini), and considered buying a pair of sandals she didn't need with money she didn't have. Still sleep wouldn't come.

It was only then that she decided to read the email.

From: KaitlinWBoston@gmail.com
To: JessieDJourno@gmail.com
Hi there, Jessie,
I hope all is good in Clooneven. I thought I might hear from you again, but I guess you've been busy. You probably have a better social life than me.

Jessie almost laughed out loud. There were prisoners with a better social life than her. She continued to read.

I got the impression from your last email that you couldn't quite understand why I'm so interested in my ancestors' stories. Some days I'm not sure myself. At the same time, it's the most satisfying project I've undertaken in years.

My interest started after my brother, Brian, got a job with an anti-immigration lobby group. That made me do some thinking. I don't know how things are in Ireland, but here it's a subject that seems to bring out the worst in everyone. (Or maybe that's just our family.)

Once I started work, I found I genuinely wanted to know more about where we came from. When I read about Alice and Martin, I was hooked. Learning that Martin was from Connemara and Alice from County Clare made them more real for me. There's every chance we still have relations in Claddaghduff or Tulla, and I'd love to be able to find them.

Today I had lunch with Brian, and it struck me that, as much as I love him, we're never going to agree. I can't understand why someone who's such a good person in so many ways can fail to be moved by what happened to our ancestors, but I suppose I'll have to accept that there's nothing I can do to change that.

What he did tell me was that a cousin of ours has also been researching the family's background. I'll probably call her and see if she knows anything that can help. I'm not overly optimistic, but you never know …

By the way, you were right about the Frobishers. I've attached a file with more details.

If I'm being honest, and I've debated over whether to tell you this, one of the reasons I've embraced the family search is that I've been at a low ebb. (Don't worry, I'm not about to load all my personal traumas on top of you!) Back at the start of the year, I had a late miscarriage. I was nineteen weeks pregnant, so if Stella (the name we gave her) had been able to hang on just a few weeks longer, she would have lived, and I'd be a mother now.

I'd love to say I've coped well with the loss, but the truth is I haven't. All of a sudden, lots of things don't feel right, if that makes sense.

Anyway, enough about me. I suppose what I wanted to say was that I feel fortunate to have made a connection with you. If you find out anything else about the lives of the people on board the Mary and Elizabeth, do let me know. Given that they were almost the same age, I like to think that Alice and Bridget were friends.

By the way, my uncle's wife, Orla, is from Limerick, and she says that when she was a child, they spent their vacations in Clooneven. She says they went swimming every day – even when it rained.

All best wishes,

Kaitlin

'So,' said Jessie, 'it seems I got her totally and completely wrong. Far from having a flawless life, it sounds like she's in a bad way.'

'Don't worry,' replied Ger. 'It happens to the best of us. Even I've been wrong once or twice.'

'Very funny.'

Whatever chance there'd been of Jessie getting a sound night's sleep had been shattered by Kaitlin's email. She'd read it twice before returning to the American woman's Instagram. On closer inspection, there was something a little off-kilter about the more recent photos. Something flat. And, while there was nothing wrong with the way she dressed, it was a bit drab, stern even, for someone who was only twenty-nine. Oh, and now that Jessie thought about it, perhaps Kaitlin was too thin. Perhaps she was more skinny than slender.

She was annoyed with herself for taking Kaitlin's life at surface value. She'd transformed her into a caricature, and judged her accordingly. Another lesson learnt.

Eight hours on, and Jessie was sitting on the prom, one hand gripping her phone, the other attempting to shoo away an obese seagull. She'd be late for work, but they'd have to cope without her for ten minutes.

'Why would Kaitlin tell you all that personal stuff, do you think?' asked Ger, who sounded as though he was still in bed.

'I guess sometimes it's easier to open up to someone you don't know. It's like the way people tell their secrets to hairdressers and barmen and strangers on trains.'

'Have you written back?'

'Ah, Ger, what sort of bitch do you think I am? Of course I have.'

'Sorry,' he said. 'I didn't mean that the way it sounded.'

'I emailed her last night, but didn't hear anything more. I hope she's all right.'

'The line about the cousin who might know something was interesting.'

'Yeah,' said Jessie, 'not to mention the stuff about the Frobishers – and the disagreement with her brother.'

'Is that any big surprise, though? The brother's job, I mean.'

'I suppose, in my unsophisticated way, I'd always assumed that Irish people, even in America, would be drawn towards the underdog.'

'I reckon that's one of the stories we're fond of telling ourselves. Like how generous and welcoming we are. The problem is, it doesn't stand up to much scrutiny.'

'Jesus,' she said, 'you're miserable this morning.'

Ger laughed. 'Nah, I'm just being honest.'

Usually Jessie tried to stay out of other countries' affairs. She had enough trouble deciphering Irish politics without getting involved in what was happening elsewhere. She made an exception for the United States. The whole world felt entitled to have an opinion on America.

'Anyway,' she said, 'I'd better get moving or Ivana will be on my tail. Ashling's taking a day off on account of the big match. She's having her nails done in the Clooneven colours.'

'It's a shame you won't be there,' he said.

'You'll hardly miss me. You'll have the whole town cheering you on … and Rosemary.'

'True, but …' Ger stopped. He'd clearly had second thoughts about what he'd been going to say. Instead, he switched the conversation back to Kaitlin's email. 'Send me a message if you hear from her,' he said.

'Will do,' she replied. 'And good luck.'

Clooneven won by three points. Although Jessie tried to listen on local radio, her nephew and niece kept distracting her. The under-tens, it seemed, were immune to the charms of a local GAA match. As far as she could tell, Ger had played well.

As usual, Ethan and Zoë had more questions than *Mastermind*. They either imagined she would provide the answers their parents couldn't, or they liked being awkward. The latter, she feared, was closer to the truth. Among the latest batch were:

The logical: 'If you're younger than Mammy, why are you taller?'

The bruising: 'You're old. Why aren't you married?'

The strange: 'How do they know it was St Patrick who got rid of all the snakes?'

The even stranger: 'Why don't people have tails?'

And the perennial: 'Why can't we stay up as late as you?'

'Because,' said Jessie, feeling on firm ground with this one, 'you need more sleep than me. It's a scientific fact.'

'Who says?' replied seven-year-old Ethan. 'Zoë's only four, so she needs lots of sleep. But I don't.'

'Four and a quarter,' said Zoë, peeping through her blonde curls. She was wearing a pink sun hat, which functioned as her version of a comfort blanket. 'And I could stay awake all night if I wanted to.'

'You could not.'

'Could so.'

'Ah, lads,' said Jessie, saying a silent prayer of thanks that she could hand them back at the end of the night, 'I tell you what. You can have another half an hour, and then it really will be bedtime.'

'What if we won't go?' said Ethan, with a giggle.

'Then I'll be very sad, and I'll have to go into town on my bicycle and find your mammy and daddy so they can sort you out. That means you'll be left here all on your own.'

'No, we won't,' said Zoë, rocking on her heels.

'Who else will be here?'

'The people out the back.'

'And who are they?' asked Jessie, assuming Zoë was referring to a group of make-believe friends. At the same age, she'd been a terror for inventing other children.

The little girl appeared to be on the verge of answering when her brother sent a pointed look in her direction.

'Only messing,' she said eventually, a bashful look on her tiny face. 'It'll just be Ethan and me. All on our ownselves.'

'That's right,' added Ethan. He paused. 'We promise we'll go to bed if we can have another cartoon first. And a hot chocolate.'

Jessie used every technique she knew to prise more information from Zoë. Nothing worked, and she decided that her niece had indeed been talking about imaginary friends.

When, finally, the two were asleep, she poured a large glass of white wine, settled into the grey crushed velvet sofa and opened her book. A wealthy Californian couple were unhappy, and their story was making her feel stupid because, rather than finding something profound in their misery, she thought they were a pair of self-obsessed bores who needed to get over themselves.

Earlier, she'd received another email from Kaitlin, who sounded slightly embarrassed at having revealed so much personal information. Still taken aback that the public-facing Kaitlin was so different from the private one, Jessie reassured her that there was no reason to feel awkward. In a spirit of share-and-share-alike, she also gave her an edited version of the events that had forced her own return to Clooneven. Somehow, she sensed Kaitlin already knew.

Half an hour passed, and then an hour, but every time Jessie tried to focus on her book, Zoë's words returned to niggle at her. On second thoughts, it wasn't so much what her niece had said that stirred her curiosity as the way Ethan had shushed his sister with a stare.

Who were 'the people out the back'? And why was she not supposed to know about them? She decided to put on her hoodie and take a look.

The ground to the rear of Clevedon remained neglected, and as she walked, the waist-high grass swished around her. She heard a rustling sound, and her muscles tightened. She cursed the fact that she was wearing shorts. It was then that she noticed a track linked to the main driveway. She hadn't seen it before. Then again, she hadn't been looking.

Once she'd joined the track, she was able to move more quickly. On she went, towards the three old sheds, a clean breeze in her face. To the west, there was still a bright streak in the sky. Otherwise, it was darkest blue, the moon a silver sliver. Something brushed against her. She jumped back before realising it was only a branch.

This is madness, she said to herself. *I'm wandering around in the dark because of a throwaway comment by a four-year-old who believes in fairies and wears a pink sun hat to bed.*

Having come this far, she decided to take a quick look at the sheds. Not that she could picture anyone living or even working there. They hadn't been used in years. The land was too marshy to support either animals or crops.

Given how close they were to Boherbreen, it struck her that once upon a time these fields might have been owned by Henry Frobisher. Nowadays, everything reminded her of Bridget. All it would take was a line on the weather forecast about conditions being suitable for the spread of blight, and she'd think of her ancestors. Small-craft warnings had a similar effect, as did news stories about women being separated from their children or a family losing their home.

By now, Jessie was ... well, scared would be an overstatement, but she was jittery. She took out her phone and flicked on the torch. The buildings were less dilapidated than she remembered. The grey stone had stood firm against decades of Atlantic storms, and the corrugated roofs, though discoloured by rust, remained intact. The thin windows had been boarded up. A thicket of brambles smothered the side of the first building, the tendrils stretching in every direction. Closer examination showed that, while the door was closed, it wasn't locked. She pulled, and it creaked open.

'Hello,' she called out. 'Is anyone here?'

There was no reply.

She repeated her shout. Again, no reply. What there was, however, was a strong smell. A distinctive smell. It was also unexpectedly warm, the heat rushing towards her as if she'd opened an oven door.

A noise like someone stamping on dry twigs went off in Jessie's head. *Snap, snap, snap*, it went.

'Oh, shit,' she heard herself say.

Everything made sense.

Chapter 32

The next day passed in a haze. Jessie made coffee, cut sandwiches and scooped ice cream. She served almond croissants, apple turnovers and pains au chocolat. Thankfully, Sundays were busy. The customers provided a welcome distraction.

It had been after midnight by the time Simon and Lorna returned. Her sister had been giddy, her teeth stained with red wine. Simon had been his usual brusque self. Jessie cycled home and spent the night staring at the ceiling, her mind refusing to shut down.

Ashling, her colleague in the Seashell, noticed that something was wrong. 'What's up with you?' she asked, when they had a quiet moment. 'You're a right mope. Seriously, a lame donkey would be faster. And you keep giving people the wrong change. They'll think you're doing it deliberately, you know.'

'Sorry, Ash.' Then, to deflect attention from herself, Jessie added, 'I'm glad you all had a good night.'

'Ah, it was brilliant. The best ever.' This was the cue Ashling had needed to revisit her favourite subject.

Jessie was happy to let her rattle on. *Talk to me about mindless things*, she thought. *Tell me again how great the match was, and how Ger had a decent game, but how your boyfriend scored 1–5 and was the man of the match. Talk to me about the crowd and the drinks afterwards, and how the next game will be a stiffer challenge. Talk to me about anything you like.*

Ashling's impenetrable positivity, occasionally a source of irritation, helped Jessie to get through the day. When closing time came, her dilemma returned. Suppose she'd inflated what she'd seen? Suppose she'd made a mistake?

But she hadn't.

What to do? What to do?

She sat on a bench, lit a cigarette, blew smoke rings and watched them dissolve. She could, she supposed, do nothing. Or she could tackle Lorna. Or she could ask Ger for advice. His judgement was sound. Even if his suspicions about Dave had been inaccurate, they were probably closer to the truth than hers. The drawback was this: Ger wasn't just the shrewdest person she knew, he was also one of the straightest.

She smoked another cigarette. All the while, she turned the dilemma around in her head.

What to do? What to do?

In the end, she decided to call him. Thankfully, by the time she did, Rosemary had already gone back to Cork. Ger, who was about to leave his parents' house, was perplexed by Jessie's refusal to talk on the phone.

'It's not about Bridget or Kaitlin or any of that stuff,' she said. 'I'll explain when I see you.'

Before she could change her mind again, she hung up.

'How many plants are we talking about?' said Ger, as they walked past the new holiday homes, an arc of lemon-coloured semi-ds, and headed towards the cliffs that bordered one side of the beach. 'Like, would you say it was a professional set-up?'

'Unless my sister has a top-secret life as a stoner, we're not talking about personal use. I didn't examine them too closely, but there were hundreds of them. Some looked ready for harvesting. Others were fairly young.'

'And you're absolutely certain it was cannabis?'

'You mean, is there a chance I stumbled across a hidden grow-house of geraniums?'

'I was only asking.'

'Sorry,' said Jessie. 'I'm still trying to wrap my brain around this, but, yes, it was definitely cannabis.'

'Did you look at the other sheds?'

'I was going to, only by then I was kind of spooked. It's very dark out there. I saw a bat and nearly lost my life. You should have seen the state of me.' She gave a nervous laugh. 'It's a perfect spot for hiding away. The only way in is via Lorna and Simon's house, which, as you know, is down a lane. On the other side, there's nothing but boggy fields. So, going back to your question, I assume that if I'd looked in the other buildings, I'd have seen more of the same.'

'You didn't say anything to them?'

'God, no. She was half jarred, and he was in bad form. I got out of there as quickly as I could. I mean, obviously I was shocked, but at the same time part of me was going, *Well, is it any big deal?* Lorna's not exactly Pablo Escobar. And, let's face it, I've smoked a fair bit of weed myself over the years.'

'No doubt you have. Most of the town has. That doesn't change the fact that what they're doing is illegal. If they're growing cannabis, they're probably working for a larger operation.'

Jessie, who was clumsy with tiredness, didn't reply. She hoped he wasn't going to get self-righteous. It wasn't as if she was at peace with what her sister was doing. She wished she could unsee the plants, the lights and the convoluted watering system. But she couldn't. The thing was, and Ger was smart enough to realise this, getting sanctimonious wouldn't make the problem disappear.

She stopped and sat down on a rock. He sat on the ground across from her. Over his shoulder, Clooneven twinkled in the dusk.

'At least this gives us the definitive answer to one question,' he said.

'What Dave has been doing around here?'

'Uh-huh. Only we still don't know who he is, or how Lorna and Simon got mixed up with him.'

'I assume he's in charge, but what puzzles me is who looks after the day-to-day stuff. He's not around that much, and both Lorna and Simon have businesses to run. Besides, I can't see Lorna in her Valentino heels wiring up the sheds or harvesting the plants.'

Ger scratched his neck. 'Do you reckon Zoë was telling the truth when she said there were "people out the back"?'

'On balance, I do. You probably know more about four-year-olds than me, but she's such an honest little thing. She only changed her story when Ethan gave her the big-brother stare.'

For five minutes or more, he said nothing. With anyone else, Jessie would have worried that they'd lost interest. With Ger, she was confident he was thinking it through. She looked down at the ocean, at its relentless ebb and flow. It had been the same in Bridget's time and would continue long after she was gone. Lapping the shore and retreating. Lapping and retreating. She allowed her mind to wander.

If she was curious about why her sister would get involved in something like this, she was also angry. Her own screw-ups had been met by endless smugness and countless lectures, yet Lorna and Simon had been growing – and selling – drugs. Meanwhile, they'd also been honing their image as upstanding members of the community. They'd been running businesses, donating to the Tidy Towns Committee and attending GAA matches. As far as their neighbours were concerned, they were as wholesome as a First Holy Communion.

She was about to say something to hurry Ger along when he stood up and wiped the dust from his jeans.

'Come on,' he said, 'I reckon we should go and have another look.'

'You're not serious?' she replied, but he was already pacing back towards the car.

He parked down a lane on the far side of Clevedon. From there, they could walk across the fields to the old farm buildings. Having spent the spring cycling the local boreens, Jessie was able to gauge where they were. The sheds were a kilometre or so to the east, while Etty's house was about two kilometres to the south.

It was almost dark, the sky dotted with stars. They used their phones for light, causing swarms of midges to rise up and billow around them.

'What if Simon and Lorna see us?' she asked.

'With any luck, they won't,' said Ger. 'But, if they do, they've more to worry about than us.'

The land was pitted with holes and clumps of reeds. Once or twice, Jessie stumbled.

A high repetitive sound, like a squeaky wheel, crashed through the silence.

'Jesus, what's that?' she said.

'A snipe. There's a share of them around here.'

Her nervous laugh returned. 'Thanks. And before you say it, I've definitely spent too long in Dublin.'

Ger strode on, his walk as purposeful as was possible on such miserable land. Jessie was beginning to fear they'd lost their way when she saw pinpoints of light in the gloom.

'That's Clevedon,' she whispered. 'And look. The dark outlines over there? Those are the sheds.'

'We should probably switch the torches off, so,' he said. 'To be on the safe side.'

'What if we tumble into a ditch or something?'

'We'll have to be careful.'

They walked on, but more slowly. Jessie's breath came in quick puffs. She told herself not to be ridiculous. She'd been less scared the night before when she'd been on her own. Approaching the buildings from this side, she noticed that some of the ground had been cleared. You could park a van here. There was no sign of a vehicle, nor could they hear anything. She got the sense that light was coming from the middle building. She remembered reading that, at various points of the process, cannabis plants required near-constant light.

As they moved closer, she saw a bright crack where one of the windows hadn't been fully boarded up. Ger spotted it too, and tipped his head in that direction. Without saying anything, they took another few steps. She heard whirring, but nothing to indicate that anyone was inside.

They glanced at each other. 'All right?' he whispered.

'All right.'

Again, the door didn't appear to be locked. Ger reached out and eased it open.

If anything, there were more plants than in the first building. Row upon row of them, tall and lush. The smell was more intense. Blinking because of the light, it took her a moment to see the woman. She was crouching at the far corner of the shed, her back towards them, her head bent over the plants, engrossed in her work.

Jessie's instinct was to back away and leave. To her surprise, Ger stepped forward.

One step was enough for the woman to register their presence. She turned around, her body relaxed, as though she'd been expecting someone. She was young, perhaps only a teenager.

When she saw them, her mouth opened, but she said nothing.

Chapter 33

April 1850, Boston

Bridget

Until she'd disrupted his Thanksgiving dinner and destroyed his business plans, Bridget suspected that Frederick Edgecombe had barely noticed her. She'd been on the periphery of his busy life. With hindsight, that had been a blessing. She feared she was ever-present in Pius Cusack's thoughts.

At the start, his interest had manifested itself in glances and suggestions, but as the weeks passed, his intentions had become more obvious, his gestures less cautious.

She had been working for Pius and Onnie Cusack since her sudden departure from the Edgecombes. Originally from Ireland, they'd been in Boston since the 1820s and, like Peggy Russell, they had a well-tended disdain for new arrivals.

It had been through Peggy that Bridget had secured the job. Finding herself with neither work nor a home, she'd fallen back on the Russells for help. Her confession had been tortuous, with Peggy determined to wring out every last detail. After a sermon about the folly – no, the absolute idiocy – of Bridget's actions, she'd announced that she had a solution.

'The Cusacks live here in the North End,' she said. 'We go to the same church. Their last girl left in a hurry, and they need someone new.' She shook her head. 'Onnie, God be good to her, has poor health, and she requires a little help around the house.'

'I see,' said Bridget, as Delia danced back and forth.

'Of course, they aren't as wealthy as the Edgecombes, so they can only afford one servant. It wouldn't be what you've become accustomed to.' Peggy stopped and met Bridget's eye. 'Then again, you're not in any position to be picky. Oh, and for fear you're wondering, I've elected not to tell them about your unwise behaviour towards your last employer. Every sinner deserves a second chance.'

It was clear that Bridget didn't have a choice. While ordinarily this would have concerned her, she knew that without a reference, finding work of any sort was going to be difficult. And she needed to work. To her surprise, Charlotte Edgecombe's parcel had contained not just three books but also a month's pay. Boston was expensive, however, and the money wouldn't last long.

Within days, it was obvious that 'a little help around the house' was a significant understatement. The Cusacks' home wasn't just shabby, it was filthy. The kitchen was encrusted with soot and grease, and the larder provided a refuge for all manner of insects. Thankfully, the workhouse and the ship had given her a high tolerance for foul smells. Onnie spent a lot of time in bed with undefined ailments. Bridget suspected she was hiding from her four children, who were as rude and demanding a bunch as she'd ever met.

If not asking about the exact nature of the work was Bridget's first mistake, failing to find out why the family's previous servant had left in such a hurry was a more serious one. Pius Cusack had a tuft of grey hair on the crown of his head, like a crested bird in one of the nature books she'd read in the Edgecombes' house. His mouth slumped into his jowls, and he was fond of sharing his views on everything from slavery to the rights of women. Loathsome as they were, his political opinions weren't the problem.

The problem was that he regarded Bridget as his property. She was there to be stroked, pinched or poked in whatever way he saw fit. When she walked down the narrow hall between the kitchen and dining room, he was there, blocking her way, pressing against her. When she climbed the stairs, he was waiting at the top, his hand on her arm, his stale breath in her face. She became skilled at contorting her body to slip his grasp. Frequently, she used Delia as a shield.

The situation was made worse by Delia's unease. In the Edgecombes' house, surrounded by kindness, she'd thrived. Here, in a house of ill-humour and distrust, she was a different girl, needy one day, withdrawn the next. Bridget tried to bring some fun to her life. Whatever free time she had was devoted to playing games or going for walks. Unfortunately, walks in this neighbourhood were never going to match Beacon Hill. There, everything had been laid out before them in a vision of plenty. In the North End, too much was grubby and run down and loud. Washing was strung across the alleyways, rats behaved as if they owned the streets, and the threat of disease was never far away.

One evening in late April, when Delia was already in bed, Bridget went to the kitchen to wash the family's dinner dishes. Although the sky wasn't fully dark, she decided to light a lamp. She liked to see what she was doing.

The voice came from the far side of the room, causing her to jump. 'There you are,' he said. 'I've been wanting to talk to you.'

Bridget put the lamp on the table. 'I'm sorry, Mr Cusack. I didn't see you there. You gave me a fright.'

Slowly, like a fox stalking a mouse, he moved towards her. 'You're a strange young woman, aren't you?'

'I don't understand you.'

'Oh, I'm sure you do. As I see it, Alice, we've been generous towards you and your child, and you've been less than frank with us.'

How could he know what she'd done? 'I still don't understand, I'm afraid.'

'For someone who claims to be a widow,' he said, 'it's queer how you never talk about your husband.' He cocked his head to one side. 'What was his name again?'

'Bernard King from Tulla in County Clare. He died from Famine fever. I told Mrs Cusack all about him.'

She hoped his wife's name might have a restraining effect, but he barely noticed.

'Most queer,' he said, his voice a low rumble. 'If you ask me, you were never married at all. You were living an improper life in Ireland, and you left to avoid bringing shame on your family. Isn't that right?'

Bridget imagined picking up the lamp and throwing it at him. 'No. That's completely wrong. I don't think you understand what the situation in Ireland has been like these past few years.'

'I understand plenty. You're a poor liar, you know that? The miracle is that more don't see through you.'

'I promise you, you're mistaken, Mr Cusack. My husband is dead, and so are my parents.' Whether she was speaking as Bridget or Alice, this was true, and she said the words with as much force as she could.

He took another step towards her. The floor creaked. He smelt of sweat and rotting food. 'If that's so, why have you been making enquiries about a man named Francie Markham? Answer me that.'

Although taken aback to hear Francie's name, she wasn't concerned. She resurrected the explanation she'd perfected the year before. 'He was the brother of a woman I met on the *Mary and Elizabeth*. She intended to find him when she got here, but she drowned. I don't know if he's aware of what happened to her. She was a good woman, and I'd like to tell him that.'

Pius took a further half-step and placed a hand on her shoulder. The triumph in his face only deepened its ugliness. Even in the poor light, she could see the purple patches around his nose, the thick veins in his temple, the brown streaks on his teeth, the dandruff on his shoulders. Would it be easier, she thought, if he had a more appealing face? No, she decided, even if he was the most handsome man in Boston, she would find him repulsive.

'I think you're lying,' he said. 'I think Francie Markham's the child's father. He ran away from you, and you're desperate to find him.'

'That's foolish talk,' she said, unable to keep the anger from her voice. She wasn't sure how much of this he believed and how much he'd concocted to amuse himself. Either way, it meant trouble.

'You ought to watch how you speak,' he said. 'You're a servant in this house and you'd do well to remember it.' His hand gripped her shoulder more tightly. 'If what I say isn't true, why did your last employer put you out on the street? I've heard you were working on Beacon Hill.' He adopted a mocking tone for the words Beacon Hill. 'And they threw you out like a bucket of slop.'

Again, she said, 'You're wrong.'

Again, he ignored her denial. His hand moved towards her breast. 'That's not all,' he said. 'I've seen you with a shell. I've watched you take it out of your pocket and look at it like it was made of pure gold. It must mean something to you.'

The thought of him spying on her was unsettling. 'It reminds me of home,' she said. 'That's all.'

'Reminds you of home? I grew up in County Limerick, and I'm familiar enough with County Clare to know that Tulla's nowhere near the sea. Who gave you the shell? Was it Francie? Was that all he had? You gave yourself away cheaply, didn't you?'

'This is silly,' she said, sounding calmer than she felt. 'Now please take your hand away. I've got work to do. Mrs Cusack might come to check on me.'

'She's asleep,' he said, as he grasped then began pummelling her breast, 'as well you know.' He squeezed hard, unleashing a spurt of pain.

'Ow!' she shouted, the sound escaping before she could stop it. She hoped no one outside the room had heard.

He released his hand then pushed her aside. She stumbled and fell against the table.

'There's something bad about you,' he said, as he left the room. 'Something deceitful. You might pretend otherwise, but you're no better than the whores selling themselves on the street.'

Given what had happened to the *Mary and Elizabeth*, and given her father's tragic death, it seemed strange that Bridget still took pleasure from watching the ocean. Perhaps it was the crispness of the air. Perhaps it was the seabirds or the tangle of different voices or the wide, wide sky. Whatever the attraction, whenever she got the opportunity, she went to the harbour. Not that it could compare to the Atlantic's other shore. The water here was greasy and coated with debris. Sometimes, she closed her eyes and imagined she could see Clooneven: the curve of pale sand, the high jagged cliffs where she had walked with John Joe and, most of all, the diamond shine of the sea.

Away from the darkness of the Cusacks' house, Delia became more animated. She pointed at ships or shouted a cheery hello at passers-by. She hopped and skipped and behaved like a small girl should. Bridget thought of the Edgecombes' home. In trying to honour her original family, she'd hurt the only family she had now. She'd let Delia down.

She'd decided that no matter how much Pius Cusack hurt her she would have to stay. The only alternative was the street. Once, she'd been convinced that if she stood up to men with power, like Captain Talbot on the *Mary and Elizabeth*, or Maurice Curry in Boherbreen, there was a chance she would be treated fairly. Her encounter with Henry Frobisher had disproved this. Pius Cusack was the same. In his eyes, she was inferior and always would be. Many in the community would share that view. He was a respected father of four, a prominent Catholic, a man with a reputation for probity. She had washed up with the rest of the undesirables. She had no money, no husband and no history. He could behave as he had the night before – he could do worse, and no one would come to her aid.

Considering his private behaviour, the way Pius flaunted his religious beliefs was hard to bear. In her time in Boston, Bridget had become fascinated by how others saw Catholics. As far as the established Bostonians were concerned, her religion reeked of superstition. It was all holy water and idolatry, incense and genuflection. Some went further, declaring it a threat to the fabric of the city. Although she was sceptical about the meek inheriting the earth, and although she took no orders from either Bishop Fitzpatrick in Boston or Pope Pius in Rome, this hostility pushed her towards her faith rather than away from it. Occasionally, she found herself dropping into the church to say a quiet prayer. She enjoyed the silence, the paintings of familiar saints and the lingering spicy smell.

She would have liked to claim her prayers were untainted by personal requests, but that wouldn't be true. While the holy souls in Purgatory received a cursory mention, she was more likely to pray for herself and Delia. There were days when she felt hollowed out by loneliness, when she ached for someone to love. She didn't want to spend the rest of her life on her own. Although she didn't expect God to find her a husband, there was no harm in asking.

She also asked for help. According to her faith, she should forgive, and while she knew she would never forgive Henry Frobisher, her continuing resentment of Mary Ellen and Thomas was weighing her down. She prayed for the grace and strength to forgive them.

She prayed, too, for Norah. Two years had passed since she'd seen her daughter. Twenty-four long months. More than seven hundred days. By now, the little girl's personality would be more fully formed. She'd be her own small person. She would probably have her own friends.

Despite their separation, Bridget's love remained constant. *Please take care of her*, she prayed. *Please give her the happiness she deserves.*

She was strolling by the water, Delia toddling along beside her, when she heard a man's voice calling, 'Bridget.' She didn't look around. No one here knew her by that name. The man persisted. When she didn't react, he tried a different approach.

'Bridget Moloney,' he shouted, 'Mrs Bridget Moloney.'

She turned to see a thin man in a loose work shirt, black trousers and heavy boots. Because the light was behind him, it took a few moments to make out his face.

'It's Martin McDonagh,' he said. 'Do you not remember me from the ship? You were good to my son, Anthony. He died from the fever. Do you not remember?'

'I do,' she said at last. This was the man who'd stepped forward when Captain Talbot had struck her. The man with whom she'd watched the light under the sea. She knew he'd survived. They'd told her so in Cohasset. They'd also said that his wife and remaining children had drowned.

He shifted slightly, and she saw him more clearly. His light blue eyes, the colour she'd come to associate with Connemara people, switched their focus to Delia. In turn, the child tipped back her head and peered up at him.

'Her not Bridget,' she said, squinting into the light. 'Her my mammy.'

Martin didn't seem to hear. 'I assumed you were dead,' he said. 'I heard the list of survivors, and you weren't among them. Your friend was, and her baby too. Did they find you afterwards? Is that what happened? Maybe I'd already left for Deer Island by the time they discovered you.

Or maybe they took you somewhere else. Was that why your name wasn't on the list?' He clasped his forehead then peered again at Delia. 'I'm confused.'

It would be wrong to say that Bridget had been waiting for this day. She'd been in America for almost two years, and she'd assumed that if anyone was going to unearth her secret, they'd have done so by now. Here, with the spring sunlight splintering around her, and Martin McDonagh's questioning face in front of her, she decided she had no choice. She would have to tell him.

'I survived,' she said, 'but my name didn't.'

They found a quiet place to sit, and she explained how she'd become Alice. She told him about Cohasset and Beacon Hill, about Charlotte Edgecombe and Henry Frobisher. She even told him about Pius Cusack. For the most part, they spoke in Irish, a language in which he was more comfortable, and which Delia didn't understand. She couldn't risk the child who'd become her daughter hearing the truth.

When she'd finished, she was nervous. Considerate as Martin was, he might be disgusted by her deceit. He might find a policeman and report her.

Instead, he said simply, 'You did the right thing.'

Then he told her about his life in America. He had considered going home to Claddaghduff, he said, but for what? He would find nothing there, only questions and hardship. And so, after his quarantine period on Deer Island had come to an end, he'd looked for work and somewhere to live.

The early months were cruel, the first winter almost unbearably so. He was unsettled by grief. Unbalanced. He despised himself for being alive when the rest of the family were dead. His work as a docker helped. It was a hard grind, relentless and physically demanding. He worked every hour he could. The other men, many of them Irish, laughed at him. There was no badness in their mockery, so he didn't mind. When he wasn't working, he slept.

He didn't drink but could see why some would seek comfort in alcohol. Why they would gamble and fight. He still prayed that one day life would be easier. He went to Mass too. He didn't, however, have faith that his prayers would be answered.

'I've never told this to anyone before,' he said. 'Unless someone's had the same experience, how can they know what it's like to lose everything?'

'I understand,' she said.

Chapter 34

October 1864, Boston

Fourteen years later

'Patrick McDonagh,' she shouted from the doorstep, 'you're to come in for your dinner.'

He looked at his friends, who were milling around in front of the house, as if to say, *Here she is, embarrassing me again.* 'Aw, Ma,' he said, 'it's not dark yet.'

'Your father will be home before you know it,' replied Bridget, 'and we'll see what he makes of you being out on the corner at this hour of the evening. He'll have plenty to say, I'm sure.'

They both knew this was untrue. Ever since Patrick was a baby, the story had been the same. Martin would spend hour after hour playing with his son or talking to him, but when it came to discipline, she took over. 'Listen to your mother,' he would say. 'She's in charge here.' It wasn't that he saw domestic matters as Bridget's responsibility, more that he was so grateful for his second family he couldn't bring himself to chastise either Patrick or Delia. As much as Bridget cherished her second chance, she believed there was something purer about her husband's gratitude.

Despite the emptiness of her threat, Patrick did as he was asked. He was too keen on his food to be late for dinner. In truth, he was a fine fellow who rarely caused her trouble. As she liked telling him, he was her favourite son.

'And I assume Delia's your favourite daughter?' he'd say.

'She is indeed. I chose quality over quantity.'

As far as the world was concerned, she was a mother of two: twelve-year-old Patrick and seventeen-year-old Delia. And, as far as Martin and Bridget were concerned, that was all the world needed to know.

She would have liked one more child, but when they'd married, Martin had already been in his forties and what they'd been through had taken a toll. While it was amazing how much the body could withstand, Bridget didn't expect most of the Famine survivors to live to old age. Too much damage had been inflicted upon their hearts and lungs and bones. At times, she felt far too tired for her years. She wanted to lie down and never get up again.

Martin had proposed two months after they'd met beside the harbour. After the wedding, they'd made a pact not to dwell on their past lives. They couldn't spend their days with one foot in Boston and the other in the west of Ireland. If they were to move on, if they were to find contentment, they couldn't become sentimental about the country that had starved them and forced them into exile. Neither could they allow their lives to be blighted by anger. Instead, they would devote their energies to becoming American. They'd also decided to use their first language sparingly. Irish became their secret code when they needed to keep something from Patrick and Delia.

After fourteen years together, Bridget couldn't claim that they'd always kept their promise to forget the past, but they'd done better than many. Sometimes, it wasn't easy. After all, they had bonded over their shared history of loss. She could choose what she spoke about, but she couldn't subdue her memories or control her dreams. Every day she thought of Norah. Her girl was eighteen now. At the same age, Bridget had married John Joe. According to everything she'd heard, conditions in Ireland had improved a little. She prayed that this was the case for her daughter. She also hoped that one day she'd see Ireland again. This wasn't a wish she could voice out loud.

Alice, the real Alice, was also in her thoughts. Forgetting her would be impossible: Bridget spent every day with her ghost. Delia had the same snubbed nose and heart-shaped face, the same cowlick in her hair and the same ability to sleep. She was also an elegant young woman with a job in a dressmaker's studio and a trail of suitors.

In their early years, Martin and Bridget had discussed what to tell her. In the end, they'd decided the truth would be unsettling. As far as Delia was aware, she was Bridget's daughter from her first marriage in Ireland. Her birth-father had been called John Joe and he'd died of Famine fever. She rarely referred to their first two years in Boston, and Bridget assumed she had no reliable memories of their time with either the Edgecombes or the Cusacks. Nor did Delia ask many questions about the country of her birth. She was young and cared mainly about the present and the future.

Bridget had reconciled herself to the fact that, in such an enormous country, she would never find her brother. In her imagination, Francie was on the plains, herding cattle, or out west, mining for gold. On other occasions, he was somewhere warm, one of those places where the air was sweet with the smell of oranges and grapefruit. Or he was in New York, working hard and raising a large family. These were comforting thoughts.

There were times when she yearned to talk about her missing family members. When she felt a sharp desire to remember them aloud. Still, if keeping part of herself locked away was the price she paid for a stable – and in many ways happy – life, then so be it.

'Shouldn't we eat?' said Delia, who was standing in front of the stove warming her hands.

'No,' said Bridget. 'It's better when we all sit down together. You know I prefer it that way. Your father will be here soon.'

'A boy could die of starvation in this house,' said Patrick. His sister sent him a warning look. He didn't seem to notice. Ireland meant little to him, and that was how Bridget liked it. Later, no doubt, he'd have questions, but she'd worry about them when the time came.

Irish people continued to make the journey to Boston. Perhaps not in quite the same numbers, perhaps not in such a wretched condition, but they came nonetheless. Like the tens of thousands who'd arrived before them, most were looking for opportunity. More were hoping for adventure. Others were running away from the drudgery and unfairness of their home place. On Bridget's street, every second family had given shelter to a family member or an old neighbour. She wondered if the haemorrhage would ever end. Or was this what Irish people did now? Had something fundamental changed so that if she lived to be a hundred and fifty, the story would remain the same?

Bridget and Martin had moved to South Boston shortly after their wedding. When they'd met, he'd been living in a boarding house basement in Fort Hill. It was grand, he'd maintained: cosy in the winter, cool in the summer. She had balked at raising children in such a cramped place. She'd wanted sunlight, a proper kitchen, neighbours with purposeful lives. They'd been in their current home on the ground floor of a brick tenement for the past five years. While modest, it was enough for their needs. The McDonaghs would never be rich, but they were respectable.

There was no point in claiming that her second marriage was like her first. With John Joe, she'd experienced extreme highs and lows. Although their time together had been brief, it was scorched into her memory. By contrast, she'd had years of getting to know Martin. While she couldn't say their relationship contained the same passion as her first marriage, it did offer other pleasures. Bringing happiness to her husband was a reward in itself. In return, he gave her contentment and a sense of belonging.

Most of the families on their street were Irish, and many had walked a hard road. A considerable number had sons fighting in the war. They were proud of Massachusetts' 9th and 28th Regiments, both founded by Irish men. 'No Yankee can accuse us of being disloyal to America,' her neighbour, Christina Kelly, liked to say. 'Aren't we giving the country our flesh and blood?' Unfortunately, she also made it clear that her sons weren't fighting to liberate slaves but solely to preserve the Union. More than once, Christina and Bridget had traded words on the issue. Finally Martin, who shied away from friction, had urged his wife to keep her convictions to herself.

Despite her firm support for the Union cause, Bridget was relieved that one of the men in her life was too old to fight and the other too young. Reports would drift back from places with magical names – the Shenandoah Valley, Cold Harbor, Spotsylvania – and she would shiver at the number of casualties.

If the war had brought death to the neighbourhood, it had also brought benefits. Every morning, thousands of men poured from their homes and headed for the factories, armouries and shipyards. They made guns, cannons and shells. There was less talk about the 'Catholic Menace' and fewer signs warning that 'No Irish Need Apply'. No longer were school children forced to read Protestant versions of the Bible or recite unfamiliar prayers. The Irish had become useful. Where once it had felt as if they'd been grafted on to the city, now they were part of it.

'Please can we eat?' said Patrick, shaking Bridget from her reverie. 'If we don't have dinner soon, it'll all dry.'

'I suppose we'd better,' she said, tucking a stray strand of hair behind her ear. 'It's unlike your father to be so late, mind.'

She was starting to worry. Martin's long years as a dock-worker meant he enjoyed more freedom than the newly arrived, and he was always home on time. She turned to the pot where the stew was simmering. Although Delia and Patrick laughed at her tendency to cook what they called 'Irish food', simple dishes were what Martin preferred. They also made fun of her cleaning rituals, but she'd been taught well, first by her mother and later by Cook and Mrs Hogan. She found comfort in her routines.

As she ladled the meat and vegetables onto their plates, she heard the door. At last, she thought. Unusually, there were two sets of footsteps. Not to worry: Martin occasionally brought a man home from work for a proper meal. Luckily, she didn't have much of an appetite, so there was food to spare.

When she looked over her shoulder, she saw that her husband was accompanied by a man with a threadbare grey beard. He had the furrowed face of someone who'd spent a considerable amount of time outdoors and the clothes of someone with neither money nor vanity.

'We have a guest for dinner,' said Martin. 'I told him you wouldn't mind.'

Bridget turned around and put out her hand to introduce herself. Then she stopped. She looked beyond the beard and the lines, beyond the worn jacket and patched trousers. For a moment, she couldn't speak. She couldn't hear. She just stared.

She was looking at someone she hadn't seen for almost thirty years.

It was only after Delia and Patrick had gone to bed that they heard Francie's full story. He'd been back in Boston for eighteen months, getting work wherever he could find it. That was how Martin had met him. Prior to that, he'd spent ten years in California. Like many, he'd been lured by the gold rush. He didn't have to tell them that he hadn't found gold.

Bridget still couldn't believe that he was sitting in their kitchen. He was a ghost made flesh, a memory brought to life. She calculated his age. He'd been twenty-two when he left Boherbreen, which meant he would be fifty next year. Although several years younger than Martin, he looked at least a decade older. His body was as thin and buckled as one of the trees in their hometown while his voice sounded as though it was fraying around the edges. His accent was almost entirely American, with only the occasional word revealing his roots.

When she'd told him about their father's death, his reaction had been muted. 'Poor Mammy,' was all he'd said. Then she'd revealed how the Famine had claimed their mother and brother and her first husband. At this, he'd cried. There'd been nothing dramatic about his tears. They'd fallen silently down his cheeks until he'd rubbed a hand across his eyes and apologised for becoming emotional.

This had irritated Bridget. *If you cared so much, why did you stop writing?* she'd wanted to say. *You could have told Mam what you were doing. You could have sent money and saved her life.* Frightened of driving him away again, she'd held her tongue.

'I never thought my own sister would be here in Boston,' he said now. 'If I'd known, I'd have come back sooner. I'd have tried to find you.' He paused. 'Sometimes, when you're young, you think family ties don't matter. You think you can go and make your own way, but the earliest years keep coming back, don't they?'

'They do,' she said.

'You were always in my thoughts. You might have difficulty accepting that, but it's the truth.'

This time, with Patrick and Delia no longer present, Bridget couldn't stop herself. 'If that was the case, why didn't you write?'

'Because I couldn't.' For what felt like ten minutes, but was probably only thirty seconds, he said nothing further.

'I hope you don't mind me saying this,' she said. 'The way you disappeared was very hard on Mam. Like I told you, Daddy had been lost at sea, so even before the Famine, her life was tough. A few lines would have meant everything to her. You must have known that.'

He peered down at his boots, examining them as though the scuffed leather held the answer to every mystery in Heaven and on Earth. Finally, he spoke again. 'I couldn't send a letter home because I was in jail.'

'You said you were in California.'

'That was later. I was in jail here in Boston first.' His gaze remained rooted to the floor. 'Between 1840 and 1848, I was locked up, mainly in Leverett Street. When I got out, I was scared to write home again. I didn't know what to say. How would I explain where I'd been? And I'd heard about the terrible situation back in Ireland. By that point, the hordes were arriving here, all in a desperate state. I decided the best thing for me was to leave the city and keep on moving.'

While Bridget's mind was alive with questions, she believed he was telling the truth. It wasn't a tale anyone would make up. 'But—' she started.

'You want to know what I did? Of course, you do. I was drunk and I got into a fight. There was a crowd of us, eight or nine or more. A brawl, I suppose you'd call it. Anyway, one man ended up dead. I didn't kill him, I promise you that. I was there, though, and I didn't run quickly enough. Someone had to take the blame, and I was the man.' He raised his sun-splotched hands. 'There's no reason why you should take my word for it, I know that. But, as God's my witness, I didn't kill anyone.'

Again, she accepted what he was saying. He appeared so defeated that not to do so would have been uncharitable. And he was her brother: he deserved her charity. She glanced at Martin, whose face was taut. Even after fourteen years, there were occasions when she found him hard to read.

'Were you out west all that time?' she said.

'I was here, there and everywhere. I worked on farms and railroads and anywhere they'd have me. I found that once I'd left Boston no one ever asked where I'd been or what I'd done. They only wanted to know if I could work.'

'And you never married?' asked Martin, the first time he'd spoken in several minutes.

'Oh, I did. That was the reason I stayed in California. Consuela was her name ... still is her name. It didn't work out. She was too young, and I was too tired. Too confirmed in my ways.'

'Do you have children?' asked Bridget.

'No. We weren't blessed with a family. That was one of the things that pushed us apart. Now I can see it was for the best. We weren't destined to be together, not like the two of you.' He smiled sadly. 'It was good that you were able to bring your daughter with you, Bridget. It's terrible that you lost your first husband at such a young age but thank God you've been able to start again.' He looked around the kitchen. 'You've done well. Mam would have been proud.'

'Delia's not my daughter.'

Bridget knew that afterwards, when Martin asked why she'd been so candid, she would claim she'd blurted out the words without thinking. That wasn't the case, though. Francie had been honest with them, and he was entitled to honesty in return.

'I'm sorry,' he said. 'I thought you said Delia was your daughter from your first marriage.'

'That's what we've told her. I did have a daughter, all right, but she's with Mary Ellen and her husband in Hackett's Cross. Or, at least, I assume they're all still there.'

For the first time in more than a decade, she told her story: about leaving Norah in Mary Ellen's care; about the shipwreck in Cohasset; about waking up to discover that everyone thought she was Alice; and about assuming Alice's identity. Throughout, she kept her voice low, scared that either Patrick or Delia would hear.

'These days, I'm back to being Bridget,' she whispered. 'Except on official paperwork – then I have to be Alice.'

'And Delia's never guessed?' asked her brother.

'No,' said Martin.

Bridget was relieved to hear his voice. She was even more relieved when he clasped her hand.

'Either way,' he said, 'her original father is dead. She's happy with what we've told her. We've built a decent life here, and I'm sure you'd agree there's nothing to be gained by dragging up the past.'

Martin was so softly spoken that no one, apart from Bridget, would have noticed the sting in his voice.

'Delia asks the occasional question about Ireland,' she said, 'but she understands it's an uncomfortable subject for us. Her own children will be American. They'll be able to appreciate their background without being held back or upset by it. And isn't that the way it should be?'

Francie raised his head. There was no light in his blue eyes. The rest of him appeared to carry the marks of every trench he'd dug, every track he'd laid, every crop he'd picked.

'Don't you ever wonder about Norah?' he asked.

After that, they saw him from time to time. He'd learnt to be on his own, he said. He preferred it that way.

As happy as Bridget was to have found her brother again, she wished he'd had a more fulfilling life. When Martin, Delia and Patrick were there, they talked about America: about their lives in Boston or about characters Francie had met on his travels. When the two of them were alone, they were more likely to reminisce about Clooneven. Mostly, their conversations centred on their childhood, but occasionally, she spoke about the Famine and about leaving Norah behind.

'I still think you should write to her,' he said one day, as they meandered down Broadway. 'She's an adult and she deserves to know about you.'

'Thomas and Mary Ellen might have shown her my letter.'

'Or they might have thrown it on the fire.'

'Please, Francie,' said Bridget, 'don't make this more difficult than it already is. I can't spend my days dwelling on what I lost or what might have been, especially when Martin lost more.'

'Martin's other children are dead. There's nothing he can do about that. As far as we know, Norah's alive.'

'You've got to think this through. If I wrote to her, and it was the first time she'd heard the truth, how would she react? She might be angry.'

'Isn't that a risk worth taking?' asked Francie.

'But even if she wanted to know more and wrote back, there would be other consequences. I'd have to tell Delia the full story. Can you imagine how upset she'd be?'

'She's a clever girl. She'd understand.'

'I'm not certain about that.'

'Please,' he said, 'take it from someone who's made every mistake possible, you'll regret it if you don't write to her.'

What her brother said was true and untrue, right and wrong. As much as Bridget loved her Boston family, Norah was never far from her thoughts. She longed to hear about her. Had she remained inquisitive? Did she still enjoy the feeling of warm sand beneath her feet? Did she have friends? Laughter? Someone who loved her?

But writing to the daughter she'd left behind wouldn't be as simple as Francie claimed. Delving into the past would be disloyal, and not just to Martin, Delia and Patrick. In a funny way, she felt it would be disloyal to Boston, the city that had provided her with sanctuary.

Chapter 35

July 2019, Clooneven

Jessie

Their names were Phan Thi Linh and Tran Duc Quan, and they lived in the third shed. Save for a table, a small fridge, an even smaller cooker, a mattress and two old nylon sleeping-bags, the building was unfurnished. They washed themselves and their clothes in a tub of cold water. There was a portable toilet in the far corner. The only light came from two bare bulbs, which cast thin shadows across the room, making the scene feel all the more unreal – and all the more pitiful.

Linh had been tending the cannabis plants in the adjacent shed when Jessie and Ger had walked in. After a few moments of panic, when they'd feared she would scream, she'd brought them next door to meet her boyfriend, Quan. They were Zoë's 'people out the back'.

They didn't know how long they'd been living in Ireland because they didn't know what month it was. They'd arrived in February, they said.

The plants and watering system had already been in place, and they had reason to believe that others had lived in the shed before them.

'That means you've been here for almost six months,' said Jessie.

This surprised them. They thought it had been even longer.

Quan, who was twenty-two, appeared to understand more English than he spoke. He left most of the talking to nineteen-year-old Linh. After an hour of coaxing, and repeated assurances from Jessie and Ger that they had no connection to the police, she began to thaw. As much as Jessie wanted to be honest and tell the couple that Lorna was her sister, she feared it would scare them.

'We live in the area,' she said, trying to explain their sudden presence. 'We saw a light and decided to find out what was happening. That's all.'

Ger and Jessie sat on the ground, Quan and Linh on the mattress. Linh spoke haltingly, occasionally opening up, then shutting down again. Jessie suspected the only reason she was talking at all was out of desperation.

The process was slow. Linh paused frequently, either because she was grappling for the correct word or because she was considering how much to say. Then a dense quiet would settle over the room. Every so often, Quan spoke in Vietnamese, and she would translate. Once or twice, he intervened, causing her to backtrack. Jessie sensed that, rather than being coercive, his behaviour was motivated by fear.

Both had the gaunt, waxy faces and red-rimmed eyes of people who rarely saw sunlight. Even the slightest noise from outside caused them to stiffen their backs and lower their voices. Every so often, one of them left and walked the short stretch to the other sheds. Their job was to keep a mundane vigil, watering plants and switching lights on and off. Hour after hour. Day after day.

While, theoretically, they could walk away, in reality they were prisoners. Surrounded as they were by fields and trees, they hadn't known that the town of Clooneven was only a few kilometres away. Plus, from what Linh had said so far, they'd entered the country illegally.

Oh, and they were growing and harvesting an illegal crop. Jessie could see why they would be reluctant to seek help.

According to Linh, they were from a province in Vietnam called Ha Tinh. Compared to the big cities, she said, life in their village had remained relatively basic.

'We grew up poor,' she continued, 'but not hungry. Our lives were ...' she paused '... good.'

Jessie did a search and brought up several images of Ha Tinh on her phone. They showed a strip of white beach, sun glinting off the water, an emerald island on the horizon. 'Wow,' she said, 'it's gorgeous.'

It took her a moment to appreciate how crass she was being. Thankfully, neither Linh nor Quan was upset by the pictures. If anything, they appeared proud to be from such a beautiful place.

As was often the case, the images revealed only part of the story. Linh told them that until a couple of years earlier people had made their living from fishing. Then, a toxic waste spill from a factory had poisoned the coastline and killed the fish. Even where the fish survived, selling them was illegal because of the risk of contamination. Overnight, people were stripped of their livelihoods. They had nothing to do and nothing to sell. There were protests, but some of the protesters were jailed.

In desperation, young people started to leave. Some were dazzled by Facebook posts showing prosperous Vietnamese communities in England and France. *Chien is managing a restaurant*, the posts would say, or *Ping now has her own salon*. Families bragged about how well their sons and daughters were doing abroad. They were running businesses and sending money home, their lives laden with opportunity. Jessie thought of the generations of Irish families who'd made similar claims. In too many cases the boasts hadn't reflected reality.

Eventually, both Linh and Quan's parents had taken out loans to pay for their passage to Europe. They'd intended to go to London where others from the area had settled. They were assured they'd make enough money to pay off their parents' debts. After that, they would save for their wedding and then they'd return to Ha Tinh and buy a house.

The young couple were reluctant to say how much they'd paid the smugglers. Quan shook his head vigorously when asked. Linh picked at the sleeve of her matted grey fleece. From what Jessie could gather, the journey had been split into several parts, with different sums due at various points along the route.

Linh referred to the organisers as 'the line'.

'They didn't tell us their real names,' she said, her voice a feathery whisper.

Their first stop was in China. After that, they went to Russia. From there, they crossed by foot into Belarus. The trip was arduous, and they rarely had enough to eat, but by the time they reached Poland, they were confident the worst was over.

Days and nights flew past, as a series of vans and lorries brought them across the continent. Every once in a while, they would get stuck in a house or apartment. Then, with a few minutes' notice, they would be moved on again. At last, they reached the outskirts of a French port where they were met by two men, the penultimate part of 'the line'. At the time, they assumed the men were English.

The container held twenty people and a wall of cardboard boxes, making it extremely cramped. They were instructed to hide behind the boxes and to make as little noise as possible. It was bone-chillingly cold, and none of them had sufficient clothing to stay warm. Nor could they see anything; their surroundings were completely black without even a hint of light. Breathing became more and more difficult. Linh remembered falling asleep, then waking with a sense of dread.

'I worried that everyone was dead,' she said. 'For a few seconds, I worried that I was dead.'

After a while, she heard a strange noise. A tearing sound. Someone was ripping up one of the boxes. She called out. Quan was using the cardboard as insulation.

The couple's eyes met, the memory causing them to share a smile.

Later, said Linh, the crossing became rough. The ferry rocked and swayed until some of the group were sick. She feared the boat would sink.

When, finally, they arrived at their destination, they were divided into smaller groups. They travelled into the countryside, believing all the while that they were in England. On an isolated road, Linh and Quan were transferred to a waiting car.

'I asked the driver if we would reach London soon, and he laughed,' she said. 'He kept laughing, like I'd told a really great joke. In the end, he said we were in Ireland. The men in France had also been Irish.'

Jessie could only imagine their confusion. It was plain that, back then, the name of their new home had meant relatively little to them. And why should it have done? Her knowledge of Vietnam was limited to a handful of tourist clichés.

'Who was the driver?' she asked.

Quan and Linh stayed quiet.

She tried again. 'Do you still see him?'

Once more, there was no answer. Quan's right leg began to jiggle up and down. Linh said something to him in Vietnamese. His reply came quickly.

'It's all right,' said Ger. 'You don't have to tell us.'

Anger rising all the while, Jessie was desperate to discover if either Simon or Dave had brought them here. But pressing Linh and Quan wouldn't just be futile, it would be heartless. Instead, she asked if they knew why they'd ended up in Clooneven.

'They told us we owed money,' said Linh, 'and that when we'd paid them, we would be free. They also took our passports and phones.'

'Do they still claim you owe money?' asked Ger.

She nodded. For the first time, she looked as if she might cry. 'They say they're putting money into a bank account, and it will be ours when we leave.'

For the next while, Ger asked Linh about home.

Without their phones, they were unable to contact their parents. 'They must think we've forgotten them,' she said. 'Or that we're dead.'

Jessie offered them her phone. Linh declined. 'It's been too long. I don't know how to ... how to explain this to them.'

She spoke about her worries for her elderly grandparents and for Quan's younger sister who had poor health. The sentences were stilted, as though each one caused her pain.

Jessie found it hard to focus. Only a few hours earlier, she'd viewed Dave and the cannabis plants in an almost comical way. She'd tried to convince herself that the enterprise was no more sinister than a poitín still or a shebeen. But this was a long way from the old fellows who sold homemade spirits or ran an unlicensed bar. This was dark.

Quan and Linh might have left Vietnam willingly, but they hadn't chosen to come here, to the very edge of Europe. Nor had they chosen to live in a damp shed where they were expected to work night and day for nothing. Their vulnerability had been exploited. What was being done to them wasn't just illegal, it was exceptionally cruel.

It was five in the morning when Jessie and Ger left. Linh and Quan insisted that if they didn't go, someone would see them.

'Some days they're early,' she said, careful once more not to identify who was in charge.

Quan spoke for a minute or two in Vietnamese.

'He says we shouldn't have spoken to you,' said Linh. 'He's worried we can't trust you.'

'We won't do anything unless you want us to,' said Jessie. 'I swear.'

'You can't stay here, though,' said Ger.

Linh bowed her head. 'There's no choice.'

'Yes, there is. If you leave – when you leave – there are people who will help you. I promise you that.'

She shrugged, her gesture suggesting that she didn't believe him.

As they trudged back across the fields, the birds were in full voice, as if this was a morning like any other. Jessie's mind roved across everything they'd heard. She rummaged for loopholes and excuses. In truth, there were none. Although she'd read about cases like this, never in a million years could she have pictured a member of her family being part of the story.

Why? she kept saying to herself. But no matter how many times she asked, there was only one answer. Money. This prompted another question: how much money did Lorna and Simon need? Would her sister really get involved in the drugs trade for a kitchen of shiny appliances and a wardrobe of well-cut clothes?

'What are we going to do?' said Ger, as the lane where they'd left the car came into view.

'I don't know. Like you said, though, Linh and Quan can't stay in that shed. We've got to get them out.'

'So you agree we should go to the guards?'

'I ...'

Her hesitation was long enough for him to read its meaning. 'You don't want to go to the guards?'

'I didn't say that. It's just ... they're here illegally and they're growing weed. What if they end up in trouble?'

'They won't,' he said, in his most emphatic voice. 'The only people who'll be in trouble with the law are the ones who deserve it.'

'Can you be sure?'

'Did you not see the state of that place? Linh and Quan aren't there through choice. They're the victims in this. And, from what they said, they aren't the first people to live there either.'

'Don't get angry with me. I'm not saying they're to blame for anything. What's being done to them is revolting. But at the same time ... well, going to the cops isn't completely straightforward.'

'Yes, it is.' They'd reached the car. He turned, leant back against it and stared at the sky. 'Okay,' he said. 'I hear what you're saying, and I get that this is awkward for you. But we can't pretend we didn't meet them.'

'I'm not suggesting we forget about them,' she said, her mouth so dry she could barely get her tongue around the words. 'But I'm also thinking of my parents. They've had a lot to cope with over the past few months. Hearing about Lorna being mixed up in something like this would be horrendous for them. And what about Ethan and Zoë? What would it mean for them?'

The implications of going to the gardaí were stacking up in front of her like a never-ending line of cards. Of course, right was on Ger's side, but she wanted him to acknowledge that whatever they did would have far-reaching consequences.

'Seriously, Jessie,' he said, 'there's no comparison between what you did and what your sister appears to be involved in. None at all. Your only crime was being a bit of an eejit. People can't get away with human-trafficking just because they happen to have sound parents or nice kids.'

'That's easy for you to say.' The phrase 'human-trafficking' hit her like a twenty-foot wave. Putting a name to something made it feel even worse.

'Look,' he said, 'I don't blame you for being shocked. Only—'

'We don't have to do anything right this minute, do we?' she said, massaging the back of her neck, which, like the rest of her, burnt with tiredness. 'It's not like Linh and Quan are going to rush up to the house and tell Simon and Lorna about us.'

Jessie was beginning to regret involving Ger. Why couldn't he understand that, for her, this wasn't clear-cut? Even as every cell in her body vibrated with shame, she had to consider what going to the police would mean for her family.

'We need to make a decision today,' he said. 'The longer we leave it, the worse it'll get.' He glanced at his watch. 'Talking of your mam and dad, I hope they haven't been looking for you.'

'Don't worry. I might be living at home, but Mam's managed to loosen the apron strings a little.'

'I take it you're working today?'

'Yeah, at half eight, though how I'm going to handle it, I don't know. I suppose I could always bunk off.'

'I don't think that'd be a good idea. You can't risk giving Lorna or Simon any reason to believe that something's up with you.'

'Fair enough,' she said, climbing into the car.

She was annoyed by his tone. Who was he to tell her what she could or couldn't do? He wasn't the one who'd have to spend the day making coffee and pretending to enjoy holiday banter. Still, she couldn't quarrel with the substance of what he'd said. She didn't want to give her sister any cause for suspicion.

'What time do you finish?' he asked.

'Five-ish, if I last until then.'

He turned the key. 'I'll pick you up, and we can decide what to do.'

Chapter 36

As the hours ticked by, Jessie's thoughts remained muddled. She was on edge, scared of saying or doing anything that would give away her secret. She drank an ocean of black coffee and took frequent cigarette breaks. What she couldn't do was eat. It was as if her throat had closed.

She'd thought she was managing the situation until, as predictable as rain, the dreaded Venetia Lillis strutted in. She ordered an oat milk one-shot cappuccino with a teeny-tiny sprinkling of cinnamon and drummed her fingers on the counter while she waited.

'Oh, behave yourself,' muttered Jessie. 'You were in the slow-readers' group at primary school.'

Venetia didn't hear, but Ashling did. She instructed Jessie to go for a walk and sort herself out. 'Listen,' she said, 'Venetia puts on an act to wind you up, and you keep falling for it. If she'd heard you, there'd have been major grief. She'd have been on to your sister in no time.'

Jessie apologised, made herself an Americano and walked to the graveyard where she believed Johanna Markham was buried. It was the best place in town for a few minutes' peace. At least, there'd been no sighting of Lorna. She wasn't sure how she'd react in her sister's presence. She sat on the grass, kicked off her sandals and smoked a cigarette. Then she got out her phone. She'd intended to read more about Ha Tinh and people-trafficking but became distracted by another email from Boston.

With all the drama of the past few hours, she'd almost forgotten about Kaitlin. It appeared that the cousin she'd mentioned did have information about Alice, Martin and Delia. She'd also hinted that the full story was exciting but wouldn't say anything further over the phone. *I'm going to see her this evening*, Kaitlin wrote. *Any news with you?*

Where do you want to start? thought Jessie, before tapping out a reply in which she wished her the best of luck and urged her to stay in touch. She promised herself that later in the week, when there was less on her mind, she'd send a longer email.

A sparrow hopped towards her, hoping, no doubt, that she had lunch to share.

'I'm sorry, buddy,' she said. 'It's not a good day.'

No matter what she said to Ger about Lorna, it wouldn't capture her true feelings because she didn't know what those feelings were. For all their disagreements, she'd remained fond of her sister and not just out of family allegiance. She considered Simon's role. Okay, he could be dour and judgemental. He was also too controlling of his wife. Oh, and he was prone to parading his achievements when most of them were the product of family money. (Etty had once described him as 'the rooster who took credit for the sunrise'.) But, hand on heart, she would never have considered him cold-blooded enough to exploit Linh and Quan.

Should she have been more observant? Had she been too wrapped up in her own life, too consumed by trivia, to see Lorna and Simon as they really were?

As she walked back to the Seashell, she told herself that for the next couple of hours she would have to bury these thoughts. She would keep her head low and try not to sneer at any of the customers, even Venetia.

When she rounded the corner, the first person she saw was Lorna. Her sister was striding into the café, one hand curled around her phone, the other fiddling with her freshly cut hair. Empty as her stomach was, Jessie thought she would throw up. Bile seeped into her mouth, and she was forced to swallow.

You've got to do this, she said to herself. *You've got to walk in there like a queen and act like everything is cool.*

Lorna was wearing a cream denim jacket, a short red skirt and espadrilles, and she looked so jaunty, so light-hearted, that it was almost impossible to believe she knew what was happening behind her house. Then again, why should her behaviour differ from normal? Nothing had changed in her world. For a second or two, Jessie considered the possibility that she was in the dark about Linh and Quan. But, no, these were delusional thoughts, a triumph of wishful thinking over reality.

'Nice of you to join us,' said Lorna to Jessie.

'It's three o'clock, Lorna, and the place is quiet. Everyone's entitled to a break.'

'As long as you don't think you can swing the lead because I'm your sister.'

Jessie dug her nails into her palms to prevent herself from snapping back. Lorna had chosen the wrong day to be snippy. Thankfully, Ashling intervened.

'Everything's grand,' she said. 'Ivana was here this morning, and I took my break earlier.'

This wasn't true. Business had been lively, and there'd been no opportunity for Jessie's colleague to have lunch.

'Thanks, Ash,' said Lorna, with her most saccharine smile. 'Just don't let her take advantage. I know what she's like.'

Although it had been voiced in a jokey manner, Jessie found the barb hard to digest. She turned to fetch her apron before washing her hands with the vigour of a surgeon scrubbing up for a heart transplant. She remembered Linh's hands, how stained and calloused they were.

'Good to know you trust me,' she said to her sister, the bile returning to her throat.

Ashling sent her a look that said, 'What's going on here?'

Lorna laughed. 'No problem. By the way, are you getting any sleep? You look wiped out.'

The desire to explain why she'd lost sleep ripped through Jessie. Right at this moment, the words would taste delicious. She would savour every blessed syllable. The temptation to say something small, to drop a hint that she knew about Linh and Quan, was overwhelming. With difficulty, she steadied herself, and focused on drying her hands.

'Don't worry about me,' she said, her voice as bland as vanilla yoghurt. 'I'll be fine.'

She left work shortly after five. Ger had messaged to say he was parked near the golf club. He looked as worn out and dishevelled as she felt. His hair was standing up in tufts, and there were blue crescents under his dark eyes.

'Ashling told me there was football training this evening,' she said, trying to sound jovial. 'Shouldn't you be there?'

'They'll have to survive without me.'

'You'd better be careful. If Ash thinks you're doing anything to jeopardise the team's chances, there'll be war.'

His expression didn't change.

'All right,' she said, 'no more jokes.'

'No,' he said, the suddenness of his response catching her off-guard. 'Don't mind me. I wanted to start by apologising.'

'For what?'

'For being too tough on you this morning. The truth is, I've no idea what the past couple of days have been like for you. If it was my family we were talking about, I'd be just as cautious about involving the guards. I shouldn't have got pissed off with you and I'm sorry.'

That his apology sounded rehearsed made it even more effective.

'You're grand,' she said. 'I'm used to people having a go at me. At this stage, I must have the thickest skin in the county.'

His forehead bunched into lines. 'You shouldn't be used to it. That's the point. I get the impression that long after everyone else has forgotten about it, you'll keep on punishing yourself over that stupid TV show and that vacuous Ivy Garland or whatever her name is.'

'You know full well her name's Hollie. But thanks.'

'Anyway, what I should have said was that you were brilliant at encouraging Linh to talk.'

'It's what I used to do for a living, remember?'

'With any luck, you'll get back to it soon,' said Ger. He hesitated. 'But I'll miss you when you go. I hope you know that.'

'Thanks,' she said.

They decided to drive to a small nearby beach where a van served coffee and sandwiches. There was less chance they'd be interrupted there – and little prospect of running into Lorna or Simon. It struck her that, even though she'd spent most of the summer in his company, she still didn't have Ger figured out. She saw now how wrong she'd been when she'd dismissed him as straightforward. He was sensible and adventurous. Blunt and kind. If his ability to state the obvious could drive her crazy, she was impressed by the way he gave himself wholeheartedly to everything he did. After years among people who possessed an almost superhuman capacity for ironic detachment, it was a welcome change. Certainly, she couldn't imagine anyone else being as useful and supportive as he'd been over the past twenty-four hours. When she left, she would miss him too.

Jessie realised then that the grit in her eyes wasn't caused by tiredness. She was dangerously close to tears.

They sat at the back of the beach to discuss their options. Several enthusiastic swimmers remained in the water. A group of teenagers gathered in a messy arc, drinking cans and swapping insults. Every so often, a motorist stopped to buy coffee. Otherwise, it was quiet.

'So,' he said, after she'd told him about her encounter with Lorna, 'what are we going to do?'

This was the question she'd been waiting for, the one she'd run around her brain a hundred times and still couldn't answer. Never had she expected to be in a situation where she needed to weigh family loyalty against doing the right thing. She thought of her favourite podcasts where people said things like 'Blood doesn't tell on blood,' and 'Loyalty makes you family.' They made it sound so simple.

'I know what we *should* do,' she said, 'only every time I think of going to the guards, I remember Mam and Dad and the kids, and my doubts return. And, yeah, I take on board everything you said last night or this morning or whenever it was. And I really do appreciate what you said a few minutes ago. But, Jesus, it's hard.'

'I hear you.'

'At the same time,' said Jessie, trailing a finger through the warm sand, 'we can't abandon Linh and Quan. So,' she took a long breath, 'I reckon we've got to call the guards and tell them what we know.'

'Thanks,' said Ger. 'I'm not going to give you any platitudes about how you won't regret this because—'

'Because I might? There's no good decision here, and that's the truth of it.'

'You don't want to confront Lorna and Simon first?'

'I considered it,' she said, 'but no. First of all, I couldn't bear the excuses. I mean, they might claim the cannabis has nothing to do with them, that it's all Dave's doing. And second, what would it mean for Linh and Quan? Assuming Dave is the guy in charge, he'd hardly say, "Right so, the pair of you are free to go." It's more likely he'd move them on … quite possibly to a similar set-up elsewhere. Linh said there were twenty people in the container, and you'd have to wonder where the rest of them are.'

'There's one thing I reckon we ought to do,' said Ger, 'and that's keep Linh and Quan informed. We told them we would.'

Jessie took a mouthful of coffee – the stuff must be running through her veins by now – and weighed her response. 'Isn't there a chance,' she said, 'that by telling them first we'll scare them? They're convinced there's no alternative to being trapped in that shed.'

'On balance, though, isn't it better to talk to them? They're already traumatised. They're entitled to be treated with the same consideration as anyone else.'

'You sound like Bridget in her newspaper interview.'

Ger smiled. 'She was ahead of her time, was Bridget.'

'Okay, then. Do you want to go now or later?'

'We should probably leave it until after dark. We're less likely to be spotted.'

'You might make training yet, so.'

'Are you having me on?' he said. 'I'm going home to get an hour's sleep.'

Jessie dug her toes into the sand. It felt good. As did the salty breeze, the early-evening sun, the rhythm of the waves, the swimmers' shouts, the teenagers' laughter. She wished she could stay there and hold the moment.

By ten o'clock, they were walking across the fields again. This was the third night in a row that Jessie had visited the sheds and, while she wouldn't claim to be relaxed, her head was clear. All they had to do was persuade Linh and Quan that, rather than handing out further punishment, the authorities would help.

To avoid her parents' questions about what she was doing with Ger, she'd cycled to the spot where they'd parked the night before.

The sky was darker tonight, the birds quieter. The closer they got, the more uptight she became. The nausea she'd experienced earlier returned. She didn't want to do this. Yet she had no choice. Even if she decided to run away, Ger would persevere.

As if sensing her doubts, he whispered, 'We're doing the right thing. You've got to remember that.' Briefly, he wrapped one of his little fingers around hers.

They'd agreed that after speaking to Quan and Linh, they would call the guards in Kilrush. There was, at best, a token garda presence in Clooneven, and the officers in the larger town would be better placed to deal with the unusual nature of their call.

Once again, they switched off the torch on their phones. Then they continued across the clearing towards the third shed. All the while, Jessie watched and listened for a hint that anything was out of place.

She knocked on the door before slowly pulling it open. Ger was a step or two further back. Inside, Quan was on his own. She assumed Linh was in one of the other buildings tending the plants.

'Hi, we're back,' she said, her voice barely more than a croak.

It took her a couple of seconds to register the panic on Quan's face.

'No,' he shouted.

Behind her, she heard Ger call out.

Finally, there was a fourth voice. A Dublin drawl. It was accompanied by a hand resting on her shoulder.

'What are you doing here?' asked Dave.

Chapter 37

July 2019, Boston

Kaitlin

Before Kaitlin could explain the reason for her call to Gina Queally, there were traditions to be observed. First, Gina revisited the times they'd met in the past. Next came the obligatory enquiries about Kaitlin's parents and other members of the Wilson inner circle. Finally, they talked about the relationships and careers of various cousins. Only when these formalities were complete were they able to speak about Alice and Martin McDonagh.

Gina ummed and aahed while she listened, throwing in the occasional remark about the people who'd gone before them. Then, with the mental dexterity of a math professor, she announced that they were both descended from Ray McDonagh, Alice and Martin's grandson, which made them third cousins once removed.

'That's fantastic,' said Kaitlin, whose brain was several steps behind. 'I wondered if you might know more about the original McDonaghs, like how they became a couple or whether they had any contact with their families back in Ireland.'

Gina gave a knowing chuckle. 'Oh, sweetheart, just wait until you hear about our girl Alice.'

The way she said Alice's name stoked Kaitlin's curiosity. 'How do you mean?'

'You do know she wasn't actually called Alice?'

'Um, no. According to every document I've found, she was Alice Ann King who later became Alice Ann McDonagh. Who else was she?'

Her third cousin (once removed) gave another chuckle. 'You'll have to come and see me. I need to show you a few things. Well, letters mainly. They were handed down through another member of the family who died last year. Do you remember Nancy O'Hagan? No? Anyway, I figure they ended up with me because no one else wanted them. Let me tell you, they have no idea what they're missing.'

Gina said that she and her husband lived in an old South Boston three-decker. 'I'm sure plenty of folks are happier out in the suburbs,' she said, 'and good luck to them. But this is where I belong.'

Kaitlin suspected the remark was aimed at her mother but decided not to probe further.

Afterwards, she called Orla, whose excitement radiated down the line.

'That's brilliant,' she said, followed quickly by 'Can I come with you?'

'I don't see why not,' said Kaitlin. 'Gina sounded quite evangelical about whatever it is she inherited.'

Having promised to keep Jessie informed of her progress, she sent an email. The reply was disappointing, its four perfunctory lines containing three misspellings. Either Jessie had lost interest, or she was distracted.

Kaitlin remained embarrassed by the email she'd sent on Friday. Never before had she been so candid with a relative stranger.

On Monday morning, she was forced to return to the boss's office. This time, Barrett Weston was less conciliatory, more abrasive. Did she realise the disrespect she'd shown to a valuable client? Did she appreciate the gravity of the situation? Did she understand that a reputation for unreliability could stick to a lawyer like tar? He spoke to her in the sort of clipped tones that she feared he usually reserved for slovenly wait staff.

For a minute, she was tempted to level with him. *Look*, she felt like saying, *I went drinking with my brother, and we tried to solve the world's problems. Or, at least, we tried to solve the ones relevant to us. Haven't you ever needed to do that?* Her sensible side prevailed, and she apologised before promising that it wouldn't happen again. She couldn't imagine anyone in Barrett's family bothering him with their problems. No doubt all emotional messiness was tidied away before he climbed into his BMW and drove home to his six-bedroom house in Wellesley.

'The company offered professional help,' he said, 'and you chose to decline. We're going to try a more proactive approach to your, ahm, difficulties.'

He referred her to the human-resources woman, who supplied the names and numbers of several psychiatrists covered by the firm's insurance plan. She also instructed Kaitlin to take a week's leave to 'refocus your energies'. The leave was with immediate effect. This gave her no choice but to call Clay and tell him.

'You keep assuring everyone you're fine,' he said, 'but that's not how you're behaving.'

She sighed. 'Everything's gone a bit ... askew. I'll do what they ask, though.'

'Kaitlin, I don't think you have a choice. Frobisher's gave you the names and numbers for a reason. Everyone has sympathy for you, but you've got to help yourself.'

'I understand.'

'Anyway,' he said, 'I'm sorry about this, but I'm up to my eyes here. We'll have to discuss it all later.'

She reminded him that she was going to see Gina that evening.

'Is that a smart idea right now?' he asked.

When she pointed out that he'd supported her family search, he said he'd made a mistake. 'I thought it would help you,' he added, 'but I was wrong.'

'We're not really talking about my family tree here, are we?' she said. 'We're still talking about work.'

'Yeah, we are. You've put so much effort into getting where you are, and now it's like you want to throw it all away. It's like your ambition has disappeared. And I can't see why. I mean, I used to think that Stella's death was the cause of your difficulties. But I don't know any more. This isn't just about Stella. Is it?'

No, she wanted to say. It's not just about Stella. It's about my whole life. And you're wrong. My ambition hasn't disappeared. It's shifted. That's all.

She didn't say this. She wasn't ready. She couldn't face another session of loaded questions and pointed observations. Not for the first time, she wondered if her job was Clay's favourite thing about her.

Before hanging up, she promised to call a therapist. She intended to honour the promise. But not today. Today was about Alice, Delia and Martin. Kaitlin's aim had been to follow the family thread all the way back, and she was almost there. When her questions had been answered, she would focus on putting the rest of her life in order.

Brian's description of their cousin was perfect. Even though slightly elevated by red wedge-heeled sandals, Gina barely passed five feet. Her white hair was cut into long spikes, like a miniature spider plant. Her lips and nails were deepest crimson.

She told them that Greg, her husband, was out with his brothers. Their daughter lived in New York, she said, her pronunciation of 'New York' making it plain that the city didn't meet with her approval. Thankfully, their son was an accountant in Dunkin' Donuts HQ and lived in Dedham with his wife and two daughters.

'Isn't that the most Boston job ever?' said Orla, who was considerably more relaxed than Kaitlin.

Gina agreed that it was.

Her house didn't match their expectations. As she'd walked up the street with Orla, Kaitlin had joked about visiting a museum of Irish Americana. They'd piled cliché upon cliché: a Sacred Heart lamp, a portrait of JFK, an embroidered Irish blessing. Orla had sung a few bars of 'With My Shillelagh Under My Arm', prompting a bemused look from a guy washing his car. In actual fact, with its bright decor, stripped floors and lack of memorabilia, the house wouldn't have been out of place on an interiors website. Even old-school Irish Americans moved with the times, it seemed. Not only that. Kaitlin had assumed that Greg and Gina lived on one floor of the three-decker. As it turned out, they owned the entire property.

The three sat at the kitchen table. A light breeze pressed against the thin drapes. Gina and Orla drank white wine, but Kaitlin declined the offer. She needed to keep a clear head. For a few minutes, they engaged in family chit-chat. Although they'd met before, Gina and Orla didn't know very much about each other so there was plenty of ground to cover. Gina had a sizeable number of friends who'd moved from Ireland to Boston in the 1980s, and it didn't take long for them to find a point of intersection.

'Oh, my God, yes,' said Orla. 'I remember Angie Farrelly. From Kildare? Super-long legs? Got a green card and worked in Filene's?'

'That's the girl,' said Gina.

'She went out with the cousin of a friend of mine. What's she doing these days?'

On and on they went, connection piling upon connection, until every county in Ireland had been mentioned. Both appeared to have endless anecdotes about myriad Gráinnes and Sinéads, Nialls and Declans.

All the while, Kaitlin sipped her water, stared at a small cardboard box, which she assumed contained the promised treasures, and told herself not to get twitchy. Just as she thought she'd explode with impatience, Gina tapped the side of the box.

'Now,' she said, 'you're probably wondering what's in here.'

Barely trusting herself to speak, Kaitlin nodded.

'Before I show you what I have, I'd better give you a little background. The contents were passed on to me by an aunt who received them from an aunt of hers. I'd love to tell you I've pieced together Bridget's full story, but I haven't. What I have done is—'

'Bridget?' said Kaitlin.

Gina broke into a wide smile. 'Like I told you on the phone, Alice was what you might call her official name. Her real name was Bridget. Before she married Martin McDonagh, she was Bridget Moloney. She met Alice on the—'

'No way! Bridget Moloney from Clooneven in County Clare?'

If Gina had been expecting Kaitlin's first interruption, this one took her by surprise. 'Yes,' she said. 'That's where she was from originally. How did you know?'

Kaitlin's breath caught at the back of her throat. 'Because I've been in touch with a member of her family.' She turned to Orla. 'Remember I told you about Jessie Daly?'

Orla gave an enthusiastic nod. 'Yes, you said her – what was it? fourth-great-grandmother? – was on the same ship. Didn't that woman drown, though?'

Gina put down her glass and waved her hands in front of her face. 'Whoa, ladies, you're moving too quickly for me.'

Kaitlin, who felt as though her insides were dancing, described how she'd made contact with a woman in Ireland. One of her ancestors had died on board the *Mary and Elizabeth*, and they'd been sharing information. When she'd finished, Gina reached over and patted her hand.

'Bridget Moloney didn't die, sweetie. She survived, and so did Alice's daughter, Delia. Then, so she could keep baby Delia, Bridget pretended to be Alice. How she got away with it, I don't know, but she did.'

'So it was Alice who died?' said Kaitlin.

'That's right.'

'What an amazing thing to do,' said Orla. 'Look after Alice's baby, I mean.'

'Absolutely,' replied Gina. 'When you think about it, Bridget was an incredible woman. It would have been an awful lot easier to leave Delia behind. From what she says in her letters, she found it hard to get work when she first arrived in Boston.'

Questions were lining up in Kaitlin's head. What letters? she was about to say. Who was Bridget writing to? Before she got the chance, Orla spoke again.

'Doesn't this mean,' she said, 'that you're both related to Jessie?'

'I guess it does,' said Kaitlin.

'I assume,' said Gina, 'that Jessie is descended from Bridget's first child, Norah? The girl who stayed in Ireland?'

'She is,' said Kaitlin. 'How do you know about Norah?'

There was a sheen of excitement on Gina's face. Her eyes slid towards the box. 'You'll find that her story – or part of it, at any rate – is in there.'

Desperate as she was to hear more, Kaitlin needed to pause for a moment. 'If Jessie Daly and I share a fourth-great-grandmother, we're …?'

'Fifth cousins,' said Gina, without missing a beat. 'Like Orla says, we're both related to her because we're all related to Bridget.'

'She's not going to believe this. She was disappointed because she thought Bridget had died before she got to America. I can't wait to tell her.' Kaitlin tapped her forehead. 'I've just remembered: she gave me her number. Why don't I call her?'

Orla drank the last of her wine. 'Because in Ireland it's almost one in the morning. I reckon you ought to leave it until tomorrow.'

'Besides,' said Gina, as she rose to refill their glasses, 'I'll have to tell you a bit more about Bridget and Norah first.'

Chapter 38

July 1865, Hackett's Cross
Norah

Norah's husband, Barney, brought the letter back from the village. It had been given to him by the postmaster, and they'd both been intrigued. In her nineteen years, Norah had never been further than Ennis, and they couldn't fathom why someone would write to her from America. Who was Mr F. Markham? And why had he used her maiden name when she'd been married for nearly a year?

When Barney got home, Norah was sitting on a stool beside the front door of their tiny cabin, the sun stroking her face. What matter that she had a hundred other things to do? It was a beautiful day. There would be plenty of grey days for scrubbing and polishing and tending the vegetable patch.

She stared at the envelope. The name was vaguely familiar, but she couldn't think why. Then it came to her.

'Markham was Mammy's maiden name,' she said. 'She had a brother who went to America before I was born. She rarely talks about him, but I'm nearly sure his name was Francie.'

'Do you ever remember him writing to your mother?'

'I don't.'

'How would he know where to find you, then? How would he even know who you are?'

'Go in and fetch the other stool, and we'll find out.'

Norah had known Barney Nugent since they were small children. She'd been eleven years old when she'd first decided to marry him. Then again, she'd always been a dreamer. Unusually, she was an only child, so she'd had ample time to think. Barney wasn't the best-looking man in the area. Nor would he claim to be the smartest. What he did have was the sunniest nature. In his view, no day was too wet, no dinner too plain. Even the most cantankerous people in the parish had their merits; the most sodden field had its uses. Having grown up with a father who would find fault with the sunrise, Norah cherished Barney's amiability. His parents and siblings were the same. The Nugents were generous people. Despite having little, they'd welcomed her to their table like another daughter.

That wasn't all. She loved the shape of her husband: his firm back and narrow hips, his thick eyelashes and long feet. She loved his hoarse laugh, his warm mouth and silly stories. She loved the way he had with neighbours, children and old people. Most of all, she loved being alone with him, kissing the hours away.

In the way that some girls obsessed about children or fine clothes, Norah had always sought pleasure in the world around her. She could spend an age looking at birds building a nest or waiting for frog spawn to turn into tadpoles. She also found joy in watching the waves lashing against the strand and in collecting shells and unusual stones. Nature made her happy. Nature and Barney.

She was aware that some would consider hers an overly simple approach to life. According to her father, she should have aimed higher. She was passably pretty, he said, and had done well at school. Could she not have set her sights on a clerk or a man with land? Why was she content to settle for a labourer from an impoverished family? But if as a child Norah had been willing to obey Thomas McGuane's orders, she was determined not to live her adult life according to his prejudices.

Barney set down his stool beside her. 'Maybe Francie's writing to say that he's become incredibly wealthy beyond in America, and he wants to leave all his money to you.'

'Oh, yes,' she said, with a smile. 'Before we know ourselves, we'll be travelling across the ocean first class.'

'Will you read it out loud, so we can both hear what he has to say?'

'I will.'

Norah opened the envelope and removed the letter. If the quality of the stationery was any indication of Francie's status, he wasn't writing to tell her that he'd made his fortune. The paper was as thin as a fly's wing.

'"My dear Norah,"' she started, '"you won't know me as I left for America nearly ten years before you were born. Indeed, you may not be aware of my existence. I'm your mother's elder brother, Francie. When I say your mother I mean Mary Ellen, as I assume she is the only mother you can remember."'

'What does that mean?' said Barney.

'I don't know,' she replied. 'Hopefully, he'll tell us.' She continued to read: '"It's many, many years since I've written a letter home, and I thought for a long time before writing this one. I hope you understand that I'm not motivated by malice or by any desire to make your life difficult. Rather, I'm motivated by concern for my other sister, Bridget."'

'Other sister?' said Barney. 'Did you know you had an aunt?'

Norah shook her head and returned to the letter. She was properly confused now. '"There is, of course, a chance that you already know the complete story. Certainly, that is Bridget's hope, but she always wants to believe the best. It is, I think, how she has managed to cope so admirably despite experiencing much hardship.

"'Bridget has lived in Boston, Massachusetts, since 1848. She is married to a decent, hardworking man called Martin McDonagh and they have a son and daughter. Therein lies another tale, but it's not my intention to trouble you with it now. Prior to leaving our home in Boherbreen near Clooneven, she was married to John Joe Moloney. I am sorry to say that, like our mother and younger brother, Michael, John Joe died during the Famine, leaving Bridget a widow. She was twenty-one years old and had a young daughter. You were that daughter.'"

Norah stopped. Despite the July heat, her teeth were chattering. She felt Barney's arm slip around her. 'Don't read it,' he said. 'Maybe Francie is mad. Or maybe he's not Francie at all. He could be an imposter, some fellow setting out to cause trouble.'

Her husband was wrong. Norah's every instinct told her that Francie was genuine. But why had he chosen to do this now? She passed the letter to Barney and nodded. She wanted him to read the rest.

"'You must appreciate,'" he read, "'that Bridget was desperately poor. The two of you were evicted from your cottage and spent a period in the workhouse in Kilrush. She only left you in Mary Ellen's care because she feared that otherwise you would die. Many of your friends and neighbours were already gone.'"

By now, Norah's entire body was shaking. Barney stopped but she urged him to resume. 'Please,' she said, 'I want to hear it all.'

He did as she asked. "'I have encouraged Bridget to write, but despite her enduring love for you, she has always refused to do so. She's scared of upsetting you. I considered writing before now but accepted that it was not my place to interfere. She is unwell, however, and this has led to my change of heart. I didn't tell her about my plan. Had I done so, she would probably have tried to dissuade me.

"'I am sorry if this letter has come as a shock or is unwelcome. Should you choose not to reply, I won't bother you again. I have included my address and also that of Bridget and her husband. To this day, she keeps a shell collected by you on your final day together. It's as precious to her as gold or diamonds. I believe a letter from you, the girl she has never stopped loving, would mean a great deal to her. Yours sincerely, Francie Markham."'

It took Norah some time to compose herself. For hours afterwards, she wandered the lanes and fields. She cooked no dinner and neglected the hens.

Barney urged her not to act too quickly. 'By all means, talk to your parents, if that's what you decide to do,' he said. 'Don't rush into anything, though. You still can't be sure that your uncle is trustworthy.'

In one way, this was correct. She didn't know the man or his motives. That didn't matter. Something about the letter told her that Francie didn't write often. She imagined him taking great care over its composition, and she continued to believe that what he said was true.

Norah's memories had only begun to fade in when she was five or six. By then, the worst of the Famine was over. While she remembered life being simple, she'd never known daily hunger. Or so she'd thought. According to the letter, she'd been in danger of starving to death.

She had only one memory from her earliest years and, in truth, it was more of a fragment than a substantial image. She was sitting beside a fast-running stream. A soft rain was falling. There was a woman with her. Perhaps that had been Bridget.

Francie's letter cast her childhood in a different light, making more sense of some elements and less of others. It helped to explain why she didn't look like either of her parents. She'd occasionally wondered how she'd been blessed with abundant dark brown curls when both her mother and father had wiry, unappealing hair. Other things were perplexing. If Mary Ellen and Thomas weren't her original parents, should others not have known? Or had her origins been erased from memory by the years of turmoil? Few in the area liked talking about those years. Barney's father said that people had endured so much and lost so many friends to starvation, disease or emigration that it was better not to dwell on what had happened. He also said that many people felt guilty. They asked why they'd been spared when those they'd loved had suffered agonising deaths.

It wasn't as though forgetting was easy. Just as the land was marked by tumbled cottages, families were scarred by the memories of those who had died or been forced to leave. Norah had always known that Barney had two aunts in Canada and a cousin who'd died of fever. She'd been aware of her own uncle in America. What she hadn't known was that another uncle had died. Neither had she ever been told that hunger had killed her grandmother.

The more Norah thought, the more she realised that there had been the occasional hint about her true origins. A neighbour had described her as doing well 'despite a bad start'. Another had asked if she intended to stay in Hackett's Cross. 'Why wouldn't I,' Norah had replied, 'when it's my home?' Back then, she'd seen nothing unusual about these remarks. Francie's letter had forced her to reconsider.

Norah had a sleepless night, thoughts jumping around her head, like moths around a candle. In the morning, she kept watch, lurking in a nearby field until her father left the house. Was he still her father? Or should she refer to John Joe Moloney as her father and Bridget as her mother? No, she decided, they were as yet unknown to her. She had no reliable image of them, no firm grasp.

Barney had offered to come with her, but he was working on a new building in the village so she'd assured him that she'd cope on her own. While times had improved, they weren't so good that he could afford to miss a day's work.

Ordinarily, she would have preferred to stay outdoors. On this occasion, she asked her mother if they could go inside. She didn't want anyone to see them, much less hear them.

She was nervous, unsure of how to start and unclear what she'd say if her mam dismissed the letter. She shouldn't have worried. As soon as she began talking, it was clear that Francie had told the truth. Her mother lowered her eyes and bowed her head. At no point did she interrupt. Whatever Norah had expected – denial? anger? contrition? – this wasn't it. Instead, her mother appeared resigned to her secret emerging. It was as if she'd spent every day of the past seventeen years waiting for this moment.

'How is she?' she asked eventually.

Norah was taken aback by the question. 'According to the letter, she's not well.'

Her mother looked genuinely concerned. 'I'm sorry to hear that. She was always the healthiest of us. As a child, she ran everywhere. No one could keep up. Even … No, I can't say she remained healthy during the Famine. Like many people, she didn't have enough to eat. But I continued to think of her as strong. She was a very resilient girl.'

'Why didn't you tell me about her?'

Even though she must have known the question was coming, Mary Ellen hesitated before replying. 'I should have done. I intended to, only the time never seemed right. And then we – your father and I – decided we'd left it too late. You were doing well, making your own way in the world. We felt it would only hurt you.'

Norah wondered if this was true. It sounded like a convenient excuse. She allowed her thoughts to drift back to her childhood. If not openly unhappy, her parents' marriage had often been tense. There had been little sign of the affection she'd witnessed in the Nugents' house. Her mother had always been anxious to please her father, as though she worried that she wasn't good enough for him. At the same time, Norah had always felt protected. And if neither parent had been especially demonstrative, their love had shown itself in practical ways: in plates of potato and herring, in clean clothes and a warm bed. Certainly, she had never doubted her mother's love. She recalled small things: a pat on the shoulder when the school master had commended her writing, the careful way her mam had combed and plaited her hair, the days they'd picked bluebells or honeysuckle together.

In her own way, her mother had been pretty, with sharp features and blue-grey eyes. Now, in her forties, she was prematurely old, her cheeks sunken, her mouth slack, strands of white in her rust-coloured hair.

'You have John Joe's hair,' her mam said. 'He had brown curls too. He was a handsome man. Otherwise, you look like Bridget. You've the same eyes.'

'I need to know more than that,' said Norah. 'I need to know why you never told me about my grandmother and my uncle Michael. And I need to know why my ... why Bridget left.'

'She left because ...' Again, her mother's gaze dropped to the ground, and she abandoned whatever she'd been about to say. 'You've got to understand what it was like in those years. To this day, I remember the silence. Everywhere was quiet, and if you heard a noise, it was probably someone in pain or in mourning. I was a young woman then. I thought that as long as we stayed alive, we wouldn't be affected. I thought we could shut ourselves off and forge ahead with our own lives. But, after all that suffering, how could any of us ever be the same? It brought a poison to the country, and sometimes I doubt we'll ever be free of it.'

Norah was growing impatient. 'I don't follow you.'

'We thought it best that you didn't know about my mother and about Michael. I was ashamed. Ashamed that they'd died such a terrible death. And ashamed that I'd done nothing to assist them. Every day I regret that we ... that I ... didn't act.'

Norah repeated her question. 'Why then did Bridget go to America? Could you not have helped her?'

Her mother clasped her hands together as if in prayer. 'I ...' The words didn't come. Presently, she stood and went to the bedroom. When she re-emerged, she was carrying a letter, its paper crisp with age. 'She left this for you.'

Norah took the sheets and read. Every single line, every single letter, hurt. It had been written by a woman in deep pain. A woman who had asked for her mercy. When she'd finished, she folded the paper and placed it in the pocket of her skirt.

'She didn't choose to leave, did she? She didn't abandon me?'

'No.'

'You made her go?'

'Yes.'

Norah watched her mother's face twist with misery. She waited for her to speak again. Finally, she did.

'What we did was wrong. I accept that. I wasn't able to have a baby of my own, and I wanted you. I'm not blaming Thomas's family, but they treated me like I was inferior. Like I wasn't a proper woman. I thought you were the answer to my problems. We could give you a home, and I would love you. You were such an engaging child. We told her ... told Bridget ... that we couldn't afford to feed you both. She'd run out of places to go ... and she was scared that if she didn't accept our offer you would die.'

'You took me and forced your sister to leave the country?' Norah caught her breath, concerned that she'd gone too far.

'Yes,' said her mother. She was weeping now, her shoulders shaking.

Norah's immediate impulse was to leave. But the woman in front of her might not be so candid again. She sat on her hands and instructed herself to stay.

'May God forgive me,' said her mother. 'What we did was wrong. I know that now. To be honest, I knew it then. We could all have lived here. It would have been difficult, but we would have survived. People survived worse. They lived ten or fifteen to a cottage and ate scraps. Still, they clung on.'

'Did you ever hear from ...' she considered her words carefully

'… from my mother again?' Mary Ellen flinched at the way she'd changed her use of 'mother'.

'No. We agreed that she would start afresh in America.' She rubbed her apron against her face. 'Does the letter say anything about her circumstances? Does she have a comfortable life?'

'She has a husband and two other children. But, no, I don't get the impression that her life has been especially easy.'

When it came to America, Norah had heard conflicting stories. Some people sent money back to their family. They wrote letters claiming their new home was filled with opportunity. Others were quieter. They gave little away – or they didn't write at all. Barney's father said that America could be a harsh place and that not everyone succeeded. Norah thought of Bridget, a country woman in a city full of strangers, and felt uneasy.

'Apart from telling me that my mother was healthy, and my father was handsome,' she said, 'you haven't told me much about them. What was she like?'

'She was lovely. Really lovely. With hindsight, I can see that I was … I can see that I was jealous. She was everyone's favourite. Not that she was a saint. We fell out plenty of times. She didn't like Thomas. I've always thought …' She paused and swallowed. 'I've always thought you got your friendly nature from her. Our brother, Michael, was similar. He was an immensely kind boy. I've come to think that the Famine was hardest on good-natured people. They allowed others to eat ahead of them, and they kept on giving when they'd nothing left to give.'

'What about my father?'

'I didn't know John Joe very well. His people were poor, even poorer than our own family. I do know that Bridget loved him. She'd always been sweet on him, like you and Barney. He caught the fever when he was on the relief works, and he didn't get long. You were only a baby.'

Norah knew every inch of the cottage, every dip in the floor, every stone in the walls. It was the only place she could remember. But she'd had a life before this place. She'd lived with her first mother and father in a cabin outside Clooneven. She'd spent time in the workhouse.

No sooner had she asked one question than another occurred to her. She needed more time to think, but her father might come home at any moment, and she was wary of facing him today. Unlike her mother, there was a danger he would be confrontational.

'What are you going to do?' she asked.

'You mean am I going to tell Thomas that you know the real story?'

'Yes.'

'What do you want me to do?'

'It's your decision,' said Norah, surprised by her own answer.

'And if I don't tell him?'

'I won't say anything.'

'Thank you,' said Mary Ellen, some of the tension leaving her face. 'What are you going to do about Bridget?'

In the space of a day, Norah's life had been turned upside down. She was not who she'd thought she was. Neither were her parents. She gave the only answer she could.

'I don't know,' she said.

'I see,' replied her mother. 'There's one other consideration. Your father doesn't know that I still have Bridget's letter. He told me to destroy it many years ago, but I couldn't quite bring myself to do that. If he found out ...'

'Don't worry,' said Norah. 'I'll keep it safe.'

Chapter 39

1865, Boston

Bridget

Bridget had difficulty accepting that she was ill. At first, she'd tried to ignore the tiredness. Then, she'd ignored the weight loss and the jabbing pain in her chest. Her family wouldn't allow her to ignore the coughing. 'You ought to go to a doctor,' Martin would say. In response, she would flap one hand and claim she always got sick in the winter. It was a legacy of the hard times in Ireland. She'd been through too many cold, damp nights. He knew that, didn't he? 'I'll be better when the weather improves,' she would argue.

But the winter became the spring, and her cough persisted.

Patrick was the first to see that she was coughing up blood. Once, she would have been able to buy his secrecy, to bribe him with extra pudding or another hour with his friends. He was thirteen now, though, and knew his own mind. He told his father, and Martin insisted she seek help.

It was consumption, the doctor said, in a voice that suggested he'd given the same diagnosis a thousand times that morning. What she needed was fresh air, a nutritious diet and a moderate amount of manual labour. Bridget explained that her life already contained all of these.

'Well, then, there's nothing else I can do for you, Mrs McDonagh.'

'Do you know what's causing it?' she asked. 'What I mean is … there are others on our street who are ill in the same way. Do you think that maybe we're infecting each other?'

'It's unlikely.'

'But, back in Ireland, people in the workhouse caught the fever from others living there. And on the ship too, lots of passengers became sick, my daughter among them.'

He gave her a cool appraisal. 'This isn't Ireland, Mrs McDonagh. It would be a mistake to assume that what occurred there could happen here.' He pronounced 'Ireland' with the same level of condescension as Henry Frobisher.

'Isn't it worth considering?' she said.

'Greater minds than ours have found no such connection. I don't think we're best placed to contradict them, do you?'

She thanked him – because what else could she do? – and went on her way. On her route home, she called into the new church. Gate of Heaven, they called it. She usually found peace there, sometimes from others, more often from herself. Increasingly, she felt guilty about Delia. There were days when she had a compulsion to talk about Alice and about the *Mary and Elizabeth*. She wanted to say, This was how it was, and I did what I thought was best. She blamed Francie, except blame was the wrong word. All her brother had done was point out the obvious. Delia was entitled to know the truth. Unfortunately, Martin was holding firm. He believed they'd left it too late to confess.

Dropping to her knees sent pain shooting up Bridget's legs, and perhaps that was why she did it. It was a form of penance. She blessed herself and thanked God for Martin, Delia and Patrick, and for returning Francie to her life. She prayed for the souls of her parents, for her brother, Michael, and for John Joe and Alice. She prayed, too, for the soul of President Lincoln, newly in his grave. And she prayed for someone whom she trusted was still living. She prayed for Norah.

The arrogance of the doctor's delivery didn't detract from the substance of his words. Bridget knew what he meant. What she didn't know was how she would tell her family. Martin had two colleagues who'd died from consumption. Delia had a friend whose mother had suffered the same fate. It was a vicious illness. 'The White Death', they called it, on account of how pale its victims became.

As she prayed, another thought crept in. She would never go back to Ireland. There was no chance of her seeing Norah again. Without thinking, she moaned. Although the sound was small, she was relieved that no one else was there to hear it. In Irish, the language she loved but rarely used, there was a special word for the sound a cow makes when her calf is taken. *Diadhánach* described a particular type of loneliness. To the best of her knowledge, there was no English equivalent.

Over the following weeks, Bridget tried to get as much fresh air as possible. Most days, she brought a kitchen chair to the front of their building and sat with the sun on her face, like she'd done as a young girl in Clooneven. With the family, she continued to put her best side forward. She gave them her diagnosis, then acted as though nothing had changed. When her chest pain was particularly sharp or she felt especially weak, she hid herself away. Oh, she knew this was dishonest, but she couldn't bear their downcast faces or anxious glances. She hated the conversations that stopped when she entered the room and the looks they swapped when she went to bed early.

Some days, she shook with anger at the unfairness of it all. She wanted to howl with rage and regret. She wanted to smash crockery and spit at strangers. Martin had already lost one wife. Delia had lost two parents. And for all his brave talk, Patrick was only a child. Not that she was completely selfless. She wasn't yet forty years old. Her hair was still red, her body still firm. She wanted more of this life. She wanted to dance and tell stories and walk by the sea. She wanted to see her children grow up and marry.

Occasionally, she found respite in anecdotes about people who'd survived for many years after becoming ill.

'My uncle got five years,' one neighbour said.

'My cousin lasted for seven,' said another. 'And she was in fine form until a month before she passed away.'

'That's nothing,' said a third. 'I worked with a fellow who recovered entirely. You'd never know there'd been anything wrong with him.'

Still, Bridget couldn't deny how sick she felt. On her worst days, the pain in her lungs was so intense that her knees gave way, and she was forced to lie down.

One day in the middle of August, she was sitting in her usual spot beside the front door when the mail came. The deliveries had begun a couple of years previously. Unlike many in the neighbourhood, the McDonagh family rarely received letters. They had no one to write to them.

That morning was different.

'Mrs Bridget McDonagh?' said the mailman, as he handed her a cream envelope. 'A letter from Ireland, no less.'

The writing was meticulous, which meant that even in the sunlight, it was easy to read the return name and address: *Mrs Norah Nugent, Gortagowan, Hackett's Cross, County Clare.*

Even though she'd decided against writing, Bridget had hoped for this day. She'd convinced herself that, while it would be wrong to contact Norah, it wasn't wrong to wish that, somehow, her daughter would find her. Francie had failed to see her logic. They'd argued and argued, until she'd told him that if he didn't bring a halt to his wheedling and cajoling, she would stop talking to him.

Despite having pictured what she would do if a letter came, she was reluctant to open it. The contents might not be what she'd wished for. Norah might be angry. She might ask why her mother had abandoned her.

While she sat there, the rag man passed with his weary horse. 'Any rags, any bones, any bottles today?' he called out, in his County Kerry accent.

The vegetable man, originally from Mayo, came too. 'Potatoes,' he hollered. 'Fresh potatoes and tomatoes.'

Groups of neighbours bustled by. And still she sat, desperate to know what the envelope contained, but equally desperate to avoid disappointment. She already had three important pieces of information. Norah was married, she lived close to where she'd grown up and, judging by the quality of her penmanship, she'd been good at school.

What Bridget couldn't understand was why she had written now, for even if Mary Ellen and Thomas had told her the truth, it didn't explain her knowing Bridget's married name and address.

Then it came to her. The letter hadn't been prompted by divine intervention but by the intervention of Francie Markham.

There were eight pages. Eight wonderful, vivid pages. Having finally found the courage to open the letter, Bridget spent the rest of the day reading and rereading. As she'd suspected, Mary Ellen had only told Norah about her in recent weeks, a development prompted by a letter from Francie.

Before writing, Norah had taken a few days to digest the information. In the beginning, she'd been furious. *How they treated you was disgraceful*, she wrote. *I wouldn't have believed them capable of such callousness. The*

*beautiful letter you left for me makes it clear that you didn't want to leave,
and I can't imagine how difficult those days must have been. My mother – I
think of you both as mother – is remorseful, however, and I have accepted
her apology. As of now, I can't forgive her but perhaps that day will come.*

Norah explained that she hadn't spoken to Thomas because she felt
confrontation would only make life harder for everyone. This worried
Bridget. Had he been a controlling father? Had he been bad-tempered
or violent? Then she told herself that, even if this had been the case,
there was nothing she could do about it.

Everything Norah wrote revealed her to be thoughtful and kind. If
this brought comfort to Bridget, it also tore at her heart. While reading,
she was in her daughter's world. She imagined her voice, her face, her
movements. She pictured her drinking tea or walking through the fields
or sharing a meal with her husband. She saw the waves washing against
the shore, the clouds drifting in from the Atlantic and the way the
grass looked at this time of year when the green had faded and burnt.
These were the images she'd never been able to let go of, and for all her
gratitude to Boston, she never would.

The letter ended with expressions of concern for Bridget's health. *I
pray that you're on the road to recovery. I don't know if you want to write
to me or if you'd like to hear more about our lives here in County Clare, but
please believe me when I say I would welcome anything you choose to put on
paper.* She signed the letter, *Your loving daughter, Norah.*

Initially, Bridget couldn't decide what to do. She considered hiding
the letter and writing back without saying anything to anyone. But that
wouldn't be wise. Francie had set the process in motion, and she needed
to talk to him.

By the time Martin got home from work, her mind was made up.

The bright evening meant that both Delia and Patrick were out with
friends, giving Bridget and her husband an opportunity to talk. While it
wasn't a word he used, it was clear he was scared. He feared that Norah's
sudden emergence would disrupt their lives and hurt Bridget's other

children. He paced the room, tension in every line on his face.

'I can see why you're pleased to have received the letter,' he said. 'Of course I can. Especially with … especially with things being the way they are. But I'm not sure you've thought this through. Your illness has been difficult for the children, and now you want to tell them that you've … that we've misled them.'

'It's because I'm sick that I need to talk to them,' she said. 'They deserve to know the full story while I'm still …' She allowed her sentence to fade away, but they both knew how it would have ended. She tried a different approach. 'It feels wrong that Norah knows about me while Delia doesn't know about Alice.'

Martin sat down and took her hand. 'Like I've said to you before, you're assuming she'll accept our explanation, and I don't think you can do that.'

'I'm not,' she said. While she desperately wanted to believe that Delia would understand, she knew she couldn't take it for granted. How many times had she said as much to Francie?

'And what about Patrick?' he asked. 'Isn't there a danger that we'll lose his trust? That he'll wonder what else we've been lying about?'

Lying. The word sounded so grubby. She'd rarely allowed herself to think of what they'd done as lying. But Martin was right. That was what it was.

The next morning, the four of them sat around the kitchen table, and hesitantly at first, Bridget spoke about her departure from home in the spring of 1848. Rather than bringing her daughter with her, she said, she'd boarded the ship on her own. She described how Delia's mother had drowned and how she'd adopted Alice's name. Finally, she revealed that the girl she'd left behind had written to her.

Patrick latched on to the details before his sister. It was easier for him. His part in the tale was more peripheral, less personal. 'What would have happened to Delia if you hadn't pretended she was your daughter?' he asked.

'I can't say,' replied Bridget. 'She might have gone to live with the richest family in Boston. Or she might have been sent to a home for the destitute. I didn't have much time to consider the situation. I did what I thought was right.'

Delia, who'd been staring at her fingers, looked up. 'I don't care that you didn't give birth to me. And I understand why you took me. I think I would have done the same. But …' She stopped and tried to compose herself. 'What I can't understand is why you didn't think I deserved the truth.'

To Bridget's relief, Martin spoke. 'We thought of you as our daughter,' he said. 'We always did. And when you were younger, we worried that telling you about your other family would unsettle you. We didn't want you to feel different.'

'If Norah hadn't written, it's unlikely I would ever have discovered the truth. That's wrong.'

'It is,' said Bridget, 'and we're sorry.'

'How much do you know about my family back in Ireland?'

Bridget sketched out what Alice had told her. She had to admit that it wasn't much.

Delia's eyes were wet. 'I'm never likely to find out any more than that, am I?'

'You're not, pet,' said Martin. 'I wish I could say otherwise, but we don't even know what Alice's name was before she married.'

As the years passed, Bridget had grown to understand that, far from being unusual, her experience of separation and abandonment was common. The Irish had been forced to scatter around the world, and while some families had remained intact, more had been torn apart by time and distance. Bonds had been severed, graves forgotten, decades of family history wiped away. Thousands upon thousands of families would never be quite the same.

She felt the urge to cough but didn't want any of them thinking she was looking for pity. Instead, she took a cautious breath. 'I feel very lucky that Norah has written,' she said, 'and it's my intention to reply to her. What's important, though, is that you both know how much I love you. What matters most to me is what I have here in America.'

It was only as she spoke that she realised how true this was.

Afterwards, Delia was guarded. She didn't ask many questions about Norah, and she was more prone to silence than before.

Bridget became flustered. 'Why can't she talk?' she would say to Martin. 'Why can't she tell me what she's feeling?'

'Give her time,' he would reply.

He didn't point out that he'd warned this might happen.

Then, one day, when they'd been talking about something else entirely, Delia looked at her and said, 'You saved my life.'

'I suppose you could say that. Then again, you saved me. I'd have been a right misery those first few months in America without you there to entertain me.'

Delia cast her eyes heavenwards. 'That's not the same at all.'

'It is to me.'

'I'll have to tell the authorities that I was stolen by a madwoman. You do realise that, don't you?'

For half a moment, Bridget feared she was serious.

Delia winked. 'Anyway,' she said, 'that wasn't what I meant. You saved my life twice. You stood up to the ship's captain, and he slapped you across the face.'

Bridget felt her lips curve into a smile. 'You've been talking to your father.'

'I have. Why didn't you tell me what you'd done?'

'Ah, it's a long time ago now. Your father was the first person to support me. Did he tell you that?'

'He didn't.' Delia paused. 'For fear I haven't said it, thanks for saving me.'

'It was no trouble,' replied Bridget, as she placed a hand on her daughter's cheek. 'No trouble at all.'

In the months that followed, Norah wrote frequently. Bridget valued every detail, from her daughter's childhood memories to funny tales about various neighbours to her thoughts on the campaign for tenants' rights and the political situation in Ireland. Reading between the lines, it seemed that, rather than shattering her bond with Mary Ellen, the truth had sent their relationship in a different direction. They spoke more often and more openly. This new honesty didn't include Thomas, who remained unaware of the shock delivered by Francie's letter.

In reply, Bridget wrote about her family in Boston and about the events that had shaped her. In a way, she was chronicling her life. After the first couple of letters, a pattern developed. She would write to Norah and then she'd tell similar stories to Patrick and Delia. At the start, she was wary of recounting some of the darker episodes. There had been a savagery about her final years in Ireland. Gentle people had been trampled upon, and they'd lacked the means to fight back. Did her children need to know about her own mother's lonely death at the side of the road? About the torment she'd witnessed in the Kilrush workhouse? About the nights she'd gone to sleep fearing she wouldn't wake again?

Gradually, her approach changed. She felt an obligation to tell the truth, no matter how difficult or ugly. She told them more about the ship and the storm; about her job on Beacon Hill and why she'd been forced to leave; about Peggy Russell's snobbery and the Cusacks' house, where she'd spent every day looking over her shoulder. She showed them her mementos: the cockle shell she'd taken from Hackett's Cross and the books given to her by Charlotte Edgecombe, *The Legend of Sleepy Hollow*, *Wuthering Heights* and *Narrative of the Life of Frederick Douglass*. Stupid as it might sound, the books had always meant more to her than the money that had accompanied them.

Sometimes the stories made them laugh. Delia, in particular, loved small, whimsical things, like the rivalry between Cook and Mrs Hogan.

'And there I was,' she said, 'trotting around in the middle of it all. It's such a shame I can't remember anything.'

To Bridget's surprise, Patrick enjoyed hearing about her youngest days in Boherbreen. She'd always assumed he had scant interest in Ireland, but her tales about their family home before the Famine appealed to him. Maybe the passage of time had gilded her memories, but there had been happy days when people gathered in each other's cabins, sang songs and played music. It was important that she recall those days too. In one of her letters, Norah had said that older people fretted because traditional songs and stories were being forgotten. The Famine hadn't just killed their neighbours, it had also changed their way of life.

There were occasions when the storytelling saddened Bridget and further eroded her energy. After all, what she was doing was an implicit acknowledgement that there would be no fresh memories. At least her reflections would give Patrick, Delia and Norah something to hold on to. She didn't want them to remember her as a fragile woman who'd struggled for breath. If she'd known cruelty and depravity, she'd also experienced great kindness and love. She needed them to understand that.

Frequently, Francie joined them. He further embellished Bridget's recollections of their childhood. In his version of events, he was always the hero, the one who warded off local villains, caught even the speediest rabbits and pulled wriggling fish from the sea.

'Don't listen to a word he says.' Bridget would laugh. 'Not one of his claims is true.'

Step by step, Martin became involved in their ritual. He opened up to Patrick and Delia about growing up in Connemara and about losing his first family on the *Mary and Elizabeth*. He told them about his home place, Claddaghduff, and about a nearby island called Omey.

'When the tide was right,' he said, 'we were able to walk across the sand to the island. There were fields there, and you'd swear they contained every flower on God's earth. On a fine day, I used to lie on the grass and listen to the sea. It was like being in Heaven.'

He spoke too about the day he'd encountered Bridget and Delia walking beside the harbour.

'I knew within a few minutes,' he said, 'that I wanted to be with you both. I went home that night feeling as though my life could begin again. *Dá fhada an lá, tagann an tráthnóna.*'

Bridget looked away then. She didn't like the children seeing her cry.

For a while, she held her illness at bay. In October, she celebrated her fortieth birthday. Thanksgiving and Christmas passed, and in January, Patrick turned fourteen.

In the first weeks after her diagnosis, she'd felt as if everything was sullied, and that even if she lived for another decade, life would be stripped of its lustre. She closed in on herself, as if her heart was shrinking. That had changed. She appreciated now that she was living on stolen time. Every additional day mattered. She was greedy for another hot summer, another scarlet and gold autumn. She wanted to watch Patrick grow even taller, and she hoped to see Delia marry Jimmy O'Brien, whom she'd been courting for more than a year. She longed for the birth of the baby Norah was expecting and she craved more time with Martin. She knew he'd be able to cope without her, but he shouldn't have to. He was fifty-six years old. He'd done enough, been through enough. For all these reasons, every day was important.

The problem was, the pain kept returning. It sat on her shoulder, sneering at her. If ever she relaxed, it swooped in again, stealing her breath and making a mockery of her intentions. Long gone were the days when she could cook dinners and clean the rooms. That all fell to Delia now.

One morning in April, she propped herself up in bed. Martin sat nearby. Spring sunlight filled the room. She would have liked to go outside and admire the blossom that decorated the city at this time of year, but she didn't have the strength. Perhaps she would ask Patrick to cut some blooms and put them in water for her. At home in Boherbreen, the whitethorn would be in flower. She imagined she could smell it.

She was expecting a letter from Norah. Because it took weeks for letters to cross the Atlantic, their correspondence could be disjointed. That didn't bother her. Any word at all was welcome, especially with a baby on the way. She was also expecting a visit from Francie, who usually called on Saturdays. She wasn't in the form for reminiscing. Her storytelling had run its course. She would prefer to hear from the others. It occurred to her that Delia and Patrick were afraid to talk about the future for fear it upset her. She would have to put that right.

There was, however, something she needed to say to Martin. It had been bothering her for days, but she didn't want him to think she was being silly.

'I haven't told you how much I love you,' she said.

Martin blinked. 'Of course you have.'

'I haven't done it enough, though. I should have said it more – to you and to Delia and Patrick.'

'We've always known.'

'Do you promise?'

'I do,' he said.

'I think I'll rest for a short while, so.'

'Would you like me to stay?'

'That would be good.'

Bridget closed her eyes. She felt surprisingly restful, as though everything she'd needed to say had been said. For that she was grateful.

Chapter 40

July 1866, Hackett's Cross
Norah

The letter arrived in July, exactly a year after the first. Norah held it against her heart, a gesture she knew was pointless. One look at the handwriting was enough for her to guess at the message within.

With Barney sitting beside her, she opened the envelope and read.

Dearest Norah,
I'm sorry to inform you that our lovely Bridget has passed on.
The final two months were difficult, but her last day was as peaceful as anyone could wish for. Father Kennedy gave her the last rites, and Martin, Delia and Patrick were there at the end. They're keen for you to know that she also asked for you.
Martin has requested that I tell you how much your letters meant to Bridget. When one arrived, she would read it over

and over again before giving the rest of us your news. Knowing you were well and happy made it easier for her to enjoy her final months. Although adamant that she was too young to be a grandmother, she was very excited that you were expecting a baby. It's a shame she didn't live long enough to hear about the birth.

She was relieved to know that you remain on friendly terms with Mary Ellen. Before she died, she told me that the only person she would never be able to forgive was Henry Frobisher. Any ill will she'd had towards our sister disappeared many years ago. Indeed, she said that when the time came, she hoped you would inform Mary Ellen of her death. If you could do that, we would be most grateful.

For my own part, I can say that no matter how many Irish people make the journey to America, the country will never send a finer person than your mother. She was loved and admired by all who knew her. Hundreds of people turned out for her funeral Mass. Everyone in the neighbourhood wanted to pay their respects.

I hope her letters have given you an insight into her character. Even though she told us what she was writing about, we all suspect she revealed more to you than to anyone here.

Despite almost twenty years in Boston, our homeplace in Clooneven was always in Bridget's thoughts. For many years, she tended not to talk about Ireland, and it was only in recent months that she started to recount some of her stories.

I don't know if you ever visit Clooneven or our home townland, Boherbreen, but should you find yourself there, please remember your mother.

By the time this letter reaches you, your baby might have arrived. If so, I hope he or she is healthy and strong.

I would like to wish you, Barney and the baby a long and contented life. Please do continue to write.
Yours sincerely,
Francie Markham

When she'd finished reading, Norah rocked slowly from side to side. For a year, she'd had a second mother. Admittedly, she'd only known her through her words. She couldn't picture her face or hear her voice. Yet Bridget had been as real to her as Barney. As real as the baby wriggling inside her or the couple who'd raised her. She knew the loss was far greater for Delia, Patrick and Martin, but still she felt a deep sadness for a woman who'd deserved a much longer life.

Her mother was more distressed than she had expected.

'I should have written to her,' Mary Ellen kept saying, as she walked the room. 'That's what I should have done. There were things I should have said.'

Norah didn't know how to respond. 'Mam, she was content. She had a strong marriage and a family who loved her. And you've heard what Francie said: she bore you no ill will. For what it's worth, I believe that. She always enquired after you.'

'Yes, only I should have written to thank her for allowing us to have you.'

Again and again, Norah tried to find the right words. She left the house knowing she'd failed, the weight of a past she couldn't remember heavy on her shoulders.

Her father arrived the next morning. Barney was at work, and Norah was in the cottage on her own. The baby, due any day now, had spent the night kicking and dancing. Not only was she tired, she remained raw with grief.

The set of his face revealed that something was wrong.

'Your mother told me about the letters,' he said, as he sat down. 'You might have let me know.'

'What way is Mam?' she replied, choosing to ignore his tone. 'She was in low humour when I left yesterday.'

'Why didn't you tell me?'

Because you're volatile, she felt like saying. *Because I knew you would react like this*. Norah wasn't able for an argument, however, and she chose her words carefully. 'Because the letters were between me and Bridget. She's gone, so it doesn't matter, does it?'

'What matters is that both you and your mother have been dishonest. Does Barney know?'

'He does.'

Her father cracked his knuckles, a habit that had always irritated her. 'And what does he think?'

'He encouraged me to write to Bridget and he was delighted that she sent so many letters.'

'I see.' Another knuckle crack. 'I don't like to speak ill of the dead, but she was a ferocious troublemaker. She had a vicious tongue on her. She was always looking to poison your mother against me. You do realise that, don't you?'

One of the things that Norah had noticed was how infrequently Bridget had spoken about her father. There were shopkeepers, neighbours and distant cousins who'd received more mentions than the man sitting beside her. That, she supposed, told its own tale.

'She came across very well in her letters.'

One more crack. 'I didn't say she was stupid. She was far from it. It's a shame she didn't put her intelligence to better use.'

'I'm mourning her death,' said Norah, 'and I'd appreciate it if you'd stop maligning her.'

He leant forward and rested a hand on her arm. 'If I were you, I'd destroy those letters. I'll do it this minute if you like.'

'No, you won't.'

'Where are they? We can throw them on the fire and be done with it.'

Norah saw that he was serious. 'No,' she repeated.

'No good will come of holding on to them,' he said, his voice steady. 'You'll only spend your time getting emotional about a woman you can't ever meet. Be a sensible girl and hand them over to me.'

She got to her feet. 'They were sent to me, and it's for me to decide what happens to them. Now, before you upset me any further, I think you should go home.'

Chapter 41

July 2019, Boston
Kaitlin

'So that was why Norah sent most of the letters back to Boston?' said Kaitlin.

'That's right,' said Gina. 'If you look at the note she included with them, she wanted to make sure they were safe. She also felt that Patrick, Delia and Martin deserved to read everything Bridget had written.'

'Jessie told me that her family still had the letter Bridget wrote before she left in 1848, the one where she explained why she had to go. I can understand why Norah held on to that one. It must have been extra special to her.'

Gina nodded. 'I assume she hid it away somewhere. I get the feeling she could be crafty when she had to be.'

For two hours, they'd been sorting through the box of letters, half of them written by Bridget, the other half by Norah. A few seemed to be missing, but not many. In all, there were more than thirty letters, most of them immensely detailed. The length of time it took for the post to reach its destination meant that occasionally the conversation was hard to follow. Norah would ask a question, and Bridget would reply two months later, during which time they'd both sent several other letters. This was a minor consideration. In the main, although brittle with age, the letters were in remarkably good condition. Even those that had been torn or stained were legible.

Bridget's letters read as though she was conscious of having an enormous amount to say and limited time in which to say it. She'd had to condense forty years of life into less than a year of correspondence. Both women had been articulate, passionate and unexpectedly funny.

Kaitlin had started the evening hoping to discover a little more about a woman who might or might not have been named Alice. Then Alice had become Bridget. Even so, she'd tempered her expectations. She'd anticipated a letter or two. A scrappy memento, perhaps. What she'd got was a first-hand account of a turbulent time in history. She was overwhelmed by Bridget's intense will to survive and her ability to rise above adversity and loss.

Over scores of pages, the letters told a story of oppression and sacrifice but also of bravery and the potency of kindness.

Orla, who'd been crying quietly, wiped her eyes. 'I can't believe she was only forty. That's a ridiculous age to die, especially given how much she'd managed to live through.'

'It is,' agreed Kaitlin. 'TB is one of those diseases we hardly think about now, but back in the day it must have terrified people.'

The letters had been handed down the generations until they'd come into Gina's possession. No doubt they'd rested in countless closets and drawers. They must have been read by dozens of people, including some of the men and women whose pictures were in Orla and Drew's box of photographs. Kaitlin felt a renewed connection to them all.

'I have this sense,' said Gina, 'that in the early years they were seen as regular letters, the sort of thing you'd find in every immigrant house. Thankfully, there was always someone who considered them significant enough to hold on to.'

'I know,' said Kaitlin. 'Can you imagine if they'd ended up in the trash?'

'It could easily have happened,' said Gina, pouring more wine. 'I'm due to retire next year, and I'd promised myself I'd try to find out more about Bridget's family in Ireland. I wondered if anyone there might be interested in what became of her. But what you've said has blown me away. Not only is Johanna in the history books, it turns out that Bridget and Norah were famous in London, and they didn't know it.'

'I can't wait to tell Jessie. Imagine, she still thinks Bridget died on the ship.'

The box also contained two of the three books given to Bridget by Charlotte Edgecombe: the Frederick Douglass autobiography and *The Legend of Sleepy Hollow*. There too, grimy and crumbling with age, was a cockleshell, presumably the same one she'd taken from young Norah's collection. Kaitlin picked it up and placed it in the palm of her hand. It was incredible to think it had been brought to America almost two centuries earlier.

'What a shame Charlotte Edgecombe didn't have the courage of her convictions,' said Orla. 'She should have stood up to her husband and insisted that Bridget and Delia stay where they were. It's clear that Bridget adored that job.'

'I hear you,' said Kaitlin, 'only if she'd kept her job on Beacon Hill, she might never have married Martin, and I'm glad she did.'

'Oh, me too,' said Gina. 'Especially given that we're both descended from their son, Patrick. And I'm glad she met up again with Francie. If it wasn't for him, Norah might never have known the truth.'

Kaitlin was moved by the way Gina spoke. It was as if she'd known Bridget Markham Moloney McDonagh and her family. Now she had read the letters that was how she felt too. For all the heartache they contained, there was something curiously uplifting about them. She'd always reserved a certain scepticism for people claiming to be proud of their roots. A truism made banal through overuse, it was something you could say without fear of contradiction, like, 'You can't take it with you,' or 'Everything happens for a reason.' But she was genuinely, justifiably, proud to be related to Bridget.

'I'll give Jessie a call in the morning,' she said. 'In the meantime, I'll take a couple of screenshots, if that's okay. I can send them to her now, so she sees them when she wakes up.'

Chapter 42

Dave stood in front of her, shoulders back, head raised as though the room was his. Jessie looked from him to Lorna. Ger looked at her.

'This is insane,' she said. 'You can't keep us here like a pair of hostages.'

'That,' said Dave, 'isn't what we're doing, but you know that. All we want is a little chat about why you were messing around on private property. It won't take long.'

That his tone was measured didn't make it any less menacing. She was baffled that she'd ever suspected him of having an affair with her sister. Now that she assessed him properly, she saw the violence in his narrow eyes, in the entitled tilt of his chin, in the impatient way he tapped on the kitchen counter. She wondered why she hadn't seen this from the start. Then again, successful criminals tended not to advertise their crimes. They wore their disguises well and adapted their personalities to suit the occasion. If you wanted to win someone's confidence, you didn't get a facial tattoo. If you wanted to buy coffee without arousing suspicion, you didn't wear a balaclava.

'Those buildings aren't private property,' she replied. 'At least, not to me. They belong to Simon and Lorna, so I've more right to be out there than you have. Anyway, what we were doing is beside the point. What matters is what you were doing.'

She hoped she sounded confident because, despite her sister's presence, she was scared. After Dave had found them at the sheds, he'd summoned Simon. To begin with, she'd been too shocked to put up much of a fight. Ger had been tougher. At one point, she'd been convinced he would hit Dave. The problem was that, short of dashing across the fields, there hadn't been anywhere for them to go. Dave had insisted on bringing them to the house, which was where they were now, standing in Clevedon's sterile kitchen, arguing about what they'd seen and what it meant.

Simon had remained with Quan and Linh. So far, Lorna had said almost nothing, and when she did speak, she was subdued.

Dave, however, was bristling with energy. He was *buzzing*. 'You can lose the attitude,' he said to Jessie. 'I don't know what rubbish you have in your head but, take my word for it, you're wrong.'

'What exactly is it I'm wrong about?'

He didn't answer.

Lorna dragged a hand through her hair. Under the kitchen spotlights, she appeared drained, her face all shadows and bone, her neck thin and sinewy. 'What I don't understand is why you were out there to begin with,' she said. 'Like, why were you rambling around in the dark? What were you looking for?'

'As Jessie said,' replied Ger, 'what we were doing isn't the issue. Oh, and for fear you're wondering, we saw the plants in the other buildings, so we know what's going on.'

'Ah, he speaks,' said Dave, cocking his head to one side. 'Now that your girlfriend's found her voice, I thought you were going to leave all the yapping to her. She's got plenty to say for herself.'

Ger gave him a watery smile. 'That's one dodgy business you're running out there.'

'Dodgy business?' said Dave, with a smirk. His face was suited to smirking. 'You haven't a clue what you're on about.'

'Yeah, I do. It's a pretty serious offence, human-trafficking.'

'Oh, I see. That's what they told you, is it? "Human-trafficking" no less.' He recited the words as if reading the television news. 'By the sound of things, the pair of them spun you a yarn, and you were gullible enough to believe it.'

'I know who I believe,' said Ger, 'and it isn't you.'

They could continue like this all night, thought Jessie, both sides tossing out questions that wouldn't be answered. Lob and volley. Back and forth. While she wasn't convinced that Lorna would force them to stay, neither could she see Dave agreeing to let them go. And he was clearly the one in charge. A professional in a room of amateurs. She returned to the idea of making a run for it. After all, Ger was fit, and she knew the terrain. She quickly dismissed it as a fanciful idea. They were unlikely to get further than the driveway, and Ger's car was in the opposite direction. Besides, she wanted to hear what her sister had to say. She decided to try a different approach.

'Lorna,' she said, 'I don't know what you're mixed up in or why, but you've got to let Linh and Quan go. If you do that now, maybe the consequences won't be so bad.'

She noticed a nervous twitch in her sister's cheek.

As Lorna went to speak, Dave intervened: 'There's no lock on any of those doors. The two of them could have walked away any time they liked.'

'And where would they have gone?' asked Jessie. 'You've got their passports.'

For a second, he seemed taken aback by her knowledge. Then he gave a dismissive wave of the hand. 'Simon has the passports for safekeeping. They could have asked for them back, no worries.'

'A likely story. They've no money and only a vague idea of where they are. Oh, and they're terrified.'

'Is that what they told you?'

'Yes, and like Ger, I trust them. Anyway, I was talking to my sister, not you. I don't even know who you are.'

As the minutes passed, Dave became more agitated. Lorna, on the other hand, appeared to be shrinking into herself, as though the consequences of Jessie and Ger's presence were sinking in. It was hard to believe that this was the woman who, only a few hours earlier, had swaggered into the café and reprimanded Jessie for taking a lunch break.

Of the four, Ger was the most together. He retained at least a veneer of calm.

'I think it's time we were heading away,' he said to Jessie. 'We're not going to get any sense here.'

He turned, as if moving towards the door, prompting a swift lunge from Dave, who seized his arm and yanked him back.

'You're going precisely fucking nowhere,' he said.

Ger struggled free, and Jessie feared a fight. A snap judgement told her that while Ger was younger and healthier, Dave was probably more experienced. And more vicious.

'For God's sake,' said Lorna, in what could only be described as a whispered shout, 'calm down, would you?'

She was, it occurred to Jessie, scared that a commotion would wake the children. The last thing she needed was Ethan or Zoë wandering in, looking for a glass of water or a reassuring hug. Her intervention worked, and the pair lapsed into a silent standoff.

'We've got to sort this out,' continued Lorna, fiddling with her rings. 'Perhaps we can come to some sort of agreement. What if—'

Before she could give full voice to her proposal, the back door was pushed open. Jessie looked around to see Simon accompanied by Quan.

Although supposedly in charge, her brother-in-law looked haunted, his shoulders sloping, his skin misted with sweat.

'What are you doing up here?' said Dave. 'And where's the other one? Why did you leave her on her own? Who knows what ideas this pair of clowns,' he nodded at Jessie and Ger, 'have been putting into her head?'

For a moment, there was quiet.

'Where is she?' he repeated, an edge to his drawl.

'Not where she should be,' said Simon.

'What's that supposed to mean?'

'It means that during the hassle down below, she disappeared. We've been looking everywhere for her without any luck. It's pitch black out there. We went as far as the back boreen, and there's a car parked there all right, but no sign of life.'

So much for Quan and Linh being free to leave whenever they liked, thought Jessie. She wondered if Linh's escape had been prompted by what they'd said to her about the town being close by – and about people being willing to help.

Dave walked towards Quan. 'Where'd she go?'

Quan recoiled as though the man in front of him was radioactive.

'I asked you a question,' said Dave. 'Where is she?'

Quan shook his head. 'I don't know.'

'I'm not swallowing that. Where is she?'

'You can ask all night if you like,' said Ger. 'It's obvious he's telling the truth.'

Dave jabbed a finger in his direction. 'You can stay the fuck out of this. It's nothing to do with you.'

'Listen,' said Simon, 'I don't reckon Quan knows anything either. He was fairly shocked when he realised Linh was gone.'

'Well, there aren't too many places she could have got to. There's nothing around here apart from bog and more fucking bog. And she hasn't had enough time to make it to Clooneven.' He picked up his leather jacket, which had been lying over the back of a chair. 'Come on, we'll go and take a proper look. Have you got a torch?'

'There's a couple under the stairs,' said Lorna. 'I'll get them.'

Again, Dave turned to Quan. 'You're to stay here with the women, and you,' he nodded at Ger, 'can come with us. But no tricky stuff, yeah?'

There was a logic to this division. Quan was unlikely to leave the house while the others were searching for Linh, but if Ger had stayed behind, Lorna would have been outnumbered. Say what you like about Dave, he knew what he was doing.

After they'd left, Lorna continued to ooze tension. Jessie remembered what Ger had said earlier in the evening about her ability to wheedle information from people. This was an opportunity to test her skills. Right now, she was operating on scraps. She still didn't know who Dave was or why he was conducting his business here. Or why Lorna and Simon had got involved.

She switched on the coffee-maker.

'What are you doing?' asked Lorna.

'Mowing the lawn. What does it look like? Do you fancy a cup, Quan?'

She glanced in his direction and was struck again by how young he was. Twenty-two, Linh had said; the same age as Bridget when she'd drowned on the *Mary and Elizabeth*. At twenty-two, Jessie's life had been a perpetual party. He seemed wary of her. Then she recalled how she'd lied the previous night when she'd denied having a connection to Lorna and Simon. He had reason not to trust her.

'You're probably wondering what I'm doing here,' she said. 'Lorna's my sister but … I didn't know about Linh and yourself until last night. That's why Ger and I came back.' She took three mugs from the cupboard and fetched a litre of milk from the American-style fridge. 'I'll make coffee for all of us.' She needed to act as though she was in charge, as though everything would be fine in the end. 'And I'll throw on a few slices of toast. Anyone else for toast?'

'Jesus Christ,' said Lorna. 'Will you stop it?'

'Stop what?'

'You know what I mean. The happy housewife carry-on. You're behaving like this is a perfectly normal situation.'

'I don't see what else I can do. What's been going on has nothing to do with me.'

'You could have kept out of it, though. Why did you feel the need to go snooping out the back?'

Jessie reminded herself that this wasn't about her. Losing her temper would be counterproductive. She said nothing. Instead, she focused on fixing the promised coffee and toast. In the background, the machine clunked and hissed. The aroma of warm bread drifted from the toaster. Quan, who had been standing a few metres apart, began to relax. When the toast was ready, he joined them at the kitchen island. He ate like he hadn't had a meal in days. Lorna stared at her plate.

For the first time in twenty-four hours, Jessie was ravenous. Also, eating saved her from having to say anything, and she was still working out how to tackle her sister.

It was only as she placed another round of bread in the toaster that something hit her. Simon had mentioned seeing Ger's car. He hadn't said anything about a bicycle. If Linh had taken Jessie's bike, she'd be well clear of the area by now. She might find someone to talk to.

When they'd finished eating, she looked at Quan. 'Is it all right if Lorna and I go over there?' She tipped her head towards a low scarlet sofa at the far end of the room. 'I need to have a word with her.'

He nodded.

Jessie felt awkward about challenging Lorna in front of Quan. It seemed insensitive to discuss someone's ill-treatment while they were within earshot. This was also a family discussion, however, and she might not get a better opportunity to confront her sister.

She took out her cigarettes and offered one to him. He declined. She lit up, took a long pull and asked Lorna for an ashtray.

'I didn't say you could smoke,' her sister replied.

Jessie blew a stream of smoke towards the ceiling. 'Are you serious?'

Lorna found an ashtray.

Chapter 43

'I could ask you a million questions,' said Jessie, as she sat down, 'except now that I think of it, there's only one: why? Why were you doing this?'

At the far end of the sofa, Lorna looked like a prisoner bracing herself for interrogation. Stripped of her normal fizz and bluster, she seemed frail. She could refuse to answer, or she could lie and obfuscate. Still, Jessie sensed she was willing to talk.

'It wasn't what I wanted,' she said. 'Whatever else you think, you've got to understand that. At the start, I didn't even know.'

'Are you kidding me?'

'Please, Jessie. Hear me out, would you?'

'Why do it, then?' she said, as she put out her cigarette.

'Because we were desperate. We needed the money.'

'Come on, Lorna, there are countless ways of getting money. Most folks could do with more cash, but they don't go into the drugs business or exploit immigrants.'

Lorna gave her a waspish look. 'I don't think you're in any position to give lectures on financial management.'

'Fair point,' said Jessie. 'Let's not get distracted, though. If you were short of funds, why not go to the bank?'

'Because it was the bank we owed the money to.'

The story that unfolded was one of bad luck and worse judgement. Simon and Lorna had remortgaged Clevedon to fund its renovation. They'd also borrowed heavily to open the café and revamp the amusement arcade. They'd been confident the figures supported their investment. Okay, they'd massaged them a little to impress the bank, but they'd remained adamant that, all going well, their gamble would yield a hefty return. All had not gone well. A series of sodden summers had hit their income, while the house had become a money pit, every job costing twice as much as they'd budgeted for.

'Why didn't you scale back your plans, then?' said Jessie. 'I mean, look around you. Every single item in this place is top of the range. I know I sound like Mam, but was all that spending really necessary?'

'It's easy to say that now,' replied Lorna. 'At the time, we thought we'd just have to ride it out. We told ourselves that everything would come good eventually. The way we saw it, our plans remained sound and the setbacks were only temporary.'

And you didn't want to lose face in the town, thought Jessie. *You couldn't bear any of the local rumour merchants thinking you were struggling, especially when your persona was built on being the woman who worked hard and persevered. The woman who'd married well and made the most of every opportunity. That this sounded so basic didn't make it any less true.*

At some point, Lorna and Simon's bank had changed its operations in Ireland and sold its bad loans to another company. It, in turn, had sold them to an out-and-out vulture fund, one of those places where sentiment is forbidden. There were no more polite chats with the bank manager. No cups of milky tea and plates of custard creams. No generous restructurings. The fund was determined to squeeze them until they squeaked. Their only point of contact was a call centre in Pittsburgh where smooth-voiced agents recited the rules and figures. There was no leeway, no nods and winks, just a teetering pile of debt. The pressure was relentless. If Simon and Lorna didn't meet the repayments, the house and businesses would no longer be theirs.

'Correct me if I'm wrong,' said Jessie, 'but aren't there protections in place to make it harder to repossess family homes?'

'We were deep in arrears. Believe me, Jessie, we got advice. Whatever way we looked, we were screwed.'

Being the queen of the brave face, Lorna had continued to work in the shop and arcade. She'd even done the occasional shift in the Seashell. Her hair had been blow-dried, her nails manicured. Outwardly, everything had been fine. Simon had focused on ways of finding cash. If you asked Jessie, it would have made more sense to reverse their roles. Lorna was undoubtedly the more resourceful of the two. Reluctant to interrupt her sister's flow, she kept this assessment to herself.

'As time went by,' said Lorna, 'I began to despair. Simon insisted that he was making progress. He told me he'd heard of someone who could help. If "help" is the right word.'

'I take it the someone was Dave.'

'Uh-huh.'

'Is that his real name?'

'It is, yeah. Dave Hodnett's his name.'

'What happened then?' asked Jessie.

Lorna looked down at her lap. 'That was when Lam arrived.'

'Lam?'

'He was here before Quan and Linh. That was how ... that was how it started. The cannabis, I mean. But, again I swear to you, I didn't know what was happening until it was too late to do anything about it.'

'I take it Lam was a prisoner too?' said Jessie.

'I don't like—'

'You mightn't like the word, but it's the right one. Don't forget I've seen the conditions in those sheds.'

'I suppose,' said Lorna.

'So, just to be clear about this: are you saying that Simon didn't consult you? That everything was in train before you knew what was going on?'

'Listen, I can see why you mightn't believe me, but I'm telling you the truth.'

'Could you not have objected? Growing weed is one thing. Keeping people prisoner is entirely different.'

'I did. I told Simon I didn't want to have anything to do with it. He said there was no other way. It was our absolute last resort. The fund was about to take us to court. Everything would have been gone. We were frantic with worry.'

Dave, it turned out, was an enforcer, a middleman. He worked for a larger operation in Dublin.

'Who runs the larger operation?' asked Jessie.

'It doesn't matter. We don't have any contact with them.'

'Of course it matters. Do you know who he works for?'

'I do, only ...'

'Only what?'

'Okay, I'll tell you. You've got to trust me, though, when I say I didn't know at the start.'

'Go on,' said Jessie.

Lorna pressed her fingertips together. 'It's a name you'll be familiar with. Vincent McPartlin. But, like I say, we only found that out later and—'

'You've got to be joking.' Vincent McPartlin was the criminal who'd been under discussion on the night of Jessie's TV disaster. He was the hardman's hardman, a ruthless gangland figure who'd left a trail of blood and ruined lives behind him. From what she'd read, cannabis was only part of his drugs roster. His gang also dealt heroin and cocaine.

When her sister didn't respond, she tried again: 'I thought McPartlin was locked up again.'

'He's in Mountjoy,' said Lorna, her voice muffled. 'Apparently, his eldest son is running the show.'

Jessie took a minute to process the information. Or maybe she took longer. Time felt distorted. Little wonder that Dave, brash, cocksure Dave, had got his kicks from making fun of her. She'd derailed a conversation about his boss and made a fool of herself in the process. Oh, the hilarity.

She remembered the evening the family had learnt about her skipping out on her landlord without paying the rent. In particular, she recalled Lorna's theatrical performance and her sermon about being responsible with money. Had that been a deliberate tactic? Deflect, deflect, deflect. Or had her sister become so detached from reality that she no longer recognised her own hypocrisy?

'Have you any notion how dangerous the McPartlins are?' Jessie said eventually, her voice louder than was wise.

'Like I told you, we've never had to deal with them. Dave arranged everything.'

'You know as well as I do that Dave *is* the McPartlins. All he's missing is the name.' She reached for her cigarettes and lit up. 'Does "everything" mean Lam, Quan and Linh?'

'Yes.'

'Great. So you're doing business with some of the nastiest scumbags the country has ever produced. Way to go, Lorna.'

Noticing the increase in tension, Quan's head jerked up. He'd plainly been following everything they'd said. This shouldn't have been a surprise. It had been apparent the previous night that, while he was hesitant to speak English, his understanding was good.

'I'm sorry, Quan,' said Jessie. 'I'll keep it down.'

'She was kind,' he said, looking at Lorna. 'Not like the others.'

'Thank you,' whispered Jessie's sister. 'I tried.'

'All the same, you tolerated what was going on.'

'In a few months it would have been over.'

'And what would have happened then? Would they have been moved on to another one of Dave's enterprises? New county, same exploitation.'

'No,' said Lorna, her voice stiffening. She crossed her arms over her chest. 'Dave assured me that their debt would be paid off by then and they'd be free to go.'

'You're too smart to fall for that,' said Jessie. 'Besides, were you not frightened of getting caught? I mean, there was Dave strutting around the town when he'd no obvious business in the place. You know what Clooneven's like. Did you not think people would say, "Hold on a minute – who's your man and what's he up to?"'

'He wasn't here that often and he tended to avoid most people. He made an exception for you … because he'd seen the telly clip, I guess. You seem to amuse him.'

Jessie blew out a stream of smoke. 'What about my question? Were you not scared that someone would cop on to what was happening here?'

'Of course I was,' said Lorna, her words embedded in a sigh. 'In particular, I was worried about Mam or Dad coming over and spotting something.'

'Why ask me to babysit, then?'

'Because you were cheap and because I couldn't see you traipsing around out the back. You'd never shown any interest before. I assumed you'd sit here with your nose pressed to your phone or a book.'

Presumably Dave Hodnett had thought something similar. Worse, he'd probably considered her too dizzy, too stupid, to notice that anything was amiss. He hadn't bargained on the observational powers of an honest four-year-old.

'How much longer were you planning on spending in the drugs trade?' she asked.

'You make it sound like we're dealing crack. I'm sure you've done far more than smoke weed.'

The honest answer was, yes, she had. Short of heroin, Jessie had tried most of what had been available. The last time she'd done coke had been with Oisín, Phelim's former friend. Looking back, she hadn't just been reckless, she'd been arrogant.

She pulled on her cigarette. 'You didn't answer my question.'

'Obviously, we weren't going to keep on doing this. Once we'd made enough money to sort out some of our debts, we'd have called a halt.'

'Does Dave know that? Because he doesn't strike me as the sort of guy who'd say, "Hey-ho, job done" and walk away?'

'I told Simon I wasn't willing to continue. I told him I'd take the kids and leave.'

Lorna's movements, Jessie noticed, had become increasingly jittery. Her hands were shaking, while one knee jiggled up and down. Dave, Ger and Simon had been gone for quite a while. Either Linh was impossible to find or something else had gone wrong. She watched a clump of ash fall to the floor then reached over, stubbed out her cigarette and closed her eyes.

As disgusted as she was by what had happened, she also felt the slightest stirrings of sympathy for her sister. Was that wrong? Lorna had been in a precarious position; everything she'd worked for had been in jeopardy. Dave and his criminal friends had taken advantage of the situation because there was always a Dave, someone who saw opportunity in another person's difficulty. Someone whose desire for money or power was so all-consuming that they viewed other people as expendable. Someone with no mercy, no boundaries. Oh, and there was always a Simon, someone who was willing to push aside his morals when life became tough.

That, she figured, was how bystanders became criminals. After all, how many news stories had there been about previously clean-living girlfriends who were coaxed into storing drugs or guns? About men who lost their jobs and drifted into money-laundering?

Jessie only opened her eyes again because she felt her phone vibrate in her pocket. She hoped it was a message from Ger. Instead, it was an email from Kaitlin titled *Amazing news about Bridget!!!!* Jessie wouldn't have put Kaitlin down as a four-exclamation-marks type of woman. She considered opening it, but this wasn't the time. Short of Bridget being resurrected from the dead, she couldn't imagine any news being that amazing. She'd read it later.

'What are you going to do?' asked Lorna.

'I'm not sure that I have a choice.'

'You do.'

'No,' said Jessie. 'I'm sorry, Lorna, I don't. Even if I wanted to walk away and forget about it, Ger wouldn't be willing to lie.'

That was the truth. Once again, she asked herself if involving him had been a mistake. Should she have tried to handle things on her own? But what would she have done about Quan and Linh? When it came to them, there was no room for ambiguity. They couldn't have stayed here. She couldn't have looked the other way.

Her sister stared at her, her gaze unblinking. A tear rolled from the corner of one eye. 'What about family loyalty? You haven't considered what this would do to Mam and Dad, not to mention the kids.'

'I've thought about it all. Believe me, I have.'

Lorna looked away. 'I'm sorry,' she said. 'I would never have chosen for this to happen. Never.'

Jessie didn't reply. Instead she sat in silence. She thought of her parents and Etty. She thought of Ethan and Zoë, of Ashling and Ivana in the café, and of Quan and Linh. She thought of Ger, Simon and Dave. She thought of Bridget and Norah. And she thought of her sister, unravelling beside her.

An hour later, the men returned without Linh. According to Dave, they'd been all over the area, first on foot and later in his car.

As he blew into the room, his eyes glittered with anger. It must have been clear to him that whatever hope he'd had of persuading Jessie and Ger to stay quiet had been shattered by Linh's disappearance.

Jessie's fears were rekindled. Everything she'd learnt about him suggested he was dangerous. Even if Linh had found someone to talk to, they might not have listened. And even if they'd listened, would they have known what to do?

She did her best to catch Ger's eye, but Dave kept getting in her way. He was patrolling the room, tossing out insults. The atmosphere between the three men was toxic, with most of Dave's anger directed towards Simon.

'Right,' he said. 'We need to sort things and we need to sort them quickly. And what we don't need is an audience. Where can we put these three?'

Her stomach turned over. 'What do you mean? What are you planning on doing with us?'

'You know you're a complete pain in the arse,' he said, taking a step towards her. 'Do you ever stop asking questions?' He looked at Ger. 'How do you put up with her?'

'Her question sounded reasonable to me,' Ger replied.

Dave took another step. His breath filled her nostrils. It smelt like cat food. She saw his fleshy nose, the flecks of grey in his beard, the minute white scar under one eye. She felt the laser-focus of his stare. She tried to shuffle backwards but she was right up against the kitchen island and couldn't move any further.

'Don't come any closer to me,' she said.

'I'll do whatever I have to.'

'Get away from her,' said Ger.

Dave laughed. 'Or what?'

'Leave my sister alone,' added Lorna. To Jessie, her voice sounded distorted, like an old-fashioned radio not quite on the station.

Dave tilted his head in Lorna's direction. 'I didn't ask for your opinion.'

He took another half-step. By now, his body was almost touching Jessie's. She was part frightened, part repulsed. Ger stepped forward, gripped a hand around Dave's arm and pulled him away. Swiftly, Dave wrestled free, turned and attempted a punch. Ger was ahead of him, however, and landed the first blow. It connected but wasn't strong enough, and Dave hit back. In a finger click, a brawl developed. They were punching and kicking. They were on the floor. They were pulling and dragging and struggling. It occurred to Jessie that someone like Dave would carry a knife.

Lorna screamed.

Simon roared, 'Stop it, would you?'

Jessie wasn't sure whether he was talking to his wife or to Ger and Dave. She was on the point of speaking when something about Quan distracted her. He was standing slightly to her right and, like her, was facing the back door. Although she didn't have a clear view of his face, she realised that his body language had changed. His shoulders tensed. In another instant, he was swerving around the fight and dashing towards the door.

It was only then that Jessie saw the car sweeping into the backyard.

Chapter 44

September 2019, Clooneven

'It's okay,' said Jessie to Ashling. 'You can get off home. I'll close up.'

Her colleague didn't need a second invitation. 'Thanks a million, missus,' she said, as she removed her apron and loosened her ponytail. 'We'll miss you when you're far away.'

At the mention of her trip, Jessie felt a leap of happiness. 'Ah, here. It's not that far away. It's practically the next parish. And I'll be back in ten days.'

'Well, take care of yourself,' said Ashling, giving her a hug. 'And have a great time. You deserve it.'

Not everyone would agree with you, she thought. She smiled all the same. 'You're the best, Ash. I mean that. The absolute best. I'd have been sunk without you and Ivana.'

Two months on, and there wasn't an hour in the day when Jessie didn't think about what her sister had been part of. Sometimes, she felt removed from reality, as though she'd become tangled up in someone else's existence while her real life – Dublin, magazine writing, Phelim – was sauntering on without her. Often, she would wake at four in the morning, clammy and unsettled, unanswered questions circling her brain.

She tried not to talk too much about what had happened. Indeed, there were details the guards had warned her not to reveal.

This didn't prevent the local gossips from having their say. They *lived* for the details.

Did you hear the latest?

Do you know what puzzles me?

Seriously, does anyone believe the rest of the family didn't know?

While some townsfolk bombarded her with questions, more turned their backs. For others, the revelations were an opportunity. Resentments stored since childhood were dusted down and presented anew. Although Jessie trusted that the full story would eventually emerge, the court case was still several months away. In the meantime, people believed what they wanted to believe, and those without time to consider the evidence were content to be nudged in a certain direction.

There was always something grasping about Lorna Daly.

Simon Keating was never the brightest. Anyone could tell you that.

What was the sister doing there? That's what I'd like to know. And the teacher? They must have been involved.

The papers were limited in what they could report, but social media had no constraints. On Twitter, people made the connection between Jessie and Lorna. On Facebook, there were suggestions of conspiracy. Maybe, wrote one grassy-knoller, Jessie had always been on Vincent McPartlin's payroll.

If Jessie was tested by the case and its fall-out, her parents were tormented. 'How did we fail?' they asked over and over again.

'You didn't,' she replied. She also pointed out that the guards didn't see Lorna as the prime mover in the crimes committed at Clevedon.

What was more, both Quan and Linh had said she was the only one to treat them with any decency.

Even as her mother and father murmured in agreement, she realised her words weren't enough. Her parents would continue to question themselves, and there was nothing she could say to heal their wounds more quickly. She didn't know how long their pain would last. What she did know was that the phrases tossed around by her profession, like 'come to terms' and 'closure', were meaningless. Who was to say how any of them would feel a year, five years, ten years from now?

After she'd closed the café for the evening, she walked the few steps to Sexton's lounge. The scattering of early-evening drinkers looked up, their eyes sweeping across her. Two or three quickly turned away again. One shouted a showy 'How are you doing, Jessie?'

'Evening, Séamus,' she said, then ducked into the snug where Ger was waiting with a pint and a glass of wine. He, too, had become used to the scrutiny of the crowd.

'I saw Simon half an hour ago,' he said, 'walking up by the campsite.'

'Did he say anything?'

'Nope. I tried to say hello, but he blanked me.'

Even though Jessie still worked in the Seashell, her relationship with Lorna was strained. In the Hollywood version of events, they would have reconciled. A long heart-to-heart would have led them to understand each other as never before. But Jessie couldn't bring herself to forgive everything. Whatever sympathy she had for her sister was diluted by her disgust at the exploitation of Linh and Quan. Lorna hadn't instigated their mistreatment, but neither had she put a stop to it.

Jessie's assumption that Linh had taken her bicycle had been correct. What she hadn't foreseen was that another member of the family would play an important role that night.

Turning left along the lane and then left again, Linh had cycled until she'd seen a bungalow with the lights on. Frightened and distressed, she'd been fortunate that the woman who lived in the house was awake. She'd been doubly fortunate that Etty had listened to her, then immediately called the guards. Afterwards, Jessie's grandmother had downplayed her intervention.

'It was obvious the girl was in a desperate state,' she'd said. 'All I did was get her a bit of help.' She was reluctant to say how she felt about her elder granddaughter's involvement. When Jessie asked, all she would say was that while some people had long memories others had memories that were very short.

As it turned out, the gardaí had already been on Dave Hodnett's trail. They'd been surprised to spot a known acolyte of the McPartlins in a west of Ireland seaside town. Assuming he wasn't there for the golf or seaweed baths, they'd begun to track him. He'd also been seen in remote locations in Sligo, Leitrim and Donegal, and they'd suspected he was operating a chain of grow-houses. Before making a move, they'd been gathering information. They insisted they hadn't known about Linh and Quan and would have acted more quickly if they had. Although Jessie and Ger were sceptical, they were powerless to challenge the official line.

That Dave had been on the force's radar explained why officers had arrived so quickly – and in such numbers. Along with the others, Jessie and Ger had spent the night and part of the next day in the garda station. The questions had flown at her like wasps. Why were you there? What did you know? Why didn't you raise the alarm when you first discovered what was going on? Finally, the police had accepted that she was a witness rather than a suspect.

She hadn't been allowed to see Linh and Quan again. As important witnesses in a significant trial, the couple had been whisked away to Dublin. A guard had told her that when the case was finished, they would return to Vietnam. Jessie wanted to know that they were all right. She wanted to say sorry over and over again. They were always on her conscience. She thought not just of the conditions at Clevedon but also of the way they'd been brought to Ireland. Of how Linh had feared they'd die in the back of the lorry and of how they'd been duped into believing they were in England.

Whenever she became annoyed or upset by the swish of gossip, she reminded herself that she wasn't the victim. It wasn't about her. She also hoped that when the trial was over, Linh and Quan would get to tell their story.

She'd seen Dave on television as he left court on the day he was charged. Even with his head bowed, he'd radiated arrogance.

Now, in the muted early-evening light, Jessie picked up her wine glass and smiled. 'Ashling was asking after you,' she said to Ger.

He laughed. 'Have I been forgiven yet?'

'Well, I wouldn't go that far, but the pain is easing with time.'

Not only had Ger skipped football training on the night of the garda raid, he'd had to miss it again the following evening. That he'd been bruised and battered from the fight with Dave hadn't helped. The manager had dropped him for the next match, and Clooneven had been comprehensively beaten by Kilmurry Ibrickane. Of course, Ashling hadn't really blamed Ger for the team's exit from the county championship, but it was their joke, and they were determined to run with it.

The consequences of the night rippled on, and not always in predictable ways. Ger's girlfriend, Rosemary, had been upset to hear about his brush with criminals, her dismay compounded by the news that he'd been roaming the countryside with Jessie. She'd lacerated him for his foolhardy behaviour and lack of commitment to their relationship. What was going on with the 'TV girl'? she'd demanded to know. (Ger had confessed this to Jessie a couple of weeks later when they'd both had a fair amount to drink.)

As was often the way, an argument that began with one issue grew and grew until it covered a multitude of grievances. Rosemary lurched from complaint to complaint until Ger felt dizzy. His father's cancer was in remission, she pointed out, so why hadn't he come back to Cork?

Or, failing that, why hadn't he suggested that she move to Clare? He was thirty years old and still living like a student. What was that about?

They broke up.

As for Rosemary's question, there was nothing going on with the TV girl. That didn't prevent people from assuming they were together. For once, Jessie was cautious. Over the years, she had approached men and been approached. She'd had one long relationship and innumerable shorter ones. She'd had one-night stands, brief flings and unrequited crushes. She'd slept with men for affirmation, adventure and just because she could. This was different. Anything further than friendship would involve taking a risk, not simply the risk of rejection, but the risk that she might lose Ger as a friend. He was the one person in Clooneven with whom she felt fully comfortable, the one person she always looked forward to meeting. She liked his sense of fairness. She liked how he saw the world. Losing his companionship would be more than she could handle right now. So she forced herself to ration the time they spent alone, and she tried to suppress the small charges of longing that popped up when they were together. She thought of it as self-preservation, something she'd shown little aptitude for in the past.

'How are your folks?' he asked.

'Not great, to be honest. Like, not as openly upset as they were a few weeks back but still not brilliant. At least they're seeing more of Zoë and Ethan, which gives them a bit of a lift.'

The children often stayed with their grandparents while Lorna and Simon prepared for the upcoming trial. It was impossible to know how much they understood. Jessie had the sense that, while Zoë was too young to follow it all, Ethan was old enough and smart enough to grasp what was happening. Although Lorna and Simon continued to live together, Lorna insisted their marriage was effectively over. Jessie hoped this was true.

Since the events at Clevedon, she'd come to realise that the sisters were more alike than either had been willing to admit. They'd both craved the admiration of their neighbours, one by planting her flag and being conspicuously successful around the town, the other by making it clear that their home place was too small for her ambitions. The reasons for this were harder to pinpoint. Their childhood had been happy if uneventful. They had been raised to be modest, respectful, self-effacing. Everything about their lives had been average. Maybe that was what they'd been rebelling against.

Ger looked up and signalled for another drink. 'Your parents do know you're planning on sticking around?'

'Ah, yeah. They're pleased about that. They're kind of iffy about my other ideas, mind.'

'I thought your mother was enthusiastic about the family-tree stuff.'

'She was, but they're both worried that I'll draw attention to myself and the family. I had to say, "Listen, Mam, there's every chance no one will be interested in what I'm doing. Nothing might come of it."'

'Maybe so,' he said. 'It's still a great idea. I only hope last year's sixth class get the credit they deserve.'

'Their teacher might have to get a mention too. If it hadn't been for him, I'd never have known about Bridget.'

It was only when Jessie had been released by the guards that she'd had the chance to read Kaitlin's email. Or emails. By then, there had been three. Understandably, Kaitlin had been perplexed by Jessie's failure to respond.

She remembered standing in the sun-bleached street reading about how Bridget had become Alice and then become Bridget again. Her fourth-great-grandmother had made it to America after all. Just as importantly, she'd been able to write to Norah. Jessie remembered her breath catching in her throat as she'd deciphered the screenshot sent by Kaitlin. And she remembered her joy when she'd read that there was an entire box of correspondence between mother and daughter.

She'd called Kaitlin – her cousin! – straight away. A blend of sleep deprivation, stress and exhilaration meant she'd blurted out far more than she'd intended about her sister, Linh and Quan.

Since then, they'd been in almost daily contact. Jessie had also spoken to Gina, the cousin who'd inherited the letters, and to Orla, the aunt with the hybrid Limerick-Boston accent who'd spent her childhood holidays at the caravan park in Clooneven.

Tomorrow, she would board a plane to go and see the letters. Not only that: she would get to visit the places where Bridget had spent the second part of her life and she'd meet her American family. She had hoped that Ger would be able to travel to Boston too, but school was back, so he was stuck in Clooneven.

The idea had been Kaitlin's. 'Why don't you write a book about Bridget?' she'd said one night. Jessie had suggested they do it together, but her cousin had said, no, she had neither the time nor the skill. 'You do, though,' she'd added.

Jessie had run the plan by Etty, who'd been so enthusiastic she'd insisted on paying for her flights.

Since then, she'd filled several pages of a large red notebook with a rough summary of Bridget's life. She wanted to tell the story from Bridget's point of view, to try to give a sense of what life must have been like for a young woman battling for survival. Given their connection, she felt that if any story was hers to tell, this was it.

'I reckon,' she said to Ger, 'that the story ought to begin slightly before the Famine so we can meet Johanna and get to the root of the disagreement between Bridget and Mary Ellen. What do you think?'

'I like it,' he said. 'Mind you, it's beginning to sound like an awful lot of work.'

She took a long drink of wine. 'What else have I got to be doing?'

At eighteen, Jessie had pledged never to spend another winter in Clooneven. Between November and March, even the fine days were blighted by a biting wind. When the rain arrived, it fell in icy sheets so that one end of the beach was obscured from the other. The hotel was boarded up, the caravans abandoned, the town deserted. And yet here she was, on the cusp of winter with no plan to leave. In truth, she didn't have a choice. This wasn't the time to walk out on her parents.

Ivana was returning to her home in Karlovac, which meant that Ashling and Jessie would run the Seashell between them. Jessie had paid off her debt, so for the first time in months, her money was her own. Ashling said that, even though it was quiet over the winter, there was just enough business to make it worth their while. After all, who else would provide Venetia Lillis with her oat milk cappuccino with a teenchy sprinkling of cinnamon? When she wasn't serving coffee, Jessie would write.

Her friend Shona was aghast at her decision to stay in Clooneven, suspecting that Ger was at the root of it. *Any action yet with the ridey teacher?* had been one of her more subtle messages. Maybe it was because she was almost three hundred kilometres away, but Shona couldn't understand how Lorna's arrest had upended Jessie's life. 'I don't see what it's got to do with you,' she'd said, as though Lorna was a distant relation. 'You can't stay in the sticks because your sister screwed up.'

When Jessie felt lonely, as she sometimes did, it was for a life she hadn't lived in many years. It was for her early twenties, a time of ambition and possibility, conviction and abandon. Of course, that was how it seemed to her now. At the time, she'd been riddled with angst, striving to fit in with her aimlessly comfortable friends.

Yes, she missed Dublin. She missed its scale and variety. She missed noisy young people. Noisy old people. A quiet cinema on a wet afternoon. She missed drinking by the canal on a summer's evening and walking for two hours without meeting a single person she knew. She missed red-brick terraces, reliable broadband and Zara. She couldn't rule out going back. For now, though, Clooneven was home.

'I'd better hit the road,' she said to Ger, as she gulped down the last of her wine. 'My case won't pack itself, and I promised Etty I'd drop up to her before I left.'

'Grand so,' he said, picking up his jacket. 'I'll walk to the end of the road with you.'

Dusk was settling in, a reminder that, as a payback for the long summer evenings, there were months of darkness ahead. By the time she returned from Boston, it would be October, and the sun's power would be further diminished.

When they reached the hotel, and the point where she would turn for her parents' house, she paused. 'I'll cycle on from here. I don't want it to get too dark.'

'Take care of yourself,' said Ger.

'I will.'

'And tell your American cousins I said hello.'

'I will.'

'And be sure to enjoy yourself.'

'I will.'

For a few moments, neither spoke. Nearby, two young fellows shouted affectionate abuse at each other. A car with exhaust trouble rattled past.

Finally, Ger reached out and ran one finger down the back of her hand. The unexpected gesture sent a series of small shocks through her body. 'Do you know,' he said, 'I'm going to miss you.'

'And I'll miss you,' she said, as she took his hand, lifted her face to his and allowed her bicycle to fall to the pavement.

Chapter 45

September 2019, Boston
Kaitlin

Kaitlin paced the arrivals' hall. She smoothed her hair then paced back again. Flight EI 134 from Shannon had landed, and within a few minutes, she would finally meet Jessie. Okay, 'finally' wasn't the appropriate word. Barely two months had passed since she'd learnt that they were cousins. In that time, however, they'd shared so many conversations, about Bridget and Norah and also about their own lives, that it felt like a more established friendship. Still, she was nervous.

The first time they'd spoken had been bizarre. Without preamble, Jessie had launched into a monologue about spending the previous twelve hours in a police station. Kaitlin had feared she was dealing with a lunatic, an exhibitionist or some combination of the two. Then she'd realised that the woman on the other end of the phone was in shock.

She continued to think about the worlds that had collided that day.

Jessie had been following a historic tale of poverty and emigration only to discover a modern migration story unfolding in front of her. Not that she tended to make the comparison. What had happened remained too personal. Too raw.

Given the unorthodox start to their friendship, Kaitlin had understood that she'd have to be more open than usual. It was hard to be reserved with Jessie. She had one of those personalities that encouraged you to talk.

The day after she'd read Bridget and Norah's letters, Kaitlin had complied with her boss's instructions and made an appointment with a psychiatrist. She was surprised to find that she could, after all, open up and discuss how she felt. More than once, her therapist had asked what she was afraid of. 'Everything,' had been Kaitlin's jokey reply. Like many jokes, it was grounded in truth. Bit by bit, session by session, she started to focus on the ideas sheltering at the back of her head. The ones she'd been too timid to pursue. She saw now that she'd been edging towards this point anyway. She'd just needed a nudge, and the doctor was providing it.

For as long as she could remember, she'd been scornful of people who claimed that, actually, life was pretty simple. To her, this was the argument of the privileged. Most people had to struggle and toil and compromise. Their lives were not straightforward.

And yet her own life had become unnecessarily complicated. In striving to be lots of different people – successful corporate lawyer, super-supportive partner, loyal daughter – she hadn't managed to become any of them. She was in danger of calcifying into a person she didn't want to be.

So what did she want?

Helpful as her therapist was, Kaitlin decided she needed to run her ideas past someone who didn't charge by the hour. She spoke to Jessie. Her new friend urged her not to do anything drastic. 'Are you sure-sure-sure?' she asked, when Kaitlin sketched out her plans.

'Well, not completely,' Kaitlin replied, 'only I need to do *something*.'

Jessie advised her to consult someone else. 'I don't know if you've noticed,' she said, 'but I'm not exactly life-coach material. I don't want to be responsible for screwing up your life.'

'There are things I've got to do differently,' Kaitlin insisted.

'Fair enough, only I think you're supposed to start with small stuff, like getting rid of possessions that no longer bring you happiness. You know, like grey underwear or ugly shoes? Throwing out your whole life is a bit extreme.'

Around and around they went until she followed Jessie's advice and spoke to Orla. After half an hour, Orla looked at her and said, 'If you ask me, you've got to take a chance ... only don't tell your mother I said that.'

The first change was the easier one. She found a new job and gave notice at Frobisher Hunter. Of course, it wasn't that straightforward. To begin with, the principal attorney at her new firm, Klein Maguire Immigration Law, was unconvinced by her application. Why did she want to do a tougher job for considerably less money? he asked. Was she willing to work in a smaller office with fewer promotional opportunities? Did she have any relevant experience? Oh, and how was her Spanish? As it happened, her Spanish was reasonable. The other questions were harder to answer, but she spoke with as much conviction as she possessed about why she wanted a change. What she didn't say was that she'd spent months trying to influence someone else's career when it was her own that had been calling out for action.

And so, just as Brian was preparing to leave for Washington, she announced that she, too, would be switching jobs. While her father's response was measured, her mother was appalled. Had Kaitlin revealed that she was moving to Montana to live off-grid, Susan couldn't have been more disapproving.

'You're tossing your career in the trash for no good reason,' she said. 'Why would you do that?'

As patiently as she could, Kaitlin argued that she was pursuing an area that interested her. Yes, she knew her standard of living would fall. Yes, it would take longer to pay off her loans. And, yes, she was aware that her new job mightn't be all that she hoped for.

Her mother, still riled up, asked if 'those old letters' had made Kaitlin overly sentimental.

'No one changes their job because of a box of letters,' she replied, 'no matter how important they are.' While this was true, finding out more about Bridget and her family had been a powerful experience, and she didn't like to hear her mother denigrate it. If nothing else, the story of a woman who'd been given few choices in life had made her focus on the choices available to her. That she was able to pursue what mattered to her placed her among the privileged few. 'You should take the time to read some of the letters,' she said. 'They might surprise you.'

So far, her mom hadn't taken up the offer.

Jessie was one of the first into the arrivals hall. For a second or two, they stared at each other, like you do when you're not fully sure how to behave. Embrace? Shake hands? Wave? Then Kaitlin felt two long arms being wrapped around her, the hug so tight she could barely breathe. Despite their many conversations on FaceTime, Jessie wasn't quite as she had anticipated. She was ganglier, with a loose-limbed energy that attracted people's attention. In the flesh, she also had an appealing goofiness that didn't transfer to the screen.

They chatted all the way to the parking garage, stopping every so often to say, 'Isn't this amazing?' or some such.

Because it was. It truly was.

As she drove, Kaitlin sketched out their itinerary for the following days. She wasn't due to start her new job for another two weeks so had plenty of time to show Jessie the city and introduce her to the American side of the family.

The day was mild for late September, the sky a deep blue. Jessie's nose was pressed against the car window, like a newly released prisoner's.

'Honest to God,' she said, as they passed a swathe of brown and cream apartment buildings, 'it really is lovely.' Then she tapped herself on the side of the head. 'Don't mind me sounding like a complete yokel. I'll have to put my sophisticated head on.'

'Admire all you like,' said Kaitlin. 'I reckoned we'd keep everything fairly low key today because from tomorrow it's going to be full-on. You wouldn't believe how many people want to meet you. And we have an awful lot to see.'

'That's fine by me,' said Jessie.

'I asked my mother not to go overboard on Saturday night, but intimate gatherings aren't her thing, so if we end up meeting every possible cousin along with half the neighbourhood and a few local dignitaries, you'll just have to go with it. At least, Orla and Drew will be there. Oh, and Brian and Riley are travelling up from DC.'

'Does this mean you're forgiven?'

'No, but your visit's a distraction … which is good.'

If her mother's misgivings about her career choice hadn't melted away, she was doing a reasonable job of suppressing them. What was more, she seemed genuinely enthusiastic about Jessie. 'Isn't she pretty?' had been her comment when Kaitlin had shown her some pictures.

The problem wasn't her mother's anger about Frobisher Hunter, it was the depth of her disappointment about everything else.

Ending her relationship with Clay had been tough, and Kaitlin knew that her mom wasn't alone in querying her decision. Objectively speaking, he was the more attractive of the two, the one who was better placed to walk away and find a new partner. He was smart, successful, solvent and good in bed. He wasn't cruel or deliberately coercive. She admired him, cared about him, wouldn't want to hurt him. But she didn't love him.

Although she'd made up her mind before handing in her notice at Frobisher Hunter, his reaction had reaffirmed her decision. It wasn't simply that he hadn't understood: he'd made no effort to understand.

Increasingly, it had felt as if they were together under false pretences. If they'd remained a couple, she'd have had to keep twisting herself into shapes to meet with his approval. Eventually, she'd have become one of those women who doesn't realise that this is what she's doing. She would have disappeared behind a cloak of compromises and feigned interests.

Despite the inertia that had settled over their relationship, and despite their silences and disagreements, Kaitlin's decision took Clay by surprise. He was irritated too, reacting as if what she'd said was a play for more attention or an engagement ring. Was that what she wanted? he asked.

'No,' she said.

Clay was sceptical. 'A few months back, we were discussing buying a house. If it hadn't been for the miscarriage, we'd have been parents by now. We'd have been talking about marriage. It's unlikely you would have given up such a top-class job.'

'Perhaps.'

His expression hardened. 'There's no perhaps. If Stella had lived, we wouldn't be having this conversation.'

'Maybe not,' she said. 'But she didn't live.'

'It's almost like you're glad about that.'

'Oh, for God's sake, Clay,' she shouted, 'of course I'm not.'

Silence hung between them. Awkward. Heavy with recrimination.

Finally, he spoke. 'I'm sorry. I shouldn't have said that. I didn't mean it.'

'It's okay. Stella will always be with me, you know that, don't you? But, even if she'd lived ... well, it mightn't have worked out for us.' He didn't respond, so she continued: 'There's no right way of doing this. I wish there was. But I need to start again.'

'I think you're making a mistake.'

Kaitlin tried to explain that the past few months had knocked something loose in her. Maybe she was being rash. Maybe she would regret her decisions. But she was an adult and would have to take responsibility for them.

After they'd parted, she cried. Not because she'd done the wrong thing, but because an important part of her life had come to an end.

Clay remained in their old apartment. He was on the fast track to better things and had few immediate concerns about money. Although small, Kaitlin's new place was bright and well-located. The Green Line ran past the end of the street, and there were grocery stores and cafés galore. She told herself that this was a temporary stop: when the lease was up, she would find somewhere better.

Her mother accused her of being unwilling to compromise, and pointed out that before the year's end, she would be thirty years old. 'You'll end up on your own or with the wrong person because all the better options have been taken,' she said. 'Let me give you some advice: you can't have everything exactly the way you want it.'

Kaitlin had to remind herself that her mother wasn't being intentionally provocative or insulting. What she was saying was coming from a place of disappointment, but also concern. When you'd been married at twenty-one and had given birth to two children before the age of twenty-six, the prospect of being thirty and single must be unimaginable.

The news reached Brian before she'd had the opportunity to talk to him. *I never thought he was right for you*, his message said. *Give me a call whenever you want x.*

She did call but, apart from the most cursory of enquiries, didn't ask how his new job was going. After months of obsessing about the Immigration Reform Alliance and its policies, she found she was no longer able to look at the website. She didn't want to see a statement with her brother's name at the end. She had no desire to see his face on the 'Key Staff' page.

From time to time, she came close to regretting what she had done. She would wake up, alone and slightly scared, ideas crashing around her head. She would miss Clay. Or, rather, she would miss the idea of him. She would worry about the future. *Did I do too much too quickly?* she would ask herself. *How did I forget what a conventional person I am?*

But there were other times when she felt confident about her choices. When she found herself looking forward rather than back. When she felt as though, finally, she might become the person she wanted to be.

That was how Kaitlin felt as she sat in the late afternoon sunshine drinking coffee and bringing Jessie up to date.

With help from Gina, she'd located where Bridget and Martin were buried. Like the graveyard in Ireland where Norah had been laid to rest, the site had been mapped out. Some of the details were on the cemetery website. Bridget, it noted, 'had sometimes used the name Alice'. The website also said that she'd been one of eighteen people to die from tuberculosis in just seven days. Thirty of the eighty-five deaths recorded in Boston that week had been of Irish immigrants.

'Martin lived for another decade,' she said to Jessie. 'Not an especially long life, but more than poor Bridget was given. Patrick was only fifty-four when he died. But Delia, believe it or not, lived to be ninety-one.'

'And to think that before she was a year old, she'd almost died twice,' said Jessie, stretching out her legs and pointing her toes.

'It also means she was alive until the 1930s, so someone in the wider family might have a picture of her. Gina's on the case.'

Jessie looked around her with an earnest satisfaction, like a child who had just learnt to ride a bike without stabilisers. 'I'd never imagined I'd find the past so fascinating,' she said. 'Did you?'

'No,' replied Kaitlin. 'I had no idea at all.'

Chapter 46

Jessie

Jessie had brought the old photo album with her so that the others could have a proper look at the picture of Norah and at Bridget's going-away letter.

While they did, she sat at Gina's kitchen table and went through the box of Bridget's belongings. She smiled at the shell and was impressed by the condition of the books. It was the letters, however, that she'd been longing to see. They were so old, so precious, that she felt she should be wearing white cotton gloves, like a museum curator or an art restorer.

She kept spotting new lines and nuggets of information. She wrote down names and locations that might help in telling Bridget's story. Some questions remained unanswered. Why, for instance, hadn't Norah told her sons that she'd written to Bridget in America? Why hadn't she wanted them to know about their family in Boston? Whatever her reasons, they were unlikely to get to the truth now.

Kaitlin and Gina had been trying to find out more about the lives of those who'd been important to Bridget. Kaitlin had tracked down a descendant of Frederick and Charlotte Edgecombe. The woman, who was called Avery Wainscott, knew a little about her great-great-great-grandparents and would be happy to meet them. Unfortunately, she'd said, the Mount Vernon Street house was no longer in the family. As far as she was aware, the current owner was a tech entrepreneur.

Later, they would go to see the street where the McDonagh family had lived. In the coming days, they'd visit the other places Jessie had been reading about, including Cohasset where Bridget's American life had begun. A few years back, a memorial had been placed near the spot where the small group of survivors had been brought ashore. One of the men on the organising committee was related to Florence Stanhope, the woman who had taken care of Bridget and Delia after the shipwreck.

The night before, Kaitlin and Jessie had stayed awake, talking and talking about the ways in which their lives were entwined and about the twists that had brought them together.

For some reason, she'd been reluctant to speak about Ger. It was only after several drinks and some determined coaxing that she'd told Kaitlin about kissing him on the street in Clooneven. 'I know, I know,' she'd said. 'We may as well have taken out an ad on local radio.'

'So this will be an ongoing thing?' asked Kaitlin.

'Oh, yes,' replied Jessie.

The cemetery was protected by a stone wall and high black gates. On the far side of the gates, a modest red-brick chapel was surrounded by scores of weathered headstones. While some were ornate, more, like the one marking where Bridget and Martin had been buried, were plain, their inscriptions obscured by time.

'This is them,' said Gina, stopping beside a thin grey stone. 'You know, I must have passed this place a thousand times, and until a few days back I didn't realise I had family here.'

'How many graves are there?' asked Jessie.

'About fifteen hundred, I think, and many of the folks buried here would have had similar stories to Martin and Bridget.'

'They were a remarkable lot,' said Kaitlin, swiping at a tear.

Gina crouched to place a bouquet of red roses beside the stone. 'They surely were. Honestly, I feel privileged to be related to them.'

Jessie took out the red notebook, which had become her constant companion. She wrote down everything that might be relevant, hoping that in the months ahead her jottings would provide inspiration. Already, sentences and paragraphs were taking shape in her head.

For a moment, she stood and allowed the stillness to sink in. They were only a couple of hundred metres away from a snarl of traffic. In the distance, she could see the towering buildings of Boston's financial district. Yet in here it was so peaceful she could have been standing on the beach in Clooneven.

She thought of Bridget and Martin and of how they'd been tested in ways she found almost impossible to imagine. She thought of the others buried here. Their descendants had become politicians and lawyers, carpenters and cooks, teachers and soldiers, quarterbacks and rock stars. Some had written newspaper columns. Some had built roads. Some had robbed banks. Their lives were woven through the city's story.

She thought, too, about what changed over the decades and what was immutable. How would Bridget feel about those who'd come after her? she wondered.

Kaitlin turned to her. 'You're very quiet,' she said. 'What do you think?'

Jessie recalled something Etty had said on the night she'd first produced Bridget's letter. It was something she'd thought about on many occasions since, and she repeated it now.

'I think what matters,' she said, 'is that we remember.'

Epilogue

June 1900, Clooneven
Norah

Norah sat on the strand, a warm breeze moving across her face, the sun's rays glinting on the water. No matter how many times she visited this spot, she always thought of Bridget, the woman who'd first brought her here to collect shells and watch the waves.

More than thirty years had passed since her mother's death. Her other parents, Mary Ellen and Thomas, were also long gone. She had no memories of the days she'd spent with Bridget, but that didn't matter. The bond between them had been firm and unbreakable.

Norah was fifty-four years old, no longer a young woman, but not elderly either. Considering that the first two years of her life had been a constant battle for survival, her health was strong.

She'd never known what to tell her two sons about Bridget, and in the end, she'd decided to say nothing. Her husband, Barney, had agreed.

'Let them think that life is fair and straightforward,' he'd said. 'They don't need to be tormented by the cruelties of the past.'

Tomorrow their younger boy, Seánie, would marry Gertrude O'Meara. Gertie was from Boherbreen, the townland where Norah had been born. Although all of Norah's neighbours from that time were dead or gone, memories lived on. There was every danger that someone would tell Seánie the truth. Norah Nugent? they might say. Wasn't she born around here? Wasn't she Norah Moloney then? Didn't her father die? And didn't her mother go to America?

That they would mean no harm was beside the point. Seánie would be confused – and hurt.

Norah had concluded that their sons needed to be told about Bridget. Discussing the rest of the family in Boston was more complicated.

James, her elder boy, had left Ireland. He was in Liverpool with his wife and five children. Five children Norah had never met. Times remained hard, and she worried that having cousins in America would lure Seánie and his new wife across the Atlantic.

She'd lost enough. She couldn't bear to lose him as well.

And so, with Barney's blessing, she'd decided to tell them about Bridget and John Joe but not about her first mother's life in America. As far as they were concerned, the next chapter of Bridget's story would remain a mystery.

There was always the chance, she supposed, that one day someone would take an interest in what had happened in these towns and villages. That they would want to know about the courageous young woman who'd been forced to leave Clooneven in the spring of 1848.

Almost as quickly as this thought came into her head, she dismissed it. Would the generations to come really care about the Famine? No, she reasoned. They'd have their own lives to lead, their own problems to solve. They wouldn't want a reminder of the years that had torn lives and families apart, the years when people had been buried without coffin or shroud.

If Norah's wisdom was limited, there were two things she could say for certain. Extreme circumstances brought out the best in some people and the worst in others. And history rarely recorded the lives of people like her and her mother.

As so often before, she picked up a shell and passed it from hand to hand. Then she turned to Seánie who was sitting beside her, his handsome face tilted towards the sun.

'I want to tell you a story,' she said.

Author's Note

Novelists are usually advised to do their research and then forget about it. In other words, nobody wants to read pages and pages of facts. They want a story. That being said, it's impossible to write a book like *The Letter Home* without focusing on the conditions endured by millions of Irish people during the Great Famine of the 1840s.

I'm originally from the same county as Jessie and, like her, I found that I lacked some fairly basic information about the scale of the devastation in our area. I'm also conscious that readers might like to read more about what happened during those times, so I thought I'd list some of the sources I used.

During the Famine, the suffering in County Clare was prolonged and extreme. It's been estimated that the county's population declined by more than a quarter between 1841 and 1851. There were also a staggering number of evictions. Of course, it's possible to measure the numbers who died from starvation and disease and the numbers who emigrated. What's harder to calculate is the trauma of the people who survived, including those forced into exile.

According to the historian Ciarán Ó Murchadha, the first death officially recorded as being from starvation was that of a widow named Mrs Conlon who was from Dysart parish in County Clare. She died in October 1846 while trying to find food for her children. Mrs Conlon inspired the character of Johanna Markham and provided the spark for the book.

The Letter Home was written mostly during two long Covid lockdowns, which made research slightly more difficult. My starting point was the Clare County Library website – www.clarelibrary.ie – which is a fantastic resource for anyone interested in learning more. It contains a considerable number of records, many of which make harrowing reading. This was where I found the records for the Kilrush workhouse and also the eviction documents for the area. In addition, it was where I first came across references to a ship called the *St John*, which sank off the coast of Massachusetts in 1849. Many of those on board were from west Clare. The story of the *St John* was the inspiration for the *Mary and Elizabeth*.

The website also contains links to a number of articles from the *Illustrated London News*. In late 1849 and early 1850, it carried a series of reports about conditions in south-west Clare. These included an interview with a woman called Bridget O'Donnel who had been evicted from her home near Doonbeg. A drawing of Bridget and her children has become one of the best-known images of the Famine. It prompted the part in the book where the fictional Bridget meets a journalist.

Although Clooneven is fictional, I think of it as being in roughly the same place as the real town of Kilkee. In trying to get a picture of what the area looked like before the Famine, I was helped by *Two Months at Kilkee* by Mary John Knott. Originally published in 1836, it's available online.

Several books were of assistance in trying to get a feel for what life was like in west Clare during the Famine. These include: *The Great Famine: Ireland's Agony 1845–1852* by Ciarán O'Murchadha; *Clare*

History and Society, edited by Matthew Lynch and Patrick Nugent; *Atlas of the Great Irish Famine*, edited by John Crowley; *Famine Echoes – Folk Memories of the Great Irish Famine: An Oral History of Ireland's Greatest Tragedy* by Cathal Póirtéir and *Clare and Its People* by Brian Dinan.

For the chapters set on board the *Mary and Elizabeth*, I received invaluable information from *Robert Whyte's 1847 Famine Ship Diary*, edited by James Mangan, and *Coffin Ship: The Wreck of the Brig St John* by William Henry. There is a database of Irish emigrants to the United States similar to the one consulted by Kaitlin in the book. You can find the real-life version at www.dunbrody.com

I began the book knowing relatively little about Boston in the mid-nineteenth century and nothing at all about the treatment of young female migrants. Among the books I consulted were: *Emigrants and Exile* by Kerby Miller; *The Boston Irish: A Political History* by Thomas O'Connor; *Bibles, Brahmins and Bosses* by Thomas O'Connor; *South Boston: My Home Town* by Thomas O'Connor; *The Atlas of Boston History*, edited by Nancy Seasholes; *A Short History of Boston* by Robert Allison; *Women and the City: Gender, Space and Power in Boston 1870–1940* by Sarah Deutsch and *Beacon Hill: A Living Portrait* by Barbara Moore.

Common Ground: A Turbulent Decade in the Lives of Three American Families by Anthony Lukas provided a powerful history of Boston. In the mid-1980s, it won the Pulitzer Prize for non-fiction as well as the National Book Award, and it's easy to see why. It's quite long, but is available as an audiobook, and I can't recommend it highly enough.

In writing about Bridget, I was also helped by the records for St Augustine Cemetery in South Boston which are available online.

When it came to more recent Irish immigration to the United States, I was helped by *The Tribe: The Inside Story of Irish Power and Influence in US Politics* by Caitríona Perry and *Irish Transatlantics, 1980-2015* by Íde O'Carroll.

For Linh and Quan's story, I was greatly assisted by a report from Anti-Slavery International called *Precarious Journeys*.

Finally, I came across the beautiful word *diadhánach*, which is used by Bridget, in *Thirty-Two Words for Field* by Manchán Magan.

Obviously, any inaccuracies in *The Letter Home* are my responsibility, but I hope that by including some of the books that helped me, I can assist anyone interested in finding out more.

Acknowledgements

Many thanks to all the people who helped bring *The Letter Home* to the page.

I'm grateful to my editors, Ciara Considine and Sherise Hobbs. Thanks also to Hazel Orme for the fantastic copy-edit.

As always, thanks to Elaine Egan, Joanna Smyth, Ruth Shern, Breda Purdue and Jim Binchy at Hachette Books Ireland.

Much gratitude to my agent, Robert Kirby, and to Kate Walsh, Amy Mitchell and Anna Watkins at United Agents.

A big thank you to the readers, writers, bloggers and booksellers who have been so supportive.

Massive thanks to my parents, Tony and Ruth English.

Finally, more thanks than I can say to my husband, Eamon Quinn.